JUN

western literature series

SUSAN LANG

juniper blue

UNIVERSITY OF NEVADA PRESS ▲▲ RENO & LAS VEGAS

WESTERN LITERATURE SERIES

University of Nevada Press

Reno, Nevada 89557 USA

Manufactured in the United States of America

Library of Congress Cataloging-in-Publication Data

Lang, Susan, 1941–

Juniper blue / Susan Lang.

p.   cm. — (Western literature series)

ISBN 0–87417–633–6 (pbk. : alk. paper)

1. Women landowners—Fiction. 2. Motion picture
actors and actresses—Fiction. 3. California, Southern—Fiction.
4. Single mothers—Fiction. 5. Depressions—Fiction.
6. Rape victims—Fiction. 7. Twins—Fiction. I. Title. II. Series.

PS3612.A555J86   2006

813'.6–dc22   2005020685

The paper used in this book meets the requirements of
American National Standard for Information Sciences—
Permanence of Paper for Printed Library Materials,
ANSI Z.48-1984. Binding materials were selected for
strength and durability.

First Printing

15   14   13   12   11   10   09   08   07   06

5   4   3   2   1

To the wildness that informs and sustains us
and to those who love it

ACKNOWLEDGMENTS

Thanks to Carol Rawlings, Carol Houck Smith, Mary Sojourner, T. M. McNally, Joy Passanante, Jan McInroy, and Sheila Sanderson. I'm forever grateful for the support and suggestions that made this a better book. Thanks to Joanne O'Hare and the University of Nevada Press for again taking a chance on my work.

PART I

CHAPTER ONE

Rain poured from the eaves in great hissing streams. A bright bolt stabbed at the bank across the wash; thunder exploded, jolting Ruth up from where she sat at the table. A pinyon flew apart across the wash, and a spear of wood sailed toward the house, dropped into muddy water rampaging down the wash. Then another pain tightened her belly, took her breath away, and she sank back into the chair, clutched the edge of the table and hung on until it finished with her.

Was this really it then—and not more of the same aggravation? Would this occupation of her body finally be over?

For days now the huge mound of flesh in front of her had been contracting erratically, shooting her through with hot buckshot. Keeping her awake. But last night's pain felt more serious, this morning's even more so. Two days ago, Kate and John Olsen had wanted to drive her into San Bernardino to see a doctor. Something wasn't right, Kate said.

"There's nothing to worry about," she had told Kate. "After all, I've heard that Indian women stop off along the trail to give birth—then just continue on." She'd even refused to let Kate stay with her. It seemed simple enough at the time to drive down to the Olsens' at the first sign.

She should have listened. This could be it, all right.

Or maybe this would ease off again. Could the Model A even make it the four miles to the Olsens' in such a storm, especially through the North Fork, where the two washes came together across the rut road? This kind of rain could sweep the car away.

Another pain sliced long fingers into her, squeezed until she could scarcely bear it before releasing her to breathe again. Getting to her feet, she looked back to see a spot of blood left on the chair. She needed no more convincing. If she wanted Kate's help, she'd better leave now, storm or no storm.

Ruth stuffed a few things into her satchel and started for the front door, flung it open just as a hand snatched her back, gripped her gut and tried to rip it out. She held on to the doorframe, gasping, while wind-whipped rain pelted her, embedded hail stinging her cheeks. When the pain diminished some, she stepped outside into the swirling water. Then the sky cracked apart, light ribboning outward to shatter it like window glass. Thunder threw her upward, brought her to her knees on the flooded ground.

Cold drops beat against her back as she tried to rise. Searing pain tore through her, and a rush of hot water gushed down her thighs, pushing her back down. For a moment, she thought she'd peed herself. Then she looked at the ground, where her bloody fluid blended into the rest.

She crawled toward her Model A, knees sliding in the muddy earth under her. The pain, constant now, intensified to wrack her again before she reached the running board. It took several attempts to pull herself up, boost herself inside, where she doubled up moaning in front of the steering wheel she could barely get behind. Her hand shook wildly as she reached for the choke, pumped it once and switched on the ignition.

Nothing. She choked again and turned the switch, choked and turned again. And again. Pushed her foot down on the gas pedal, as if the car might already have started, the rain and growling thunder drowning out the sound of the engine. But it was stone dead. She let go of the switch, sat shivering with cold and agony. Then another dagger thrust deep and hard inside her, twisting as it traveled. She yelled out, yelled out more as it stabbed and twisted again.

Ruth pushed open the door and stepped out, but her legs wouldn't hold her. She slid onto the ground, her shouts swallowed up in the swollen storm. Unable to propel herself further, she lay on one side and felt herself surrender.

Some Indian woman she turned out to be. So much for the family rumors, she thought bitterly, as a wave of nausea hit her. Then even that was swept away by the tidal wave of torment that carried her toward a place without thought or word or emotion. Where there was only pain, pain, pain, her own animal cries and dry heaves, the cold wet coming down and pooling under her, the hot flow slushing out between her legs.

Through a thick haze of anguish she watched drowned ants float by, inches from her face. Her eyes drooped shut, but she had recognized something just ahead and opened them again. She began edging closer. Scarcely able to endure the throes each movement brought, she dragged her wracked body forward, immune to its protests. Ruth reached out as she neared the floating strands of black hair outside her cabin door, grasped them in her fingers, and hung on as if they alone would save her. Now her blood would soak into the earth to mix with his. Closing her eyes, she drifted away into stark and unrelenting pain.

The sound of the big engine slit open her eyes enough to vaguely recognize the Olsens' truck pulling up. When John Olsen lifted her from the ground, she kept Jim's hair locked tight in her fist. Inside they fussed over her, wrapped her in blankets far too hot, rubbed her skin and hugged her to them. She tried to tell them to stop, it was all right now, she had his hair in her hand; they shouldn't worry. "Along the trail," she heard herself say.

"What, Rute, what did you say? She talking, John. Get more water. You have to come back, Rute."

Of course she was talking. What was the matter with them, she wondered, a bit irritated. She clutched the hair tighter. The blankets were making her hurt worse again, pains coming hard again. Shivering now. She wanted the numbness back. Ruth felt her legs pushed apart, held there; something jammed inside her. "No. No." Behind her eyes lurked that smirking face, that mass of orange hair. "No!" Then clawing pain chased the memory from her, seized her very breath.

"Stop, Rute. You have to help." Someone was slapping her. Was that Kate? Surely not Kate slapping. "Come on, Rute. You have to push it out."

Push what out? Push out the pain? It was too strong. Too long. Warm hands squeezed her cheeks, and she opened her eyes to find a big face inches from her own. Kate's face. She blinked to bring it into focus.

"I can see the baby's head, Rute," Kate said, squeezing her cheeks again. "The baby has black hair. You hear me, Rute? The hair black."

"Black, Kate. Is it black?" she tried to whisper.

"You push down next time, Rute, you hear me. Push it out."

Next time? It was all one long hurting.

"Now, Rute. Now push. No. Not kick. Push. Have to push." She felt it ease enough to let her breathe. Something cool swiped across her forehead. "I know you tired," Kate said. "But you can do it, Rute. You have to. Just a big push and it all be over.

"Okay, time now. Push it now," Kate said as pain pinned her again, held her there squirming. "Ya, that better, ya. Harder now, Rute. Goot, goot. More hard . . . okay, wait, wait." It eased and Ruth began drifting again, until pain snatched her back.

"Now. Push again. Hard, Rute, that's it. . . . Again, harder . . . push, push . . ."

A baby's cry filled the room. Ruth raised her head to see, laughed out at the child with dark skin and black hair Kate laid on her belly. John Olsen stood behind with a basin, his face beaming.

Kate cleaned and wrapped the baby, placed it in Ruth's arms, the same relief on her face that Ruth felt inside. "A boy," she said, opening Ruth's closed fist. "I take this now," Kate told her, as she pulled away what looked like blades of grama grass.

So it had been Jim's all along. Ruth looked down at the infant in her arms, smiled at the way its face was smashed out of shape, bent down and kissed the top of its lovely dark head. Then pain gripped her again, hard, and she heard herself gasp for air.

"It just afterbirth, Rute. I get it now."

When Kate began massaging her belly, another excruciating wave took hold. Ruth felt the urge to push this time, while before it was forced. When she did, there came a slick *sloosh*, and she heard Kate cry out in surprise, looked over to see her lift up a screaming infant smaller than the other, hold it out to inspect. Ruth watched in horror as Kate swiped a hand over the infant's head, as if she might wipe away that red-orange fuzz, the color of rotting peach. Eyes welling, Kate looked over, steadied her gaze.

"This one a girl, Rute," she said.

CHAPTER TWO

An excited chittering and clucking hiss turned Ruth's attention to the window. On the sill sat a red squirrel, its forepaws against the pane. It scolded again, scratching tiny claws at the glass. The strange sight was almost enough to lift her mind from the wailing bundle wriggling in the corner cradle. Take her thoughts off the tiny head with orange-red fuzz. Almost. The other bundle in the cradle was quiet—despite the near continual racket that went on beside it. She glanced over, reassured herself that the hair on the quiet one was still thick and black. At least she had that.

Her need to pee finally dragged her out of bed as far as the slop jar. She cringed at the sight of the belly that hung there like a huge flap of thick skin whenever she unbuttoned her pants. Kate had laughed and said it would tighten back up. But Ruth was glad Jim wasn't around to see it. At least she could pee again without so much sting—Kate told her a doctor would have put in stitches—and she could walk without as much soreness. Her bleeding was lessening. Maybe things were healing down there. She wished she could say as much for the rest of her.

Ruth went to the stove and lit the fire, filled the coffeepot with water, not because she wanted the beverage but because that was what she did in the morning. She had few desires these days, save relief from her life. But as she reached across for the coffee can, her arm glanced off the stewpot, sending it clanging to the floor.

The wail in the corner became a terrified shriek, and the dark head next to it began to move. Ruth rushed over and snatched the cater-wauling bundle, jamming it to her shoulder as she marched to the other side of the cabin.

"There, there," she said, trying to pat and soothe this helpless creature thrust upon her. "It's only a stewpot. It can't hurt you," she crooned in a voice so false that it made the child struggle and cry even more.

They had both been thrust upon each other, she and this girl child—who hadn't chosen her for a mother any more than she had chosen it. That was the one thing that connected them. The rest . . . well, Ruth just didn't know what would come of it.

Kate said it would pass, this blackness that had come over her after the birth. Said it happened to many women. Ruth knew it was more than that. She could no longer remember what it felt like even weeks ago, who she was before the babies came. Let alone who she had been before the rest happened. She sometimes forced herself to recall things she had done, times she had laughed. But it was like remembering from the outside, watching some other woman she had been. Each time she lay down to sleep, something in her still hoped to wake and find that the last few months had been nothing more than a nightmare.

Ruth held the baby out and looked into its frantic little face, the translucent skin deep red from screaming. To stop the squalling, she pulled a breast from her shirt and put a nipple to the tiny, quivering mouth. She looked over at the other dark-haired bundle in the cradle to set the milk flowing. Ruth didn't want to hate this child in her arms. She was trying not to.

She was certain the other child, the boy, was Jim's—and not some throwback to her mother's rumored Indian lineage. She could sense his spirit in the child. But the other, the red-haired one, was definitely not Indian, and the hair color too significant to deny.

But how could this have happened, she asked Kate? She'd never heard of such a thing—twins from two different fathers. Yet the evidence was unmistakable. Kate told her she'd heard rumors of it among women, but had never seen it before herself.

Ruth placed the quieted child back beside her brother. The girl was smaller and hungrier than he was, always needed more. That had been a problem from the beginning. Ruth's breasts would tighten and hold on to the milk whenever she tried to feed the girl, while milk would pour down when the boy was at her breast. It was Kate who came up with the idea of substituting the one for the other in her mind, though it had taken some practice to accomplish. Even Ruth's own body did not want to keep this child alive.

Taking up the slop jar, Ruth walked out through the fine mist to empty it behind the outhouse. Water still dripped from eaves and trees, the sky hidden behind a thick paste of cloud. Would these rains never stop? She dumped the slop, watched it sink slowly into the rain-washed earth.

Just beyond the cabin sat her Model A, its custom yellow paint the one bright sun in the gray day. If only she could hop in it and drive away from these creatures who confined her with their obligations, who bound her with invisible chains. She wondered if she would ever be wholly herself again, if there would always be parts of her somewhere outside herself, needing and wanting and being, parts embodied in those voices from her cabin.

As huge as she'd become, the babies were easier to carry when they were inside, quieter too. Now she would have to lug the two of them everywhere, along with diapers, blankets, and cloths. Thank god she had the Model A. Except for those final two weeks, the pregnancy seemed almost a breeze when she thought about it now, her climbing around the mountains—even with a bellyful of babies—hiking down to the Swedes' to keep fit for birth. That walk would be impossible today. For a moment she imagined herself traveling down canyon with the kind of cradle board she had seen some Indian women use in El Paso. She could envision the boy's black hair above the pack strapped to her back. But what about the girl? Another image appeared: the crying girl bundle bouncing along behind, dragged over the rocky terrain on a rope. A laugh escaped before she could clamp it back.

Ruth knew she had to fight this mean impulse—even if these shots of black joy were the only relief from the darkness that had overtaken her. How bizarre and complicated life was, after all, a bit like those Russian novels she'd read, where lives other than her own had been twisted out of shape by circumstance. She had been in the midst of her happiest moments, when along came an evil that planted its seeds. It had taken months to mitigate the hatred she felt for Charlie Stine, but the girl's birth had brought it all back. Now hate kept rearing its head, hard set against what nature meant her to love.

The drizzle had stopped. Clouds were lifting, though a steady rumble still came from the flooding wash. She walked over and stood on the bank. She would have to dig to find her spring again when the flood stopped. Behind her, diapers snapped and flapped on the rope she had strung between trees to skin rabbits and other game. She guessed it had truly become a clothesline now. Jane Thompson and the other townswomen could gloat over it, Ruth mused blackly. She was becoming as domestic as any of them.

Muddy water poured off Rocky Mountain, the ground already saturated from last week's storm, rolling rocks and branches fast down canyon. Ruth thought about the way forces from far away gather strength and finally come do their work to change people's lives, the same way they change the shape of a canyon. And even when they were repaired, the lives were never the same as they'd been. The spring inside her would be harder to dig out than the one across the wash.

A chorus of bawling had started up within her cabin. For a moment Ruth stood her ground, continuing to watch the storm's destruction, the splintered pinyon across the wash, the changed terrain of the banks of the streambed, as gathered rainwater poured from the mountain rising on the other side. She felt the pull of her children's claim on her and turned around to confront it, though she made no move toward the cabin—despite her body's urge to get there on the run.

"Oh, Jim," she whispered. Ruth looked at the sopping ground in front of her cabin, remembering the horror that took place there only months ago. She felt herself start to dissolve, liquid inside her rushing to join the torrents around her. Then a section of her hair lifted slightly in back as by a current of warm breath, and she felt herself steadied, as if strong hands gripped her shoulders in support.

Where but in memory was her lover? And mere memory was insubstantial, unsatisfying—could change shape if a person wasn't careful. Still, memory was all she had left—of her Jim, and of the woman she had come to this place to be. Ruth breathed in what she could of the wind's promise and went inside to attend to the cacophony.

CHAPTER THREE

D̲espite her qualms, it felt good to be going somewhere in her bright shiny car again, even with two infants bedded down on the floor of the passenger side—though it had taken forever to get herself and the two of them ready. After two months, she had finally managed to button up a skirt she had worn before the pregnancy. Although the fit was tight, it hid the flabby belly that appeared to be shrinking back, but slowly. Both babies lay awake on the passenger floor, their eyes widening in surprise whenever she hit a buried rock or swerved to get out of one's way. To save gas, she had turned off the engine after climbing the bank at the North Fork wash and let the car find its own momentum down canyon.

She hadn't been to town since long before the babies came, letting John and Kate take care of her supply needs, which they had insisted on doing anyway. Why should she want to face small-minded townsfolk? The Olsens had continued that duty when the thick blackness descended on her after the birth. Even now Ruth felt it sitting above her like the flat black bottom of a thunderhead. She hoped Kate was right about despair being natural after giving birth, hoped that soon the light skin of that baby's face and the red-orange hair on its head would cease to sicken her spirit.

At any rate, she had to get out of that cabin, away from the place that felt more like a prison each day. How strange that the place she loved most in the world had come to feel like an iron-jawed animal trap, its teeth sunk into her flesh.

Kate came lumbering out as Ruth pulled into their yard. The minute the car stopped, one of the goats reared up and placed both forelegs on the passenger window, then slid off sideways and disappeared below the window glass. Both babies began to cry. Kate flung open the passenger door, shooing away the goat and two others that had joined it.

"For heavensake, Rute, on the floor?" Kate said, when she saw the makeshift nursery. She reached inside and lifted the nearest baby. Ruth had tried to get the cradle into the car, but it was about an inch or so bigger than the space she had for it.

"They were just fine, Kate, until they saw that goat. I think they enjoyed the ride down here." Ruth got out and walked around to pick up the other infant. She was always surprised at the way the girl calmed down whenever Kate took hold of her. "I finally named them last night." Ruth picked up the boy left on the car floor.

"You're holding Madeline," Ruth said as they walked toward the door of the rock house, "and I have J.B." She didn't mention that Madeline was her mother Cally's middle name—one she hated.

"What kind of name is J.B.?" Kate asked. "Even for American boy."

"I always think of him as Jim's boy. That's where the name came from."

"Why you not just name him Jim, then? A real name."

"Because he's not Jim," Ruth said. "That's why."

Inside the house, Kate stuffed a few pieces of pinyon into the stove and poured water in the coffeepot, setting it on a burner, the infant's head bobbing with each movement as the girl reared back to stare at

Kate's face. The boy on Ruth's own shoulder continued to gaze out the open doorway behind them.

"I won't be staying, Kate. I'm on my way in for groceries. I'll pick up whatever you need while I'm there. Of course, I'd love it if you want to ride in with me . . . ?"

Kate sat down across the table from her. "Why you not leave babies here with me? Make trip easier for you."

Ruth's heart lightened at the thought. She imagined herself walking unencumbered into the general store. She might even try out Mrs. Rose's Cantina that she heard opened in the back room of the store. Matt must have found a way to profit off his mother-in-law's cooking. Then she remembered her own role as a general store for her new babies and shook her head. "They might get hungry before I get back."

"You be back in time. If not I use goat milk mix with water, ya." Kate rose and walked to the stove, dumped a scoop of coffee grounds into the pot and pulled it to the side of the burner. "I miss them every day."

"I couldn't have got through this without you, Kate. I'll never forget that," Ruth told her, remembering the nights Kate slept beside her on a cot, how she got up each night to bring the newborns to Ruth's bed for nursing when she was so dazed and numb she could hardly tell one infant from the other in the dark.

"You look thousand miles from here, Rute." Kate set a cup of steaming coffee in front of her. When Ruth looked up, the girl was asleep on Kate's shoulder. *Madeline*, Ruth reminded herself, she had to get used to thinking of the girl that way. Naming her made the child's existence all the more real.

"Not so far." Not far enough. She picked up the cup and blew ripples across the surface of the liquid. The boy, J.B., had closed his eyes and breathed softly against Ruth's cheek. She turned her face toward his and brushed her lips over the soft skin of his forehead, then returned to test the heat of the coffee, savoring its bite on her tongue.

"John and the men gone all day to the mine. Your twins keep me company. You feed them again before you go," Kate said as if it had all been settled. Ruth changed the subject so she could think about it.

"Do you suppose those desert mines will open this winter?" she asked, and they spent the next few minutes discussing the effect the

New York Stock Market crash was having on the usual winter work in the desert mines, the rumors of closures and cutbacks. It was work the Swedes counted on to supplement the meager living they were able to hack out with John's onyx mine up the North Fork. The price of onyx had tumbled with the stock market, but they had hopes that a necessity like salt would keep its price, and hence the desert work, fairly stable. They would know soon, Kate said. Next week John and Ingmar would drive down to the desert and talk with the mine managers.

Conversation fell off and the two women sat listening to the sounds from outside, the occasional bleat of a goat, the nearly constant clucking of the hens, the mixed background of running stream and light wind in the willows. A fly droned by. "It's so peaceful when the babies are asleep," Ruth said wistfully.

"You need time away. Leave them with me, Rute. I take good care of them."

"I can't keep taking from you, Kate."

"You do me the favor, ya. I miss those babies."

Ruth considered for a few moments more. "Well, keeping them today might cure you, then," she said suddenly. She stood before she could change her mind. "All right. I suppose I ought to feed them and get going." She walked to the car and carried in the blankets, spread them on Kate's bed. Then she sat on the edge and poked J.B.'s mouth with her nipple until he was awake enough to suck. She kept having to give him little shakes to keep him nursing. When he would take no more, Kate brought Madeline to her other breast. The girl attacked the nipple greedily. It was Ruth who struggled now, keeping her eyes and heart trained on J.B. so the milk would continue. Finally, Madeline's eyes closed, and Ruth felt the baby's sucking ease. The infant let out a burp, then made a long shuddering sigh before her head lolled to one side.

Ruth laid her down beside her brother, got up and walked to where Kate stood mixing bread dough at the table. "Thanks, Kate," she said, starting to put her arms around her.

Kate stepped aside and waggled her away. "Go. Go, Rute. You get flour on you."

She leaned in and kissed Kate's cheek, then ran out to where her shiny car sat waiting, pulled open the door and swung herself inside.

Releasing the hand brake, she let the car roll for a few yards, switched on the key and let out the clutch. The engine caught. She pushed down the gas pedal and whipped around the bend, out of sight of the old stone house.

The road ahead drew her forward, and Ruth traveled over its familiar contours, the bends and dips in its ruts, as if renewing acquaintance with an old friend—one who had taken on new meaning with absence. Without the infants in the car, she could tip back the front window and savor the wind in her face, the scent of freedom heady and enticing. She could feel some of her old self returning, that sense of her own power that had always been with her before the ugliness. Its return burned tears into her eyes and tightened her throat. She was ready to face anything townsfolk might dish out.

When she arrived in front of Matt's General Store to find the front parking area devoid of other vehicles or horses, she was relieved. Yet when she pulled open the screen door, she found Jane Thompson talking to Mrs. Rose, the store owner's mother-in-law, at the front counter. The Thompson woman was, without contest, the desert town's most stalwart upholder of the social norm, and the nastiest busybody to boot.

"Hello," Ruth said to Mrs. Rose, nodding as she walked up the aisle. Both women looked surprised. Mrs. Rose nodded back. Neither invited her to join their conversation. That wasn't a surprise. Ruth opened her satchel and began selecting staples, while the women at the counter continued conversing about the effect of last year's economic collapse. Apparently it had affected much more than the price of onyx. They didn't lower their voices, which at least invited her to listen, Ruth decided. Mrs. Rose was saying that jobs were becoming so scarce that many husbands were staying in the Los Angeles area to work, returning occasionally on weekends. Some families had already moved out altogether.

"Lucky folks," Jane Thompson said. "I keep hoping Harry will decide to move back home to L.A. Mother would be glad to let us stay with her until things get settled. But he insists we can make a go of it, thinks he can find work building that new dam up on the Nevada line."

Ruth had nearly forgotten how bad things were everywhere. She was fortunate, she thought; she had her place and her garden and the nest egg from the inheritance she kept hidden in her bottom drawer, a nice one too. She'd hardly touched the five thousand, except for buying the car and her supplies. Must have most of it left, though she hadn't counted it lately. What would she have done if that inheritance hadn't come? As she gathered up her list of staples, Ruth pictured herself back in El Paso with her two babies. Her mother would have put her to work, all right. Ruth could see it now; as a trained nurse, she would be a front for the rest home, while she doubled in the brothel at night. An apprentice madame—or worse.

"I haven't seen you in some time, Ruth," Mrs. Rose said politely, as Ruth began unpacking her groceries on the counter. "You're looking well. You just missed Lily and Matt. They left only minutes before you came."

"It's good to be out again," Ruth said and meant it. She was surprised at the woman's civility, appreciated it. Noticing the closed door behind the counter, she remarked, "Kate said that back room was a cantina these days. Ingmar and John raved about your casseroles."

"We open it on weekends. You'll have to come back and try out our food sometime." Mrs. Rose began ringing up the groceries.

"Who knows when I can get back this way?"

"Indeed. Where are those new babies of yours, Ruth? Out in the car?" Jane Thompson asked, with pointed politeness. "We heard you gave birth to twins."

"That's right. Kate's got them for the morning."

"She's a good soul," Mrs. Rose said. "That will be twelve fifty, Ruth. I could never stand to be away from my babies when they were that small. Of course, I never had to handle two at the same time."

"I'm not getting much sleep," Ruth said, counting out the money. "Sometimes I hardly know which end of the baby to feed. One night I woke to crying and picked up the wrong one—the one who wasn't crying. Woke him up too. Then I had both of them hungry and screaming to contend with."

"Too bad you don't have a husband to help out," Jane Thompson remarked.

"Why, Jane! You know husbands are never good at those things," Mrs. Rose said. "What Ruth needs is a mother to help out. I'll certainly be there when Lily's time comes. You must have a mother around somewhere, don't you, Ruth?"

"God forbid. Not my mother. She's worse than any husband. That witch can stay right where she is—back in El Paso." Ruth began filling her satchel with the purchased provisions.

Mrs. Rose paled, raised a hand to her chest and held it over her heart, while Jane Thompson continued to watch Ruth with pursed lips. "I'm so sorry to hear that, Ruth, dear. Do you have other family you can count on?" Rose asked.

"I can count on myself. Kate tells me they'll sleep through the night soon."

"Well, you'll just have to bring the babies with you next time," Thompson said, with a knowing smile. "I, for one, can't wait to see what they look like."

"I'll just bet you can't." Ruth kept her voice as sweet as the venomous words would allow. *Who* they look like, Thompson might as well have said. Thompson and her ilk *might* forgive Ruth a child that resulted from force and violence—though even that was doubtful. But they would never forgive a child born of her love for an Indian man. Suddenly Ruth knew why Kate insisted on keeping the infants.

"But I guess you'll just have to be patient a while, Jane," Ruth said, forcing the same honeyed tone. "To get the rest of the juicy story to spread around town."

"Gracious sake." Mrs. Rose crossed both hands on her chest.

"I'll bring them with me soon enough, though. Maybe I'll take little J.B. over to the reservation in Black Canyon when he gets older, so he can learn his father's language. I always loved hearing Jim speak it." Ruth forced a smile, then found herself imitating, badly, something close to the rhythms and sounds of Jim's words when he spoke Yuiatei. "You see what I mean?" Ruth hefted the satchel over her shoulder. "It's been a real pleasure seeing you again."

She wheeled around, marched down the aisle and out the store door, leaving its bells jingling behind her. Reaching her vehicle, she yanked open the door and climbed in, slamming it firmly behind her. The motor caught and she spun the car around and out of the parking lot in a cloud of dust that trailed behind as she sped away from Juniper Valley. By the time she reached the turnoff to Rattlesnake Canyon, the heat on her cheeks had cooled enough for her to consider. She decided she wasn't sorry she had declared war on that awful woman. Why waste time pussyfooting while Thompson sprinkled her remarks with insult?

Poor Mrs. Rose though . . . she'd been genuinely friendly. Too bad the woman had been caught in the middle. How could she set foot in that store again now? Yet how would she get her provisions without going there?

And whatever had come over her to pretend she was speaking Yuia-tei? Some desire to rub the fact of her Indian lover in Thompson's face? How ridiculous. As if she were a young child sticking out her tongue at the woman, rather than a grown woman with two children. Well, she sure didn't feel like a grown woman with two children—she was still only twenty-two. Was she supposed to be changed completely by the mere act of birth? How could everything have changed so quickly? She had just begun making her life and suddenly it was over—or at least laid out before her as limited as a dress pattern.

Ruth kept her eyes dry. She swallowed hard and clamped her teeth. She would not become one of them. A creature tamed and leashed who gloried in its own captivity as it became warped out of shape. This would not be her fate. She remembered the silly ladies' teas in her Aunt Myrtle's parlor—then pictured her mother's dim rooms at the so-called rest home, where men slipped stealthily down the dark passageways each night. Surely that wasn't the only way to escape what society prescribed for a woman. There had to be better ways. Her brief flapper period been exciting, but hollow. Then she discovered Glory Springs and a life with substance. She hadn't counted on her own fertility to trap her. But she couldn't let it, wouldn't let it. And she did have the money her father left her, something neither Cally nor Myrtle had. That changed things. She had her own car. She'd trained as a nurse—could work if it came to that. And Glory Springs, she still had her Glory Springs—even if she *was* trapped in her cabin with two infants. Even if right now her breasts were tight and heavy with the duty of them, her body blindly obeying its own plan.

Under her blouse, milk dripped from one nipple, tracing a pathway down her skin, a liquid tether beyond her control. What would her life be like now if Jim were with her? She pictured them holed up together with the one child they would have had, both social outcasts. But they would have had each other. They would still have climbed Rocky Mountain together, would have driven over to visit his people in Black Canyon, a place closed to her without him. She imagined the two of them laughing as they drove, the child between them, Jim's long dark hair whipping back in the wind as he looked over and smiled at her.

But was a trip to meet his people really impossible, she wondered? What if she went on her own to Black Canyon with Jim's child? Maybe when J.B. was a little older? What would Jim's people say to such an intruder? Did they even speak English? A wave of pain choked off the rest of her thoughts. What would be the use going back to see where Jim had come from—when what she really wanted was to have him back?

Tipping the windshield open wider, she let in wind to dry her eyes. Air flowed back to whisper in her ears, and she swore she heard in it the sound of Jim's voice.

Ruth skidded the Model A to a halt, the steering wheel jerking out of her hands as her tires met the edge of sandy shoulder above the ruts. Fingers trembling, an ache welling in her chest, she switched off the ignition and got out. "So just where are you now, Jim?" she shouted toward the mountain looming in front of her. Dropping to her knees, she looked up at the distant ridges. "Why did you take him from me?" she demanded. The only answer was the whine of wind in pines high on the mountain.

CHAPTER FOUR

Ruth's eyes kept returning to the high slopes of Rocky Mountain, with an occasional glance at the diapers she rubbed up and down the scrub board. In her mind she was back with Jim at his hut, the two of them again together at that lake hidden high on the mountain. For a moment she imagined herself scrubbing these same diapers there by the petroglyphs, stars of sunlight reflecting from the water, Jim's presence as substantial as the ground under her knees. The feeling swept over her and was gone, the time they had shared far more distant than the mere top of a mountain.

"Times like this can't last forever," he had said on one of those magic ten days they spent together at that place. He'd kneeled behind her, and she could still feel the sensation of her breasts cupped in his hands while she coiled a rope of clay onto the olla in front of her. Letting go of the clay, she leaned back into him, looking upside down into his face.

"We'd better make the most of it, then," she'd told him glibly, turning so he could pull her to him.

Ruth swiped one shoulder across an eye, then the other, turned her head to check that the babies weren't doing something harmful—choking on acorns picked up from the ground, or grasping and chewing the pads of beavertail cactus. The girl, especially, was prone to testing out such delicacies. A few days ago Ruth had come across Madeline chewing something, and when the girl looked up and smiled, the black legs of a stink bug stuck out from between her white baby teeth. And each day it seemed Ruth had to stop to remove the hairlike beavertail spines from the children's fingers. Now that she'd weaned them both from her breast, maybe Kate would keep them for the day so she could go up the mountain. But could she bear to see the ruins of that place that had brought her so much joy? It might well break her heart all over again.

Both babies were fairly steady on their feet now, though there were still days until their first birthday. They were quick, Kate said. At least their walking allowed Ruth to let them run diaperless in the yard most summer days, even if they still required cloth protection at night. Winter had been a nightmare of diaper duty in icy water, garnered sometimes from melted snow and icicles. When she hung the wet diapers outside, they often froze solid, and she found herself bringing in stiff icy sheets that had to be thawed, then dried by the stove. Finally she had surrendered and hung the white flags everywhere inside her cabin. Well, not exactly white, since the stains never came out altogether, like the stain she turned back now to work on.

Ruth had come to understand her neighbors' insistence on plumbing and electricity. It would certainly make caring for children an easier task. John Olsen said that electricity would soon come into Juniper Valley, and there were days when she would have paid every cent of the inheritance she had stashed away just to bring electricity to her cabin. An expensive impossibility, of course, Juniper Valley being twelve miles away, but she could at least look into having the water piped from the spring to her house.

A frantic cry, followed by a duet of sobs, pulled Ruth from her thoughts. She looked around to find Madeline and J.B. flat on their backs, her new nanny goat having run between them, knocking each child aside as it raced to claim the clump of grama grass where the children had knelt, pretending to eat the grass like goats. Ruth jumped up and sprinted toward the commotion. "Get away from there, dammit," she shouted, kicking at the goat as it pulled out a mouthful of grass. "There's grass all over the place, you silly thing. What are you worried about?"

The goat leapt over the patch of grass and joined the other nanny in attacking an antelope bush. The babies quieted and sat staring up at her with tearstained faces. "For heaven's sake," Ruth said. "Do you have to be such babies about it?" She bent and helped J.B. to his feet, brushing the pebbles from his bronze back and buttocks. "Oh, I guess you do, don't you," she told him.

Madeline continued to stare up at her with pale blue eyes, as if she too deserved the same attention. "Oh, come on," Ruth said, reluctantly. She gave Madeline the same lift and brush-off, but a bit more briskly. "You're all right. It was just the goat."

Both children remained squinting up at Ruth in expectation, the July sun seething over their heads. She closed her eyes and sighed. How was she ever going to finish the wash? Their damned wash. She looked back at what used to be her bathtub, now filled with stinky diapers only half scrubbed. "Okay," she said, "let's go inside."

She scooped them up, one in each arm, and marched toward her cabin door. A little food and maybe she could get them to nap, have some time to herself. "How would you like a biscuit—some nice goat cheese maybe?" She had some milk to spare from the morning milking, though most of it she had put aside for making cheese. She had purchased the two nannies in order to get the twins weaned, but liked to reserve as much milk as possible for the cheese she so loved.

Ruth set her children on the floor, then half smashed a hunk of the zucchini she had cooked the night before, leaving enough chunks so they could pick up the food with their fingers, along with pieces of the goat cheese-smeared biscuit. She placed a bowlful on the floor in front of each baby. She'd rather feed them outside so she could finish the wash, but that usually ended in red ant bites, and once even a yellow jacket sting on J.B.'s tiny toe, which grew somewhat less tiny for a while.

On her bed, alongside the new modern novel she'd purchased when she took Kate to San Bernardino, lay the volume of *War and Peace* that had got her through the winter. She'd been grateful to have the huge saga to keep her occupied those cold winter months, hating to see the pages dwindle near the end, and she enjoyed the book so thoroughly she'd read it immediately a second time.

Ruth walked over and put the book back in the box under her cot. She picked up the new novel, ran her fingers over its colorful paper jacket, then opened to those pages that had intrigued her enough to buy the book in the first place. She looked down now and saw not print on paper but the colorfully dressed men and women she had read about, as they jitterbugged in a room filled with curling cigarette smoke, champagne glasses clinking on the sidelines. It was certainly a classier version of the flapper world she'd sampled briefly in El Paso, and even El Paso had its lure. Today the world in the novel seemed as fantastic as the one she encountered in the pages of the Russian novel. St. Petersburg didn't seem any more exotic than New England.

Ruth closed the book. She looked around the inside of her cabin, at the lower rock walls that reached up to greet the rough-hewn planks that held up the roof, at the cement floor with the two new throw rugs. J.B. had emptied his wooden bowl and was banging it on the floor near Madeline's foot. Squeals of laughter accompanied quick kicks of her legs. A hunk of half-chewed biscuit dropped from her mouth. J.B. let go of his bowl, leaned over and snatched up the gooey gob of food. He had it in his mouth before Ruth could get there. Madeline's laughter changed to sobs.

"Oh, icky, icky, J.B." The baby swallowed and smiled up at her.

"Kkkkk," he echoed. His sister continued sniffing, pointed at her brother.

"All right, you two. I've about had enough of all this." Reaching down, she yanked them each to their feet. "Let's go pee pee," she said, half dragging them back out into the yard.

When the pre-nap toilet was completed, Ruth brought the children inside and settled them onto opposite ends of their small cot, gave each a small cup of goat milk to drink before sleep. After smearing goat cheese on a biscuit for herself, she lay on her bed and picked up the novel she'd closed earlier. She might as well read until they fell asleep. The glamour of jazz and snappy conversation, the dramas of the rich, a welcome relief from the soiled diapers awaiting her. She wished she could as easily find solace in that other exotic world she longed to know, the world of Jim's people in Black Canyon.

"Those people not like strangers to come, Rute," John Olsen said when she told him she wanted to drive over there, and he went on to relate a story of a woman captured by other local Indians long ago. Kate had heard somewhere that the women in Black Canyon wore only grass skirts and the men considerably less. But Ruth had trouble reconciling these things with what Jim had told her—which, she had to admit, wasn't much. Yet there was no easy way to know what was true, no book to pick up about that place and the Yuiatei people. No way to know short of going there. She sighed and opened the novel before her, falling into pages that took her far from her cabin and the bed she lay upon.

Ruth found herself standing by the front tire of her Model A, listening to the hiss of the tire that had gone flat. But why was it still hissing, then, she wondered, and so violently? She walked around to see if the others were going flat as well. But they showed no sign of leakage. She felt a puzzlement so intense it managed to wake her, and she opened her eyes to discover the inside of her cabin. She realized the hissing was still going on. Only this time she recognized the sound at once. A rattler. And close by outside.

She jerked up from the bed, glancing as she did at the children's cot across the room. Empty. Then she heard their whimpers. In an instant, Ruth was at the door. The twins stood holding the front rim of the washtub, motionless except for hiccuping sniffles. Slightly around the bend of the tin tub, the rattler curled in the basin's wet shade.

Ruth snatched the .22 from the chest by the door, had it aimed and the trigger pulled before she stopped to consider. The shot took the snake's head off and made the babies howl out in loud body-shaking sobs they had instinctively held back. Ruth ran to the tub and, using the barrel of her rifle, flung the rattler over the bank of the wash, the head attached by only a thin strip of skin.

How had the babies got out without waking her? Would she have to close and latch the door from now on—even with the summer heat? And how had she fallen asleep in midday? The last thing she knew

Gatsby was standing on his marble steps, then suddenly a rattler was attacking her children. The goats that were supposed to alert her to snakes were grazing peacefully along the bottom of Rocky Mountain. Ruth took a deep breath and leaned her .22 against the tub, turned back to the red-faced panic she now had to soothe. Kneeling in front of the youngsters, she curled an arm around each one and hugged both tightly to her. When they calmed some, she held each one out from her, examining legs, arms and torsos, just in case.

"You're okay. You don't need to cry anymore," she told them, but they continued to cry. "The bad snake is dead. Come on. I'll show you." She led them to the bank of the wash, where they could look down on the dead reptile. When they saw it, they howled louder.

She sat them on the bank and walked down the trail into the wash, where she used her hands to hollow out a small hole in the sand. It wasn't a bad snake really, just some creature trying to find comfort. But snakes just create more snakes, she reasoned. She could eat the snake. She'd heard cowboys sometimes did. Then the meat wouldn't be wasted. But even from two feet away, the gamy smell made her stomach queasy.

Both babies screamed in terror when she used a small sage branch to lift the drooping rattler into the depression and cover it, first with sand, then piled rocks. "See," she said. "It's gone now." But the wailing babies couldn't possibly hear her over their commotion.

Her feet like stones, she climbed the bank of the wash and dragged herself toward her children. It wasn't their fault the rattler had terrified them, or that they woke up and she didn't. She shouldn't be irritated with them because of it. After all, they were just babies.

She had worked up a degree of compassion by the time she reached the sobbing pair. She took J.B. and Madeline into the house and broke up another biscuit, this time swabbing on some of the precious tomato jam Kate had given her. When the trauma finally receded, they all went back out into the yard, and Ruth finally managed to finish and hang the wash. By that time, the sun was sitting close to the mountain ridges. It was time to start the campfire and heat the stew. She had still to gather zucchini and tomatoes to add to the pot, and to get the goats off the mountain and milked before dark.

CHAPTER FIVE

Insides writhing, Ruth turned off the paved highway onto the dirt road that led to the Black Canyon Reservation. J.B. lay curled asleep on the seat next to her. She owed it to the boy, she reminded herself—and to Jim—to bring him here. She had seen no reason to bring the girl.

J.B. had traveled nicely through the long hours, spending much of his time standing at the window watching the desert pass by. Occasionally, he would turn to her in excitement and point out some animal. "Cooat," he would say, "cooat," when they saw a coyote, or "raba" for the many rabbits, so many Ruth was glad she'd brought the .22. She could pick up a couple for supper on the way back.

The road was now approaching the mouth of a canyon which looked very much like her own on the opposite side of Rocky Mountain, though the canyon walls were taller and steeper. More mesquite and manzanita interspersed with pinyon and scrub oak.

The rut road in front of her didn't appear much traveled. Sandy patches revealed some sign of automobile tires. Yet even these signatures of habitation and mobility were overlaid with the tracks of animals, and she tilted open her windshield to study them as she drove. Only the large curvatures of horse hooves within the mishmash of track were clearly identifiable.

Just what would she find when she arrived, she wondered, causing another invasion of butterflies in her belly? Despite her determination to put aside the stories she had heard, images of half-naked savages kept popping into her head.

Just ahead, the canyon curved sharply at nearly a right angle and continued on. Ruth followed the bend around the side of the mountain, then found her Model A dwarfed by huge cottonwood trees alongside the road, the diameter of each ancient trunk nearly the size of her car. Magnificent canopies of luminous gold leaves met and locked above the vehicle, their glow suffusing the air with an incandescence that made Ruth pull in her breath. Below the trees, and around them along the road, stood thickets of willow, their lemon color a subdued reflection of the leaves above. A single cottonwood leaf, deep amber and heart-shaped, floated in through the space above the tilted windshield, drifting down to settle on her lap. She brought the car to a halt, let out her breath. Drew in deep, as if she could bring all that beauty inside her with the air.

She sat for a moment, listening to the whispering slap of leaves, then quietly pulled down the door handle and stepped out of the car. Pushing the door closed, she muffled the click as the latch caught. Putting aside the purpose for her journey, Ruth walked up the road ahead of the Model A, looked overhead and stood marveling at the continuous ballet of deep ocher flecked with occasional green leaves. She held out her arms and watched the light dance across her skin, the pattern's movement accompanied by the tinkling chitter of tiny birds and the bouncing notes of a canyon wren. The ground around her wore a quilt of golden shapes, and she kneeled down and began to gather up handfuls of long, tapered willow leaves, began to weave and tangle the golden fingers into her hair. She stood, then, and began to whirl, flinging her arms out in celebration, swirling and leaping and laughing until at last her breath gave out and she collapsed gasping to the ground.

Her eyes burned with happiness. It had been so long since such wild exuberance had come over her. She had forgotten the intoxication of joy. Her own canyon had once brought her small daily doses, but so much had happened there that it had become simply the place she lived. She had ceased to see it—to really see it, the way she once had. The willows and cottonwoods at the Swedes' had turned gold like these, but she had barely noticed. She supposed wrens had sung there too. She hadn't heard them. Now this gladness had come upon her like a belated gift from her dead lover. Jim's gift to her, bringing her to this place so she could feel again. His way of telling her she was still alive. That he wanted her to be alive, to feel joy, even without him. She hoped she could carry this feeling with her to her own canyon.

A stirring from the car brought her back. J.B.'s head became visible at the passenger window. Above the car, the sun was nearing the ridges of the canyon. Not only had she not yet reached her destination, she realized, but she was hours from home in a strange canyon even wilder than her own. And nearing people it gave her shivers to think about. Yet she felt in no hurry to leave.

Ruth lifted her son from the window, gave him a hug and set him down to pee beside the vehicle. Shades of umber leaves over his head drew her eyes to the trunk of a cottonwood draped with many strands of vine, where wide leaves were turning a lovely red-orange that stood out among all the gold. Clusters of small purple fruit hung behind the leaves. Grapes? She walked over and looked closer. The globes were smaller and darker than any grapes she'd seen, so purple they were almost black. Ruth reached up, stretching onto her toes to get hold of and yank down a cluster.

The flavor was definitely grape, though more tart and with a fuzzy aftertaste. The seeds larger, the flesh less. She pulled down a few more clusters, handing one to J.B. "Spit out the big seed, J.B.," she said, demonstrating. He spit out the half-chewed grape instead. "No, J.B., not the grape," she told him. "Watch me." She placed a plump grape on her tongue, then ate and enjoyed it in an exaggerated way, exclaiming "mmmm" as if it were the finest chocolate, finally spitting the seed out into her palm. "See. Eat the grape and spit out the seed." She put one in his mouth.

"Mmmm," he said, going through the same demonstration of embellished savoring that she had, in the end spitting the seed into his palm, then looking up at her, his eyes expecting approval. She kneeled and hugged his small body to her, buried her nose in the thick dark hair that looked and smelled so like his father's. What a strange thing this was between a child and its mother, she thought, something never brought up in any of the books she read. This child had been given no choice, had been born to love and trust her. She winced inside, thinking of what that meant in Madeline's case.

"Come on, J.B.," she said, reaching down for his hand, "let's go see Daddy's people."

"Da peep," the boy said, "da peep," his smile bright with anticipation.

"I wonder what you think a daddy is," Ruth said sadly. She lifted him in through the passenger window and walked around to her own door. She didn't know if he'd understood any of what she told him on the way over as he stood gazing out that window while she went on explaining where they were going and why. It didn't matter. She'd tell him again when he was old enough to understand.

They drove on through the willows and occasional cottonwoods, though none so ancient as the first stand. As they rounded a bend at a spot where the small stream crossed the road, a bobcat raised its head. Ruth coasted to a stop, watched the cat fix its eyes on them, its whiskers still dripping. Then the animal turned and padded into the trees. She turned to J.B., who was grasping out the window for yellow fingers of willow that reached out toward the car. He hadn't seen the bobcat.

The line of willows dwindled and disappeared around the next bend, and they came to a place where the canyon widened. Ruth could make out signs of human activity, small dried fields where something had been grown, footprints, and a few ramadas for shade—brush-covered roofs, raised on long poles. A few horses grazed by the foot of the mountain. The canyon opened up even more around the next bend, bringing the little community into view. A number of small wooden houses, rectangular and boxlike, were scattered about. Most had the shade structures on the side or in back. Some of the houses had near them huge clumps of brush, woven and battened down with rope and poles. Looking more closely, Ruth noticed they had openings, doors, and appeared to be some sort of dwelling place. In the center of the community sat a large round building made of loosely woven brush, palm fronds and cattail tules. A tin chimney stretched up above the domed thatch roof.

Ruth drove toward the group of people—none appeared to be wearing grass skirts or loincloths—who were gathered at a campfire at the end of the village. She pulled up next to a rusted truck, the only other motor vehicle she had seen here, and switched off the ignition. The ensuing silence unnerved her.

From out her open window she heard nothing but the popping of wood in the campfire and the squawks of a jay nearby. The faces of the people were dark and unreadable. Campfire smoke curled up behind them into the twilight. She saw no sign of welcome, and their indifference appeared to express a hostility that ordered her away. Even the children had stopped in their play and gone silent. Such formidable self-possession was foreign to her own culture, which plastered suspicion over with a spurious sociability. She removed her hand from the door handle, ready to start the ignition and drive away.

"Da peep," J.B. cried out from beside her. "Da peep." He began jumping up and down on the seat. Before she could turn to quiet and correct him, the sound of language and laughter started up from the people at the campfire, as if J.B.'s voice had released them from some frozen state. Children appeared at the passenger window, a few talking animatedly in their own language, others in English, as they nodded toward J.B., who continued to bounce up and shout in his baby voice, "Da peep, da peep." A few of the adults started toward the Model A, and Ruth opened the door and stepped out to greet them.

Only a young woman and one man returned the hand she offered, giving it but the lightest of shakes, a subtle squeeze really, seeming uncomfortable with her own firm grip. From the beginning, Ruth suspected language would be a problem, even if it turned out that they spoke English as perfectly as Jim had. It was her own language that was the problem, and all words deserted her once she had nodded and smiled her hellos. She had no idea how to articulate her reasons for being there, and for a few moments stood dumbly looking over the group, while they appraised her as well.

In addition to the children chattering at the passenger window with J.B., there must have been nearly a dozen adults, including the few who stayed back tending the fire. Most of those who had approached the Model A were women, dressed similarly in long dresses, though a few had pinafores over the dresses. Many wore necklaces of bead and shell. The men wore belted pants and long-sleeved whitish shirts, some with vests. And hats, beaten and battered from wear. The group's attire was quite different from Jim's khaki pants and plaid shirt—and far different from the grass skirts and loincloths she had been warned about.

A white-haired woman that Ruth had noticed particularly for her presence and bearing stepped forward and spoke to Ruth in the language she remembered hearing Jim speak. The sound soothed her ears, brought tears to her eyes. She wanted to respond with like sounds that the woman would understand. But this woman that the rest deferred to was no Jane Thompson to be fooled by sounds made in childish defiance. Strength and leadership had patterned the weathered lines of her face.

"I'm Ruth," she said, holding her palm to her chest. Ruth turned back to the car and pointed inside, "and this is J.B., Jim's boy." But the passenger seat was empty. She whirled back around in time to see J.B. carried toward her by a young boy, who came up surrounded by the rest of the children. The baby was laughing and waving his hands about. The woman walked over and studied J.B. closely, as did the other adults.

The boy carrying J.B. said a few words of Yuiatei to her and, when she didn't answer, said in English, "The baby's hungry. Can I feed him?" He pointed toward the campfire. Ruth considered for a brief moment, then nodded. The boy seemed to know what he was doing.

Once the children left, the woman who had spoken to her before called out toward one of the dwellings, and a moment later a young girl came out, holding an infant who couldn't have been more than days old. The girl herself could have been anywhere from thirteen to sixteen, Ruth thought, admiring the long braid that hung down her back to her waist. The woman spoke again and the girl turned to Ruth. "She wants to know why you come here and how you got this child."

"J.B. is my son," Ruth said quickly, looking from the girl to the older woman, "mine and Jim's. He never got to see his son. I've come here because Jim told me this place was his home. I wanted J.B. to see where his father came from. To meet his people."

As the girl translated, the old woman's eyes gazed into the distance. Then she looked Ruth over again and said something to the girl. "Grandmother Siki wants to know more about this Jim. She doesn't know this name," the girl with the braid told her.

"He'd been sent to school. Even went to college, but came back here. Jim worked for some miners on the other side of the mountain," Ruth said, pointing at Rocky Mountain, "where I live. He used to return here before each winter, even though his parents are dead. He said his mother died of diabetes. I think his father died long ago. A sister married a white . . ." Ruth stopped, considered the word Jim told her was used for whites, then continued, "a Teske and moved away. That's all I know about them. Daniels was their name."

The deep lines in the old woman's face shifted into a smile as the girl related Ruth's message. Members of the group began to confer, and Ruth relished the sounds of the exotic language. She took in the place more deeply as she breathed in the smells of campfire smoke mixed with something mouthwatering she could see being roasted there. Near the campfire, J.B. was seated on a small rock, the group of children sitting in a half circle around him.

"She said your Jim must be our Ni'jini." The girl's voice brought Ruth back. The others had begun walking toward the campfire. "He used to work in the mines way back there." She indicated the outline of Rocky Mountain with her head. "Used to come back here before the snows. Over there, that's his place." With her eyes and lips she directed Ruth to one of the brush clump dwellings up against the mountain, barely visible in the thickening twilight. "No one's there now but *iti'situi*. Mice."

"My grandmother said for you to come eat with us now," the girl said. "Oh, my name is Brenda." She shifted the baby to one shoulder and started toward the campfire, looked over her free shoulder at Ruth to follow her.

"Thank you. That's very nice of her, of all of you," Ruth said, awkwardly, as they walked. She was famished, but had been too preoccupied to notice until she'd smelled the food. "You must have gone away to school somewhere, to speak English so well." Not as well as Jim,

Ruth thought. But she loved the way the girl's English words retained the rhythms and inflections of her native language, something Ruth could barely make out when Jim spoke.

"In Banning for a while. My mother works at the agency," the girl said without looking over. "Before this happened." She patted her baby, and the quickening of her pace told Ruth she didn't want more probing.

When they reached the campfire, Ruth went directly to J.B., who was chattering happily in his English baby talk while the children gathered around him, occasionally speaking to him in a language as foreign to him as his baby talk was to them. Clearly, something more basic than language was being understood. Ruth watched a girl who looked to be about five lift a small rock and give it to J.B. "Na'di," the girl said.

"Nnee," J.B. imitated, the heavy stone dropping from his hand to the ground, initiating a new round of laughter. J.B. looked up at Ruth and chirped out a string of words that she barely got the gist of, then went back to ignoring her in favor of the group. She had never seen him so excited, or so full of words.

When the boy who had carried him arrived with two small bowls of food, the other children dashed toward the campfire. He set the wooden bowls down and helped J.B. from the rock, placing him on the ground with a bowl between his legs. J.B. needed no coaxing, reached down and chose a morsel. Ruth kneeled and looked closer: a few kernels of corn, squash, and a small section of some kind of hard bread, which was what J.B. had picked up. But it was the strange lump of stringy meat in the bowl that intrigued her. She was wondering just what this mystery meat might be when Brenda walked up and handed her a bowlful of her own. Ruth saw she no longer had the baby with her.

"Thank you," Ruth said, getting to her feet. "It smells delicious." The sound of her polite words seemed oddly out of place.

Brenda led her over beside the campfire, where the Yuiatei adults sat, and Ruth settled cross-legged onto the sandy ground at the periphery of the gathering, cradling the heavy wooden bowl to her. She picked out the slender cob of parched corn, bit into the sweet kernels. Heavenly, as was the squash. She tried a bite of the bread, which took some doing. It was less hard than extremely chewy, and the taste was like no bread she'd ever eaten, heavy and wild and slightly sweet—interesting and not at all unpleasant. Yet the meat continued to concern her. Its texture, shape and color were foreign to her experience. "What is this meat?" she asked Brenda, who had settled beside her.

"*Bki'situi,*" she said, with a slight smile. "It's very good." Ruth was relieved that she hadn't said *iti'situi,* but the sound was too similar to comfort Ruth much, given the size and shape of the meat. She chose not to ask for a translation. It really could be a very small rabbit, she told herself, and not one of the other creatures that Jim said were sometimes eaten, squirrel or wood rat. Everyone else seemed to be enjoying it along with the rest of the meal, even her J.B. When Ruth noticed that Brenda glanced down occasionally to see what Ruth was eating, she put a morsel into her mouth and chewed it as casually as she had the corn, all the while fighting her stomach's churning. It wasn't that the sweet flavor repulsed her in itself, nor the meat's dry and stringy texture, but the ideas her imagination continued to conjure up. Rabbit, Ruth insisted to herself, small rabbit.

Ruth knew others in the group were observing her, though so subtly it was hardly apparent. She was a likely subject of the occasional conversations that occurred. Yet she felt no less comfortable here than in groups in her own community, where people attempted to engage her in conversations laid with traps to test and accuse her. At least here there was reason for her to be subject to observation. Ruth watched as Grandmother Siki removed a moth from her bowl, placed it carefully on the ground beside her, and went on eating. She liked the fact that these people weren't adverse to their surroundings, didn't squeal at lizards or squash the moths and other insects that landed on their food, which had happened frequently at community potlucks. Some townsfolk even threw out the food afterward. And if Ruth's suspicions about the food here were correct, she herself had a lot to learn from these people, that is if they allowed her to.

How distant and unreal that world on the other side of Rocky Mountain seemed as she sat enjoying this place and its people. Its substance seemed to have disappeared into the darkness that swallowed up the outline of her mountain. The fact that she was far from her cabin, that Kate would be wondering if Ruth would return to take

Madeline home tonight, didn't seem at all important. After all, it was Kate who'd insisted that Ruth take blankets along "just in case." "It a long way, Rute. Who know what might happen, ya? Might have to stay somewhere." And Ruth knew Kate would bed Maddie down with her. Ruth was free to bed J.B. on the car seat and throw a blanket on the ground somewhere for herself. At the moment she had no burning desire to return to her own canyon and cabin, which had come to feel too much like a cage. Yet the instant that thought occurred to her, an intense longing for Glory Springs came over her. To never see it again would mean the end of her.

Ruth recognized the familiar smell of coffee, as Brenda came toward her from the fire, and carefully removed the hot cup from the girl's hands. These were modern Indians; after all, it was 1932. Around the glow of the large campfire, she noticed the crowd had thinned, could detect the pale light of kerosene lamps and a flicker of candles through the windows of some of the cabins.

J.B. toddled over and settled into her lap as she drank. She stroked his bare arm as he lay against her. His skin felt cool to her touch after the hot coffee cup. The air was beginning to chill. She supposed she should get his little jacket from the car, or put him to bed there. Then what, she wondered? Drive somewhere and bed down herself? Stay here for the night? But how could she without being asked?

Ruth had been dimly aware of a droning, a sound like that of an approaching motor in her own canyon. As the sound grew louder, she became certain it was indeed a vehicle and trained her eyes on the road down canyon. It wasn't long before she saw headlights flash on the mountainsides as the vehicle rounded the bend, then the yellow-orange orbs of light coming toward the camp. A small truck pulled up next to the old rusted one, a number of men spilling out from the bed. A woman and two men got out of the cab and started toward the campfire, one man tall and lanky, the other short and stocky, walking with a jerky limp. Some of the Yuiatei who had gone inside the cabins came back to the campfire, and conversation surged as food was served to the returned group. Ruth thought she detected a faint smell of alcohol while women and children unloaded boxes of groceries from the truck.

J.B. was sound asleep in her lap. Ruth pulled herself to her feet and carried him to the Model A. He barely stirred as she wrapped him in a blanket and kissed his cheek, leaving him curled on the passenger seat. Ruth closed the door quietly and went back to say her good-byes. She picked out Brenda's silhouette from the group around the fire and came up beside her. "I'd like to thank your grandmother before I go," she said. "Will you translate again for us?"

"This is my mother," Brenda said, indicating the woman beside her. "I just told her about you." It was the woman who got out of the truck cab.

The woman held out her hand. "I'm Martha Naubel," she said. "You've already met my little grandson here, Brenda tells me."

Ruth took her hand, tried not to squeeze too hard. Grandson? The woman didn't look much older than Ruth was. "Pleased to meet you," she said. Martha wasn't dressed like the other women either but wore slacks and a tailored blouse. Her shoulder-length hair had been curled.

"This is my brother, Lem," Martha told her, and the stocky man with the limp rose and took Ruth's hand, gripped it firmly. Modern, Ruth thought. "Jackson, my husband . . ?" She exchanged a look with her brother, glanced out into the darkness, and sighed, "Well, he's out there somewhere.

"Come on," she said. "I'll translate for you."

They walked around to the other side of the fire, where the old woman sat talking with the tall, lanky man, who looked up, openly scrutinizing her as she approached. Ruth met the intensity of that gaze, then squatted before the old woman, whose face was even more impressive as the fire illumined its sculpture in light and shadow. Ruth hadn't noticed how much humor lay dormant in the patterns on her skin. "I want to thank you for letting me stay and eat with you," Ruth told her. "For being so kind to me and my son. I hope you'll let us come back."

Brenda's mother translated and the woman responded. The look on the old woman's face gave Ruth the idea that she would have said more if Ruth could only understand. "You can come back anytime, Grandmother Siki said," Martha told Ruth. "You don't have to leave now, either. You can stay up there if you want." She nodded toward the darkness next to the mountain. "Why don't you stay around so we can get to know you?" she added.

"Thank you very much," Ruth said, gratitude deepening her voice. But she had finally decided it was time to leave. Now she was confused.

"Where is your boy?" The tall man's voice was resonant and firm, and without a trace of Indian inflection.

"He's asleep in my car." Ruth regarded him closely. He appeared taller than any of the others and wore no hat to cover the loose black hair that glinted in the firelight as it dropped to his shoulders and chest. Light lines at the corners of his eyes and etched below his cheekbones indicated he was older. Somewhere in his late thirties, maybe?

"What happened to Ni'jini?" he asked. Ruth sensed the man's position in the group, knew by his tone that his question demanded an answer.

"He was murdered by a cowboy named Charlie Stine. Stine also . . . well, I would have killed him myself but he left the area. Someone shot him dead in Kansas a few months later. I only wish I'd got see his rotted body to make sure." Ruth found herself shaking. Would this consuming hatred ever leave her? Maddie's image completed her bitterness.

The man's eyes narrowed slightly as he listened. He said nothing when she finished but continued to observe her. "Where did this happen?" he asked finally.

"At my place, my homestead, Glory Springs, on the other side of Rocky Mountain. He's buried there across the wash from my cabin." Then Ruth remembered. "Jim said his people—that would be you folks, I guess—used another name for the place. I can't remember the words he used exactly, but I remember he said they meant something like 'small rocks rising.'"

A look of recognition crossed the man's face. He turned and conferred with the old woman, who nodded at his words. "She has heard of the place. I went there many times when I was young. You're welcome to stay here tonight," he said. "But Ni'jini's old place isn't a good idea. Full of bugs and rodents. You'd need to clean it out first. I'll go up there with you so you can look at it, then decide."

"Oh, yes, I'd like to see it." Ruth stood, realizing now that some of what she'd thought fire glint in his hair was scattered strands of gray. "I can sleep anywhere. It doesn't have to be inside. I have blankets with me."

They walked together through the darkness, the tin kerosene lamp the man carried casting a bright circle around them. "This was his mother's *ki'takii*. Ni'jini would replenish it each year when he came back. We wondered why he didn't return last winter. Their place should be burned now that he's gone."

"He did leave a son," Ruth said, surprised by her own boldness.

"These old *ki'takii* are meant to be renewed. Not many use them anymore, except for ceremonies," he told her as the brush dwelling became visible in the lamp's peripheral illumination. "When people move out, other creatures move in fast." He lifted the lantern and held it up next to the door, while Ruth examined the construction of the dwelling. What had appeared to be a huge pile of brush from the distance showed itself to be sturdy and intricately interwoven beneath the brushy exterior. She wondered if the apparent crude surface had originally been meant to camouflage the structure's purpose to outsiders.

The man held the lantern inside the door. Ruth stepped over and peered into the *ki'takii*. She was surprised to see that the floor was not level with the ground, but dug down a foot or two. They walked down the dirt incline that led into the roughly circular dwelling, past a rusted tin stove in the center, to a small table on the other side. The man set the lantern down and turned up the wick, expanding the range of illumination. Ruth ran her palm across a section of the dusty tabletop, cleaning away a place where her fingertips could feel the grain of the wood. The table had been fashioned from the trunk of a manzanita, just like the one Jim had made for Ruth's new cabin. Her own was larger and more finely finished, but she recognized Jim's work.

"There's not much left here." He lifted a tin mug from the table, set it inside the wooden bowl beside it, then handed both to Ruth. "Except for these, Ni'jini always brought with him whatever he needed. You can have them for your boy.

"I'm going back now," he said. "You can keep the lamp and come back when you want. Or stay up here." He started to leave, then stopped, turned back. "By the way, Thomas is my away name. You can call me that. They didn't tell me your name."

"Ruth. My boy is J.B., that's for 'Jim's boy.'"

Thomas smiled, regarded her for a moment more. "If you do leave tonight, we want you to come back. You are welcome here, you and Jim's Boy." He turned and disappeared into the darkness beyond the doorway.

Ruth brushed dust from the upended side of the apple crate next to the table and sat on it, listening to Thomas's retreating footsteps until they were swallowed up in the song of fall's final crickets. Occasional gusts of conversation wafted up from around the fire glow visible through the open door, the meaning and words as mysterious to her as the meaning of cricket chirp. The air inside the dwelling absorbed the smell of campfire and roasting pinyon nuts, dulling slightly the odors of rodent and stale dust.

She wondered if Jim had ever sat on this same crate, watching the glow of campfire out this same door. But it would have been nearer winter when he came back here, she remembered. He would have hung something over the door and made his own fire in the rusted stove. Ruth got up and took the lantern from the table, held it up to better illumine the rest of the empty room. Her eye was drawn to a scattering of dry leaves across from her, and she walked over, kneeled down to examine them in the lamplight. At first she thought the leaves had been pulled out from the walls by the rodents whose odors were so acutely present. Except that she could see a definite depression beneath the leaves—about the length of a man's body. Then, on the tule wall behind them, Ruth caught sight of strands of red cloth. She reached over and pulled one free, felt its texture between her fingers. It might have come from the very blanket Jim was buried in. She rubbed the strand against her cheek, picturing her lover wrapped in that red blanket as he lay asleep in this depression—so shallow and innocuous compared to the depression he lay in now.

Ruth fit her own body into the pattern Jim's had made, turning to one side and snuggling her hip into the sand. Of course, he would have lain on willow boughs and sage that he cleared away when he left. On boughs like the ones in his hut on the mountain, boughs they had never cleared away. The two of them had intended to return, never imagining what was to follow. Here she had only a few dried remnants to cushion her from the ground's hard reality. The leaves near her eyes were mostly willow, like the ones so bright and lemony in the canyon. But these were pale and grayed, taken when they were still green, the way Jim had been. Ruth let her quiet tears water the willow leaves now, as if her bottomless longing could make them spring up green anew.

CHAPTER SIX

R uth forced her feet beneath the chill stream, glad winter's ice had finally melted. She had stopped to let her children pee on the way back from town, deciding to test the water's temperature while she was there. A rustling across the creek drew her attention, and she looked up just in time to see the blue face part the willows and stare down to melt her with enormous brown eyes. At once Maddie was at her side pointing and attempting to whinny, while next to her J.B. squealed out "huss, huss." The horse shifted its gaze to the children for a moment, then stepped out of the willows and lowered its mouth to the water. It was the bluest roan Ruth had ever seen. So blue it made all other roans she'd seen seem gray, its coat the exact color of juniper berries, blue dusted slightly with white. Her hand ached to touch it, to run a palm along the length of neck, still soft with winter coat, to feel the smooth velvet of its nose against her skin.

"Pretty horse," she told it. "Pretty, pretty, pretty." The horse ignored her and went on sucking up water from the stream. She wanted to pull her feet from the cold water, but was afraid of scaring off the animal. It took all the will she had left to let her feet freeze in order to keep the creature in her sight. When at last the horse raised its head, she quietly slid her feet from the stream, grasping one in each hand to warm it, keeping her eyes trained on the beautiful animal.

Mouth still dripping, the roan nodded, shook its head from side to side, nickered, then turned and disappeared into the willows. The horse had excited the children beyond control, and they continued to giddyup circles in the sand, whinnying and neighing, until it left. Then they stood on the stream bank pointing and crying as if their hearts had been carried off by the animal. Ruth had an urge to run after it herself, shouting *Come back, come back,* as she listened to the sound of hooves trotting off behind the willows. She wanted that animal like nothing she had wanted for a very long time.

Comforting the children with a quick hug, she took their hands and started toward the Model A parked in the road. "Huss, huss," J.B.'s teary voice kept repeating after she eased them in the passenger window, their little fingers still pointed at the spot where the horse had stood.

"Yes, yes, the horse. I don't know where he went either," she told them as she walked around and climbed in. She shut the driver's door and switched on the ignition. "I don't even know where he came from or what he's doing in this canyon. Or who he belongs to, but I intend to find out." She'd start with Kate and John.

The two children kept their eyes on the willows as Ruth drove, while she went on explaining the situation to them the way she always did, which was really a form of talking to herself. She kept the car moving slowly, so she could peer through openings between the newly leafed willows for some sign of that splendid blue coat. The fact that the coat was so thick, only about half shed, she guessed, meant the horse must have run wild and unprotected for the entire winter. It was hard to believe anyone would let such a gorgeous creature run free. She could only think it must have escaped from somewhere.

Neither John nor Kate had any idea where the animal had come from, nor who owned it, though both had caught sight of the horse more than once since they returned from the winter mines two weeks ago. Their return had been earlier than usual, as had been the appearance of spring after what had been the mildest winter Ruth had yet seen in the canyon. Snow had been as scarce as money seemed to be these days, worsening month by month for the Olsens. And the newspaper she read in town said the rest of 1933 was likely to be worse yet. Already the Swedish miners could hardly find work or sell the onyx from their own mine. Only their goats and chickens and the garden kept them from dire straits.

Ruth unloaded the staples she had picked up for the Olsens at Matt's store, shaving a small amount of its cost from the price she asked. Not enough to notice. They insisted she stay for a lunch of pinto bean soup and biscuits, and she hadn't the heart to refuse. She knew the Olsens loved having J.B. and Madeline around, as did the other miners, and the meal was filled with laughter at the children's antics and attempts to string words together. Even she found the children more amusing in that appreciative company, where at home she might not have noticed, or been annoyed at the distraction.

Ruth was glad to see Maddie getting a good share of the attention. It helped to relieve her own nagging guilt, something she struggled with daily. She forced herself to treat Madeline fairly and equally, though often it was hard to dredge up much heart for it. Little things the girl did annoyed Ruth terribly, like her constant imitation of animal sounds.

The animal imitations, Ruth realized now, had started as far back as the incident with the rattler at the laundry tub, though she'd thought nothing of it then. But the next day, she remembered, Maddie began pointing at sticks and twigs, making a *sssssing* that sounded little like the frightening imitation of a rattler the girl could affect these days. Other creatures too. Just last week, Ruth had crept quietly to the spring and peeked around the oak bush, fully expecting to see the quail she'd heard calling there. Instead, she found Maddie making those damn mouth noises. Ruth hadn't realized the girl had become so adept at it.

It chilled her to remember her own treatment by Cally, and she fought hard against the meanness that tried to seep out into her actions. Such meanness was in her, though. She felt its presence every time her eye met the red of Maddie's hair, although she was glad the girl's hair was more a coppery auburn than the ugly orange of her father's.

It was midafternoon by the time Ruth pulled up in her own yard. Both children had fallen asleep after they left the Swedes', and Ruth was careful not to wake them as she left the car. That was probably a mistake, she told herself, lifting groceries from the rumble seat; it would mean they would both be awake late into the night. But a moment's peace was too much to pass up.

She was carrying her sacks, one in each arm, toward her front door, when she saw the man across the wash standing over Jim's grave. He seemed to take no notice of her, but continued to sprinkle something over the pile of stones. She could make out the sound of a low chant. Ruth went inside and put her groceries on the table, then came back out to watch. She had recognized Thomas right away, although his hair was now pulled back and braided.

Ruth walked across the wash, where he seemed to be waiting for her. "You found Jim's grave," she said as she walked up.

Thomas nodded. "Words had to be said for him."

"Thank you."

"Over there too." He looked back across the wash. "If that's where it happened."

She looked over at her cabin and yard, unlocking the feel of the men attacking her body beside the cabin, pictured Jim dragging himself out the door with the shotgun, aiming that final shot at the attackers before collapsing. "Yes," she managed to whisper.

They walked back across the wash. Thomas's expression contained a contemplative calm, as if he were somewhere far off in his thoughts, yet at the same time fully set on his task in the here and now. "Sit there," he said, when they stood in front of her cabin. She obeyed, easing herself onto the ground, still hard and cold from the long nights of winter.

He remained standing and chanted for a few minutes, sprinkling something from his feathered pouch over the ground, and more over her head. She looked up at the light powdery substance drifting above her in the calm air, then closed her eyes as his finger came down to touch her forehead and the bridge of her nose. Her breath caught when she felt the caress of a feather brush the skin of her cheeks. He turned and walked to each side of the yard around her cabin, still chanting and stopping at some invisible boundary to scatter a bit of the substance. Ruth reached up to examine the powder he'd placed on her forehead, which felt like silk to her touch, its color a golden yellow on the tip of her finger. She found the taste sweet and dusky.

When his ritual was complete, Thomas came and sat on the ground beside her. "I hope that will help," he said. "Evil events leave a power behind them. The rest will be up to you."

"Some events are harder to erase than others," she told him, thinking of the red-haired child asleep in the car, of her daily struggle.

"They can't ever be erased. They have to be *niihi'ahi,* turned back." He seemed to be studying her. "Where is your boy?"

"In the car. Asleep."

"When he wakes, I'll say words over him."

Ruth started to protest, but clamped her mouth shut. Madeline would wake too. If only she'd left her with Kate. But how was she to know Thomas would be here? The last thing in the world she had expected. "How did you get here? Did you come over the mountain?" she asked. "That's such a long way."

"I go up there each spring—but on the other side," he told her, "to get the *bi'hi* that come up under the snow. They dry up fast once the snow goes. Usually I don't come all the way over here, though."

"Except this time—because of Jim?"

"It took two days. I stayed on the mountain last night. Up there." He looked over his shoulder, at the far eastern ridge near the top. "I could see your cabin's light from way up."

Ruth realized she had forgotten her manners. "Would you like a cup of coffee, something to eat? You must be hungry."

"I'm fine. Coffee would be good though."

They went inside, and Ruth built a fire in the stove and put the coffee water on to heat, while Thomas stood examining the books lined up on the top of her dresser beside the olla Jim had made. The ollas she'd made herself lined the small natural shelf between the roof and rafters. She still felt awkward about Madeline, but there seemed no way to avoid his becoming aware of the girl's existence.

"What you were doing earlier . . . are you what they call a medicine man, then?" she blurted out when she turned from the stove and found him watching her from across the room.

"I suppose your people would call me that. *Cafika,* in our language." He walked over and sat in a chair by the stove. "My skills are pretty basic, I'm afraid. I was away at school some of the years I should have been learning. But I have what's left of the old knowledge. Much has been lost."

"What kinds of things have been lost?" Ruth set two cups onto the table in front of them.

"Old songs of knowledge and history. Special learning about some of the plants, the ways to prepare them and what to use them for. Many of the old customs and healings."

"I don't understand how they get lost," she said. "They aren't the kinds of things that can just be misplaced somewhere."

"They get lost when people, when whole families, die suddenly of diseases they have never seen before," he told her, his voice hard. "Lost when people are moved from their home lands and made to live in places foreign to them for long periods. When they're forced to learn new ways to survive. Then people forget the old ways and the reasons for them. Some just go live away like Ni'jini and one day stop coming back. Are never heard from again. Who knows what happens to them?"

"You know what happened to Jim."

"Thanks to you. But no one else would have driven over to tell us he'd been killed. To them he would only have been some dead Indian."

Ruth opened the coffee can and scooped out grounds. Pouring them into the pot, she gave a quick stir, then moved the pot off the burner. "Coffee always tastes better made on a campfire," she said. "But this will have to do."

"I think I heard a child's voice out there." Thomas got up from his chair. Ruth pushed past him and was out the door before he could take another step.

She heard both children whimpering as they woke to find themselves in the Model A, and hurried around to the passenger door and yanked it open. "It's all right," she assured them quickly. "You're right here in our yard." J.B. sat rubbing his eyes, kicking out at his sleepy sister to move her out of his way, which made her cry harder.

Ruth lifted J.B. from the car and set him beside it. She glanced over to make sure that Thomas remained by the cabin. "Go pee pee, J.B., there, behind the tree. Come on, Maddie," she said. "You're home. It's time to get up now." She snatched Madeline up, set her down next to her brother. "Go pee pee," she ordered. She didn't look over to see if Thomas was paying attention to this undignified but necessary ritual behind the car. She would have liked to pull down her own pants and join the children, but thought she could hold out a while longer.

When the children finished, she herded them over to where Thomas was standing by the cabin. "Da peep," J.B. said, when he saw Thomas, and began running toward him. Maddie stayed close by Ruth's side as they walked.

"It's good to see you, J.B.," Thomas said when the boy reached him, but his eyes never left the girl at Ruth's side, even as he lifted the boy from the ground. Once in the man's arms, J.B. patted at Thomas's head and repeated the phrase that Ruth was surprised he remembered. "Da peep," he kept saying.

She swallowed hard, clenched her teeth, then lifted up and presented her shame and nemesis for Thomas to behold. "They're twins," she said, as his eyes inspected the red hair and light skin of the child.

Finally, he brought his gaze to Ruth's face and an understanding passed between them. There was much she couldn't read in those dark eyes, but she did see a comprehension and an empathy beyond anything she had found elsewhere, even within her own heart. "I'll say words over them both," he told her.

They took the children to the front of the cabin, and Ruth sat on the ground with one arm around each child, while Thomas performed the ritual. The two children remained fascinated the whole time he chanted and sprinkled pollen, even laughed occasionally, especially at the end when the man left a streak of the powdery substance on each of their foreheads. Did she imagine it, or did his hand linger longer with the pollen over the girl's head?

Pulling out that feather so large it could only have come from an eagle, the man brushed it lightly over each of their faces and along their shoulders and chests.

Once the ceremony was over, the children left her side and began imitating the sound of the chant and sprinkling pinches of dirt over each other. Maddie picked up a jay feather and the two of them took turns patting it over the other's face. Thomas stood examining the plants along the bank of the wash. Unable to ignore her full bladder a minute more, Ruth started toward the goat pen.

"I have to milk the goats," she called out, escaping with her bucket to relieve herself behind the pen before any milking got done.

"You'll stay for supper, won't you?" Ruth asked later, after she had returned and put on the coffee to reheat for them. She strained the milk into a jug while the coffee was heating, and gave each child a cup of it to drink. The rest she would clabber to make more cheese, like the lump of it left hanging in the window. "What are you going to do, go back over the mountain? Would you like me to drive you back tomorrow? I'd been thinking about making another visit anyway.

"At any rate, you're welcome to do both," Ruth continued, "have supper and stay the night." She heard herself chattering, but didn't know how to stop. Something about him or about the situation made her feel awkward, though she wasn't sure what it was. Maybe because she'd learned he was a medicine man . . . and because he seemed to understand more about her than she wanted him to. "Supper won't be much more than ordinary stew and biscuits, nothing so interesting as I had with your people. I only planted my garden a couple weeks ago, so there won't be any fresh vegetables I'm afraid. Then . . ."

"Whatever you have will be fine. I'll go back over the mountain though. I plan to get more *bi'hi* on the way back."

"But it will be dark soon. Surely you won't leave tonight."

"I can stay across the wash, if it's all right with you. That's where I left my pack and blanket. I'll leave at dawn."

"Of course, it's all right," Ruth said. "I'm curious, though. What are these 'bee hee' you're after? What do you use them for?"

Thomas smiled at her pronunciation. "I think you folks would call them snow flowers, but they have to be gathered before they rise much above the ground. Their medicine gets lost when it hits the sun. They're used for a number things," he ended mysteriously. Ruth had never heard of snow flowers any more than she'd heard of "bee hee" or however it was said.

"There are vegetables growing around your spring, by the way," he said. "Come, I'll show you."

Before following him out into the twilight, Ruth pulled the chairs away from the table and made sure the children were busy on the floor near the bed with the chunks of wood John Olsen had cut and colored for them—they liked to pile the blocks high in different formations until they finally crashed to the floor.

"See all this," he said, squatting by a patch of newly sprouted weeds beside her spring. "These are *bi'hatii,* very good. You can cook and eat them. Roast them with or without meats, as we do. Or boil them up like spinach probably, though I haven't had them that way."

"I pulled out a lot of these to plant my garden." She kneeled and examined the plant more closely. The stems were red and the arrow-shaped leaves had a V of white stamped on them. She picked a leaf and chewed, spitting out the slightly bitter residue.

"You have to cook them first," he said, smiling. "Over here." He pointed to another kind of plant close by. "These sprouts too, just coming up. These are good even without cooking."

Ruth looked closely at the odd leaves, shaped somewhat like the foot of a duck or goose. "Yes, goosefoot. I hadn't noticed them. Jim and I ate these. My mother boiled them too sometimes. She did a lot with plants and herbs—which meant I ignored such things because of it. It wasn't until I met Jim that I became interested."

"Teske children show little respect for their parents' knowledge."

"Sometimes the parents don't deserve respect." Medicine man or not, his preachy tone brought blood to Ruth's face. She raised her eyes to meet his. "I think it's wrong to give respect to someone just because she's your mother. Besides, most people in my culture do respect their parents' ways, follow those ways even if the ways are stupid. You can't judge other Teske by me," she said, using the Yuiatei term for "White." She knew it meant something like "Peeled Ones" because of their light skin. "I've never been much like anyone else."

She took in a breath and looked back at the plants. There was that discomfort again. Something about the way he heard her words seemed to absorb and neutralize her defiance. At the same time, he mirrored the words back sounding trite, almost silly. Was that how he heard her, then? And his remark. Its judgment was clear, but it was not the kind of judgment she had heard and resisted her whole life. This judgment probed deeper, unsettled her.

"Anyway, why don't I pick some of these while we're here?" She reached down and began pulling up the plants, red root and all. "I can plunk them in with the stew and see what they're like," she said abruptly.

"The small and tender ones are best," he said. "Break them off above the root and they'll grow again." He helped her pluck some from the sand.

While they waited for the stew and new biscuits to finish, Ruth unwrapped the lump of goat cheese and smeared some on the rest of yesterday's biscuits to quiet everyone's hunger. Such a treat was always welcome with the children, and Thomas ate his with as much relish as she did.

"Those ollas," he said, looking over at the project she'd abandoned long ago, "do you make them?"

"I did for a while. Jim showed me how. I never did get very good at it. He's the one who made the only good one, that big one." She glanced over at the clay pot, looking through it, back to the day of its making. "I brought it down the mountain," she told him. Those words carried nothing of her treacherous journey through the blizzard, told nothing of Jim's appearing to take her hand and lead her home, then disappearing into thin air.

"I had someone once," Thomas said. "It was a sickness that took her." He pulled in a breath. "Our child too. I was away laying track for the railroad. It happened a long time ago."

"Does it ever go away?" Ruth asked. "The sadness? Sometimes I think I feel him around me. I even hear his voice . . . though not like you'd hear a regular voice."

"Ever is too far away to know. I'll let you know if mine goes away," he said, his smile tinged with a sad bitterness that was not very medicine man-like. He got up and walked over to the ollas. Watching him handle the clay pots brought back to her the feel of wet clay in her hands, the gritty yet giving body of it, flesh of earth yet unborn as creature or plant.

Ruth rose and pulled out the hot biscuits. She tasted the new wild vegetable in the stew and found it really was delicious when cooked, then checked the potatoes, found them done enough to pierce with her fork, though further cooking would improve the stew's flavor. The children were bickering over the blocks, so she decided to dish the stew out as it was. She made sure each bowl contained a portion of the dark green leaves she had added, then cut the children's ingredients into small bites before handing them their bowls and fresh biscuits.

The supper felt somewhat awkward with a stranger there. She was not used to company in her own home, at least not adult company. It was pleasant enough, J.B. and Maddie occupied with his presence, J.B. holding up biscuits and spoons and naming them to make conversation. And Thomas seemed to enjoy the children as well. It made Ruth realize how isolated they had all been. Except for trips in to the store and an occasional meal with the Swedes, they stayed away from other people and the wagging tongues she disdained.

After Thomas left and the children had fallen asleep, the silence of the canyon weighed heavy on her. Ruth found herself remembering the dances she used to attend around the desert. For the first time, she found herself wondering if there were something perverse about her need for isolation. Why did she prefer the company of wild things to that of her own kind? The deer and squirrel and birds were more naturally her companions. And except for Kate and John, she felt more connected to the Indians in Black Canyon—some of whom she could barely converse with—than to her own neighbors in Juniper Valley.

She had hoped Thomas would let her take him back there. But he said she should wait until midsummer to come, when all the people came up from the desert. Martha and her daughter would be there then. With mild desperation, Ruth opened the novel she had picked up that day with the mail at the general store. The new Fitzgerald book had taken weeks to get to her from the bookstore in Los Angeles. She fell deep into its pages and didn't put the book down until the candle flame finally flickered and went out. Then she dropped off into busy dreams that came back to her when she woke the next morning.

Her dreams had not been filled with modern cities and characters from the book she had spent hours with the night before, but with the blue roan. In her dream, the roan appeared at her spring, inviting her to ride it. She found herself on its back, and they had traveled many places together—to Jim's hut on the mountain, and Jim had been there along with J.B. In the dream, the four of them had lived there, the horse making the fourth. Ruth rode the roan also to the reservation in Black Canyon, and in the dream she lived there too. They rode to other places she only vaguely remembered. And wherever she and the roan went, the horse's hooves barely touched the ground, nearly flying over the landscape as they traveled.

Maddie wasn't in the dream, Ruth realized, as she lay with her eyes closed against the day, guilt seeping into her. At the same time, she joyed at that absence, hugged the memory of the dream tighter to her, lay there longing for its return.

CHAPTER SEVEN

"But she your mother, Rute, ya. How can you not go see her? It not right." Kate shook her head, looked at Ruth with incredulity from across the kitchen table. "You know I keep the children."

Ruth looked out into the yard through the open doorway, where Maddie was clucking at Kate's chickens, J.B. attempting to pick up a red hen whose wings slapped his face. In her goodness, Kate could never conceive of a mother like Cally. Ruth wished she had never brought it up. She should have just thrown the letter in the fire and forgot about it, instead of letting it keep her awake all night. And now telling Kate had trapped her into considering it.

"It's such a long way to L.A.," Ruth said lamely, "and you know how I hate that city."

"Your mother come all the way from El Paso on that train."

"But she's not coming all that way only to see me, Kate. She'll stop in L.A. for a few hours on her way to Las Vegas. It's convenient for her to see me." Ruth took a sip from the cooled coffee she had forgotten, the dark liquid become bitter at that temperature. "Oh, maybe she does have something to give me, like she says. But I'll bet she makes sure I know how beholden and incapable I am while she's at it."

"So you go show her how wrong she is, how strong you are, by yourself up here with two little children." Kate got up from her chair, walked over and peeked into the oven, then poked another hunk of pinyon under the burner. "You only a girl when you left El Paso."

Ruth flinched at her words. She was already twenty-four. How old she was getting. "I'll think more on it, Kate, I promise. If you knew Cally, you'd know why I don't want to go. But I'll consider it. I promise. It's another week before she arrives."

"No mother perfect, Rute. Just woman like you and me. No different." Kate returned to the table with a pan of strudel, calling out the door to J.B. and Maddie.

If only her mother *were* like Kate. Ruth sighed, got up and tossed her cold coffee into the yard, narrowly missing J.B. as he came in on the run. After filling the cup with hot brew, she settled into her chair again and tried to pull her son onto her lap. He would have none of it and headed back out the door with his strudel, his sister beside him.

Ruth had been shocked to find her mother's letter at the general store. It took days before she could bring herself to open it. How many years since her mother had written, sending those nasty herbs to help remedy Ruth's pregnancy? Not that they'd worked. The letter had thoroughly chastised her for getting herself in that trouble. Ruth didn't think Cally had ever forgiven her for claiming her own allowance when she came out west. And Ruth had never told Cally about inheriting the rest of her father's money. Nothing she had ever done pleased that woman. She had no use for Cally in her life, saw no reason in the world to drive one hundred and fifty miles to see her, even though she was curious about what her mother might be wanting to give her. The letter seemed serious enough about that—*something important to you,* Cally had written.

When John Olsen and the miners showed up for lunch, Ruth helped Kate dish out the stew and pour coffee. Then, while they were finishing the meal, Ruth was chagrined to hear Kate tell them about

Cally's letter and invitation to meet her in L.A. They were thrilled with the idea, John even offering to grease up the Model A and change the spark plugs for the trip.

"It long way, Rute. You want car to be in good shape, ya," he said, nodding, as if it had all been settled. And in effect it was, since Ruth found it hard to swim against that current of goodwill that wanted to send her off. And later, at home, when she thought more about having a few days unencumbered by her offspring and the endless daily chores, the idea of making the trip to see Cally didn't seem as onerous. She began to favor Kate's idea of confronting Cally with the woman she had become. And maybe she could buy some books and see a movie or something while she was in the big city. She could afford it.

Ruth was still of two minds when she left the children with the Olsens and set off down canyon a week later, though one of those minds seemed to have enough control to lead her toward Los Angeles and her mother. And once she was out of the canyon and gassed up in Juniper Valley, she began to feel she was off on an adventure—as long as she didn't dwell on memories of her mother. Then a hundred scenes would play out in her head, and a helpless frustration crept over her that she thought she left behind years ago.

She kept her thoughts on what else she might do while she was in the city, after she met with her mother the following morning, wondering if the city held places like the jazz clubs she'd read about in the novels. Then, for a while, she drove with glamorous scenes in her head—envisioning herself in clubs with laughter and music, dancing while surrounded with Gatsby-like glitter. Champagne glasses clinked around her, though she knew well they had been outlawed by prohibition.

Los Angeles had expanded at the edges, with many more houses now sprouted among the orange and avocado groves than there were when she arrived there four years ago from El Paso briefly to meet up with the Baxters. Then she got on her way to the desert and her new job as May Baxter's care nurse. Tuberculosis was a common reason why people left the city for desert places like Juniper Valley.

When she neared the city's center, the labyrinth of streets and the chaos of crowds walking in all directions, the endless stream of automobiles, scoured the feel of her quiet canyon from her mind. The confused sight of so many other human beings swarming in all directions reminded her of an ant colony gone mad.

Ruth hadn't thought out what to do after she arrived. Where to stay. She couldn't just throw down a blanket and sleep on the ground. Certainly, that wasn't the kind of impression she wanted to make on her mother. Ruth glanced down at her faded pants and shirt, clean but stained and worn from work—her last skirt had finally fallen apart when she tried to wash it. She could smell the pine pitch that had blackened a patch of threads just inside her shirt pocket. Washing had only driven the pitch in deeper. She could just imagine the look of disdain on Cally's face. It had been some time since she'd considered such things as fashion. Everything she owned was either handsewn to begin with or nearly handsewn from being stitched back together so many times.

She drove down Main Street with its solid front of buildings. The smart clothing worn by women along sidewalks in front of the department stores told her that styles had changed since the late twenties. When she spotted the big May Company building, the place she'd purchased her red dancing dress years before, she pulled into the empty slot in front and switched off the ignition.

The store was every bit as intimidating as she remembered, with rack after rack of dresses and slacks and tops, table after table of sale items, lingerie, and shoes. What she really wanted was to walk right up to any given rack and find exactly what she wanted, but that wasn't the way it worked, she remembered. She had found her old dancing dress quickly enough, only because of its bright red color, which had drawn her eyes immediately. She'd been lucky. Now she found herself going from rack to rack and back again, without ever being terribly drawn to anything in particular.

She finally located a pair of slacks that weren't so thin and delicate they'd fall apart the first day she wore them in the canyon, along with two blouses that would never do except for trips to town. She was looking around for a salesclerk, when she spotted a rack in the far corner of the store with fabrics that had a certain satin sheen she recognized. Ruth rifled through the short rack of evening dresses. These were indeed what a woman might wear to a club. She held a red satin fabric against her arm. Nice. Setting the slacks and blouses aside, she sorted through to something silvery white and pulled it out of the rack, admiring the sleek simplicity of its lines. It pleased her to see that breasts had been freed again from the binding of flapper styles. Holding the gown up to her shoulders, she assessed where the length would fall, then returned it to the rack and picked up the slacks. A gown was not what she had come for.

Ruth had vaguely noticed two women and a man standing together a couple racks away, conversing and occasionally looking in her direction. Now, one of the women and the man began walking toward her. The man, in his suit and tie, looked to be a manager of some sort.

"May we help you, Madam?" the man asked. Almost imperceptibly, but not quite, his eyes assessed Ruth's rustic attire. She became acutely aware of the dust and sweat her hours of driving had wrought, overruling the brief splash bath she had given herself the night before.

"Certainly," she said, drawing herself up and confronting his eyes. "I'd like to try on these slacks and blouses. Could you direct me to the fitting rooms?"

After just enough hesitation to convey his suspicion, but not enough to deter an actual customer, he pointed Ruth toward the wall at the back of the store, directing the woman with him to "go along in case she needs help."

"That won't be necessary," Ruth said as she headed for the fitting rooms. The woman followed along at a distance anyway, no doubt intending to hover over her the whole time. Obviously, someone so dusty and uncouth could not be trusted. After an initial flash of anger, Ruth settled into a mild amusement over the matter as she tried on the garments.

The slacks, dark brown enough to hide dirt, and the pale blue blouse looked classy and attractive. The rose blouse as well. If she'd come in wearing these, even unwashed, the management would not have been suspicious. At the counter, she found the price reasonable for two pair of the slacks and two blouses, lingerie, stockings, and a few other items she selected. Ruth knew a dress and heels would be more likely to impress her mother, but she was unwilling to compromise herself further simply to stave off Cally's contempt.

After studying the map she'd picked up at a gas station, and the addresses of hotels advertised in the *Times* she bought at the same place, Ruth marked out a route that would take her to what seemed the most centrally located good hotel, a place called the Biltmore. Getting there, she found, was much easier on the map than on the actual maze of streets packed with automobiles going in every direction—some streets even had trolleys coming and going in the middle—and pedestrians stepping off curbs to walk across in front of her. Keeping track of all that kept her from seeing some of the street signs she needed to guide her, and she found herself having to make turns and go around blocks to backtrack and find which street signs she'd missed. This led to other problems, since she learned that some blocks were really triangles and going around them didn't lead back to the same place at all. Some turns also led to one-way streets going in the wrong direction. Others wouldn't allow her to turn left when she needed to. All this had her constantly pulling over and studying her map to figure the route out all over again.

How did all these people get where they were going, she wondered, with all these artificial rules, and without mountains and peaks to guide them, except the range far to the north—and that wasn't much help. It felt foreign to rely on street signs to find her way, so much harder than finding her way along the mountain ridges back home. Ruth felt great relief when she finally pulled up in front of the Biltmore and parked her car. She ran a brush through her hair and checked her face in the rearview mirror, then stepped out of the car and straightened the new blouse and slacks that she'd made it a point to wear from the department store. She was pleased that the slacks hung just low enough to cover any scuffs on her worn black dress shoes.

The hotel lobby was marble with high ceilings, expansive windows and tropical plants. She wondered briefly if the onyx ashtray on the reception counter might have come from John Olsen's mine up the North Fork. He had mentioned that his ore was put to such use. It made her cringe to think that here people might jab the lit ends of their cigarettes into a piece of the mountain she loved. What a odd thing to find, really, that she and that Rocky Mountain onyx had traveled this far to wind up in the same hotel.

The desk clerk, once he'd ascertained that she didn't have a reservation, stepped over to confer with a manager. Ruth smiled as sweetly as she could in their direction, noticing that the manager, a young and classically handsome man, was watching her with something besides suspicion. He walked over with the desk clerk and stood behind the

60

counter with what Ruth registered as an admiring smile, while the clerk assigned her the room she would be staying in for the next two nights.

"A bellhop will help you with your luggage," the clerk said as he handed her the key, motioning with his other hand to a short, compact young man who stood in uniform by the door.

"That won't be necessary. What little I have I can handle myself once I see the room," Ruth told him, the May Company bag in her hand containing all she had with her. "But he can show me to the room."

It had been years since Ruth had experienced the jerky lurch of an elevator that dropped her belly to its floor. "Does your hotel have stairs as well?" she asked the bellhop as he opened the accordion iron gate and they stepped into the upstairs hall.

"Certainly. Right at the end of this hallway."

Relieved, Ruth filed the information away and followed him to a door about halfway to the stairwell. The bellhop went in and, without giving it so much as a thought, switched on a lamp next to the doorway. What ease such people had with modern conveniences, she mused, remembering her own tendencies when she lived in El Paso. While the bellhop was pulling open the drapes that covered the layer of chintz window curtains, Ruth walked on into the bedroom and peeked into its adjoining bathroom. At the sight of the smooth porcelain tub, all her qualms about making the trip gave way to an image of herself ensconced in that tub, surrounded by bubbles and steamy air. That bath alone might well make her whole trip worthwhile.

She tipped the bellhop and, when he shut the door, turned to savor the luxuriousness of her surroundings, the plush sofa and small dining table, where another onyx ashtray sat next to a vase of irises. She found it a great delight to pee into the sparkling toilet and flush it all away, though she had to deny instincts that fought against such a frivolous use of water for her own comfort. But for the next two days, she would not be Ruth the rural drudge who washed clothes in a tin tub, with water hauled from a spring and heated on a campfire, would not be the homestead woman who milked goats and killed rabbits to feed her children in some wild place. She would be a woman who wore satin underwear to meet her mother at the train station, then went home to a room with cushioned sofas, where windows were hung with chintz curtains and heavy damask drapes, and where a porcelain tub awaited her.

Ruth soaked until the water went from hot to cold, then added more hot and soaked some more. Her wet hair wrapped in a towel, she lay back against the cool porcelain, thinking how nice it would have been to have the bubbles she hadn't thought to purchase. But oh how wonderful her long hot soak had been after years of occasional sit baths in a tin tub. Then her stomach rumbled and her thoughts turned to satisfying that hunger. She sat up and used a small brush to clean dirt from underneath her fingernails, while she considered where to go for food: maybe to one of the three restaurants here in the hotel. As she was getting out of the tub, it came to her. Room service. The bellhop said all she had to do was dial down and food would be sent up for her. Could anything be more luxurious? Afterwards, she might even go to that movie, *City Lights,* in the big theater she'd passed a few blocks away. A laugh escaped her. How easily she'd gone from drudge to decadent, she thought, reveling in the idea.

By the time Ruth heard the knock on the door an hour later, she was truly ravenous, ready to yank the door off its hinges to let in the bellhop with the tray of food. Only it wasn't the little bellhop who stood there when she flung open the door, but a tall man in a suit, with dark hair that flopped down just above one eye, somewhat like the forelock on a horse. He looked to be about her age.

"Your cuisine, Madam," he said, in an overly formal manner, and with what appeared to be an English accent. "Shall I serve you at the dining table?" he asked, surveying her attire, which happened to be the deluxe robe she had been delighted to find furnished with the room, "or would you prefer"—she watched his tongue push out behind his cheek—"that I prepare a bed tray for Madam?" His face showed no hint of a smile, but she sensed mockery hidden somewhere in those dark eyes.

"The table will be fine," she said, stepping aside to let him in. He swept past her and, with an exaggerated flourish, arranged the covered dishes on the small dining table, then pulled out the chair and stood waiting for her.

Reluctantly, Ruth followed his nonverbal instructions, feeling compelled by the situation to do what was expected, when she would much rather have taken the tray from him at the door and attended to herself. She walked over and sat, let herself be pushed up to the table. Was this the way rich people lived, then, she wondered, being ordered around without knowing it?

After he had removed the lids from the dishes and straightened the salt and pepper shakers, he poured out a cup of tea, then moved back from the table. "Is there anything else I can get for Madam?"

Impatient to dive in, without looking up, Ruth shook her head and pulled a bill from her pocket to hand him. He didn't take it, and she glanced up to find him looking at her like she was a wayward child. She felt her face flush as she snatched the paper he held out for her to sign. "Unless Madam would like something special from me?"

When Ruth handed back the signed bill, he didn't make a move to leave.

"Yes?" she said, with puzzled impatience.

"Does Madam?"

"Do I what?" She looked up at him fully now, noting the way his face registered nuances she couldn't quite fathom.

"Want anything special from me?" His expression was pointed, but his crooked half smile erased any pretense of formality and for a moment arrested her, hunger and all. Confused possibilities raced through her, one in particular igniting another dormant hunger she'd forgotten.

"I don't think so," she managed to say, with more bewilderment than conviction.

"Very well, then," he said in a return to formality. But just before he shut the door, his tone changed completely. "If Madam thinks of anything special, just call down and ask for Ben."

What an odd man. Handsome, though, in a roguish way.

Before attacking her meal, Ruth got up and slid the safety bolt shut. She returned to find the food excellent, though it had cooled some during that strange exchange. Still, it would have been perfect if only she had something stronger than tea to accompany it. The awkwardness of the encounter had left her restless, somehow reminded her that she had to face her mother the next morning. She struggled against her restlessness until after sunset. When dark came on, she made up her mind to see that movie after all.

CHAPTER EIGHT

Despite her luxurious bed, Ruth spent a restless night, visited in dreams by all she'd managed not to dwell on when she was awake. The man who had served her food was now trying to pry her legs apart, open her up to an extraordinary penis, which unfolded the way she'd seen horses' do. Then she found herself there with the blue roan in her canyon, trying to ride away. Suddenly Cally was scolding her, pushing her down a dark hallway toward those rooms she never wanted to enter. After that there were more men, all with dangling horse penises. When dawn finally outlined the drapes, even the dreaded visit with Cally seemed preferable to the places she had just been.

From outside her room came the murmur of many voices, the sound of feet walking the hotel halls and floors, and from the windows that infernal buzz of traffic, perpetual and insistent, punctuated occasionally by horns and sirens. How different from the morning sounds of her canyon, the chirps of birds and chattering of squirrels, the musical hum of wind in pines that accompanied the waking sounds her children made each morning. There, everything seemed to be of one piece.

Last night, she had meant to see *City Lights* at the Los Angeles Theater, but instead got caught up in another drama lurking behind the lights of the real city. She couldn't get into the theater without seeing the destitution just outside. Wandering through the opulent theater lobby, with its silken tapestries and fountains, and several restaurants, she found it hard to fathom that while patrons inside it peed in marbled restrooms built like tiny palaces, across the street stood long breadlines, where scruffy men and even a few women and children waited impatiently for bowls of watery soup. A few yelled out at the theatergoers, most of whom ignored them. Ruth wished she could have. She escaped back to the Biltmore, and from its lobby watched men with ties and women in shimmering gowns going in and out of her hotel's nightclub doors.

She supposed the breadlines were what people in town had in mind when they spoke about the hard times they were now calling the Depression. She'd had no idea how bad it was. But how strange to see that reality smack up against the world of the well-dressed crowd who went about their business indifferent to it, she thought, as she got out of bed. The street seem to serve as a line between light and shadow.

After she combed the tangles from her dark hair, tamed the willfulness of its direction, and otherwise made herself presentable, she found herself pacing from window to door. Just what would she say when she saw Cally? She had nothing in particular she wanted to say to that woman—nothing she would dare say anyway.

Nearly two and a half hours remained before nine o'clock, so she went down and ordered breakfast at the hotel's coffee shop, the least formal of the three restaurants inside. Yet she found eating impossible, since she couldn't make herself sit still. She slammed down some of the horrid weak coffee and decided to drive over to the train station and wait there.

It turned out she had less time to wait than she imagined. On the way, she somehow lost her bearings and again became caught between the snarl of streets and the representation of those streets on her map, found herself driving in circles, squares and triangles, so confused that she arrived first at the wrong train station, a trolley station for local routes only. By the time further wanderings through the labyrinth of concrete and asphalt led her to the right station, she had less than an hour to spare.

An army of downtrodden milled outside the depot, selling anything they could. She thought about the Indians in Black Canyon and the way they survived on what grew around them. Little grew here that was edible, except for what was owned by growers. She first purchased pencils from a woman who had several children stairstepped beside her, then a bruised apple from an old man who could hardly stand, then more pencils and a card of hairpins from others who approached her.

At two minutes before nine o'clock, she heard the scream of her mother's train outside the station. Everything in her tightened, as if she had suddenly become one of the strings on the fiddle at a community dance. She clenched her fingers into fists to stop their shaking. What was happening to the woman she had become? She hadn't driven all this way just to let her mother affect her like this, she reminded herself, taking in a deep breath. With a screech of brake and roar of engine, the train bellowed into view through clouds of steaming smoke. She almost expected it to paw the ground with great steel hooves.

Closing her eyes, Ruth put herself back at Glory Springs, wrapped herself in its sights and smells and sounds. Quieting, she kept that memory before her as she scrutinized the people exiting the train. "You go and show her how strong you are," Kate had said. That was what Ruth had come here to do, not to fall apart like some young girl still at her mother's mercy, a girl who could be yanked around, slammed into a chair and slapped silly for reasons that had nothing to do with her. All that was years behind her.

Her resolve thinned out again when she spotted Cally walking among the crowd on the platform. Even in new fashion, a respectable longish skirt and smart suit top, with matching navy hat and heavy veil—quite unlike anything she'd seen her mother wear before—Ruth easily picked her out from the rest. Something about the way Cally moved gave her away, sliding quietly along, like a cloud shadow over a sunny meadow. Ruth made no move to start toward her, even when Cally looked up and saw her, nor did Cally quicken her pace.

Ruth stood her ground as Cally approached, though butterflies belied her calm exterior. She still had no idea what to say, so she said nothing as Cally came up, stopped in front of her and set down her suitcase, nor did Cally speak, and the two of them stood assessing each other. Ruth noticed that she had more clearly defined lines on her copper skin, especially around the eyes and mouth, as if the last few years had not been easy ones. Cally's gaze remained neutral as she assessed Ruth's attire. She wondered again just why her mother had left El Paso to start the new "business" she'd written about, what scandal had chased her out.

Finally, Cally drew a cigarette and lighter from her bag and lit up. "Well, take me someplace to eat. Somewhere with fine food," she said, sending a cloud of whiskey-scented smoke in Ruth's direction. "I'm sure you can afford it. That is, unless you've already managed to waste all that inheritance." She left her suitcase on the platform and began walking into the station. Ruth snatched it up and followed her.

"My car is this way," Ruth said, passing her mother to redirect her and lead her out the station door. How in the world had Cally learned Ruth had that money?

"Too bad you're not dressed in something besides slacks. Then you could take me somewhere elegant," her mother said offhandedly as they walked toward the Model A. She stood looking the car over, one hand on her hip. She tapped off her ash as Ruth opened the passenger door for her, made a little "mmmph" as she got in.

"Why don't we just go to my hotel, the Biltmore? They have good restaurants there. We could order room service, if you like," Ruth said, straining to keep the triumph from glaring on her face. "It's hours before your train."

"Now I do wonder if you have any of it left," Cally muttered.

"I've little reason to spend it," Ruth said before she could stop herself. "I've most of it."

"Glad to hear that," her mother said. She flicked her cigarette out into the traffic. "The Biltmore, then."

Cally's concern over the money continued to trouble Ruth as she retraced the route through the tangle of streets toward the hotel, making only two wrong turns onto one-way avenues. Neither spoke, though she could feel Cally's disapproval at her driving.

Ruth couldn't help but gloat a bit as she showed Cally through her elegant rooms, letting her mother see she was no longer the same young girl who left for California to work as someone's nurse. Her mother didn't comment.

Ruth ordered lunch while Cally freshened up. When she came out, the smell of whiskey on her breath had strengthened. With her hat and veil removed, the full force of her mother's striking looks became apparent. Even with those new lines in her cinnamon skin, Cally was still stunning, her dark hair now highlighted with strands of auburn that Ruth imagined covered up emerging gray. She would have been beautiful if not for the meanness in that face, like some evil queen in a folktale.

Ruth was relieved that the waiter who delivered the meal was not the man from the night before who had offered her something "special" but an older man who merely laid out the dishes, removed the lids and promptly left with a quarter tip. Then the two of them were alone, eating in a silence that Ruth found increasingly strained. Yet she didn't want to fall into the trap Cally had set, didn't want to fill up the silence with chatter that diminished any advantage she had. Ruth felt each bite hit her stomach with a thud.

"I only came all this way because you said you had something you wanted to give me. Something I would find important," Ruth said, once the absurdity of the situation got to her. She put down her fork, unwilling to force down another morsel.

"Maybe I just want to see my daughter after all this time. See what kind of a woman you've become." Cally fixed sharp eyes on Ruth's. "After all, the last time I heard from you, you were carrying a child that belonged either to some Indian or to someone you claimed had raped you."

Ruth threw her napkin onto the table. "I didn't come here so you could spew out your disapproval and nasty temper." She curbed an urge to rise from her chair. "And I don't believe for a minute that you have any interest in seeing me. Though you do seem to have kept up on the financial aspects of my life well enough," Ruth said.

Cally smiled. Her eyes dropped their accusation. "You haven't exactly been friendly toward me the last few years, you know. Or now either, for that matter."

"I don't feel friendly," Ruth snapped. "And you've never been friendly to me."

"Then have you forgotten all the times I used to get you out of bed at night to play canasta with me?" Cally sighed, looked out the window. "Remember, Ruth, before you went to live with your Aunt Myrtle?"

"Before you sent me away to live with her, you mean. Before whiskey became more important to you." Ruth had always known it was whiskey that uncovered the witch inside her.

"She poisoned you against me. Made you hate me."

"If anyone poisoned me against you, it was you."

"See, you take her side."

"I do not. But any side is better than yours."

"Ah," Cally said, studying her. "Have it that way. It's your call." She lit another cigarette. Her mouth twisted into that mocking smile Ruth found so daunting.

"Well, then, how does it feel to be responsible for a child you never wanted?" Her mother's eyes hardened again, and all trace of smile left her face. "Maybe now you know what I went through with you," she hissed through a stream of smoke. "Only I was just a girl, sixteen. At your age, you had no excuse, especially with what I taught you after that German boy. But I couldn't stop you from running headlong into trouble."

"After what you *taught* me? You would have made me one of your whores."

"At least my girls don't have children. I see to that. But I had bigger plans for you. You could have helped me run the business. Maybe if you'd been there when . . ?" She stopped and drew in a breath. "All that doesn't matter. It's in the past now. I didn't come here to chastise you."

"It seems you can't help yourself."

"I came here with a business proposition for you." Cally took a long drag and stabbed the rest into the onyx tray in front of her. "To offer you something you've always wanted."

Ruth felt the cigarette's burn clear through her belly. "A proposition?" She folded her arms in front of her. "I thought you meant to give me something tangible. Otherwise I would never have come. I wouldn't have come anyway, except for . . ."

"It's right here in my purse," she said, patting the bag beside her. "Aren't you even a little curious?"

Ruth bit her lip and looked away. Most likely nothing was in that purse, and Cally was only taunting her. But when Ruth looked back, Cally had set a heavy, folded paper on the table in front of her. "Open it," her mother said.

Inside the folded paper was an oval photo about the size of a large sardine can. A dark but faintly familiar face stared back at her from the yellowing print. Somehow Ruth knew this woman.

"This is the grandmother you've pried so much about. Since you're hell-bent on ruining yourself as a white woman, I thought you'd better know what it was like for her, as an Indian woman. Maybe that will scare some sense into you." Cally reached over and snatched the photo away, stuck it back in her purse. "I will tell you about it, but first the proposition. It will be an exchange." She pulled out another cigarette, held it between fingernails so red Ruth almost expected to see them drip blood onto the light carpet.

Chewing the inside of her cheek to keep quiet, she took in a breath. She had to see that photograph again. Getting up to choke the life out of her mother to regain it wasn't an option.

"You can see how much you look like her, especially around the cheekbones and eyes," her mother said. "The smile too, the little I saw of it from either of you." She held the lighter to her cigarette. "That likeness always worried me."

"What do you mean, an exchange. What will it cost me?" Despite her efforts, Ruth felt her fingers trembling. She kept them on her lap, out of sight.

Cally's face tightened and her eyes went cold. "Rightly, that inheritance should have been mine. I'm the one who married your father and got into that rich family." She took a drag, blew smoke across the table. "I'm the one who bore you, don't forget—then had to raise you without any help. Imagine, just what kind of a fool walks in front of a damned taxi. That's the only reason I had to start the business."

Ruth rose and walked to the window. "Some business! And what do you mean, without any help? After his death, you were sent an allowance every month—for me. Until I left El Paso. You didn't have to start any *business*. You started that disgrace on your own."

Cally reached down and ground her cigarette into the onyx, got up, walked over to stand in front of Ruth. Her dark eyes narrowed. "If I wanted us to live like paupers. I deserve that money, Ruth, and you know it. In your bones, you know it."

A wave of guilt and obligation washed over her. Ruth let it, trying to rid herself of its traces with a shake of her head. "Well, you're not getting it," she said. "And you don't deserve it. I do, for being raised by a witch." She met Cally's steely look. "I need that money to raise my own children."

"Children?" Cally's eyes glittered. "I hadn't heard that. Are they papooses—or rapist brats?"

Ruth's hand flew up and landed smack against her mother's cheek, seemingly of its own volition. Cally's slap back was more deliberate. Then the two of them stood glaring, Ruth pulling in huge gulps of air, her entire body shaking.

Without warning, Cally pulled her eyes away. She seemed to sag, to shrink into herself. Turning, she walked to the table, sank into her chair and fixed her eyes out the window. Ruth stared after her, impotent in her fury.

"I'm not asking for all of the inheritance, Ruth," Cally said, after some time. "I simply need a justified portion of it to get a business going again. I lost everything I had in El Paso, thanks to that bastard of a mayor. Men are never to be trusted. In the end, they blame you for their own weakness. Remember that, Ruth."

And you are to be trusted, Mother? Ruth thought, but didn't say. She came over and sat across from her, struggling to still the turbulence that filled her. She had never seen Cally look so tired. Whatever happened had cost her.

"I need it, Ruth. Without that money, I'm ruined. The business is all I know—and I'm good at it. Prospects are excellent in Nevada right now, where they're building that dam. If I get in on the ground floor, there's money to be made." Ruth saw little trace of the Cally she knew, until her mother looked up and said, "Unless you'd prefer I come stay with you. That would be my only other option."

Ruth bit the inside of her lip, waited until the chills on her back diminished. "What do you consider a justified portion?" she asked.

"A couple thousand if you have it. And I'm willing to trade. I'll tell you all you want to know about what happened to your grandmother." Seeing the look on Ruth's face, she added, "And, of course, a share of the business."

"One thousand," Ruth said, "but I don't want any part of that business. And I do have a condition: that you never contact me again, ever, for money or for anything else." Even as she said it, Ruth felt her heart contract.

Cally looked away for a moment, then back. Her face seemed naked, maybe even sad as she nodded in agreement.

They spent a few minutes working out the logistics of getting the money out of Ruth's stash and just where to send it to Cally when she stopped in Las Vegas. After that was settled, Cally brought out the photo and handed it to Ruth. "My mother's name was Lolinda," Cally began, "probably a mispronunciation of some stupid Indian name, but I can't remember what that was."

She stopped to light up, took a drag, blew it to one side. "She was what they call a breed. Died when I was ten. That's when Father took me to live with his white family, your Aunt Myrtle's family. They hated me from the start."

"Did you live with the Indians before that?"

Cally's laugh was caustic. "We lived out on the edge of town by ourselves. She only took me to see her tribe once. And it was no wonder—they treated us with contempt. To the Indians she was a half-breed whore who lived with a white man, bore his child—as her mother had done before her with another white man." She drew out another cigarette, set it on the table in front of her. "To the whites, she was a dumb Indian whore. That's what she did to herself for a man."

It was from Lolinda, Cally said, that she had learned about herb medicines and foods. Cally despised those native ways, said she hated every moment spent gathering plants, preparing the potions. She hated the rituals that went with them, too. "Though I did find use for some of the herbs later," she told Ruth with a wry smile.

"But what I hated most is that she made no attempt to become

72

anything like the white women we lived around." Not that she would have been accepted, Cally admitted, but she could have tried.

"I was tainted. Even after Father brought me to El Paso, civilized people always suspected me. In the end, it took my business to make me part of the community."

"Your business made you an outcast. Both of us. Not part of any community."

"Don't fool yourself. That business is part of every community. People might pretend it's not, but if it's run with enough discretion, it can be a respectable place."

"Is that why you had to leave El Paso, then, because you were so respectable?" The words left Ruth's mouth before she could stop them.

Cally's eyes narrowed again. "If I was an outcast, it was never by choice. But you had a choice. You had a chance when you came out here, to put all that behind you, to be respectable—and white. With that light skin of yours." She shook her head. "But you threw it away for an Indian man. That's worse than what your grandmother did. She was only a hopeless Indian woman. You were given advantages. Why do you think I allowed you to live with Myrtle's family those early years?"

"But I had no desire to be that kind of respectable—to be like Myrtle's family. All those other women I saw there. No desire to be like you, either. I just want to be myself . . . live my life the way I want to. And I like being with Indian people better than—"

"And look where that's got you."

"Yes, look where that's got me." Ruth felt herself swell with pride. "Here we are, sitting in a fine hotel. I have a car, a place of my own that I homesteaded. My own animals and garden. I take care of my children—and without starting any kind of *business*."

Cally held up a hand. "You came into that inheritance through none of your doing—it was my doing. Without the money, you would have been ruined. You've always had your grandmother's blood in you. I could see it in your face. And you're still headed straight for trouble, mark my words."

Cally rose, picked up her hat and the ashtray, went into the bathroom and shut the door behind her. What was left of Ruth's confidence dissolved with the click of that lock, and she was left helpless before a familiar frustration. It wasn't only her body that was trembling now. Cally's words left her whole self awobble, who she was and what she had made of her life.

She should have been overjoyed to know she had her grandmother's Indian blood in her; it made her closer to Jim's people. But Cally had made it seem shameful, a curse. Ruth wondered what Thomas would say about that. She wished he were here to say words and sprinkle pollen over her. Some residue here needed to be *niihi'ahi,* turned back fast.

The only words spoken between the hotel and the train station concerned the transfer of money, repeating again what had been agreed upon. Once Cally's dark presence left the car at the station, Ruth began finding herself again. But the calm that came to her felt as tenuous as her pathway back to the hotel through the confusion of streets. She tried again to imagine the quiet of her canyon, but nothing came to overrule the quagmire of sights and sounds around her, which had now come to mirror the tangle inside her.

Back at the Biltmore, Ruth shunned the elevator for the stairs, grateful for the dimness of the passageway she climbed. Maybe she wouldn't stay in this grand hotel another night after all. She couldn't imagine simply luxuriating in her room again—and the idea of actually going to see that movie as she had planned seemed particularly ludicrous as she opened the door to the third floor and started down the lit hallway.

She was walking by an adjoining passageway of suites when she heard a knock that caught her attention. A man stood in front of one of the doors, and she saw at once that it was Ben, the waiter from the night before. Just then the door opened, and she saw a quick exchange as she stepped past the hallway and out of sight: Ben handing in a brown paper bag and the hand from inside holding out currency for him to take.

So that was what he meant by *something special.* The man was a bootlegger. Something inside her perked up. If ever she needed a drink, it was now.

Although she was not the least bit hungry, Ruth called room service and ordered something called Shrimp Louis and coffee, "strong, please. And would you have Ben bring it up," she added casually.

She found the wait intolerable, found being in this busy city intolerable, didn't know how she would get through another night here. She tidied up the room, emptied her mother's mess from the ashtray—polishing the onyx clean again—and started stuffing her clothes back into the May Company sack. Maybe she would leave this afternoon. Then she realized that she'd need to gas up twice on the way back and stations would close by evening. Somehow, she would have to wait it out until morning.

When the knock came, she yanked the door open and, before the man could go into his routine, said, "Just put it on the table and leave the lids on. But I would like something special, if you have it." She pushed the door closed behind him.

He placed the food as she requested, turned to speak but stopped when Ruth held up a hand. His formal look dissolved into a crooked smile that matched the sudden spark in his eyes. He reached behind the lapel of his jacket and pulled out a small paper sack, held it out.

Having no idea how much the going rate was in a place like this, Ruth reached into her purse and pulled out a five-dollar bill, twice what she'd pay for a bottle that size at the general store.

He took the bill, thanked her, but hesitated.

"Is that not enough?" Ruth asked. She reached back in her purse.

He shook his head. "Plenty," he said, all trace of that formal English accent gone now. "I just wondered if you'd be needing anything else."

"This will be more enough to get me through the night," she told him. Then the image from the dream of his unfolding horse penis superimposed itself, and she struggled to keep her face straight, but lost the battle. "I'm fine, really," she said, and broke into an outright laugh. All at once everything seemed terribly funny. Especially with him staring at her, varying shades of puzzlement flickering across his face. She lost control completely and laughed even harder, stumbling toward the table, where she plopped down into a chair. "And I haven't . . . even . . . taken a drink yet." She could hardly get the words out. Tears started down her cheeks as she looked up at him.

"I think you need more than a bottle of whiskey," he said, which convulsed Ruth further, as she imagined him pulling out his horse penis. She managed to point to the door and wave good-bye, before she doubled up and almost fell to the floor.

When the door closed, she snatched up the whiskey bottle and unscrewed the top, poured a shot into her coffee cup, her hands still shaking, but now with hilarity. She'd needed a good laugh, couldn't remember ever needing one more. Now all she had to do was pay the witch off and she'd be rid of her for good, she thought, as she raised the cup and took a swallow of the improved brew. But it wouldn't go down, and she felt it spew out over her as her guffaws changed to sobs, equally uncontrollable, as were the kaleidoscoping images that overtook her—Jim lifeless on the ground, the men holding her down, J.B.'s first cry, then the other—and behind it all, Cally's knowing look.

Coming to this city had unhinged her, she decided, some time later, when she had begun to get hold of herself. This would never have happened back in her canyon, no matter what her mother had said. In the bathroom, she splashed water on her face and gave her nose a good blow. She returned to the table, where she gulped down the doctored coffee, poured a shot into the empty cup and gulped that. By the time the knock came, the edge of her pain had dulled.

"Who is it?" she called from where she sat.

"It's Ben. I just wanted to check on you."

"I'm fine."

"Will you open the door then, please?"

The request left her puzzled. She must have scared the man. She got up and went over to the door. When she pulled it open, she was surprised to see him dressed in street clothes. "You see," she said, forcing a smile, "I'm good as new."

"I wondered if you'd like to have a little fun tonight," he said. "Take your mind off whatever is eating you."

"Who said anything's eating me?"

He rolled his eyes. "Hey, could I come in minute?" He looked around behind him. "Walls have ears."

"This room has walls, too," Ruth said, but she stepped aside to let him in. Out of uniform, he appeared a different man.

"I'm meeting some friends at the Coconut Grove tonight. I'd like to have you on my arm if you want to come. We'd have some fun," he said. He slid a cigarette from his pocket and lit it.

"I don't even know you."

He shrugged, walked over and sat in one of her chairs, pulling the ashtray closer. "Let's get acquainted, then." He pushed back her whiskey bottle, pulled a flask from his coat pocket and poured some into her cup, then took a swig from the bottle. "Look, you probably think I'm just some waiter. Well, I'm really an actor, see. From Chicago. This is one of my roles—a gig till I hit it big. The right movie comes along—and I'm off," he said. He tapped his ash over the onyx tray. Ruth averted her eyes from this further desecration, better his than Cally's, and sipped at her whiskey.

"No more lard sandwiches for this kid," he said. "My mom won't have to scrub toilets back there, either. Someday I'll bring her out here, put her in a classy house too, wait and see." Ruth tried to listen as he launched off into stories of his parts in various movies, none of which she'd ever heard of, and of his plans to become a star. She could see now that he was quite young, really, younger than she was, though his size and looks belied it. He was a survivor, like she was, though his methods of surviving were far removed from hers.

"Now you," he said, after he had run down. "Just where do you come from? I could tell from the start you weren't just your average rich bitch."

Ruth laughed and encapsulated her life into a few sentences for him, told him about the beauty of Glory Springs and the rustic nature of her life there. "Why, you're the cat's pajamas, doll," he said when she paused. "But where is this place, somewhere near the Springs, maybe? You know, Palm Springs. I've done shoots out there." He reached up and pushed back the forelock, snubbed out the cigarette. After all, Ruth reminded herself, this was what the ashtray had been put there for. Hundreds of cigarettes must have been ground into its surface.

As they talked, Ruth began to entertain the idea of a night out in a club, as if she could step into the pages of one of the novels she'd been reading. She could picture herself dancing in a long shimmering dress. Then it dawned on her. "Look," she told him, suddenly, "I can't go to any nightclub. I just remembered I didn't bring anything suitable to wear."

"If that's all that's stopping you, you can borrow a gown from the boutique downstairs. Shoes too." He looked at his watch. "After they close at seven. What do you say, baby?" He held up the whiskey flask. "I'll show you a real good time."

Baby? Ruth clinked her coffee cup against his flask, slammed the rest, and nodded her assent. She could feel something in her ready to break free.

CHAPTER NINE

Ruth slid the slinky gown over her head. It beat anything she'd seen at the May Company. But could she really wear such a dress now? Pregnancy had taken its toll, shifting the proportion and layout of her body. Yet whiskey had bolstered her courage to find out.

Her back to the mirror, Ruth glided the dress down over her hips, gave it a final smoothing with her hands, and turned to face the mirror. *Daring* was the first word that came into her mind. The dress front was cut into a huge V that sliced down between her breasts—whose nipples asserted themselves through the revealing fabric—and ended just inches above her navel. If the cut had gone any lower, it might have shown the marks of stretched skin on the small bump of belly barely seen between breaths that shimmied the fabric as she stood there.

Ruth turned, looked back over her shoulder at the way the back of the gown dropped down to begin just where her waist met her hips, the brown skin of her back complemented by the silvery white of the satin. The dress came with a small cape that she wrapped around her shoulders and hooked in front. She turned again to examine its effect. Not nearly as striking. Removing the cape, she continued her inspection.

She turned again a time or two before the mirror, pictured herself shocking the crowd at some dance in the desert—although that place, like the two children there, seemed far away and not quite real at the moment.

The price tag on the dress with its matching change purse and glittering high heels was considerably more than on the one at the May Company. She was glad she wasn't paying for it. Promising Cally that money had already decided her to land a deer when she got home, to count her money, too, since she hadn't for some time. All she knew was the pile was slowly shrinking. Before she left the boutique, she chose a pair of silk stockings to fit over the thickly calloused soles that allowed her to walk barefoot in her canyon—she might leave a dollar with Ben for the stockings.

Walking into the Coconut Grove was indeed like entering a jazz club in a Fitzgerald novel, and every bit as glamorous as she had pictured it. In the dining area, formally dressed couples sat at tables with cloths and candles and flowers. Beyond lay the dance floor with its dazzle of lights that extended their glitter by means of a few well-placed mirrors around the sides. Surely no part of her mother's prophecy could find her in a place such as this.

She had worn the satin cape and chose not to check it at the door to reveal her daring dress. That would come later. She noted that her gown was more revealing than the ones on most of the women who were leaving their fur wraps at the hatcheck counter. Her escort checked his coat there like the other men. All these fancy but very warm coats amazed her, since it was balmy enough outside to wear short sleeves.

Their table sat midway to the dance floor, a good view, but not too close, and Ruth found herself overwhelmed by the sights and sounds around her. The belts they'd taken from his flask on the way added to the dreaminess she found herself in. She smiled inwardly at the thought of Cally seeing her now in this classy nightclub. There was no foundation to Cally's claims. Heading for trouble indeed! Who was that woman to talk, anyway?

When the waiter set an iced tea before her, Ruth was delighted to find that it contained the definite taste of alcohol. She glanced up at Ben.

"It's who you know," he said, winking. "And how you order." Remembering his story of growing up with lard sandwiches, Ruth forgave his bluster.

She took another sample of the embellished tea, held up her glass. "Perfect," she said. "Here's to a real good time." They clinked glasses and drank up.

"I just can't picture a dish like you out in that wilderness, except maybe at the Springs," he said a few minutes later. "You look like you were born for a place like this."

Ruth threw back her head and laughed. "Right now I'm finding it hard to picture me there myself," she said. And although she could easily remember only two days ago, kneeling barefoot at the washtub after skinning a rabbit that hung at the edge of the clothesline to leave enough room for the children's clothes, she could no longer believe her own memory was real. "But then I'm not thinking so clearly right now," she added.

More iced teas appeared soon afterward, just as two couples stopped by the table, the men wanting to be introduced to Ben's new friend, and then not leaving until she promised them both a dance later on. One of the men had hair the butter color of Matt Baxter's, that spineless snake she once mistook for a lover. The other man's hair was dark and wiry as pubic hair.

"I knew you'd be a smash," Ben told her when the group left for their own table. He gave her a look so smoldering that she thought he must have practiced it for a movie scene. "I thought their eyes would pop out."

"You must come here often."

"As often as I can. Everyone who is anybody comes here. It's the only way to get somewhere in this town," he said, and went on to tell her of the contacts he'd made in this place, the big stars he'd seen and talked to here. Ruth was having a hard time keeping track of the conversation, alcohol having blurred what little focus she had. But focus was the last thing she wanted right now. She was reminded of the first time she had been sent to live with Aunt Myrtle—she must have been around five—when she had dressed herself up with makeup and jewelry and walked into the parlor, interrupting one of her aunt's tea and bridge parties.

"I'm a hussy like my mother," she had told them when they asked what she thought she was doing. Her little girl's idea of a "hussy"— something she had heard Cally called—had been the most glamorous role she could think of. Her aunt made her wash off the makeup and spend the rest of the day in her room. She had cried then, but tonight she was finding the incident rather hilarious as Ben crowed and glowed over rubbing shoulders with celebrity. It occurred to her that she hadn't changed that much; here she was, pretending to be a hussy—this time a classy and glamorous one.

All this was still flickering around her head in a jumbled way, when Ben leaned over and kissed her square on the mouth. A quick kiss, just long enough to tickle her lower insides. Especially with his hand on her thigh. She managed to push it off.

"Oh, baby," he said. "I just couldn't help myself . . . I just had to see what those lips would taste like."

Fortunately, the waiter arrived just then with the food Ben had ordered earlier. Suddenly ravenous for the first time that day, she dug into the puffy round of beef with its mushrooms and tangy sauce, overriding another kind of hunger the kiss had stirred in her, the kind of hunger she had once given in to recklessly. Yet, until now, that particular appetite had gone dormant after her rape.

"I'm glad they finally fed us," Ben said a few moments later. "I don't think I've ever seen anyone attack a filet mignon like that."

Ruth looked up from the plate she'd just cleaned, put down her fork and knife, and picked up her third glass of tea. "Maybe now you can picture me in that wilderness." She took a drink. "Except this fancy meal isn't what I'd be eating."

"What do you wilderness people eat, then? Rattlesnake?" That cocky smile appeared.

"Sometimes, though I haven't. But goat and rabbit are more common than beef. Rabbits are easiest." She lifted her arms as though she were aiming a rifle. "*Bam*. Then you skin and eat it." She took another drink of tea, pleased to see the look of confusion and distaste on his smug face. Pushing even further, she added, smiling sweetly, "Local Indians even eat squirrel and other rodents. They don't taste too bad either. A little sweet maybe."

Relief overtook his face. With a jerk of his head he sent his forelock into place. "Oh, for a moment you had me going there, sweetheart."

Ruth continued to smile. She took a sip from her tea. "You'll never know," she said.

"What I do know is I want to dance with you, baby." He stood and held out a hand. "Let's go, as they say, 'cut that rug.'"

Ruth slid her change purse under the tablecloth and got to her feet, steadied her balance in the high heels, and pulled loose the string that tied her cape, which she draped over the back of her chair. "Let's," she said, letting him take her arm, enjoying the moment his eyes all but devoured the body she had exposed.

"You are some doll, sweetheart," he whispered into her neck as they walked toward the dance floor. "That's all I can say."

And more than you should have said, she thought, laughing at the idea of herself as a "doll." She'd been called that, too, back in El Paso during that flapper period, and each time she would picture the rows of china dolls in her aunt's glass cabinet. As if she were a fragile thing to be handled delicately. They ought to see her gutting a deer or shooting a rattler that they'd probably run from. Oh, well, she thought, as he slid an arm around her waist and whirled her out onto the floor, maybe it was best they didn't know that.

Ben was a damned good dancer, leading her through several new steps. Other than learning the Charleston in El Paso, she had confined her dancing at desert gatherings to various speeds of two-step to fiddle music—which she liked well enough. But even that had ended with her pregnancy. She found it a joy now to let herself go with the beat of the music, as if her body itself were remembering her former freedom. This, oh this, was better than any novel, she thought, as her feet kept wild time with the jazzy band.

Even with all the liquor, she was able to stay on her feet well enough, though the high heels were a great annoyance, like weights binding her feet and hampering the ease and flexibility of her step. Not that she had time to be concerned about it, dancing every dance with either her partner or one of his friends who cut in, all of them determined to show her they were the best dancers on the floor.

By the time the band stopped for a break and Ben returned her to their table, Ruth could feel sweat trickling down under the satin cloth below her breasts. In the ladies' room stall, she pulled down the straps of her gown and used towels to dry her skin. Some china doll she was. Back at the table she drank down another glass of tea thirstily and had Ben order yet another. She could no longer taste the alcohol, so Ben added a bit more from the small flask concealed in the pocket of his jacket.

The two other couples brought their chairs to the table now. Ruth listened to the friends chatter about people she didn't know. She found the jaunty tone of their conversation an interesting and welcome change from the dullness of conversations at desert gatherings. Not that she'd been to one for a while. She tried to remember names—she had been told earlier—but found her mind too foggy. Everything in the room seemed slightly out of focus. In a gesture of friendliness, she turned to the woman closest to her, one with long platinum hair, and complemented her on her gown, another satin that was a sky shade of blue, but with a cut much more subdued than Ruth's own.

"Thank you," the woman said, with a slight smile, her eyes tracing the outline of Ruth's gown. "I think understatement is more effective, don't you. Why be glaring?"

"Why indeed," Ruth said, tightening, "unless of course one has something outstanding to be glaring about. Or just glares naturally." So things were not so different here after all. They remained smiling at each other for a moment, then the woman turned to her date and asked him to order her another glass of *tea*.

The band started up again, and Ruth felt herself swaying to the rhythm as she listened to the conversation, which had turned to film and the latest releases, none of which she'd heard of until they got to *City Lights,* which she hadn't actually seen either. All the while she was craving to be out on the floor, moving to the music, until the pull of it was so excruciating that she found herself on her feet by the table, straining toward the dance floor.

"Looks like the lady wants to dance," the butter-haired man said to her partner. "I'll be happy to accompany her." He got to his feet. "You don't mind do you, Sally?" he asked the woman in the blue dress, then turned toward Ruth without waiting for an answer.

"This time I don't want these," Ruth decided suddenly, kicking her high heels under the table. "Why, indeed," she said again to the blue woman, before heading for the dance floor.

Her new partner was not as agile as Ben, and while Ruth found she could move with amazing fluidity without the heels, and with hose that made her feet slide, her partner was having trouble keeping up with her steps. He seemed more interested in trying to engage her in conversation—she at least learned his name was Paul—and in letting his hands glide across her dress often, passing suspiciously near her breasts. Ben soon broke in, and their pairing made a better match that other dancers gave berth to. Yet even having to match her steps felt like a restraint of sorts, and she was glad when the man with pubic hair cut in. For several songs the vying men passed her back and forth among them, always holding on to her whenever possible, their hands slipping and sliding over her satin dress.

While her body was intensely present, fully engaged with the music around her, Ruth's thoughts floated freely above the notes she danced to, flickering continuously and vividly through her mind. She saw herself building her cabin, saw Jim bending to kiss her, saw herself jerking a deer, bathing in the tin tub, and a hundred other things. She remembered sitting around the campfire with the Indians in Black Canyon, dancing under shimmering gold cottonwood leaves, saw again the imprint of Jim's sleeping body there in the *ki'takii*. She pictured Thomas sprinkling pollen over Jim across the wash, her children sleeping at the Olsens'. This is why I'm dancing, she thought, to celebrate the life I've made. Cally and her predictions be damned. Suddenly Ruth wanted to dance her way back to the desert mountains where she belonged.

She was surprised when the music stopped again and Ben began leading her back to the table. She didn't want to leave the self she had just rediscovered. He leaned against her slightly, his arm around her waist, his gait not as precise as it had been earlier. Then they were all back at the table, the others laughing and bantering with the ease of frequent association, and the boisterousness born of considerable alcohol. Ruth's thoughts were murky as she watched them, no longer bothering to break in with a remark occasionally. In truth, this whole place, these people, had come to bore her now. Their conversation seemed inane, nothing like conversations in the novels. Not a word they said interested her in the slightest now. Ready to go home, she didn't know exactly how to extract herself.

There was a playful tussle between one of the couples and an empty glass crashed on the floor beside the table. Paul bent down to retrieve the larger fragments, placing them one by one on the tabletop. The buttery color of his hair brought back bad memories.

"I just don't believe these feet," he said suddenly, getting to his knees beside his chair. "You have to see them for yourselves."

While the others leaned to look under the table, Ruth paid little attention to his antics and looked across the room for a waiter, thinking that at least she might quell her boredom with another drink. There was an explosion of laughter. Then she felt one of her feet being raised slightly, then the other. She kicked the hand away, doubling Paul over with laughter. The others continued peering under the table.

"What are those things anyway, hooves? I've never seen anything like them." The man with the head of pubic hair looked up at her from the edge of the tablecloth. "What the hell are you? Some kind of savage?"

"They are rather *glaring*," said the woman in the blue dress.

"Oh, leave her alone. Who cares what her feet look like when the rest of her is perfect?" Ben chucked Ruth under the chin. "You're my little wild woman, aren't you, baby?" He hiccuped, looked down at her feet like the others.

Ruth moved the tablecloth aside and looked down at the feet they were all staring at, feet whose calloused soles had darkened with the sand that had callused them, and whose ragged edges around the heels were so sharp and tough they had torn through her hose to expose themselves, leaving the bottom of her stockings around the rims of her ankles. She was proud of those feet, could walk miles barefoot with them if she chose—and never wore shoes anymore unless she went somewhere. And here these city people were making fun—while not a one of them had so much as skinned a rabbit in their entire lives. Fools.

"You could probably walk over cactus in those things," Ben said, causing another outbreak of laughter.

"That's right." Power surged through her in a sudden rush of blood to her head. Ruth reached down and took hold of her shoes, picked up her change purse. Snatching her cape, she stood beside the table. "Walk over glass too," she said, and deliberately tromped across what remained of the shards. She stopped, then, to step into her high heels, pulling down what was left of the bottoms of her stockings and trapping them under her feet as she slid them into the shoes.

All three men rose and followed her, protesting, as she marched off toward the front door—which took some doing after so many drinks and with her feet freshly stuffed into high heels after she'd set them free to dance. But she'd be damned if she'd stumble in front of that crowd. Ben caught up and took hold of her arm, turning her toward him. "Oh, baby, don't go. We were just funning you, sweetheart. No one meant anything by it."

The two friends came up beside them. "I'm sorry," Paul said. "I didn't mean to offend you. But you have to admit those are impressive feet."

Ruth drew herself up. "They certainly are. Much too impressive to waste dancing with the likes of you city boys." She looked up at Ben, whose face was only slightly blurred. "Thank you for bringing me. It's been fun. Really it has. But I've had enough now."

She took another step toward the door and felt his arm slide around her waist. "At least let me take you back," he said, his eyes trying to smolder through their glaze. "Please, baby. The evening can't end yet."

"It already has," she said, removing his arm. She loved the idea of leaving the three of them standing there helpless as she flounced the rest of the way to the door.

"See you in the movies, then, kid," she heard Ben call after her.

The attendant found her a cab immediately, and she watched the city lights stream past as they drove toward the hotel. She'd had her fill of the place. Her pride was only slightly bruised and even that dissipated in the wake of her escape. Things might have gotten complicated otherwise, she realized, giggling quietly to herself—especially with Ben and his horse penis.

She paid the taxi driver in front of the hotel, then stood for a moment looking out at the city around her, everything slightly out of focus, but at least not whirling around.

The first thing she did, after she locked the door of her room behind her, was to kick off her high heels on the way to the bedroom. She switched on the lamp beside the bed and folded back the grand bedding, then pulled down her straps and let her gown slide to the floor. As she sat on the edge of the bed to take off what was left of her hose, she noticed dark footprints trailing across the soft carpet from the door, fading slightly before they reached the bed. When she got down to examine them, she found they were the prints of her own bare feet, inked in blood. Maybe she needn't have been so dramatic, she thought, smiling; there were probably more genteel ways to extract herself. She felt along the bottoms of her soles but could find nothing more than a couple of small cuts that were no longer bleeding, though the clarity of the tracks told her she must have bled pools into her high heels.

After washing her feet in the bathroom basin and peeing once more in the kind of toilet she would not see again for a long while once she left this place, Ruth slid between the luxurious bedsheets and pulled the covers up. How appropriate, she thought smugly, as she let her head fall back onto the satin pillow and closed her eyes, that she, like some wild creature, had left fresh tracks to mark her trek through this treacherous city.

CHAPTER TEN

T he drive back to the desert, past citrus and avocado groves and countless fields of vegetables, seemed interminable. She had risen at first light, her head pounding loudly from the night before, and taken one more steamy bath—who knew how many years until she got another like it—before setting off, her eyes craving the sights and sounds of home.

She stopped again for gas and sandwich makings in Beaumont, where the open stretches of grass had given way to sand and cactus and other desert flora, and she felt more at home. The town of Banning brought her into the pass between the two grand mountains, San Jacinto on her right, and Grayback, San Gorgonio, to her left, both massive mountains trailing their own chain of lesser cousins behind. Her eyes focused on one distant peak in particular, the rugged outline of Rocky Mountain against the light desert sky. A glance to her right brought into view the spread of Palm Springs at the base of San Jacinto—the Springs, Ben had called it, as if it were some mythological place on high. She'd found his note slid under her door when she woke, asking her to leave the dress and shoes so he could slip them back into the shop. He also offered to meet her at the Springs anytime, left a phone number scribbled at the end. She'd crumpled it, tossed it into the wastebasket.

Ruth shifted the Model A into low gear and climbed the hill leading into Devil's Garden. Signs of the coming summer's infernal heat were already apparent. Only patches of yellow blossoms remained on creosote and brittlebush, left over from the spectacular display of wildflowers that appeared in spring, a palate to seduce the eyes a week ago. Now only the legion of barrel cactus remained fully crowned with delicate petals, and even they would soon shrivel and blow away in the ever-present winds. Once she'd turned north off the pavement and lost the tailwind she'd had through the mountain pass, Ruth had to struggle to keep the warm wind from pushing her car into the sandy shoulder along the dirt road.

By the time she came over the long grade into Juniper Valley, the sun sat just above the mountain ridges. The last light of sunset, trapped in thick dust blowing up from the desert, cast a red-gold net over the valley, suffusing the air with rich color. Ruth drew in a breath at glowing Joshua trees, trembling wildly in wind gusts, at creosote and juniper that seemed lit with inner fire. She had an urge to wave back at the dancing branches that appeared to be waving her a welcome. Beyond the valley, the high ridges of Rocky Mountain radiated sun, a beacon guiding her home.

She turned north again and headed for the Rimrock and the road up Rattlesnake Canyon. Home, but not quite home, the car seemed to deliberately crawl along the landscape. Fly, fly, she wanted to tell it. She was ready now, ready to reclaim the life she had made here in this canyon. She would take both children, too, in her stride. Show Cally just how not headed for trouble she really was. Ruth Farley was back on her feet now, she told herself, tough feet too, and for the first time since Jim's death, she felt stronger than ever.

She gunned the motor when she caught the sight of the willows in her headlights, then slowed again when the road curved away from the stream and climbed the bank. If she hadn't eased up on the gas, she might have hit the blue roan that stepped out of the willows into the road in front of her and stood there as if blinded by her lights. Ruth braked hard and felt the rear of the car swing around to the side, burying the back wheels in the loose dirt of the shoulder and coming to a dead stop.

When she got out of the Model A, the horse was gone, though she could hear it crashing away through the underbrush. Her car sat sideways in the road, its headlights illuminating the brushy bottom of a mountain. She couldn't make out anything in the moonless dark outside of the headlights, so with her hands she assessed the depth to which her tires had been buried in the shoulder. It appeared considerable. She got back in the car, hit the ignition, and stepped on the gas, slowly at first, then gave it more punch. The wheels spun sand, but the car wouldn't budge. Getting out again, she felt to see if the wheels had moved at all. They'd moved, all right—deeper into the soft shoulder.

She had left behind the shovel she usually carried, thinking there would be no need for it on the paved highways in Los Angeles. With her bare hands, she scooped away as much of the loose dirt and small rocks as she could, though her hands were not adequate for the job. She did more breaking of fingernails and scraping of skin than moving dirt. When she again tried to drive the car out of the shoulder, the same thing happened as before. Ruth switched off the motor, pushed in the knob for the headlights, and sat in the darkness. The upsurge of positive feeling and resolve she had felt only minutes before seemed to have drained away. It troubled her that her spirit appeared to be fragile and transitory, dissolving like frost crystals in sun.

She got out of the car and climbed onto the hood, leaned back against the windshield. Above her, countless stars hung throbbing against a black velvet sky, the Milky Way draped across the canyon like a filmy bridge stretching from one ridge to the other, where it disappeared into the inky blackness of solid mountain. Cricket song rang loud around her, mixing with frog calls from along the stream. Warmth radiated up from the motor under the hood, buffering her from the damp chill of the air around the willows and giving her a few minutes of comfort.

That blue roan again, she thought. Here she was rushing madly up the road, and the roan had simply stopped her in her tracks. Left her here to get reacquainted with the canyon. What did it all mean? Or did it mean anything at all?

She thought she heard sounds in the brush around her, things moving—or maybe it was wind. Or pure imagination. She didn't have her rifle with her, which would have kept her calm about such noises. But what would she have done, anyway, fired shots into the dark? What if she hit the horse, or some little fox out there? Ruth decided it was time to walk to the Swedes', which had to be less than a mile up the road. The miners would probably have her car out in about two minutes.

She got down off the hood and felt along the shoulder for a few small rocks to carry—just in case—then began walking up the rut road. In the pitch black, she negotiated more by sensing the emptiness of the road than by sight, sometimes tripping over half-buried rocks in the dirt, sometimes brushing into pinyons or scrub oaks when she got too near the road's edge. She tried singing for company, but found it distracted her senses, so she quit and walked, surrounded by the chirp of crickets, the swish of blown branches, and the crunch of her own footfall. It was company enough, she told herself. Yet when she rounded a bend and caught sight of the Swedes' lighted windows, a joyful relief came over her.

She stood listening to their voices, the laughter of the men, Kate's quiet speech, her own children's small utterances, then more laughter. The air smelled of wood smoke and cooking food. She took off down the road at a run.

For a moment, her wild-eyed appearance at the door, without her car, was cause for alarm, but she brushed their worry aside, shaking her head and smiling and giving hugs to everyone she could get to, first her children, then Kate and John and the closest of the miners—the enthusiasm of it giving the crusty men a bit of pause. But her gladness at being welcomed was uncontainable.

"So where your car is, ya, Rute?" John Olsen asked, when things had calmed down slightly.

"Stuck in the shoulder down the road," she said, laughing, and explained to them about the roan's sudden appearance.

"Nearly every day we see him now," Kate said, as she set a big pot of stew on the table. A tray full of biscuits followed, and everyone began filling their bowls. Ruth sat on the bench, one child on each knee, all three of them finding each other a hindrance to getting food from the bowls in front of them into their mouths, but caring more for the physical closeness than their appetites. Every few bites, Ruth found herself leaning down to kiss the top of a child's head, making sure she kissed Maddie as much as J.B. Even the near auburn tangle on her daughter's head would soon be precious to her, Ruth promised herself.

"Now, Rute, about Los Angeles," John Olsen said, when they were finishing up their meal.

"And your mother," Kate said. "She must be glad to see you."

"See my money, you mean," Ruth told her, hearing the bitterness creep into her words. She really didn't want to talk about Cally at all, but knew she had to tell something to these people who cared about her. So she began with Cally's plan to borrow money from her—which brought a bit of bewilderment and head shaking to the table—then went on to tell about the picture and the stories about her grandmother Lolinda. "I'm glad I went," she said. "And I'm even gladder to be back again." She hugged her children tighter, but by now they were bored with the homecoming and wanted free of her. She allowed them to slide down onto the floor.

Ruth went on to tell details about the breadlines and people selling whatever they could along the streets, about the magic line between rich and poor. She told them of the sumptuous hotel room, and remarked about the way people were moving into Los Angeles and expanding its boundaries the way ants can expand the circumference of a picnic ground. She didn't tell them about the night of dancing at the Coconut Grove, or the fancy dress she'd left on the hotel floor along with her bloody shoes.

Later the men went out to retrieve the Model A, refusing to let her accompany them. When they returned, Ruth gave out the presents she had for everyone, and some of the pencils. By this time, J.B. and Maddie were cranky, and Ruth was tired herself. After allowing Kate to bestow on her a pastry to heat for breakfast, Ruth thanked them again for taking care of her children and animals, then said her good-byes and led the two children out to the car.

The car's headlights cast a small circle of illumination ahead of her as she went, highlighting briefly the shapes of brush alongside as she passed. Occasionally, at the light's periphery, she caught a glimpse of eyes peering out, the red of fox or raccoon. That was all anyone could ask for, really, a brief glimpse into what lay ahead—which was far better than earlier, when she could only grope in the darkness and hope she didn't walk into something hurtful. Suddenly her hands ached to make more of the clay pots she had once found joy in fashioning. She would learn to make them beautiful. She wanted to learn more about the ways of Jim's people, who were J.B.'s people too. She wanted to love her daughter, would make herself. Like Ruth, the child of a wicked parent. And the blue roan . . . strange as it seemed, the animal called out to her—in the real world of the canyon and in that other world of her dreams spoke to her of some brand-new Ruth she could sense at the periphery of her vision.

CHAPTER ELEVEN

Ruth was still unsure about bringing Madeline with her to Black Canyon, but Kate and John had gone into San Bernardino. And she had waited long enough. The urge to be there again was too strong in her to put off, as if she were being pulled there by an invisible cord. After all, she and J.B. had been invited back. . . . She smiled, remembering the way the Indians seemed to love J.B. But what would they feel about this girl—who was about as "not Indian"-looking as anyone could get? That hadn't made a difference to Thomas when he learned about her. Would the others accept her in the same way?

At any rate, it was far too late to do anything about it now, she told herself, as she drove under the canopy of giant cottonwoods down canyon from the small settlement. Leaves that had been golden when she was here last fall were now fat and dark green, clapping against each other in the breeze as her car passed under them. Just past the stand of trees, at the water crossing where she had seen the bobcat last fall, a coyote lay in the damp earth beside the stream. It stared for a moment at her approach, then stood and slid into the surrounding brush.

Many fresh tire tracks embossed the ruts as she drove up the canyon. The last time, the few tire tracks had been laid over with a pattern of animal prints. Near the settlement, she found a number of cars and trucks parked beside the road, and when she rounded the bend that brought the community into view, she could see a large crowd of people milling about. Maneuvering the Model A into a space between two trucks, she switched off the engine, the children still asleep on the seat beside her.

From the camp came the sounds of people talking and laughing, of children's play—she could see quite a few running about. And men with hats standing around. The air was filled with smoke and the aromas of roasting food, along with a haze of dust from all the activity. She had pictured the same small group as before, had seen herself being welcomed by the old woman, while Brenda or Martha interpreted. She had imagined Thomas might be there to greet her. But this large gathering was something else entirely—here she was an intruder. Ruth sat quietly in her disappointment, trying to decide whether to turn the car around and head back.

J.B. stirred, raised his head. He sat up and looked over at her, rubbing sleep from his eyes. Then, as if he'd heard or remembered something, the boy stood up and looked out the window. "Da peep," he said, his face igniting with excitement. He reached down and pulled at his sister's shirt to wake her. "Da peep, Maad," he told her as she got to her feet beside him.

"Not da peep, J.B. Daddy's people. Daaa dee's pee pull. Anyway, I don't think we're staying this time, after all. Something's going on, and I have a feeling we shouldn't be here now."

J.B. pointed out the window, his face suddenly distraught. "Da peep," he pleaded. Looking back at her, he amended, "Da dee peep."

"That's better, J.B. Da dee pee pull. But that still doesn't mean we're staying." She pumped the choke and reached for the ignition.

"Da dee pee pull," he moaned, in one last attempt to persuade her. A tear escaped and made a track down his cheek.

Ruth hugged him to her. "Look, J.B., I want to stay too. I drove all this way. But it's not a good time. We'd be intruding and . . ." Words failed her at the sight of his crumbling face. It mirrored back her own distress at leaving. Beside them, Maddie gave out two sharp barks, and Ruth looked over to see the girl peering out the back window. Maddie bounced once and gave another bark.

Ruth looked over her shoulder at the dog running ahead of a group of children who were fast approaching the car. "Stop barking, Maddie. They'll think you're a dog," she scolded. Why couldn't that girl use words like a normal child? It wasn't that she didn't know any. Ruth had heard her speak perfectly clearly to her brother while they played in the wash.

By now J.B. had one foot over the edge of the sill. He slid down into the arms of the same boy who had carried him around last time. The boy gave Ruth a nod and a smile as he took hold of J.B. Filling in her brother's place at the car window, Maddie stared at the children with wide eyes. Then the boy with J.B. said something in their language, and they all laughed. He walked up to the window and touched her red hair, then said the word again, which brought more laughter.

"She Maad," J.B. told them.

Maddie pointed at the dog and gave another bark. The children laughed again. One of the girls reached in and ruffled Maddie's hair, then pulled her out the passenger window. The children started for the central area, J.B. and Maddie in tow. Relieved, Ruth pulled the key from the ignition and pushed down the door handle. It seemed unlikely that anyone would arrive to pull her from the car window, she mused.

She walked toward the cloud of smoke and dust, part of her wanting to creep up, concealing herself behind things as she went. It was funny the way she was intimidated by groups of people, her own neighbors included. Maybe especially. She was convinced that she wouldn't have been nearly as worried walking toward a bear or mountain lion as she was walking into a group of human beings.

Ruth stopped at the edge of the gathering and looked for someone she recognized. Her children were no longer visible. She didn't see Thomas anywhere either, but thought she spotted the old woman in a cluster of people near the circular thatched house at the center of the settlement.

Affecting a thin air of confidence—and reminding herself that she had been invited to bring J.B. back here—she walked toward the woman. Still, the distance seemed impossibly long. It wasn't until Grandmother Siki looked over and smiled at her approach that Ruth felt some of her tension dissolve.

She glanced at the array of unusual foods laid out on the long table, the several flat breads and dried meats and what looked very much like roasted cicadas or grasshoppers, while the old woman continued speaking in her own language to the others. She nodded and motioned toward Ruth as she spoke. Many of the women were dressed no differently than women in Juniper Valley—in flowered dresses or in slacks and a blouse, the way Martha had been, rather than in the long loose dresses with pinafores worn by the old woman. Rather than covering their heads with scarves, these women wore their hair short, cut in modern styles.

Ruth noticed Martha coming out of a little dwelling. She smiled at Ruth as she walked toward her and the group of women. "Grandmother says to tell you that you come at the perfect time," Martha told her, after first speaking a few words with the old woman. "She was hoping you would get her message and be here with us tonight for the Whirling Bird Dance."

"A message? Did she send me a message?"

Martha laughed. "Not that kind of message. It's different in our language, but there's no word in English for it. 'Message' comes the closest—but it's a different kind of message. One that comes from here"—she put a hand on her chest then nodded toward Ruth's—"to here without words. *Heart-calling* might be a better way to say it."

"Jim used to say that, too—that words don't translate, I mean," Ruth told her. "But why would she want me here tonight?"

"This is the last night. That's why so many of us have come up. For the big dance," the woman said. "It really goes on all week. The relatives who live here all summer have been getting things ready. Something happens each day." She stopped to adjust her glasses before explaining, "The *ni'hiha* was presented to the *cafika* two days ago, the *ta'nama* after that—that's the naming of all the new babies. Yesterday was the *ka'niha*."

The old woman smiled again, spoke a few words to Ruth that

98

she couldn't understand. "Grandmother says they'll take you to the *kit'catact* later—that's the big house here," Martha explained. She nodded toward the circular hut. "And show you. But we have to be dressed traditional first." She stopped and looked at Ruth. "By the way, Grandmother calls you Dlah'da, willow leaf woman, but you must have a name of your own."

"Ruth. But why does she call me that?"

"That one's Ruth too," Martha said, nodding toward another of the modernly dressed women, this one quite plump in her flowered dress, with a matching hat. She also wore glasses. "That's my sister. We work together at the agency. Translate and cook. Even do paperwork." The other Ruth looked over and smiled. The two of them looked to be only a few years older than she was.

Behind Martha, at the periphery of the larger gathering, Ruth could see several children chasing after each other; J.B. and Maddie, along with two other children about their size, lagged behind a few yards, their little legs doing their best to keep up. She remembered last fall—how unsteady J.B. was on his feet then.

Ruth looked away from the children. "There are so many people here today. The first time I came there weren't nearly so many. Not so many children either."

"Most of us don't live here anymore. Just come up for the *ni'hihata*, the Whirling Bird—or to be here sometimes in summer. I come up more, sometimes stay here for a few weeks. Hardly anyone stays in winter. We all go down to the desert, where it's warmer. Even in old times most people did that. But now some of us have jobs down there."

The old woman said something and everyone laughed. "She said, 'No more pounding acorns and mesquite for you'—that's me she meant—'you pound type keys to eat.'" Seeing Ruth's confusion, Martha added, "Maybe 'grinding' would be a better word. But that's not it. For us it's the same word as your 'chew.' I guess it's not funny unless you know the language." She stopped and nodded at someone approaching from behind Ruth's shoulder.

"Anyway"—Martha smiled and looked back at her—"Grandmother Siki calls you Dlah'da because she says you had willow leaves stuck in your hair the first time you came here." Ruth felt heat rise to her cheeks, remembering her wild dance of joy among the willows.

When Ruth turned to see Thomas walking in their direction, she was surprised to find him wearing a colorfully striped scarf draped over each shoulder and feathers woven into his hair and headband. But the biggest change was his face, which had been painted in the same colors as the scarves, rust red, blue, ocher, white, and black. The nod he gave to her and the rest of the group, before he went into the circular building, was formal and reserved. Ruth remained staring after him through the doorway into the dim interior, where she thought she could make out colorfully dressed people standing in a row toward the back, all quiet and unmoving.

She looked back to find the women walking away in various directions. "We have to get dressed now," Martha called out to her. "You can come with me and Grandmother Siki."

Ruth looked around for J.B. and Maddie, located them sitting on the ground nearby to watch some of the older children kick around what looked to be a rounded stone. She hurried after Martha and the old woman, who were disappearing inside one of the small conventional houses made of unfinished wood. Beside it sat one of the older dwellings made of brush, like the one Jim had stayed in.

Inside, the one-room cabin was simply furnished, somewhat like her own, with a bed near the door and a table and chair farther on. The two women were already searching through a rack of clothes in the corner across from the bed. The far side of the room had a woodstove and small standing basin for a sink, and above it something Ruth didn't have, a large tin container that looked to hold water for use in the sink. What an excellent idea for her own place.

"This is Grandmother's other house," Martha told Ruth, "so she can be more comfortable. But she likes to sleep there, in the *ki'takii*"— Martha nodded out the door toward the brush dwelling—"most of the time anyway. Especially in summer."

The old woman was laying out clothes on the bed beside the clothes rack. She pulled out a long green gingham dress with a white pinafore and looked at Ruth, motioning with her head for Ruth to come closer. When she came near, the old woman held the dress up to Ruth's front. Though Ruth couldn't understand a word she said, the tone was one of approval.

"She says this one will fit you okay," Martha said. "It used to be my sister's before she had all those children." She took the dress and held it out to Ruth.

Ruth accepted the dress but stood there not knowing what to do with it next. Apparently, they wanted her to put it on, but the dress was not the kind she would ever wear on her own—and she wasn't sure she wanted to now. She wondered if Lolinda had ever worn such a thing. The photo showed to just below her shoulders, and she appeared to be wearing what looked like a peasant blouse—but then she was from a different tribe entirely.

"These are the dresses we use for the *ni'hihata* these days," Martha told her. "The Whirling Bird. When Grandma was a girl, she says some wore the old grass skirts. But she never did. Only the old ones."

"Tell me about the Whirling Bird Dance."

"Oh, you'll see. We'll show you what to do. It's better not to talk about it, just to do it." She began gathering up clothing from the bed. "Go ahead. Put it on. Me and Grandma have to go into the *ki'takii* to get dressed. You can get dressed here in the other house."

The dress seemed entirely unsuited for her, and the comfort and belonging Ruth had experienced earlier disappeared completely once the women left her alone in the cabin—the other house, as they called it. Whatever was she doing in this strange place, wearing this outlandish costume? What of Jim did she hope to find here? Why did she feel she belonged in this place when even Jim had rarely spent time here? Ruth walked to the door and looked out at J.B. and Maddie kicking at the stone ball while the older children laughed and encouraged them. At least they seemed as at home as they did in their own canyon—a place Ruth missed greatly at the moment.

How odd that she should suddenly feel so alienated when these people clearly wanted her here. The townsfolk in Juniper Valley were not at all welcoming, had only tolerated her at the best of times. Now she was considered a ruined woman and most excluded her completely. And she them, to be honest. Yet, she could hardly walk away from this—whatever it was—when these people had sought to include her.

She looked over at the large circular hut that Thomas had gone into, his face painted and somber. That one they called a *kit'catact,* she remembered, and tried the word out on her tongue. Some deep drumming seemed to be coming from within the place, and she could see others heading in that direction. Ruth stepped out the door and began walking toward it as well.

Not much happened until the sun dropped the rest of the way to the horizon. Until then, the crowd turned its attention to the foods laid out on the long table. Martha explained to her that these were the old foods, now prepared mainly for ceremonial occasions. Only a few of the old ones, like Grandmother Siki, ate them regularly. Most were dried foods that tasted of the place around them. Ruth recognized venison in the brittle strips of meat, but other chunks and strips were not as apparent. She bypassed the small roasted lumps where the legs were still visible. Several grains and flat breads beside them she found hard when she bit into them, but each had a delicious and exotic flavor that stayed with her long after. She thought she recognized dried yucca blossoms from their familiar color and shape, though she had never thought such a thing might be edible. They tasted slightly sweet and a bit soapy. Sweet also were small strips of something fuchsia and chewy, and sweeter yet were sticky brown chunks of something else that Ruth had no idea about. Occasionally, a child would come over and help itself to these foods, and she noticed that the brown chunks and red strips were especially popular with them.

She called J.B. and Maddie to her in the twilight, lifting them to see the foods on the table, then chose for them things they might like. They tolerated her interference with their play just long enough to satisfy their hunger, then went back to run with the other children, leaving Ruth as free and unencumbered as if she had no children. Even at Glory Springs the two of them had become more independent of her attention lately, except for necessities like food and bathing. But here their need for her seemed to have vanished completely.

Ruth turned with the others when colorfully arrayed men began filing from the *kit'catact* to surround the large fire ring that had been prepared earlier. Flames seemed to explode into life as they circled. At least she thought they were men—with all the feathers braided into their hair and draped from arms and shoulders on beaded leather bands, they seemed more the embodiment of the birds they were meant to represent than human men. Even so she noticed that the lead dancer had the limp of Martha's brother.

Some dancers wore the shiny black feathers of ravens and made sharp caws and clucks and gurgling sounds as they whirled in circles and flapped wing arms while moving around the fire. The brilliant blue of jays was another popular color worn by several swirling dancers, and there were yellow and black orioles, and birdmen the color of cardinals and another red bird Ruth had seen once, and many the duller color of sparrows and wrens and even gray doves and speckled quail and birds she didn't know by name or by the calls that were being imitated so well.

Then from the door of the *kit'catact* came a high, shrill cry and out flew—for that was how she perceived it—a reddish hawkman, and several other hawkmen of types she'd seen, one black with white wing tips, another gray with light underfeathers. The hawks created a flurry among the other birdmen as they joined them, whirling and circling the fire, causing the lesser birds to chirp and squawk and fly in circles out from the fire and back, while the people watching laughingly approved. By now the children had gathered to watch the show, and Ruth glimpsed hers there with eyes as wide open as her own must have been. After some time, the smaller birds returned and the whole group settled into a more harmonious relationship as they circled the fire, with only an occasional flurry of chirps and wing flaps when one of the hawks got a bit too close. The people seemed especially to enjoy these incidents of commotion and laughed and commented among themselves at each one. Ruth couldn't help but laugh over their antics.

Another shrill cry sounded from the door of the hut, and she looked over in time to see a large eagle appear. Now all the birds stopped moving entirely. The eagle stood in the doorway, making high cries, each one stronger than the last, then flew out toward the campfire, wings waving as slowly and gracefully as if he were really soaring through air.

All the other birds flew off from the circle, chattering and squawking as they went. Ruth could hear them somewhere out in the darkness that had come to enclose the gathering, while the eagle soared around and around the campfire, magnificent in its dignity and power. Gradually, the other birds returned, one by one, until all were whirling and dancing and calling and chirping around the campfire while the people looked on.

By now Ruth had come to regard the whirling dancers as something other than men adorned with feathers, and something other than birds or even the spirits of the birds depicted. She had moved into a place beyond words or categories and could only open herself to the spectacle and accept the wonder on its own terms.

When a low chanting began to emanate from the *kit'catact,* the bird dancers slowed the pace of their whirling movements, eventually ceasing to whirl at all and, in the end, simply waved wings and moved around the campfire so slowly that Ruth felt her own heartbeat and breathing ease up to keep pace with them. Then they began to leave the fire, snaking away single file toward the door of the hut and disappearing into its interior.

Things went back to ordinary again. People began talking and laughing, some moving back to the food table for more. Soon Ruth smelled coffee and went to look for the source near a smaller fire ring in front of one of the wooden houses. She lined up with the rest and was given a steaming cup whose tin sides were too hot to touch. She could barely hold it by the handle and had to let the liquid cool a while before she could manage even a cautious sip from the cup's metal lip. It was coffee all right, and delicious, but with something else added that left a delicate sweetness.

"You're going to need that," Martha said, walking up with a cup of her own. "The dancing goes on till dawn."

"The dancers must get awfully tired by then."

"We'll all be dancing later. You too." She laughed mischievously and gave Ruth a nudge with her elbow. "Grandma said I ought to tell you what happens next, since you'll be involved in that part."

"Me? Why would I be involved?"

"Because of Ni'jini. Don't worry, it's just a short part before we all dance—but it's real important. The dancers will come out and get all the *haa'iit aki.* Just follow along what the others are doing. We thought about your boy being the one to do it—because he's the real relative. By blood, I mean. But we decided he's too young. He's just been named. Besides, he never knew Ni'jini. So you're the one."

Ruth stood in puzzled silence, watching the way flickering firelight cast mystery onto even the homey scene of people eating and drinking coffee, leaving so much of everything in shadow. All this was so

strange, yet familiar at the same time. "But what is all this about? This
. . . this . . ?" She searched for the right word but could only come up
with "this dance," though clearly it was much more than any kind of
dance she knew about.

"We already did the naming of the babies last night. Thomas gave
your boy his name—it had to be done even though it's way past time
by now. Sometimes that happens these days," Martha said. "He's
called Nii'giia, makes places." Glow from the fire gave the lenses of her
glasses a light gold sheen as she spoke. "Thomas told us about your
girl. Called her Taha." She laughed. "Like your paintbrush flower."

When Ruth didn't laugh back, Martha's face became serious again.
"What's happening now is we're freeing the taken ones. The *haa'iit*
like Ni'jini. He should have been let go last year, but we didn't know
then."

So they had called Jim's son Nii'giia, makes places. How did they
decide that, she wondered, and what then did Ni'jini mean? Martha
started to walk away, then turned back. "Drink up. It will start again
soon. And don't worry," she said. "It will all work out like it's supposed
to. You'll see. It always does." Ruth breathed in deeply and downed the
rest of her sweet coffee. She returned to the line for another cup, then
went to search out her children.

She found J.B. and Maddie sitting with a group of other children
near the big fire ring, where people had already begun to gather again.
She lifted the long skirt of her dress and squatted beside the circle the
children had made. They were playing some game that involved rolling small rounded stones into each other. It reminded Ruth of marbles
games she had seen boys play in El Paso. Her children, like the others,
were so intent on the game they paid little attention to her presence. She
remained watching them a few minutes more as she drank her coffee,
enjoying the way the older children coaxed the younger ones in their
clumsy attempts to spin their rocks into clusters of other little rocks.

Maddie had been perfectly accepted, and she and J.B. seemed happy.
Although Ruth had hardly paid them mind since they arrived, their
smudged faces and dirty clothes gave a clear report on the pleasure
taken. She left them and went to stand at the fire with the others.

A chorus of chanting came from the hut now, soft at first, then
gaining in volume each time a certain phrase was repeated. Although

Ruth hadn't an inkling of the words' meaning, she felt them becoming so deeply ingrained in her memory that she would probably be able to repeat them in her sleep. *Ni'hihata ki'catacti haa'iit aki, ni'hihata ki'catacti haa'iit aki.* By this time, everyone had returned to the fire ring, and she could feel anticipation growing in the quieting crowd. Eventually, the children stopped their game and kept their eyes trained on the door of the hut.

Then, with a sudden flurry of motion, the dancers burst from the door of the hut and swooped through the crowd. Just as Ruth registered surprise at the addition of a huge vulture to the bird dancers, she felt herself being swept toward the fire ring in a flurry of feathers, an irresistible movement carrying her to the center, where others in plain dress were also merging into the line of dancers and beginning to circle the fire. She continued around and around the campfire, her feet set on a course her head didn't yet understand, matching steps with the rest in the flickering darkness, all the while smiling inwardly in amazement to find herself in this place with these people, doing what she was doing, without even knowing why. The long green dress that she had felt so uncomfortable putting on, had now become part of her—as if she had been born wearing it. And dancing around and around the fire soon came to seem as if she had always been there, her feet keeping beat with the rest. Yet no sooner had this thought occurred to her, than the eagle stepped out from the circle and made his shrill cry, and all the birds began stepping out to make their cries, falling into line behind the eagle and starting for the big hut, the buzzard trailing the rest in silence, while the plainly dressed dancers followed along after, Ruth with them, toward the door of the *kit'catact*. As she went, she caught a glimpse of her children's wide eyes.

Inside, the floor of the *kit'catact* had been dug out even deeper than Jim's *ki'takii,* and the dancers led her and the others down a dirt ramp into the large round room, lit only by a fire in the center and by four tall torches, one set in each direction. When the others began seating themselves on each side of the woven palm frond and willow walls beside the door, Ruth followed suit and settled cross-legged on the soft soil, while the bird dancers went to stand farther on, now shaking rattles held to their sides. A tall man—it took her a moment to realize that it was Thomas under the paint and bright scarves that adorned him—stood chanting and sprinkling powder over a row of still figures already standing at the far side of the hut. With the torch in back of the far figures and with their distance behind the fire so great, they were at first little more than darkened silhouettes that she strained vainly to make out. When her eyes adjusted, Ruth was able to determine what the presence she felt had already told her. Jim was there among those figures.

It was a mystery to her, just how she determined that figure was Jim in the dim light, but the moment she did, she heard herself gasp, and her body tensed to spring upward and run toward him. At the same moment she felt herself held back, as if hands as firm as granite had clamped down on her shoulders. She heard the words clearly in her head, "sit down, Ruth," though she had no idea where they came from or whose voice spoke them. It may have been Jim's or Thomas's or her own, but its authority was enough to keep her seated on the ground. All the while, her eyes bored intensely into Jim's image, which, even though constructed merely of feathers and tules and dressed like him in khaki pants and plaid shirt, was so remarkably real to her that she could barely restrain herself. She wanted to clasp that beloved image to her breast, as she would a child, and bring it back to life with the love she felt rushing into her. She had forgotten how precious that feeling had been until this moment. Even the small doses that used to come to her in dreams had deserted her of late. But that love was with her again, back in all its force, pumping steadily on the fountain of her blood with each heartbeat, as if keeping time with the thrumming that came from a drum somewhere.

Jim, oh, Jim, you've come back to me. You've come back to me, her heart sang silently over and over again as she sat enraptured, while the tall painted man sprinkled pollen and words over the darkened figures, his motion and words accompanied by the quiet roll of the rattles and the somewhere drum. The high sweet melody of something flutelike mixed with the rest. Memory brought the past to life, and Jim was with her again—everywhere all at the same time. Her skin felt his hands travel its surface once more, her ears absorbed the sound of his voice, and she breathed in his scent as surely as if he were there in the room with her.

Ni'jini, she said inwardly, using the name that belonged with him in this place, feeling the word form silently on her lips.

Thomas now faced those seated along the sides as he chanted and sprinkled pollen from a feathered bundle over each of the plainly dressed dancers. When he neared her, Ruth peered deep into his eyes and face, trying to find the man she knew from before, yet found he had been replaced by someone with the same outward appearance, but whose eyes were focused far inside, even when he looked right at her, and she felt the light brush of his finger on her forehead, his eagle feather caress her skin. The steady hum of the rattles and thumbing of the drum lulled the high pitch of her emotion into a steady pulse of feeling that streamed through her with each thump of her heart.

Everything taking place around and inside her now took on an aura of utter significance. Each sight, each sound and smell, each movement, however foreign and strange, seemed preordained, as if she had always known them. The feathered dancers with their rattles, the tall man chanting and dropping pollen, the dance of light and shadow in the air that cast gold sheen onto the braided walls of the hut, even the way smoke rose and curled away from the popping fire made her draw in her breath at its beauty. She felt the scene being etched permanently inside her, the way petroglyphs are carved into rock.

Thomas turned and threw something into the flames that made them flare high, then lifted a large clay bowl that had sat on the ground by the fire. Flames reflected on the surface of liquid inside as he offered the bowl to the closest of the dancers. The dancer drank from the bowl and passed it on to the next dancer in line, and the next, until it reached the first of the plainly dressed people, who also drank and passed the bowl on to the next in line. When the bowl reached her, Ruth found the liquid inside as black as a no-moon night, except for bright flames playing across its surface in reflected light. She held the bowl in front of her for a moment, marveling at its nature—the earthen vessel holding this merger of fire and water that shimmered lightly as she breathed out air upon it. Then, like the rest, she lifted the bowl to her lips and took a sip of this dark wonder into her body, and passed it on to the one beside her. Its strange, bittersweet taste lingered long after.

When the bowl had been returned to its place, the bird dancers appeared in front of the rest, their feet keeping time with the drum as they stood there. From somewhere came the wail of a flute. The others began rising to stand before the dancers, and Ruth found herself echoing their motion without a thought, found her body following the flow of sound and movement that surrounded her. One by one, each of them was chosen by the feathered dancers, who drew them out from the rest and encircled them, then sent them back with the others. When they had finished, the dancers led the group toward the figures behind the fire. Ruth's heart picked up its pace as she neared her beloved, and she could not contain her quiet tears as she reached out and touched Jim's image. So real he had become that what she saw before her was skin and flesh and hair and was entirely surprised that her fingers and hands encountered instead the scratchy surface of the strawlike material beneath the clothes, and the face of woven feathers hung on the rack. In that moment, she knew the image for what it was, but that quickly passed, and she pulled her beloved to her, holding him tight to her heart that was doing its best to pump enough life for them both.

She was not allowed to remain in that place for long, as she felt the rest turn with their images back toward the door of the hut. They were all in motion now, and she with them, her legs and feet keeping time with the dancers despite the resistance she felt, her urge to stay in that place and savor the return of her lover, however delusional it might be. Instead, she felt herself thrust from the hut with the others, expelled from that place of warm and magical light, outside into the waiting night, and she crushed the image to her breast as if it alone might save her.

The crowd outside opened a pathway as the dancers swept the group from the hut to the fire, where they all began circling again, and now the whole crowd took up the chant from before, *Ni'hihata ki'catacti haa'iit aki. Ni'hihata ki'catacti haa'iit aki,* as they went around the fire. Then, after a few turns, a voice called out something, and the first person in line let go the woman figure he had been carrying and threw her into the fire. Ruth watched in horror as the image turned over in the air, its arms outstretched, its skirts flapping and wrapping back around as it sailed steadily into flames that reached up to grab and then quickly consume it. She searched the faces of the ones next to her, but those faces revealed none of the pain that sight had stirred up in her. She hugged Jim's image tighter to her as they all resumed moving around the fire, and the chant began again: *Ni'hihata ki'catacti haa'iit aki, ni'hihata ki'catacti haa'iit aki.*

As Ruth was afraid might happen, after completing a few more circles, a voice again cried out, and the dancers came to a halt once more. Then the next person cast her figure into the fire—this image so small the woman had held it bundled in her arms, with only a black feathered patch visible above the face. Now it arced above the fire, turned end over once, then descended into the orange fingers waiting to grasp it. Ruth shuddered and looked back at the woman. She thought she saw a glistening on her face in the firelight. Then they were all in motion again, and the chanting had resumed. Ruth thought she understood now what this ceremony was about.

The realization left her with a deep affection and appreciation for these people. At the same time, her own resistance to it began to crystallize. This ritual had had the power to bring her love for Jim back into being, when the horror of his death had nearly erased it, and she had no intention of letting it go again.

In the first place, she told herself, as her feet and body moved mindlessly on, Jim had been the only one in her whole life who had ever truly loved her. And he had been the only one she had ever truly loved. If not for that love, she could have gone on with her life as before indefinitely. But their love had changed everything for her. She suddenly understood why she had been floundering like a polliwog out of water ever since. It hadn't been the murder or the rape or even the birth of the babies that had ripped from her the self she knew. It had been the loss of that love that had changed her. And now it had been restored to her. She wasn't about to simply toss it into the fire and watch it disappear again. If it took this . . . this tule and feathered thing in her arms to bring it all back, then she would cling to it as long as she needed. These people weren't about to keep her from doing so. She wouldn't let them.

It was funny, the way all cultures were alike in that respect, had rules everyone had to mind—or they would not remain a part of it. Even Jim had told her that. Although she had never felt a part of any group, she had begun to feel that here; it had been a new and comforting feeling. Yet if that comfort meant giving up all that she had just regained, she would give up such belonging in a minute.

It was some time before the voice called out and brought the circle to a halt again, and when it did, Ruth found herself strengthening her grip on Jim's image. She was still two down from her turn to let go and fling her figure away into the universe somewhere, watch it become smoke and ashes in front of her eyes, the way she'd seen Jim's blood drain out into the earth in front of her doorway. Even as they began moving again, she wasn't yet sure what she would do when her time came. But she wasn't going to throw this image into flames, that much she did know. For a moment, she pictured herself running with the figure through the darkness toward her car and driving away as fast as she could. But that picture didn't include J.B. and Maddie, and she couldn't just leave them there for the Indians to raise—though for a flash the thought sorely tempted her.

Searching the edges of the crowd, Ruth saw the two of them sitting in front with the other children, all the young eyes huge with wonder at the spectacle. She rearranged her escape to include them, picturing herself scooping the two of them into her arms along with the figure and all of them running into the darkness. But that wasn't realistic. She could never carry the big figure and both children as well. What if she left Maddie—the Yuiatei seemed to like her well enough—and ran off with J.B. and Jim's figure? But it was J.B. who belonged to these people. Could she leave him instead and run off with Jim and Maddie? That was unthinkable.

Maybe her children could just chase after her as she carried Jim's image. Except—in the dark it would be difficult. For all of them. She could almost hear their voices crying behind her as they stumbled over rocks and into cactus. Then she remembered that she had no idea in which direction her car was parked in the first place. She would be as lost out in the dark as they were.

By now the circle had stopped again and gone on, and there remained only one stop in front of Ruth's own time, and soon that was done and her turn was coming up without anyone else in front of her. Her muscles were so tight with tension she thought she might simply spring upward, her legs propelling her body higher and higher, rising up and up like the sparks from the campfire until she disappeared somewhere into the starry night overhead. But that was merely what she wished, and she knew she would soon have to confront the moment for real. Her choices did not include floating away into space, but options left to her standing on solid ground. Then the voice cried out from somewhere—and the circle of dancers all came to a halt.

Clutching Jim's image to her, Ruth stood stubborn while the people waited. She would not, would not give it up. They could not make her do it. They would just have to start moving again and continue on with the person next to her, she decided, clenching her jaw to firm up her resolve. Maybe the man behind her could throw his figure now, in place of hers.

Everything had come to a complete stop now, inside and outside the circle. She had brought it all to a halt. Waiting was thick in the air, the collective breath held. Defiant, she looked out over the faces in the crowd. Though their eyes weren't on her, she knew they were all watching. From somewhere nearby a coyote howled, then more joined in, filling the night with plaintive chaos.

A movement at the edge of the crowd caught her eye, and she saw J.B. rise to his feet and run toward her, his little face set with determination. With deep relief, she realized he was showing her the way, and she loosened her grip on Jim's image a bit in order to lift her child up and run with him into the darkness. She bent and opened an arm to grab him and, when she did, she felt the figure lift from her other arm and fly toward the fire. Ruth turned to snatch it back, but Jim's image had already left her son's hands and was plummeting into fire. She took a step, meaning to fling herself after it, but before she could take another, what had been a replica of her lover became a fat mass of flame, a blur of orangey-yellow tipped with roan blue that seemed to reach into her as well, searing its way clear through her being. She stood in stunned agony while its heat burned her clean inside. Then the image was gone. All that remained was the love it had reawakened, now pumping steadily through her veins.

Ruth glanced down at her son, who looked up at her with eyes that appeared as wise as they were innocent, then he ran back to take his place beside Maddie, and the circle started moving forward again.

CHAPTER TWELVE

Ruth gave up on sleep, sat on the edge of the bed, yawned and rubbed her eyes. A week had passed since she returned from the Whirling Bird Dance, and still her nights were filled with dreams of fleeing the campfire with Jim's image, pursued by feather-clad dancers. She placed her bare soles against the concrete floor, rose and tiptoed to the stove for a pan and matches, stuck the coffee can under one arm so she had a hand free to slide up the latch on the door, and snuck out into the front yard, where she could move freely.

Setting the can of coffee and the matches on the rock table by the campfire, she took the pan across the wash to her spring for water. All around her, the canyon glowed with the pink-wash of dawn. As she walked back with the water, a gob of buttery sun appeared over the ridge, and she allowed her eyes to remain on it long enough to see its shape solidify, become round and begin lifting into the clear sky.

She could still see the sun's dark afterimage as she walked back, superimposed on everything she looked at—the sky, the mountain, the cabin door, behind which her children yet slept, though she expected them any moment to wake and wander out to pee. She found it strange that a shape as bright as the sun would leave itself imprinted on her sight as a phantom vacancy. When she tried to focus on the blot of blank darkness to better make out its contours, her eyes were unable to do so, the way her mind could not quite grasp the remnants of dreams left impressed on her day, letting them fade away like the specter of sun that was slowly disappearing from her eyes.

When water began hissing in the pan, Ruth pulled it from the fire, dumped in the coffee grounds and stirred them into the developing foam. As if on cue, J.B. appeared at the cabin door, Maddie behind him. Ruth had hoped to sit out alone with her coffee, but the day was already making its demands. The nanny had started to bleat a few moments before, though she had been able to ignore her until the children came out. Now it was clear that her precious time alone was over. Another day was calling her into itself.

Ruth spent the next few hours numbed in daily routine. Milking the goat, straining, starting new cheese, fixing pancakes for Maddie and J.B., hauling bucket after bucket of water, washing the clothes she'd left sitting far too long, preparing lunch and dinner. She did find herself pleased when she experimented with the pancakes, adding in some of the mesquite and acorn flour that Martha had given her. The results were so tasty that Ruth wondered if she should begin harvesting and grinding acorns and mesquite flour of her own—although it struck her as somewhat peculiar that she might choose to embrace the arduous work of the Black Canyon women when she had so much distaste for the far easier duties of women in her own culture. Or what was said to be her culture. Who knew how much of Lolinda was in her?

Eventually, the day wore on her, though, and she looked up from her scrub board at Rocky Mountain, remembering the day Jim showed her a place near the top where bright red ladybugs beaded the green fir branches, like rubies from some magical kingdom. She remembered how the two of them could see the land around them in every direction as they sat on rocks at the highest peak, how they looked down on Jim's lake and the lean-to where her world would shift forever.

But those days were gone, and without the freedom she had come here to find, there was tedium, no matter what she kept telling herself. If only Jim were here to share her life, then it would not oppress her so.

None of these thoughts were new to her; in fact, she thought them almost daily as she went about her chores. Round and round she went with the same ideas, still hoping for a way out of such obsession, much the way she hoped for a way out of the tedium—and remained equally trapped in both. The only relief for her came when she visited the people in Black Canyon. But those were only visits. She couldn't base her life there, though she'd like to bring more of what she found there to enrich her own life in Glory Springs.

Ruth finished rinsing the clothes, wrung them, and walked over to hang them over the clothesline. She dumped the pile of clothes on a rock so she could first untie the rabbit's feet she'd broken off at the ankles and left dangling, after skinning the creature for dinner the night before. She noticed, as she hung the clothes, that J.B. was building something out of sticks by the pine tree across from the clothesline, and that Maddie occasionally walked over and handed him something that looked like bread. She hoped it was bread; both children seemed to be eating it. After Ruth hung the last of the children's shirts, she walked over to make sure.

The food Maddie was sharing turned out to be petals of yucca blossoms that had dropped from the plant next to the wash. Not bread at all, but also not harmful, and the children weren't doing much more than tasting the flowers, then J.B. would lay the wilted petals over his mounded sticks. He looked up at his mother as she squatted beside him. "Da peep," he said, then, remembering her correction, "Da dee pee pull howse." And sure enough, the little mounds of sticks did look a lot like those tiny brush dwellings. Ruth smiled and ruffled his hair, letting her hand linger a minute to feel the coarse texture that was so like his father's.

"*Ki'takii*, J.B.," Maddie muttered suddenly in her child's voice, pronouncing perfectly the words from both languages, and shocking Ruth so that she fell from her squat to a sit. She had heard Maddie speak occasionally with J.B. in play, enough to know the girl could do more than create the sounds around her—animals and insects and wind. But Yuiatei? Why wasn't it J.B. who said it?

"What did you say, Maddie?" Ruth asked when she recovered herself, but the girl had rushed back to the yucca for more of the blossoms. She must have misheard her, she thought, getting up to follow her.

The flavorful yucca blossoms they had eaten at the feast in Black Canyon had been either boiled or dried—maybe both—or mixed into stews. But none of them, she was sure, had been gathered from the ground.

"You have to use the ones still on the plant, silly," she said, keeping her distance from the crowd of green daggers at the bottom, leaves that served to protect the cactus-like plant's progeny, as she reached in to pluck several thick cream-colored petals from the stem rising at the center. "The ones on the ground are all wilted." Avoiding the shiny green beetles who were enjoying their own feast, she leaned in to gather blossoms closer to the heart of the flower cluster. Ruth straightened and held the handful of petals out. Maddie seemed surprised at her mother's sudden interest.

"Maybe I'll boil up a few for supper," Ruth said, already walking toward the campfire, without waiting for an answer. She wasn't going to let this little red-haired twerp be the Indian in the family. Something in her wanted to tell the girl that she wasn't Yuiatei at all, that her brother was the only real child of a Yuiatei father. Yet shame at her own meanness was enough to glue Ruth's mouth shut.

To the leftover rabbit stew they ate at late-afternoon supper, Ruth also added a few of the yucca petals, which turned out to be much tastier than the ones they'd boiled for a few minutes earlier, then dotted with butter and salt. But she would have to learn more about the ways the Black Canyon people fixed yucca flowers—that is if they were going to eat them any other way than in stews. The ones she boiled and buttered were edible but retained too much of that semi-soapy flavor she didn't much relish. Ruth tried her best to savor the flavors this plant produced from her beloved canyon's soil, but her palate resisted. Raw potatoes or beets were not so tasty either, she reminded herself. She would just have to learn more about how to prepare her canyon's delicacies.

By the time Ruth had settled J.B. and Maddie into bed—she always made a point of getting them down early so she could have more time for herself—and come back out to reheat the coffee, sun was casting the last splash of gold light over the mountains around her. She walked toward the wash, thinking to gather wood and bolster the campfire, but stopped short when she discovered a coyote lying on top of Jim's grave, as calmly as if it owned the spot. A storm of conflicting emotions whirled through her. She wanted to pick up a rock and heave it at the animal, to scream at it to get off the resting place of the only human being she had loved completely. Yet a cynical despair told her to turn away and leave the coyote be, that under the earth beneath the creature were now only bones, wisps of hair, and withered flesh.

She hated the tears that welled up, the way her voice cracked when she choked out the words, "Get away from there," which came out more as a plea than a demand.

The coyote raised its head and looked at her, though it made no move to leave. She bent and picked up a small stone, tossed it at the animal. The rock flew halfway across the wash, dropping far short of its target, but the coyote stood then and considered her more seriously.

"What do you want here? Why pick that spot," she asked it, "when you have all of this canyon, these mountains to lay down on?" She spread her arms as if to show the creature what she meant. "Why pick the one place I need to keep . . . keep . . . ," She searched for a word, rejecting the ones that came to her—*sacred, hallowed*—finally settling on "untouched," blurting it out in a way that caused the coyote to take a step back, though it continued to regard her without alarm.

By now the coyote had blurred beyond recognition from tears as hot on her cheeks as fresh blood. She took a step toward the grave, hesitated, then slid down the bank and into the wash, stumbling her way over the mounds of rock and debris, half blind.

She scrambled up the far bank near the grave, wiping her eyes with a forearm. By the time she arrived, the coyote was disappearing into the underbrush like some apparition. Next to the grave, Ruth dropped to her knees, savoring the pain caused by sharp sticks and pebbles. Martha had told her that *Ni'jini* meant something like "belongs to the rock." But he didn't belong to the rock; he belonged to her.

Ruth began tossing off the warm stones the coyote had lain on, the smoothly rounded rocks they had once pulled from the wash to protect Jim's fresh grave from being ravaged by scavengers—stones not so different from the ones she had placed over her heart to survive the pain. When she reached the soft sand of disrupted earth, buried so long beneath the rocks, Ruth flung her body onto its yielding substance, positioning herself along the length of Jim's grave. She lay her cheek against the chill sand that for years had had no exposure to sun and air and let memories of the times they'd spent together seep into her. Arms hugged tight to the mound of dry sand covering her lover's body, she let herself weep, as if she were draining away water that had stagnated somewhere deep inside her.

"I could never have thrown you in the fire, Jim," she whispered through her weeping. "Never. I'll not leave you behind. No one can make me do that. Not even your son, when he threw you in. Not even him. He never even knew you. I'll keep you here with me, Jim, always. I promise."

After some time, she began to calm, and a quiet came over her, broken only by occasional gusts of memories that continued to waft through her. Then one particular memory came on so vividly it took over every sense in her body. She and Jim were kneeling beside the lake in midday heat, Jim pointing out the differences between bobcat and coyote track, showing her the two nail prints directly in front on the coyote track, the slightly askew shape of the softer cat print. He'd leaned over and touched the back of her hand. The smell of him came back to her, the sight of sweat glistening on his bare upper torso, as if she had memorized that sight and scent and touch of her lover's body, engraved him into her being the way the sun's image had marked her eyes. But she didn't want that memory to slip away like the sun's shape had; she wanted to hold it fast inside her body forever.

And as she lay remembering him on the cool sand above his body, Ruth felt the stirring of what had dormant in her since Jim's death. An erotic remembering that visited her with definite physical longings that shook the foundation of her grief. Shocked at this unexpected return of desire that seemed so inappropriate at the moment, Ruth turned away from the patch of earth that housed her lover's body, facing the sky and the canyon that surrounded her with its abundance. All that was left of Jim's body had now merged with this place that she loved so dearly. From now on, she would give the fullness of her passion to this land he was part of, to the plants that rain drew up from its rocky soil, to the pitchy pinyons whose bodies furnished her shade and fuel, to the wind and the sky that brought water to her spring. These things she would take into her as she had once taken him, and to them she would give herself, the hours and labor of her life.

Ruth opened wide her arms and raised her breasts up toward the sky, unbuttoned her shirt so the air could caress her taut nipples. As the sun slid behind the mountain, she lifted her skirt, opened her legs to the earth around her, shuddering as warm wind took hold of her thighs and thrust long fingers of pleasure deep inside her.

Afterward, she lay watching the sky's cerulean darken to sapphire. Pinpoints of light began to prick its surface, and the pale risen half-moon luminesced. These things, the ground beneath her, the sky overhead, and all that existed between them here, would be her lover now. Maybe they had always been, and the intimacy she craved she would find completely with this place—even without the freedom to roam its contours.

For a long while, Ruth lay quiet on the sand above the grave, aware of each breath she drew in from the canyon's lungs as it inhaled and exhaled somewhere in the high pines of the mountain, aware of the sand that cushioned her back and buttocks, the sounds of crickets around her, and an owl somewhere down canyon. Gradually, drowsiness drowned out her awareness. It wasn't until later that the chill air woke her, and she made her way back across the wash in moon and starlight, to the empty bed that awaited her.

PART II

CHAPTER THIRTEEN

Ruth pulled another willow pole off John Olsen's flatbed and dragged it over to the pile the men were using to construct the corral. The poles were fairly straight, except for a few twists and knots where branches had been sawed off. This morning she had helped to dig postholes, but she planned to stay out of the men's way as they pounded in the poles, then nailed and baling-wired together the cross slat joints. Her son had no such intention, and J.B. was at their elbows every step of the way—which was hardly surprising, since he spent hours every day building tiny dwelling structures as part of his play. The men tolerated his presence, even seemed to enjoy his eager interest in their work.

She was glad the miners had agreed to take pay this time, though not much. When they helped her dig the well and put in the windmill in the spring, they had refused. This time Ruth convinced them that she needed the chicken coop, barn, and corral constructed—but would do without them if they didn't accept pay. She knew they needed the money desperately, hadn't taken out but one shipment of onyx all summer long. And no one knew whether the desert salt mines would reopen at all this winter. John Olsen said they should have heard by this time. The Depression had spread everywhere, even to this isolated place.

The truth was, Ruth wasn't even sure she should be building this corral to fence in an animal that had chosen to make Glory Springs its home in the first place. It seemed a betrayal. After all, the horse had appeared at her spring two years ago, shortly after she returned from the Whirling Bird ceremony—and had remained without such measures. No one ever claimed the animal, and so the roan stayed, as if it had decided to bind their fates together.

Building the barn was something she could justify without qualms. After two mild winters, they were due for a doozy, people were saying, and the horse might well need some protection from weather this year. She had gathered in enough wood for such a winter, and now, with the new well and its windmill and water tank, felt prepared for whatever was to come. She hadn't been so the last two winters and was only lucky a bad one hadn't struck—which was why she finally decided to dip into the inheritance. Until now, she'd been frugal—except for that trip to L.A. two summers ago and the money she'd given Cally. She really should count that money again soon, she told herself, remembering how diminished the pile of bills looked after she'd taken out enough to buy the building supplies.

Down near the spring, the blue roan grazed on bunchgrass, raising his head occasionally to glance over at what the men were doing, as if he knew the structure's purpose and was there to inspect the building of his new quarters. A ridiculous thought, Ruth told herself as she walked into the wash to rub her palm on the roan's silky nose. Juniper Blue gave a quick nuzzle of his head into her belly, then lowered it to rip out another mouthful of the grass. She gave him a pat. She could always leave the corral gate open for him. Then he could come and go as he pleased, which meant she would have to buy less feed for him as well.

Maddie was in her usual spot on the bank above the spring, her hair glinting auburn in the sun as she pounded stone on stone. Ruth walked up to see what the girl was grinding this time in the *na'dai* she had discovered a few months ago. Ruth must have walked by that rock a hundred times without seeing anything but a rock, but Maddie scraped out the dirt and debris that had gathered over the years and revealed the treasure. The girl's eye must have been sharpened for such things after all the trips to Black Canyon. Well, at least Ruth still had her table rock for grinding her own acorns and mesquite into flour—and it served her perfectly fine.

Maddie glanced up but went on with her pound and grind of the mesquite pods that they'd gathered last week in Black Canyon. Ruth and the children had arrived in time for the final mesquite harvest, a small second harvest really, that had come about because of abundant summer rains, Martha had told her, and they had joined the others in gathering the dried pods that drooped like clusters of fingers from the thorny tree branches. Inexperienced at the task, Ruth bore scratches on her arms for several days afterward.

She watched the girl's determination as she slowly made meal of the pod's pulp, stopping occasionally to remove bits of fibrous shell from the pile of granules she was creating. Maddie glanced up, a flash of bright green eyes, then went back to her task. The girl was never happier than when she was at work with some plant. How surprising that a child as young as Maddie could imitate the Indian women's work so faithfully, even if her motions were a bit awkward and inefficient. Maddie was such an odd child. Ruth saw no sign of her father's meanness in the girl. She wished she could love her.

J.B. was unusual, too, Ruth reminded herself, as she walked into her garden to gather a few tomatoes—unusual in a more normal and interesting way. She hadn't ever been around children much, had had no sisters or brothers. Sometimes her Aunt Myrtle made her play with cousins, but that would often end in disaster. Even as a child, she had preferred to keep her own company. Her children were like her in that regard—except they had each other's company, seemed to understand each other in ways that she couldn't.

As she gathered vegetables, Ruth was vaguely aware of the drone of a motor, but it had not fully registered until the sound got louder and became the unmistakable strain of an engine challenging the upward pull of the canyon. She kept one eye on the bend while she walked back to her cabin with the squash and tomatoes. The miners, she noticed, were glancing down canyon as they worked the cross slats of the corral into place. The unexpected arrival of a vehicle was always an event. Usually, Ruth could pretty much count on any arriving vehicle to belong to John Olsen, but today his flatbed already sat in her yard. It was rare that someone from town would wander up the canyon. She put the vegetables inside on the table and went back out to watch for the vehicle's appearance, adding a few small chunks of wood to the low-burning campfire as she waited.

The tan van wagon rounded the bend and slowly made its way toward Glory Springs, its motor still struggling with the long uphill haul. When it finally pulled up behind John Olsen's flatbed, the engine quit with a shotgun blast of backfire. Clouds of steam billowed from beneath the hood. A man jerked the door open, jumped out, and with a nod toward Ruth and the others, rushed around to the front and raised one side of the hood—which released an even bigger burst of steam. He stepped back fast and swiped an arm across his eyes and forehead.

Instinctively, Ruth took a step toward him—he could be scalded. The man looked over and flashed her a smile, his teeth gleaming white in a face darkened by sun even more than her own. His chocolate hair seemed almost as unruly as well, where it poked out from beneath a cloth hat.

"Guess I should have left that motor alone for a while," he called out, walking toward her now, still revealing those gleaming teeth.

Ruth nodded. "You were lucky," she said when he came up to her. "It must hurt though," she added when she saw the red tinge beneath the brim of his hat.

He reached up and touched a few places on his forehead. "No more than a sunburn." He looked over at his van wagon. "I didn't realize the damn thing was that hot. By the way, I'm David Stone." He held out a hand. "You must be Ruth Farley."

Ruth shook his hand, which felt as rough and calloused as her own, approving of the dirt packed beneath his nails. "Yes, and this is John Olsen," she said as the Swede walked up. "He lives in the rock house down in the willows."

"I know." He reached for Olsen's hand. "Glad to meet you, Mr. Olsen."

"Ya, just John, I am," the Swede said. "How you know us?"

"Clare Gooden told me about you folks up here. I stopped down at your place, Mr. Olsen—John—and your wife said you were up here at Can Tree Springs—which was where I was headed in the first place."

"Kate wouldn't call this place 'Can Tree.' This isn't Can Tree Springs anymore, Mr. Stone, hasn't been for years. I named it Glory Springs when I filed the homestead claim six years ago." Ruth felt her cheeks flush with the memories the old place-name brought back. She took in a breath to calm herself. "Just what is it you want here?"

"Well, the last thing I want is to upset you." He smiled sheepishly and shuffled his feet as he spoke. "I found the name on an old map. Anyway, Clare told me this was once an Indian camp of some kind. And I just wondered . . . well, if I might look around here for artifacts."

"Most certainly not. This is my home, Mr. Stone, not some kind of museum."

"Guess I've upset you again." He pulled off his cap and held it with both hands down below his waist as he spoke, glancing over at John Olsen for help. "Clare said this might be difficult, that you wouldn't much like it."

"I don't even know who this Clare woman is . . ."

"She the Indian agent, Rute, in Two Bunch Palms," Olsen told her. "Fine woman, too."

"But how would she know me? I don't understand—"

"Oh, everyone seems to know who you are, Miss Farley." Stone replaced his cap and gave her another flash of those teeth. "You seem to be pretty famous for a person who keeps to herself up here in this isolated canyon."

"Do you practice always saying the worst thing possible, or do you just have a natural knack for it, Mr. Stone?"

"Looks like when it comes to you, I must have a knack for it."

Repressing a smile, Ruth looked over at John Olsen, who hadn't held back his grin at the predicament of this exasperating man. "Indeed you do," she said, releasing her hold on humor. "Just who are you, anyway? Besides the name. Are you one of those pot hunters the folks in Black Canyon talk about?"

"You're not an easy woman to converse with," he said, "truth be told. I happen to be doing fieldwork for the University of California— I teach archaeology there—and I'm gathering artifacts that represent a history of the original inhabitants. For placement in the university museum, eventually. If it isn't done soon, all that history will disappear into the homes of collectors." He looked over at the line of newly fired ollas Ruth had sitting on the table rock beside the campfire, then back at her. "Like the ones you have there."

"You don't seem to be much of an expert at what you're collecting, Mr. Stone, if you think those are artifacts. But that doesn't surprise me, somehow." She shook her head and glanced at John Olsen, who was enjoying the whole thing. She shot him a look, then met Stone's eyes. "You're welcome to stay around until your truck cools. Use any water you need to fill the radiator before you go. But you're not welcome to look for artifacts while you're here—unless you count those pots on the rock." She began walking toward the house, then stopped and turned back. "I'd have a closer look at them first if I were you."

Ruth went in and gathered up bowls and spoons for the chili beans with rabbit she had simmered on the campfire all morning. She pulled the chili off the coals, threw on more wood, and set the pot of water on for coffee. She'd left the ladle inside with the loaf of bread made the night before, and when she came back out with them, Stone was examining the ollas. He picked one up and turned it slowly between his hands.

"Nicely done. No wonder I thought they were old ones. You must be using methods similar to what they used," he said. "Who was it that taught you?" He set the olla down and looked at her. "I do feel like a fool—but that's been true since I arrived."

Ruth bit down on the acknowledgment threatening to escape her lips. "You're welcome to stay for a bowl of chili if you want," she told him instead.

"I guess I didn't say the wrong thing that time." He set the olla down beside the others.

"I wouldn't press your luck, though." She ladled out a bowl of chili beans for John Olsen, then one for Stone and handed it to him. "Help yourself to the bread. Coffee will be ready in a minute." The other miners had begun walking over when they saw her appear with the bread. Ruth ladled out two half bowlfuls for the children and began filling the bowl each man held out to her. "There's plenty for seconds," she said when they were all eating. "Just help yourselves to the rest."

J.B. took his bowl and sat on a rock near Ingmar and John Olsen. She stirred in coffee grounds and moved the pot back to settle, then sliced up the rest of the bread. Handing J.B. a slice, Ruth looked around for Maddie and found her still across the wash pounding mesquite pods.

"Maddie, come get your lunch." The girl looked up once, but continued her grinding. "Now, Maddie!" Ruth said with more emphasis. Not that it would do any good. The girl wouldn't come until she felt like it. Such a stubborn child.

Ruth filled the coffee cups and ladled out a bowl of the chili for herself, pulling the pot to the edge of the fire. She leaned over to cover what was left of the bread with a cloth. Jays had already found the picnic and were creating a cacophony of squawking in the pinyons overhead. The miners seemed to enjoy throwing out an occasional crust and watching three or four birds dive for it at once to do battle, leaving a cache of blue feathers on the ground in its place.

Settling cross-legged in front of the flat rock that held the ollas, she leaned back and listened to the men discuss the general state of things caused by the Depression. The miners had heard at the general store that a steady stream of trucks—all overloaded with poor families and their belongings—was being turned back at the state border, at least the trucks that arrived without enough cash. Ruth had seen two such truckloads of people herself when she was in Juniper Valley a few weeks ago, folks who had come for the early harvest in the Imperial Valley. Men desperate for any kind of work, and families who looked out on the world with hungry eyes.

"It's just as well they don't go to L.A.," David Stone was saying. "There's no work, and the soup kitchens can't feed the ones there now."

"I saw some of those breadlines when I was in Los Angeles a couple years ago. Right across from the fancy hotels," Ruth said, sobered by the memory. "Otherwise I would never have believed it."

"It's much worse now than it was two years ago." Stone took in a breath and shook his head. "I'm glad I'm out in the field, so I don't have to encounter it for a while. Gladder still that I have work with the university."

"It seems strange to me that you would get paid just to dig up Indian artifacts to put in a museum someday, when so many people are about to starve for lack of useful work." Ruth stood and helped herself to more chili. "Just like it was strange to see so many well-dressed people going into that fancy theater—while others were selling pencils on the streets just so they could eat. It's hard to understand such a thing."

Stone nodded but didn't reply, leaving a silence that felt somber and awkward, until Maddie appeared on the bank of the wash. "That's your bowl of chili there," Ruth said, pointing, once the miners had greeted the girl. "Come sit with us."

Maddie's eyes looked from Stone to his truck and back. "That's David Stone, Maddie," Ruth said, struggling to keep the annoyance out of her voice. "Surely you saw him drive up."

"Hello, Maddie," Stone said, gifting the girl with a gleaming smile.

Without answering, Maddie took her bowl and sat beside her brother. Where were those words now that she spoke with such precision? Well, at least she wasn't imitating the jays in front of company. It was bad enough that the girl began picking at her beans, examining each one before putting it in her mouth, tasting and chewing it with deliberation. By now, J.B. had finished his chili and was on his hands and knees, having turned the bowl upside down over a small depression he'd dug out in the dirt, and was creating a tiny ramada-like structure beside it out of pine twigs and needles.

The subject changed, and the men began talking of rumors they'd heard about some kind of work program Roosevelt wanted to establish, one that would pay local men to improve roads even in outlying areas such as this. Ruth's mind wandered across the wash, where Juniper Blue was running up canyon in the soft sand, kicking up powerful hind legs as he went, then swinging around to run again in the direction he'd come from. She loved the way his mane and tail flew free in the wind as he ran, loved the bold and graceful curve of his neck. His unrestrained play was the closest she'd seen to the freedom she craved.

Scenes from dreams came back to her where she and the roan rode over the mountains, the horse's hooves touching down as they all but flew across the land. In real life, riding the roan felt nothing like it had in dreams. In the waking world, she could feel the jar of his hooves pounding ground hard as they went, especially when he ran. It had taken months of coaxing before Blue would allow her up on his back, and then the first few times, he only stood there, so tense she was afraid he might just toss her off. But he did not, and after some weeks they relaxed into each other's ways and became comfortable together.

She had purchased a light saddle, but most of the time she rode bareback, usually for short distances around her place but sometimes down to the willows to visit Kate and John. Blue allowed her to include the two small children for that trip. She yearned now to go down into the wash and swing herself up on his back, imagined riding up the mountain to Jim's lake, a place that in her mind always waited for her return.

Ruth's attention was yanked back when Stone asked if she'd heard anything about the new movie set to be built out by the Rimrock area. The question dumbfounded her, and she looked over at John Olsen, who only stared back blankly. Why would anyone build a movie set out in those boulders? Whatever was this man talking about now?

Stone went on to explain that while he was out in the Rimrock examining petroglyphs and digging for artifacts, he came upon a crew of surveyors who said they were hired by someone in Hollywood.

"Hollywood people stop by the general store, Matt Baxter say," Ingmar affirmed. "Said they bought some land."

"Well, the men I talked to said they were laying the measurements for some kind of movie set—claim it will be built to look like an old western town." Stone shrugged and flashed his teeth. "That's all I know. Anyway, I have to stay around and guard that dig before they ruin the place."

"If they're looking for an old western town, why don't they just make their movie in the middle of Juniper Valley?" Ruth asked, wondering more to herself than asking the others.

"That isn't the kind of town depicted in movie westerns I've seen.

These towns look older—like the ones in Arizona during the last century," Stone explained. "I guess you don't get to see many movies out here."

"Don't they want things to be real? There weren't any towns in this area last century. Only Indian settlements." Ruth got to her feet and walked over to refill her coffee cup. The talk had brought back memories of her nightclub adventure in Los Angeles, with those actors some years ago, the dress and bloody shoes she had left on the hotel floor.

"About hour more we finish the corral, ya." John Olsen stood and set his empty bowl on the flat rock next to the ollas. The other miners followed suit and began ambling toward the corral, the stop for lunch having taken much of the purpose from them. Ruth saw how tired they looked and wondered if it were simply the morning of work that accounted for it—more likely it was the bleak subject of the Depression weighing down their walk.

"What if I come out and help you finish up?" She set her cup down on the rock.

"You come look over corral, but we do the work," Olsen called back over his shoulder.

"Mind if I have a look, too, before I leave?" Stone got to his feet, then the two of them walked out toward the corral. "You seem to have quite a spread here," he said, stopping to look around at the collection of structures that Ruth had accumulated in the few years she'd been there.

"My own little L.A.," she said, wryly. "At least it's getting to look that way." It had begun to worry her lately, what was happening to Glory Springs, this place that had once been so untamed—which was what she had loved about it. Loved about it still. Yet without meaning to, she had done her share to tame it. First the cabin and outhouse, then the goat pen, now the corral and barn that served as a wall for the chicken coop. The windmill for the well, too, which sent its creaks and shudders out into a canyon where wind in pines had once been the only pristine music. Oh, it was all necessary, she supposed, to enable her to live here with her children. But it worried her. And if one person had been the cause of all this—well, one person and her offspring—no wonder the rest of the desert grew less wild by the day. She was glad the road ended with her cabin, and that beyond stretched a range of mountains that would remain wild only because they were inaccessible. She looked up gratefully at Rocky Mountain, its massive presence a barrier to human intrusion—remembering how the mountain had barely tolerated her own intrusion that first winter and almost didn't let her off alive.

"You seem far away," Stone said.

Ruth looked back at the man beside her. He appeared entirely out of sync, as if he belonged to another time and place altogether. "I guess I was," she said. "I was remembering how . . . but that doesn't matter, really." Then, unable to contain her concern, she added, "It's just that this place used to be so wild."

Stone threw back his head and burst out laughing. "Used to be," he said when he calmed some. "Why, this place is one of the wildest I've ever seen. How much more wild could you want?"

Heat flamed her cheeks. "Then you've not seen a truly wild place, Mr. Stone. Clearly, you don't know what you're talking about. But then I'm not surprised, given that you're from Los Angeles."

"I wish you'd call me David." His amused smile infuriated her even further.

"Let's inspect the corral, shall we?" she said, and resumed walking, this time picking up her pace so that he remained just behind her.

The willow pole corral was complete, though for added strength, the miners were still wrapping baling wire around a few of the nailed-together sections where they joined. Willow, she explained, had been chosen for the corral because of its flexible strength and because it saved the cost and trouble of purchasing and hauling up more long planks, like the ones used to construct the barn. Besides, the flood several years ago had changed the course of the wash down by the Swedes' and left a huge clump of willow isolated from the stream to die.

John Olsen was dragging over a long tin tub to be used for the water trough, and Stone went to help him lift and place it just outside the corral. That way the horse could reach it from inside or outside the fence. Ruth watched the men struggle with the weight of it for a moment and found herself imagining the muscles in Stone's back underneath the shirt as he lifted the trough. Her eyes liked the way his face was darkened with sun, and she had noticed how his tan skin dove under the open V of his shirt collar. Then she caught herself and pulled her eyes away, unsettled by the nature of her thoughts. The man—though well meaning—was an insensitive clod. But more important, she couldn't afford that kind of thing again. How needy her body must be—and the tight tingle below her belly told her just how physical the need was—to entertain such an impulse—especially for someone so unconnected with this place she loved.

She closed her eyes, trying to conjure the memory of muscles rippling in Jim's back as he unloaded onyx from John Olsen's truck, but nothing came to her. Well, no matter. The image burned in the ceremony at Black Canyon had allowed her to go on with her life, but it couldn't erase all that Jim meant to her. He belonged to Glory Springs forever—and she would not desecrate her connection to him and to this place by hungering after someone who clearly did not belong. It was like desecrating Glory Springs itself.

Ruth put her hands around the willow pole post beside her, pressing her palms tight against the rough peels of bark curling out from it, as if she could somehow push the curls back where they had been, so they could heal into place again. She took in a deep breath of pine air and opened her ears to the chittering cactus wrens.

Maddie had gone back to her grinding rock, Ruth noted, with grudging admiration at her persistence. J.B. now had a little *ki'takii* settlement built under the pinyon. Soon all the men would be gone, she reminded herself, then she could fling her legs up over Blue's back and ride up the wash toward the *ciénaga seca,* turn and run him back down to the bend. Afterward, she would settle herself beside Maddie at the spring and begin another olla. Just the thought brought back the feel of slick, wet clay flesh squishing between her fingers, a sensation she found herself hungering to experience.

CHAPTER FOURTEEN

T his trip to the *natsata,* the leaving feast, would be the last time
they could get to Black Canyon before winter set in and before their
friends left for the lower desert, Ruth explained to her children as they
pulled away from the Swedes' stone house. Kate waved from the doorway until they drove around the bend and out of sight.

Winter would soon be upon them, Ruth knew. She sensed a change
that the lemony leaves of the willows seemed to validate. Although
days were still warm, brisk winds occasionally blew in, and nights
brought a steep drop in temperature that left a thin film of ice on
the horse trough. Already she had dragged their cots from under the
pinyons back inside the house. She would miss watching the bowl of
stars turn slowly in the summer night sky.

The Swedes would leave for the desert mines in a few days. After
that there would be no one to feed chickens and goats and milk the

nannies while she was gone. Ruth was relieved, though, that the mines were reopening; now she didn't have to be quite as worried about Kate and John's finances.

By the time Ruth reached the crossroads where Rattlesnake Canyon intersected the wide dirt road that led from Juniper Valley out to the Rimrock area, desert heat had already spread a film beneath her breasts. The contrast between the high desert's climate and the canyon's never failed amaze her, and she tipped the front window toward her before she turned right onto the wide road to head toward Juniper Valley.

She had gone only about a half mile, down one deep dip and up another, when she saw the tan van parked along the shoulder, its driver's door wide open. A khaki shirt hung over the open window frame. Ruth slowed as she neared the van, coasting to a halt across from a pair of leather boots that protruded from under the vehicle onto the edge of the road. J.B. and Maddie climbed onto her lap behind the wheel and the three of them watched as the boots began to wriggle toward them, followed by a trunk and torso and finally the shoulders and head of the man.

Ruth tried to avert her eyes as David Stone sat up, snatched the shirt down from the window frame, then raised his arms to towel it quickly across his back and loosen embedded pebbles. Finally, he covered the tanned skin and taut muscles she had kept her eyes from. She couldn't tell whether the smile he flashed was tinged with a bit of embarrassment or prideful awareness—or something else altogether.

"Trouble?" she asked.

"Don't know exactly." He got to his feet, brushing sand and pebbles from the seat of his pants. At least he had kept those on, Ruth mused, despite imagining the scene had he not. "There's a loud clunk when the wheels turn. Think it might be an axle."

"Sounds serious."

"I'm afraid so, though I don't know for sure."

"Can I ride you on in to town? Maybe you can find help there."

Stone stood scratching his chin. "Well, the thing does still run," he said, looking out toward the Rimrock, "and I left everything at camp pretty unprotected, thinking to be back soon. Then there's all these groceries I bought." He looked over at her and took in a breath. "I'd like try to make it back out there with them."

"Then you'll be even farther from help with your clunking vehicle."

Stone shrugged. "True. But I've hit a vein of artifacts. I don't want to leave them out there exposed much longer. Especially with those movie people nearby." He scratched the back of his head and glanced toward the Rimrock again. "You don't suppose you could follow me out in case this thing quits on me?" he asked, turning the full extent of his boyish smile on her.

Ruth steadied her eyes on him as she considered. She had wanted to get an early start on her long drive. It had already taken more time than she planned to feed and milk the animals. Then she couldn't refuse Kate's offer of coffee and strudel. This side trip would take another hour or more—at least—and she still might end up taking the man, boyish smile and all, into town. Yet it was hard not to be neighborly when called upon. That wasn't how things worked. She just didn't want him to think his charm was working on her.

"We'd better get started, then, Mr. Stone. I'm hoping to get to Black Canyon while it's still daylight."

Ruth pulled ahead and turned her car around, easing up behind Stone's van. As they drove slowly toward the Rimrock area, she backed off farther, staying behind the cloud of dust his wheels were spinning up, until she could no longer hear the repetitive clank of metal on metal. She'd always had a mild curiosity about the Rimrock, though it struck her as odd to now be driving out to this unknown area behind this outsider whose sole purpose was to take away what belonged to this place.

They drove on by the turnoff that led to the Hudsons' and several other cabins, the main road continuing to wind between clumps of huge boulders scattered over the land like piles of petrified droppings from some giant, ancient deer. Maddie had abandoned her stance of displeasure—sitting arms folded on the seat staring upward—over the delayed trip to Black Canyon and was now at the window beside her brother, the two of them examining the new landscape. Ruth, too, settled into the mood of exploration. On another day, this could have been an adventure of sorts, Ruth mused, rather than an inconvenient side trip.

The vehicles rounded a boulder clump and Ruth caught sight of a huge patch of dust nearby on the left from a bulldozer clearing the land for the new movie town. Stone made a turn to the right, heading over toward a mountainous pile of rocks—with several boulders as large as her cabin. A cove opened in front to reveal a patch of green plants, and Stone drove up to them and shut off his engine—which produced the same blast of backfire as last time. It certainly would be hard for the man to sneak up on anyone, she thought, as he got out of the vehicle and began walking toward the Model A.

"Thanks," he said, laying a hand on her window frame. "Looks like the truck made it just fine. Sorry to put you out of your way, though." He stepped back and looked over at the rocks. "Since you've come all the way out here, why don't I show you what I've found?"

"Not today. I've got to get back on the road. Maybe some other time," she told him. "We've got a long ways to go." She glanced over at her children just in time to see Maddie follow her brother over the open window frame.

"Looks like they have other ideas." David Stone flashed his smile, reached over and pulled down her door handle.

Ruth felt heat creep into her cheeks. How was this man so able to get under her skin? "I guess I'd better go round them up, then." She pasted on a smile to match his as she stepped out of the Model A. The air was warm with late-morning sun, but high wisps of cloud had veiled the sky, and she could sense a stiff breeze brewing, a latent turbulence that ruffled her clothes and hair.

J.B. and Maddie had run straight to the boulder pile and were scrambling up and around the rocks as Stone followed Ruth in their direction. They disappeared through a space between boulders, then reemerged in a different place altogether before the adults reached them.

"There's a multitude of small caves between those rocks," Stone said when J.B. disappeared again. This time Maddie didn't follow her brother, but on her own headed for a spot near the base of the rocks. "I suppose they're not real caves, but natural shelters created by the way the boulders are placed."

"Maddie. J.B. Get back in the car," she shouted. "We have to get on the road now." Ignored by both youngsters, she stood helpless in front of the boulder mountain. It was getting to be quite a problem, this independence they insisted on, though she knew it stemmed from the same force of will that gave her a small measure of freedom.

"I'm sure they'll come down in a minute," Stone said. "Meanwhile, come see what I've dug up."

Ruth walked with him into the patch of green plants, which turned out to be a mixture of broom and sumach and some other small trees she had never seen before in the region, deciduous trees, with yellowing leaves. He had a small white tent pitched next to the rocks, under one of the few pinyons that grew at the edge of the rock pile. Farther on in the cove, Ruth recognized a patch of wiry grass, the kind that grew around a water source.

Stone took her to a folding table that he had set up behind a clump of scrub oak and sumach and showed her the collection of large shards and arrowheads, and even a small clay pipe he had found, then unwrapped an olla that he had left half concealed in the brush. She found it annoying that he referred not to the objects themselves, but to notes and drawings he had made about them, as he explained to her what the various shards told him about the tribe that had made them and why.

Ruth tried hard to listen and interest herself, but in the end could not hold back her comments. "But of what importance is any of that?" she asked, fully aware of her rudeness, yet unable to stop herself. "What does that tell you about the people who made them, really, about who they were? About the life they led in this place. Just identifying the name of the tribe seems so . . . so impersonal. As if it were a brand of coffee or flour."

She looked around the cove, pictured it peopled with folks like the ones she knew from Black Canyon. Their great-grandparents might well have been the ones who had lived in this place.

"I don't understand why you're not more interested in the people who are still alive," she told him, explaining about her friendship with the Yuiatei in Black Canyon. "Why you don't learn more about the Indian people who are still around, hear their stories while they're still alive, rather than try to piece together their lives from remnants from the past."

"But that's not what I'm trained to do, Ruth. That business is for anthropologists." He shuffled from one foot to the other, his face reddening slightly. "I wouldn't know how to go about it."

"Or you're not interested in doing it."

"Perhaps." Stone stopped shuffling and met her eyes. "Are you always so hard on a man? Or does everything about me simply displease you?"

"Not everything. I think you mean well," Ruth said quickly. Suddenly contrite, she added, "I don't mean to be hard on you, really. It's just that I find so many things frustrating about you. Things you say and . . ."

"And things I do," he finished for her. "Such as my life's work, for instance. This *is* my life's work, you know. Trying to understand more about the cultures that were here before we were."

"But they're still here, Mr. Stone. They aren't gone. Not yet, anyway."

"But they're not here, Ruth. Not really. Their culture is not the same at all since we came. We've changed them, changed the way they live. What I want to understand is how they lived before that." He looked over at the spring, where Maddie was now kneeling on top of one of the flat rocks. "You see that rock?" he said, his face gone serious. "That's where they ground their flour out of god-knows-what. Now I'll bet they buy flour the same way we do. Only by seeing what they left here will I know what they found to sustain them in those days."

"It's true that we've changed the way they live," Ruth admitted, "but not as much as you think. My friends in Black Canyon still grind acorns and mesquite pods, other things too—like berries from these sumach trees, even if it is only for ceremonial occasions. If you went to Black Canyon, you'd see all that still exists. I'm surprised your Indian agent friend doesn't tell you these things."

"Clare doesn't work with the people in Black Canyon. She's out in Two Bunch Palms, and what I've seen there tells me their ways are going fast. The big oasis where several tribes camped is damn near deserted now." All traces of that smile now gone, Stone's face looked pained as he spoke.

"I think some of them went to Black Canyon. Martha said that—" Ruth began.

"And where are the Indians who used to camp at your place, before it became Can Tree Springs—or Glory Springs, as you now call it?"

"The Yuiatei People still remember the place, in fact, have a name for it. Jim said it meant something like 'small rocks rising.' Later I learned what that name referred to, at least on some level." Ruth smiled, felt the joy well up inside at the thought of those tiny hopping insects camouflaged as pebbles that she discovered on the ground that day, and of all she had understood in the moment she first saw them.

"I'm sorry about what happened to your Indian man, Ruth. Just the way you look when you talk about him tells me how much he meant to you." Stone stopped speaking and looked at her. "I do understand, Ruth, why you want to be with the Indians who are alive now," he said.

Ruth couldn't utter a word. How dare this man suggest it was only because of Jim that she felt this way.

"You don't understand at all," she said, when she could speak again. "There's so much more to it. Maybe I went there first because of Jim and his child. But I found something else there." She felt a tear start to slide from one eye and turned her head away so he wouldn't see it. "Something I was looking for when I first came here—though I didn't know it.

"Those people, the Yuiatei, are the only ones who understand the way I feel about this land." She looked out at the cove and opened her arms to include its scope. "About rocks and trees and animals, and . . . and . . ." Ruth looked up to find him open to her words. "Well, the people in Black Canyon understand their place that way too, you see, and know more about it than I do. Jim did too . . ." Ruth stopped, her voice faltering. "I learned so much from him in the short time I knew him." Ruth felt Stone's hand on her shoulder, felt the gentle pressure of his compassion.

"Maybe we're both looking for the same thing in different ways," he said quietly. "But the kind of direct experience you seem to require has never been a part of my nature. I admit, I'm more comfortable in the world of books. They're more permanent. Even now, I'm hoping to use all this to make a lasting record of what these things all mean. A book. Collecting for the university's museum merely allows me to get the book written."

"But you'll take away what belongs here to do it."

"What difference does that make? Do you really think these things are better off buried and hidden than out in the open where people can view them and perhaps understand more about how people once survived on this arid land?"

Ruth had no words for him, yet something inside told her there was a difference, an important one. She could only leave his question unanswered and turn to search out her children. Stone walked with her to the spot on the grinding rock where Maddie had remained. J.B. had come down from the boulders, and they found him on the sandy ground below the *na'dai* stone, arranging small rocks into piles.

Stone squatted down to watch J.B.'s work, while Ruth climbed up to fetch Maddie from the rock. She wasn't surprised to find the girl trying to pound acorns into flour.

"It's time to go, Maddie," she said impatiently. "I thought you wanted to see Grandmother Siki and Martha up in Black Canyon."

"After I make acorns," the girl told her, with annoying precision, then repeated her message in Yuiatei.

Ruth wondered what was motivating Maddie to speak; she had expected that to wait for Black Canyon. More and more Maddie seemed to be picking up the Indians' words and inflections and their unusual uses of ordinary English, much the way she had picked up Kate's Swedish.

"You know scrub oak acorns aren't the kind to use," Ruth said, as sweetly as she could manage. "They taste awful."

"I know. I like to practice."

"Well, take them with you. You can practice at Black Canyon—or when we get home."

The girl stopped to consider. "I like this rock," she said.

"Maybe we can come back to it sometime. Come on, now, it's getting late."

Maddie set the small grinding stone into the depression and scrambled down off the rock. "Come on, J.B., we have to get on the road now," Ruth said when they reached her son, who was still working on his pile of rocks. When he saw that Maddie was already down and running toward the car, he took off after her.

"That boy sure likes to build things," Stone said. He was still squatting in front of J.B.'s rocks. "Look at all the little openings he made here—a lot like the natural shelters in the rocks." He looked up at the boulder pile. "And he was constructing small brush structures around the pinyon at your cabin that day I was up there. Maybe you have an architect in the making."

"Maybe he just likes to play that way. Or maybe he takes after his father," Ruth said with a burst of pride, remembering the little hut Jim built at the top of Rocky Mountain. She followed the children toward the Model A. "At any rate, we really do have to be going now."

As they walked, Stone thanked her again for seeing that he got safely to his camp. She thought he wanted to say more, so she kept her eyes averted until she was safely in her car and the ignition had caught.

"I enjoyed our conversation," he said then. "I hope we have more of them. You're welcome here anytime."

"Thanks," Ruth said. She knew he hoped she'd follow up with a similar invitation to her place.

"When winter sets in I'll have to break up camp, though, and go back to the dig in Two Bunch."

"Well, good luck to you, then," Ruth said, and began backing up the vehicle. She waved to him once as she pulled away. She was glad to find there was substance behind that flash of smile, but at the same time relieved to break a connection that made her uneasy.

"We can have the sandwiches now," she told her children when they reached the main dirt road. "Give me one, too," she said as they began rifling in the flour sack on the floor. In the distance across the road, gusts of wind were carrying huge clouds of dust high into the sky. As she changed direction, she caught a glimpse of the big machines scraping away brush from the land. What fools those movie people were.

Ruth watched a moment, then shook her head and turned the Model A onto the road toward town, and her attention toward their visit to Black Canyon. With this late a start, they wouldn't get there until dark. Still, she looked forward to bedding down in the *ki'takii* they'd helped build, then waking up to a fresh new day in the place, surrounded by friends dear to her.

CHAPTER FIFTEEN

B y the time Ruth reached the lower desert, the turbulence latent in the high desert had fully manifested. All through Devil's Garden she had to hold tight to the steering wheel to keep the Model A from being pushed off the road by gusts embedded within a steady but strong sidewind. She had rolled up the windows and latched tight the windshield, but that didn't keep out the grit they had to breathe. Even the dirt road in front of her lifted its surface to meet her as she drove over it. Especially bad were sections where the road was torn up for the new Colorado River pipeline. Ahead of her, the air in the lower desert was so choked with dust that she could barely make out the mountains lining the pass she would soon turn into. Then she would have to point her vehicle straight against the wind's force. Palm Springs, usually visible ahead to her left as the road turned right toward San Bernardino, had been completely obscured by a thick curtain of blowing sand.

Sand pinged the tin hood and fenders of the Model A, pocking the windshield glass. Ruth gunned the car up the hill where the road turned right into the pass, pushing the gas pedal to the floor to give the vehicle enough momentum to reach the top, she and the two children coughing as they went. Ruth assumed that once they started down the other side and reached the paved highway, the dust in the air would lessen because she would be driving on blacktop. Yet when she went over the top of the hill and across it, the high viewpoint offered no glimpse at all of highway at the bottom. The only thing visible below was a boiling soup of green-brown dust.

For the first time, she wondered if she should turn back, questioned seriously if she would be able to get through the murky tempest that lay between her and the road up Black Canyon. She had been through dust storms before, but nothing like this one that pitted her windshield with pebbles and made the air more impossible to breathe with each mile she drove.

The problem didn't lessen when she reached the paved highway. The tarred surface in front of her was barely discernible beneath the steady layer of low-blowing sand streaking straight toward her over the road. The headwind slowed the Model A to a crawl, but the reduced speed did not enable her to see any more of the road ahead. Now she understood that she *would* have to turn back, at least for the time being. The distance out of the dust storm was much shorter back the way she had come.

Ruth began looking for a turnout, where she could safely swing the car around, but couldn't see well enough where the pavement ended and the soft shoulder sand began. Not wanting to get trapped in the treacherous sand trap beside the road, she continued struggling slowly forward, all the while searching for a widened edge of paved road. Without disaster, she managed to get the children's shirts up over their noses, telling them to breathe through the cloth, though her own shirt would not stay put there without her holding it, and she needed both hands to hold the wheel steady against the vicious gusts. Even taking a hand off the wheel occasionally to wipe grit from her eyes was risk enough to stir up butterflies in her belly and shoot streaks of heat into her armpits.

When at last, in a small pocket of near visibility between gusts, Ruth caught a glimpse of a wide turnout across the road, she swung the car around toward it. She'd been lucky to see the road widening, she realized, as a wave of sand closed her view about halfway through her turn, and the air became even murkier than before. She trusted the vision she'd had and made her turn. Changing direction brought the wind behind her, which kept pushing the car to greater speed than she dared on a highway she could barely make out. Only a change of texture when blowing surface sand met pavement then left it again gave any clue to where the road was, and sometimes even that was hard to make out. It puzzled her, though, that instead of the low-blowing sand streaking from straight down the road behind them, the sand now crossed at an angle. Had there been a slight but sudden shift of wind?

The children's coughs had become less frequent, though she found herself choking and hacking and clearing her throat constantly as she drove on, straining to keep the vehicle on the highway, while she waited for the hill that would lead her away from the lower desert. She could see nothing farther than a few feet around her now in the darkening brown-green thickness. It seemed, after a while, that she should have reached that hill some time ago, but without any visible external references, she found it hard to trust her own perceptions. Time seemed to have been carried off on the wind along with the rest of the world. Ruth was reminded of a day years ago when she struggled through a snowstorm, and time and direction became as unreal as they were now. At the moment up, down, sideways were all the same, and she started to wonder if maybe she had climbed the hill without realizing it, since she had no clear reference point. Had she simply not noticed the car rising above level ground? That seemed entirely possible under these conditions, even probable.

A moment later Ruth noticed a diffuse light somewhere just ahead to the right of her. She assumed what she saw was the headlights of a vehicle coming toward her—another traveler about to enter the tempestuous landscape that had forgotten its stationary place—and she meant to stop and warn whoever it was not to go on any farther toward the pass. Her decision to turn back had been a wise one; already the air was lightening slightly, and she was relieved that the sand traveling over the pavement had thinned from a steady stream to scattered trickles snaking their way across. Through blurred air, she was now able to make out creosote and other brush several yards away from the highway. Visibility improved enough for her to realize, as she came closer to the light, that it was both singular and stationary. She had expected the highway to curve toward the light to her right, but it did not, and she found herself driving past the dim glow that came from somewhere just past her range of visibility. Had someone driven a vehicle off the highway and become stuck in the sand? Entirely puzzled, she considered stopping to investigate, but looked over at J.B. and Maddie, who now slept leaning one on the other. It seemed she had no choice but to keep her vehicle moving on the pavement. Pavement?

Realization came to her at the same moment that she saw another dim light, this time to her left, with another close following it. Then ahead of her more lights yet, and the double lights of an actual vehicle coming toward her on this road. A road that should not be paved at all—if she really had turned and gone up the hill. Somehow she had lost her way. But how had she become so disoriented as to not realize that fact the moment the sand had cleared enough to see the pavement under it? And where *had* she gone then? Just where was she?

The air cleared a bit more as she drove farther, though the thick haze of dust retained a strong hold. And the sky seemed especially dark. She could make out the sides of a huge mountain whose top was lost in the darkness overhead, and now Ruth understood that she had driven into the shelter of its cove. Blurred buildings began to appear on each side of her, most of white stucco, restaurants and shops and even some small hotels. She saw another Model A in the lane ahead of her and a truck coming her way. Beside the highway, a line of palm trees waved frantic fronds. Other fronds lay along the side of the road. She began to understand and vaguely recognize this place, though she had come here only once, and that was several years ago. The clearing she'd seen when she turned must have been the road to Palm Springs, Ruth realized with great relief, and she had wandered into Ben's mythological Springs.

It wasn't such a bad thing, she told herself, as accidentally as it might have happened. It got her out of the main dust storm—and it occurred to her that if she found someplace to spend the night here, it would be easy enough to go on to Black Canyon in the morning. If the storm ended.

Other than a few passing cars, Ruth saw no one out on the street as she drove through town, though most shops and restaurants appeared to be open. It was no wonder the streets were so bare, with all the wind and dust in the air, an occasional palm branch flying across the sidewalk like some giant bird. She drove through town until buildings became more scattered along the road, then turned the Model A around and headed back the way she had come, searching for a hotel for the night. She had liked the name of one she had passed—the Cricket Club. Such a whimsical name for a hotel. She liked the clean lines of the place too, without fancy signs or elaborate buildings.

The hotel front did seem more classy when she actually pulled up into its driveway and killed her engine. But quietly classy, she thought, as she looked at the two stately palm trees guarding the door, the green, green lawn, and beds of colorful flowers bordering the building. Wind had speckled many of their petals over the grass and layered the concrete drive with soft ribbons of color. A gust of wind rocked the car as she looked down at the children waking beside her. J.B. sat up, rubbed his eyes and looked at her. Both eyes were ringed with dark grit. Maddie's were too, and she had a smudge of mustard on her cheek. Ruth tipped the rearview mirror to look at her own face, and burst out laughing.

"We look like a family of raccoons," she said. She turned the mirror toward them, had them stand and see their faces.

J.B. laughed at the sight of himself. Maddie made claws of her hands and began hissing and imitating the low chatter of the animal, the sound eerily accurate.

"This isn't Black Canyon," J.B. said after he'd peered outside the car windows. He looked over at Ruth, puzzlement spreading over his sleepy face.

As she wiped their faces, Ruth tried to explain how she'd thought she was turning back toward home, away from the sandstorm, and ended up in Palm Springs—at least she thought it was Palm Springs.

"I want to go see Grandmother Siki," Maddie said, with that adult clarity she affected when she deemed it necessary. "I want to go to Black Canyon."

"We can't get there now, I told you. The sandstorm is too bad. Maybe we can stay here and go in the morning." But already Ruth was reconsidering that plan. The three of them were dressed for Black Canyon. Even their one change of clothes was not appropriate for this place. She had no tolerance for the kind of snobbery their worn denim and faded cotton might encounter in a place like this. Maybe she should drive farther, even closer to the mountain and see if there was someplace less classy.

Before she could decide, a man came out the door of the hotel and hurried toward the Model A. Ruth swiped at the edges of her eyes to get off more of the grit as he approached her window, which she unrolled as he stood there, his short hair blown forward to frame his face, like some kind of carnival mask. She smiled, despite her predicament, at the sight.

"Are you with the movie crew, Madam?" The man asked, his eyes registering but not judging her appearance. A gust rushed in, shoved hard against the passenger window to get back out.

Ruth shook her head. "We had to turn back in the storm," she half shouted, indicating the children with her eyes. "Now I'm not sure what to do."

"I suggest you come inside, then. The wind's still quite strong. The radio reported a hurricane along the coast of Baja." He looked over at Maddie and J.B. "Would you like some help?"

"Thanks, but no," she told him, pushing at the door to open it. The door would barely budge against the wind. The attendant reached over and yanked it open, then held it back so it didn't slam into her as she got out, reached in and slung her knapsack over her shoulder. She went around and pulled open the passenger door for the children. It took all her weight to shut it again.

"Where are we going?" J.B. yelled as she tugged the two of them through the wind toward the hotel's front door, where the attendant stood ready to do battle with gusts and open it for them.

"Out of the wind," she shouted. They reached the building just as a huge blast spattered them with debris. She was surprised to see a group of people gathered behind the big glass window watching their approach.

Once she had the children inside and the door closed behind them, the three of them were greeted by several of the crowd, who seemed to be relieved they'd made it inside. Ruth was surprised to see such small-town, neighborly concern in a highbrow place, and she warmed to them enough to describe in detail her harrowing attempt to make it through the pass in the storm. "But we're not with the movie crew," she finished, the thought suddenly occurring that such a misperception might be behind all the attention.

"Of course not. Nevertheless, we hope you'll remain with us until the storm passes," a woman with a massive gold necklace said, while others were murmured in agreement. The woman gave Ruth and the children's appearance a once-over, then said politely, "You needn't worry about paying under these circumstances."

Ruth laughed, allowing pleasure at the friendliness to override the insult—what else would the woman expect of such ragamuffins. Especially in these hard times. "Don't worry," she said. "I can pay for a room if we stay the night. But thank you. I appreciate your concern, all of you." She stopped then, puzzled at the way people appeared to be smiling at her. "Is something funny here?"

The tall woman who spoke before stepped forward and opened a palm toward Ruth, clattering the numerous gold bracelets on her arm. "The flower petals," she said, her smile broadening. "They're all over you. It's quite striking—and lovely."

Ruth looked down at herself to find tender speckles of deep and pale blues and others of violet and white, pink and yellow scattered over her arms and chest. Maddie and J.B. were also sprinkled with color. Ruth reached down and plucked out a purple petal caught in her son's dark hair.

"You look more like fairy people than victims of a fall windstorm," the woman said. "A princess and her two attendants." Ruth liked her strong face with its high cheekbones, tanned skin and expressive hazel eyes. She was older, but ageless at the same time. "Either way, welcome to the Cricket Club refuge, though there will be no cricket today."

Ruth was just about to say something about the playful name of the place, when Maddie gave out the most perfect imitation of a cricket chirping Ruth had ever heard. She felt her face heat as the girl kept it up, one hand placed over her mouth. The crowd around them first looked at Maddie in amazement, then burst out laughing.

"What a wonderful sound joke," the woman said. She bent her knees and lowered herself to Maddie's level, long linen skirt and all, so she could look directly into the girl's face. "That's so clever of you." Holding out her hand to Maddie, she said, "I'm Esther Golden."

"I'm Maddie," Maddie said, just as formally.

"Maddie who?"

The girl stood a moment considering. "I don't know," she said, finally. "Maybe Cricket."

That got another laugh from the crowd and from the woman, who now rose, heavy jewelry and all, as agilely as she had descended. "What a superb child," she said. She offered Ruth her hand. "Esther Golden. The Cricket Club is my hotel."

Ruth accepted the hand. "Ruth Farley." She looked around for J.B. and found him by the wall, running a hand along the stucco surface as he examined the room's high ceiling. "And this is my son, J.B.," she said. Everywhere, it was always Maddie with her weird little ways who got the most attention. J.B. was even more interesting—yet his quiet introspection brought him less notice. Sometimes Ruth couldn't help but wonder if it was his darker skin that kept eyes away from him.

"Yes," the woman said. "Such a serious boy."

Ruth opened her mouth to take issue with the woman's statement, when light flashed from the walls. At the same instant thunder boomed through the room as if it would fling the stucco structure to kingdom come. No one said a word, but they all turned to look out the big bay window just as another thudding clap came, this time stabbing a wavy knife of light into the ground across the highway. A huge gust swept leaves and flower debris against the windowpane and held them squirming along the glass before sweeping it clean again. Ruth noticed a few splotches of water remained on the pane.

"My word!" the woman exclaimed. "We're likely to lose our electric if this keeps up." She called the attendant over and told him to bring the kerosene lamps out of storage. Turning to one of the middle-aged men in the crowd, whom Ruth had noticed because of the cream-colored suit he wore, Esther said, "You'd best give up on the rest of your entourage, George. Most likely they won't be arriving today. If the pass is as bad as this woman says, they'll not get through any better than she did." She turned back to Ruth.

"You, sweetie, I'd like to have stay in the Willow Suite. Joey here will show you the way. Bring her one of those lamps too, will you, Joey?" she said, as another bolt of lightning lit up the window and thunder crashed down around them, rattling glass panes and the vases beside them.

"Dinner will be served at seven, come hell or high water," she called as the attendant led Ruth and her children from the lobby into a hallway, "and high water is likely." By now rain was washing over the glass sheets that formed one side of the long corridor, while bursts of thunder and flashes of light followed one after another.

Their rooms were large, with a living space and divan in addition to the bedroom, very much like the Biltmore's, except for the glass door leading to a large patio, which at the moment had a fast current washing leaves and debris across it. Excited exclamations turned Ruth's attention from the rain to the bathroom, where Maddie and J.B. had had their first-ever sight of a real toilet and a porcelain bathtub.

Ruth demonstrated the use of the toilet, and the children delighted in copying her waste-letting. Then she stripped them, filled the large tub with hot water that miraculously waited behind the faucet with the red center dot, and all three of them wallowed and played there, splashing and laughing as if they had never seen such a thing before—which of course two of them hadn't—until thunder became only a constant and tinny grumble against the huge mountain that helped shelter the town from the virulent effects of the sandstorm. By then the water in the tub was nearly as cold as that coming down outside.

Dinner seemed relaxed enough for the few guests who had made it to the hotel before the storm strengthened, though for Ruth the white tablecloths, candles, and china dishes served to underscore her own now clean but rustic attire. The only thing that enabled her to relax was the glass of ruby-colored liquid in front of her, and she found it difficult not to gulp it down at once and ask for more. It was truly the most delicious-tasting wine she'd ever had. Of course, for years during prohibition, she'd been able to get only the crude wine and moonshine whiskey that Matt Baxter's brother furnished. She remained clear-headed enough, however, to understand from conversations around the large round table that Esther's brother was the producer of the film that the missing crew had been coming to shoot. He and a few others had driven out from Hollywood the evening before.

Ruth half listened to the moviemaking talk—dominated for the most part by the producer brother, who had more words to say than anyone she'd ever seen—and immersed herself in food without speaking for most of the meal. It had been some time since she had tasted such a thing as slices of roast beef floating in gravy, accompanied by potatoes au gratin and asparagus dribbled with yellow sauce. She ate the food out of politeness and curiosity—and considerable hunger. She was attuned to the tastes of goat and game and of the wild plants that grew around the zucchini and tomatoes she planted in her garden. She'd come to prefer them as she had the mesquite-pod flour she'd learned to prepare in Black Canyon. It greatly enriched the flavor of the breads she made. For special occasions, she even added coarse flour made from dried sumach berries. Though she had stocked up on canned food, she wouldn't use any until the foods from the canyon ran out, as she knew they would when winter came on in earnest.

J.B. and Maddie certainly had never seen such foods. They sat at a table near the window, cautiously picking small bites of the exotic meal. The two of them had spent the hour before dinner bouncing up and down on the beds in the hotel room and now seemed content to quietly observe the adults.

Ruth was just swiping the last of the gravy from her plate with a slice of bread when Esther turned toward her during a brief pause in the director's monologue and firmly announced—in a voice obviously meant to put an end to the man's verbal domination, "Now tell us about yourself, Ruth. My instincts tell me you have an interesting story."

Caught completely off guard, Ruth almost choked on the bread she'd jammed into her mouth. But she swallowed and smiled, took a drink of water from the crystal glass, then patted her lips with the cloth napkin—as if this were the way she behaved at every meal, as if she really had china plates and cloth napkins in her canyon when clay bowls and the back of a hand served just as well.

"Oh, I've nothing exciting to tell. No interesting story, really."

Esther laughed. "A fairy princess with two wood sprite children appears in the middle of a storm, telling us she comes from the far-away wilds to the north and is on her way to the wilder wilds of Black Canyon. And you say nothing's unusual or interesting about that? It sounds like a plot for one of George's movies. One of the better ones, before he turned to westerns."

"Now, Esther," the director said. He turned to look at Ruth for the first time during the dinner. "Yes, do tell us your story, before my sister writes your script herself."

"Only because you're so wrapped up in your own importance, George." Esther wagged a finger at him.

"Don't be unkind, Esther. Your brother has a lot on his mind with the new project," the woman sitting beside the director said. She reached over and squeezed George's arm. "And the stories he tells are fascinating."

"Well, he doesn't have to lord it over everyone else. He misses a lot that way, Barbara. In fact, I'll bet a new Ford that this young woman has a more interesting tale to tell us than any of his." Esther turned toward Ruth expectantly. The others looked at her also, though not expectantly, but as if they were waiting for her to make a fool of herself—which seemed quite possible. Ruth found it hard to appear collected with a torrent of blood rushing to her head. She was sure everyone could feel the heat her cheeks radiated.

"So, tell us, young woman, just where it is you live up there in that wilderness country. And *why* you live such a place?" Esther's brother demanded.

"Because I want to live there, that's why." Ruth set her chin and continued on in the only way she knew how to respond to such idiotic patronization—a word she'd gleaned recently from her novels, but an attitude she'd long encountered. "And as for *where* I live, I doubt that you'd have any idea if I told you."

Esther's delight was registered in her melodic laughter, though others at the table were brought up short by Ruth's curt reply.

"I know more about the area than you seem to think, young lady," the producer countered. Ruth thought she detected high color in his cheeks as well. "It so happens I'm involved with a project we're building smack out in the middle of that wilderness. A rocky area past that little town, Oak Valley or whatever it's called."

Could he mean the movie set? Could this flabby city man be responsible for those huge machines that were fast scraping away the rocks and wild plants, she wondered? She pictured the clouds of dust released by the dozers as she drove by the place. Machines scraping away all remnants of earlier residents so someone could make a pretend version of a place that had never existed? Looking at the man across from her in his cream-colored suit and silk shirt, Ruth could almost understand how and why such stupidity could be happening. The thing that startled her, though, was the fact that she had just left that place, only to have a ferocious sandstorm drive her here to encounter the agent responsible for its making. The thought sent a chill up her back.

"Near Juniper Valley, you mean? Perhaps a movie set?" Ruth kept her tone casual. She sipped at her water, glanced at her empty wineglass. She could use something stronger than water at the moment.

"Not your ordinary movie set. A genuine frontier town—and it will be a permanent town. All Frontiertown buildings will be functional for the people who live out there." Golden's face lit up with enthusiasm as he went on describing the place. "The Dirty Dog Saloon will be a real bar, now that prohibition has ended. The General Store will have actual groceries. We designed some of the set buildings as living quarters, like the Land Survey Office and Dr. Brown's Medical Office."

"What people who live out there? Nobody lives out in the Rimrock. There are a few homesteads left around the periphery, maybe, and in Juniper Valley, but . . ."

"You build the town and the people will come," Golden announced proudly.

"Meanwhile your dozers are scraping away an archaeological site."

"So I've been told. Merely a few broken pieces of primitive pottery. Nothing compared to what I'll build in its place."

"Enough, George. You've taken over again. But you, Ruth, you haven't told us just where you live out there," Esther insisted once again, waving him quiet with clatter of bracelets.

This time Ruth welcomed the distraction from Golden's abomination. The idea of it made her sick at heart. Yet she wasn't so innocent herself. At the Coconut Grove, she'd sampled again the hollow world she'd homesteaded to evade. Now she felt as if she had somehow been contaminated, brought back Hollywood on her clothing to violate her desert and canyons. David Stone had been the first warning of intrusion and led her to the rest. She was only now beginning to understand the extent of it, not so much an intrusion as a full-scale invasion.

For the moment, Ruth put aside her concern over what the area might become and went on instead to explain how she'd found her homestead, describing her struggles to build and remain there. She told them about midwifing her nanny's two new kids, about the bobcat she chased off with a broom when he tried to escape with one of them, how the cat came back later that night and took them both. Deliberately vague about just where her place was located, she hoped that would keep Glory Springs inviolate. She left off also any mention of how the children came to be and how all that fit into her story. Ruth sensed that Esther was on the edge of probing, but the woman didn't push, seeming satisfied that Ruth's story was as unusual as she had promised. Other guests, including Golden himself, became quiet and listened, though his expression was one of puzzled amusement.

When she could, Ruth escaped to her room with Maddie and J.B., both of whom fell asleep almost as soon as they lay on their soft mattress. Ruth spent hours awake, listening to the hard rain that was still coming down steadily. She couldn't stop worrying about the effect such a movie town could have on the small desert community and on the wild landscape she loved, cringing again over her own intrusion there— the buildings and windmill she had put on the barely touched land of Glory Springs. How different was that from what she hated to see others doing? As much as she had despised the tin cans that cowboys had hung from the pines to catch pitch before she homesteaded the place, she herself had put much more than a few tin cans on that land.

She remembered the strong sense of destiny she'd felt at her first sight of Glory Springs, the passion unleashed when she found her place. In what way was that different from the passion shown by Golden for his foolish Frontiertown? She remembered what Thomas had told her about the changes the people of Black Canyon had seen, remembered what Jim had said about civilized encroachment in the area. And suddenly she wasn't sure of anything, of her own role and purpose, of what was right for herself or for the rest of the world—which kept turning out to be far more complicated than she had imagined. The only thing she *was* sure of was that she wanted to be with her friends in Black Canyon tomorrow, wanted to pound mesquite pods on the *na'dai* and bake the wild flour into bread, to drink tangy liquid made from that mesquite as they sat around the campfire while night came on. She wanted to eat with her friends the sweet flesh of plants and small wild creatures—some she had never dared ask about. All she could do was lie awake and wait for morning so she could get on her way. Only when she heard the rain dwindling away enough to allow her to make the trip did she let herself fall asleep for a short while.

CHAPTER SIXTEEN

Every particle of yesterday's sandstorm had been washed from the air when Ruth drove away from the Cricket Club early the next morning. The entire desert had been scrubbed—and rather brutally, as if the rivers of moving ground had been pounded down to stay where they belonged under the stark blue sky. She left the little desert city and drove into the pass that had been so impossible to traverse the day before. In many places, the pavement now lay buried under the thick quilt of wet sand that had flooded over it in the night. If it weren't for a few tracks made by cars and trucks that came before her, Ruth wouldn't have known just where to drive in those sections, and she held the steering wheel and gas steady to keep her tires in the grooves, while surrounding sand tried to pull her into its vast expanse.

J.B. and Maddie seemed content to stand at the window and watch the changed landscape, J.B. pointing out an occasional raven or hawk overhead, and Maddie imitating the bird's call. Esther had sat with the three of them at breakfast, then insisted they take a basket of sandwiches, fruit and fancy cookies that she had the kitchen pack. Without the others there, the two women had actually been able to converse. Ruth learned Esther was a reader too and had read several of the books Ruth liked the best, which gave them much to talk about. Ruth had also learned, in the course of conversation, that the hotel was named after a kind of cricket played with a ball—and had pieced it together without having to reveal her initial ignorance. In the end, Esther wouldn't let them leave until she had made Ruth promise to come again—promise also that someday she would take Esther to see her little cabin in the canyon. But then, Ruth would have promised anything to get on her way to Black Canyon.

Once they reached the raised ground of the main highway, the patches of sand on the pavement lessened, disappearing altogether by the time she came to the first gas station. She replenished her tank, then got back on her way. By starting out from Palm Springs, she had cut hours from her travel time, but she was still impatient to be with her friends, and she sensed the same impatience in the children.

When J.B. asked to pee, Ruth spotted a clump of lush creosote bushes and stopped. The three of them walked around behind one, J.B. watering its base while she and Maddie squatted. When they rose, Maddie made a sound so close to flushing that Ruth was taken aback. J.B. laughed. Exactly the kind of response the girl wanted.

"Why do you always do that, Maddie?" she demanded. "It's not really funny, you know."

"Because I want to," Maddie said clearly, without looking up from the creosote bush she had stepped up to examine. "I like to."

"I think it's funny," J.B. said.

Ignoring him, Ruth walked over to the girl. "Well, I don't," she said. "Why don't you just use plain English? And what are you doing now?"

Maddie had begun to pluck a few of the rain-washed leaf clusters on the creosote. "Grandmother Siki told me the ends are the best part. We might need some for winter medicine."

"Just pick some at home, Maddie. Why carry it around with us all the way?"

"It doesn't grow in our canyon."

Ruth curbed a sudden urge to shake the stubborn child, even if she was right, maybe *because* she was right. "Get in the car, then, if you want to see Grandmother Siki and the others," she said, setting her jaw. A glance at J.B.'s face told her she was losing control again. In defiance, he pulled off a few sprigs of creosote and handed them to his sister before the two of them followed Ruth to the Model A.

The boy had always been protective of his sister. Not that she would ever touch the child. Her old anger rarely asserted itself anymore, and she went out of her way to be fair. Months went by now without her being seized by resentment. But then, just when she thought it was gone forever, out of nowhere the old rage would reappear, despite her resolve. It was well understood, this unspoken thing between the three of them—Maddie meeting it defiantly head-on, and J.B. standing beside her against their mother.

Ruth switched on the ignition, and they drove the next few miles in tight silence. She swung from shame to rage over her behavior. But what more could she do than what she had been doing all along? Control anger with reason and will and hope it withered away. She couldn't deny that if it had been J.B. making the animal sounds, she might have found it charming. Yet it changed nothing to tell herself it was wrong to dislike the things Maddie did. She had no one to talk to about her impulses—not even Kate, who was the person closest to her. Certainly not Kate.

Each time it happened, Ruth thought of Cally. Her resentment toward Ruth had been similar—still was, for that matter. But it was without justification—Ruth's father, after all, had not raped Cally. Even though Cally claimed to have been "just a girl," Ruth suspected that, if anything, it was Cally who had initiated the coupling that had brought Ruth into being. That poor Easterner hadn't had a chance. Ruth couldn't let herself become like that woman. She shook the thoughts from her mind, glad that her mother was out of her life for good.

Ahead, to the right of them, the opening in the mountain range that sheltered Black Canyon came into view, helping her regain some balance. She looked over at the children, whose faces, while not sad, had become impassive, without the open and expectant expression they usually wore. "I think Esther put some fruit and fancy cookies in the basket," she said. "Why don't we have some while we drive? We can save the sandwiches for a picnic by the stream."

The effect was not immediate, but a few minutes later, J.B. reached into the basket and took out a cookie, then handed one to Maddie— who reached in and dug around until she came up with a plum. "What about me?" Ruth said. "Don't I get something?"

The children looked at each other, then Maddie picked up the cookie she'd rejected and handed it to Ruth. At least it was a start, Ruth thought.

When she turned off the highway onto the dirt road that worked its way toward the mountains and up Black Canyon, the way became rough. The widespread rains had done their work here, littering the dirt road with washed-up rocks and small rivulets—and occasionally deep gullies that she had to maneuver around carefully. She was glad they'd made such good time earlier, since they could proceed only at a crawl from now on. And they hadn't even entered the canyon itself. It made her uneasy.

J.B. and Maddie had regained their usual inquisitive mood, now standing at the passenger window pointing and talking—J.B. in words and Maddie with animal sounds and a few phrases thrown in. They seemed to be enjoying the slowed pace of the trip, without any of the worries Ruth had about what the road so far might portend. She could have relieved her own anxiety by talking it out at them, but hated to spoil their cheerful mood—when it might turn out that they would have no problem at all. Instead, she suggested they eat the sandwiches as they drove, since getting to the cottonwoods was taking far longer than expected.

The first part of the canyon road remained rough but passable until she came to the place it crossed the dry wash. Then things got tricky. The wash was wide enough and the bank low enough that she could maneuver the Model A down into sand that now held no sign that a road had ever been there. The damp sand pulled at her tires, but she kept the steering wheel firm as she drove steadily across to the high, firm hump in the middle. She told the children to sit back down and hold on, then made a run to the far wash bank, gunning the vehicle up the slope. The Model A bucked violently over the top edge of the bank, Ruth's head smacking against the roof, and Maddie and J.B.

were thrown onto the picnic basket on the floor. Ruth took her foot off the gas pedal just as the steering wheel ripped from her hands. The motor died and they coasted to a stop a few feet over the top.

Ruth sat rubbing her head as the children extracted themselves from the car floor, whimpering slightly and rubbing bruised places. Except for when they were infants, they had never been criers. She helped them up, brushed them off, and wiped away the tears. "You can stand again," she said. "But be ready to sit back down when I tell you. Bumpy road ahead." The engine caught and they started up, proceeding smoothly enough on the higher ground beside the wash, dodging the few rocks washed up by the rain, and negotiating the tires out of small gullies. Ruth kept her pace slow and steady.

She started up a conversation with J.B. about the storm and the rains responsible for the changed configuration of Black Canyon. Her son seemed rightly awed by the power of water to move the whole sections of land they saw ripped from the banks of a usually dry wash. She told him the story of the thunderstorm that had turned her tent and all in it topsy-turvy and ruined her first attempt at the foundation of the cabin they lived in now. Maddie sat listening quietly, as if she knew that storm came soon after Ruth had threatened to shoot the terrible man who was destined to became Maddie's father. It had never occurred to Ruth before that Charlie Stine must have been caught out unprotected in that same violent storm. Too bad lightning didn't strike him dead on the spot. How different life would have been then. In a sudden burst of compassion, Ruth reached over and ruffled Maddie's hair. They were, after all, both involuntary victims of the bastard's act.

She drove along the high bank skirting the mountain's bottom, looking at areas below in the wash where water had cut deep, slicing away ground that had once been solid bank. Corpses of Joshua trees, mesquite and willows—even a few pinyons—were a testament to the water's destructive power.

Shadows laid long dark shapes across their path by the time she finally caught sight of one of the giant cottonwoods ahead, the last rays of sun filtering through the few leaves left on branches stripped nearly bare by yesterday's wind and rain. She nudged the gas pedal just past the snail's pace she had set earlier. As she got closer, she saw that her earlier fears had been realized. Slowing more, she drove forward and stopped the Model A just before the dirt road dropped off into nothingness.

They got out and walked to the edge of the dropoff. It must have been fifteen or twenty feet, Ruth guessed, down to where the road had once been—though there was no sign it had ever been there. Instead, virgin sand had mounded over piles of rocks already rounded by eons of floods. The thickets of willow Ruth had driven through before had been ripped away and only a few branches remained near the bank. But the biggest shock was the sight of two of those giant cottonwoods, uprooted and partially buried under debris. The other three remained upright, though the bottoms of their thick trunks had become traps for other branches and detritus. The sight was beyond anything she had imagined. There was no question of driving farther.

Ruth looked down at the children beside her and found Maddie looking up with welling eyes. "Grandmother Siki," she said. "I want to see her."

"And Thomas and Himiki and Jeff and Della." J.B.'s expression was pained.

Ruth felt her own eyes burn with disappointment. "You can see we can't go any farther," she said. "The road is completely gone. I can't drive over all that."

"We can walk," Maddie said, and her brother nodded in agreement.

The idea brightened her. The little settlement was only another mile or two. Yet already the sun was easing down behind the far ridge. "We'd better hurry, then," Ruth told them, "so we can get there before dark."

Ruth gave each child a heavy shirt to put on and a blanket to carry, then picked up the knapsack and her own blanket, along with the tin kerosene lantern she always brought to light the *ki'takii* they slept in. They made their way down the concave cliff the flood had carved from the wash bank, sliding one at a time to the sandy bottom, then picked their way across the tangle of willow branches and brush left by the flood. The stream that once ran through the middle had doubled in size and strength and moved close to the far bank of the wash, which was a lucky thing, Ruth realized. One thick branch of an uprooted cottonwood angled across it, up the far bank of the wash, and they used the branch as a bridge to climb over the stream and up the bank. Above the wash, the road was again semi-intact.

Although they walked as fast as they could—the children's small legs working double time to keep up with Ruth's pace—the canyon had darkened by the time they reached the harvested gardens a bend away from the camp itself. Just enough light remained in the blue dusk to make out the land around them dimly, and a full moon was lifting up from the horizon, the moon that signaled the night of the *natsata*.

The heavy rains had washed away any sign that humans had ever set foot in the field to plant or harvest, just as it had cleaned off all sign of human travel on the road ahead of them. The freshly sterilized ground gave Ruth a chill that she sensed the children shared, and the three of them quickened their pace even more, her senses expecting to soon find the smells of campfire and food, her ears alert for the sound of murmuring voices and quiet laughter.

The smell of campfire still hadn't manifested by the time they came around the bend and into what, at least in daytime, would have been a clear view into the Indian community. Even in semidarkness, campfire and lantern light should have been visible. Ruth slowed at the sight of the darkened camp, then stopped altogether, listening for some sound of human voices. She heard nothing more than a few crickets and the soft crunch of J.B. and Maddie's footsteps on the wet ground. Without Ruth's higher vantage point, the children were rushing on ahead.

Ruth tried to convince herself as she hastened after the children that maybe, for some reason, everyone had gone to bed early—maybe the wood was still too wet to make a campfire—and they would find the camp occupied. After all, the group hadn't planned to leave for the lower desert until after tonight's feast. She just hoped that the storm hadn't hastened their departure.

As they came closer to the settlement, the children slowed, then stopped and the three of them stood looking out into the darkness. "But where are they?" Maddie moaned. She cupped her hands around her mouth and yelled Grandmother Siki's name.

"They're gone, Mad," J.B. pronounced. His child's voice carried a somber conviction that surprised Ruth, who was still straining to change things, to bring back what she had so longed for.

"But I want to see them," Maddie said, as if she would not accept any other possibility. She called out other names into the darkness, her voice tearier each time. J.B. walked over and stood beside her.

"Why did they leave?" he said. "It was the *natsata*. They knew we would come."

"It must have been the storm. You know how they go down to the desert for the winter afterward—just like John and Kate go to the mines. We'll see them again next summer." Ruth's attempt to comfort them with reason was a weak one; an ache inhabited her chest that reason couldn't reach.

"But where down in the desert? I want to go see them there." Maddie stamped her small foot. In the light of the risen moon, Ruth could make out a glistening on the girl's cheeks. The ache in Ruth's chest could easily translate into tears. She had so counted on seeing her friends again, Thomas and Martha and Grandmother Siki especially, on being at the *natsata,* their leaving feast, as they had been last fall and the fall before.

She squatted between the children and hugged them to her, each of them alone in private sadness as they huddled in the empty darkness, remembering the same place lit with fire and warmed with conversation. Ruth wondered why she had never thought to ask more about where to find her friends when they were not in their canyon. She knew they went to several different places, but had no idea where any of them were, didn't even know at which agency Martha and her sister worked.

When they walked through the deserted encampment with the lantern, Ruth could see that although the wooden houses remained, along with the big round ceremonial house in the center of the settlement, all the *ki'takiis* had been taken down and the brushy materials scattered, then further disbursed by flooding. It had to have been the storm that made everyone leave early. Or had something else happened? The full moon told her this was the right night. Yet they'd left no sign, no message for her. But then the rains might have washed away any signs they did leave. The place appeared so forlorn, as forlorn as she felt, as if something precious had been erased, and she was left without a shred of hope that they would return. But the people always come back in the spring, she assured herself. Somehow nothing inside her believed it. It seemed to her at the moment that the people had dissolved, would now remain scattered throughout the lower desert forever, spread out as diffusely as the rains had scattered the remnants of their traditional dwellings.

From nearby, a coyote began to howl. Another joined in, then yet another, and soon the whole pack were howling mournfully. Maddie got into the spirit of it first and sent her own painful wail into the night air. J.B. added his voice, merging with hers in plaintive harmony. Without hesitation, Ruth looked up at the luminous moon, tilted back her head, and gave forth with her own throaty lament, the three of them continuing to bellow out sorrowfully long after the coyotes quit.

CHAPTER SEVENTEEN

The caw of ravens woke her, a bird foreign to her own canyon, and she turned her attention to other small chittering birds, some she didn't know. The unfamiliarity of their songs and calls unleashed a longing to be back on land that was truly home to her. The night before, she and the children had stumbled their way back to the Model A by moonlight and lantern, leaving the deserted camp behind them. She gave J.B. and Maddie the car seat to sleep on, and spread her own blanket on the ground beside the car. The night was chill after the storm, and the ground still damp underneath, so she hadn't slept well or long, barely enough to refresh her for the long drive home at dawn's light.

Later, as she negotiated the rivulets and washed-up rocks on her way out of Black Canyon, she began to wonder for the first time if the storm had reached as far as Rattlesnake Canyon, subjecting it to the same intense flooding. The idea brought mild alarm, but she told herself that most storms did not affect such an extensive area. Yet everything she saw along the way home implied that this one had.

They drove up to the general store just as it was closing for the day, and Matt Baxter's wife, Lily Rose, allowed them in for groceries. Matt hadn't returned from making deliveries yet, she told them anxiously, and she was afraid he might be stuck somewhere on a washed-out road. The rains had wrought severe flooding many places in Juniper Valley, Lily Rose told her, even washing out families foolish enough to build too near a wash bank. Roads weren't the only thing that Matt might be stuck in, Ruth mused grimly, noticing how tired the young woman looked in her second pregnancy, her former golden curls drooping and straight as wet straw, all the pretty shine gone. The mother who was always there to help was bedridden with gout, Ruth had heard. She couldn't quite stifle the strain of glee that mixed with the sympathy she felt for the woman, along with gratitude that this former flame hadn't pursued her as a wife instead of Lily.

She was already fairly stocked up for the winter, but she had an urge to buy even more flour, sugar, lard, coffee and canned goods. John Olsen had brought up her winter's hay last week on his flatbed, and Ruth picked up two more fifty-pound sacks of chicken feed. She still needed a supply of wine and whiskey, but was hesitant to mention it to Lily Rose. Though prohibition had been over for some time, alcohol was still treated like an illegal commodity, fetched from under the floorboards in the back room, just as before the law was changed. Ruth wondered if Matt lacked the license for selling it, if there were such a thing. Or maybe he simply wanted to continue selling his own brother's goods beneath the law—the whiskey came in the same kind of jugs the moonshine had. At any rate, Lily Rose turned out to be accommodating, asking only how much Ruth wanted—though the deep flushing of her face and the set of her dainty jaw let Ruth know how the young woman felt about the matter.

The road up Rattlesnake Canyon was every bit as bad as Ruth feared, with large rocks she had to maneuver around, and ruts that had become sizable rivulets. Twice, the high ground beside the rivulets was too weak to hold the weight of the car and caved in under her, leaving her with two wheels in a small gully and the Model A tipped badly to one side as she drove. She held her breath each time, as if that would keep it from tipping over the rest of the way. Even though she hoped to get closer to the Swedes' place before full dark, it was difficult to make good time without putting them all in danger, especially with twilight making it hard to see the changes in the road.

When the canyon narrowed at the willows, driving got even more difficult, and she came around the second bend to a sudden view of the water's power. Willows had been wiped clean from the bottom of the canyon where the road was supposed to go, and the stream that had flowed dead center through the willow grove, the way a part separates hair on a head, had been rerouted to the far side of the wash. The flood had removed a section of land in the process, slicing away the road in front of her. She saw no sign of the ruts that had traveled along the clay bottom beside the stream, following as it meandered around the next two bends, before heading up an embankment to high ground at the Swedes'. All traces had been swept away or buried in mounds of sand and rock and remnants of tree and willow branches.

Ruth got out to better determine if there was a way to get the car across the mess in front of her. J.B. and Maddie scrambled out and down the bank into the wash before Ruth could stop them. She was still on the bank straining to see a route in the dim twilight when J.B. called out to her.

"Look," he shouted. "There it is. They made a new road."

Ruth walked along the bank until she stood above the children. From there she could see a makeshift route hacked down the bank and along the wash on the side opposite the stream. In a flood of gratitude and relief, she slid down the bank to see more clearly what the miners had done, and if it would be enough to allow her vehicle to pass.

She had the children remain out of the way in the wash—just in case—as she cautiously eased the Model A down the steep incline the miners had constructed. When she reached the wash bed, J.B. and Maddie got back in. The rest of the drive to the Swedes' was slow but without incident. They arrived to many hugs and smiles of relief—and considerable scolding about her making the trip in the first place, then for staying away in such terrible conditions. Once she'd followed Kate's commands and the three of them were seated at the table with bowls of stew in front of them, Ruth began telling the story about how she had turned back in the sandstorm and mistakenly taken the wrong road, ending up in Palm Springs at the Cricket Club. Maddie, of course, supplied the chirping effects, and Ruth didn't bother to correct her interpretation. The sound of whopping cricket balls wouldn't be nearly as charming.

When J.B. supplied details about the flood destruction in Black Canyon and how they arrived to find no one at all at the Indian settlement, Maddie's eyes teared. Kate reached over and pulled the girl onto her lap, spoke to her in Swedish, with Maddie answering in the same. Sometimes Ruth wondered if Maddie had uttered as many Yuiatei and Swedish words as she had English, seeming to choose whichever language most fit the situation—though her animal sounds outnumbered both by far. It was a wonder.

"We leave for desert mines in two days, ya," John Olsen said. "Kate worry you not be back. We have to go look in Black Canyon for you."

"Well, we're back now. Made it up here just fine." Ruth got up and poured herself another cup of coffee. She walked back to the table with the pot and refilled the cups for the rest.

"Ya, you don't get back if we not fix that road. Sometime I think you crazy woman, Rute," he said, shaking his head. "Driving around in all kinds of weather with these two."

Ruth started to defend herself—after all, they could have walked the rest of the way home if they'd had to, but Olsen interrupted her and went on to describe the condition of the road the rest of the way to her house—barely passable, he said, up to the North Fork, where there was now an impossible twenty-foot dropoff. He and Ingmar had to walk from there to do the milking and feeding for the last two days.

"Even we work all day on that road tomorrow, don't know if your car get up that far bank. Very steep, that bank is," he said.

"You have to stay here, Rute, for tonight," Kate told her. "I give you extra blanket."

Ruth sighed. "I guess you're right, Kate," she conceded, letting go of her longing to be home. "We have enough blankets with us, though."

Ingmar and Olaf doubled up in another tent and gave their own to

Ruth and the children. Having the shelter was a good thing, too, Ruth realized when they went out to bed. A greater chill was in the air. In the morning she noticed ice crystals around the sides of the chickens' watering tin next to the house. But she'd slept deeply and was happy enough to wake up to the chirp and chitter of familiar birds.

Ruth left Maddie and J.B. with Kate and went up to the North Fork to work with the miners reforging a way across the chasm that water had dug. When she stood on the bank there, surveying the area where the flooded washes from both canyons converged, the sight almost stopped her breath. It might be twenty-five feet maybe, she thought. And so steep; it reminded her of the drop she'd seen at Angels Flight in Los Angeles. Repairing the way to her cabin would not be easy. Before she could do anything else, though, the animals at her place had to be attended to.

Ruth walked down canyon a few yards, to a place where the bank of the wash hadn't been sliced as deeply, and eased herself down to the sandy wash bottom, then took the fork up Rattlesnake wash until she found easy access to the road that ran alongside the two miles to her Glory Springs.

About halfway, she was surprised to find Juniper Blue galloping toward her; he was supposed to be penned up until she returned. He was not happy, either, and whinnied and neighed out deep guttural complaints as he trotted around and around her, not letting her touch him, and even taking an occasional nip at her clothing. She would have loved to fling herself up on his back and ride the rest of the way home, but he would have none of it, so she quickened her pace. He continued to show his displeasure as they went. When she rounded the bend and brought her cabin into view, her ears were assaulted by the bleating of desperate nannies and hens squawking madly in accompaniment.

The warm swelling in her chest at the sight of her home deflated at the sound of the animals' demands. She ignored them for the moment and went in to make sure her cabin roof had survived the storm without leakage. Yet even her relief at finding her cabin intact was disturbed by the cries outside. She sighed, remembering her days here before someone always wanted something from her, when she had endless time to sit out under the pines and listen to birdsong and the sound of wind in the pinyons, breathe in the scent of piney air. Without that, sometimes her spirit felt as withered as a nanny's milked teat.

Ruth walked to the chicken coop and scooped up some mash, spreading it onto the floor of the pen, sectioned off hay for Blue and tossed it into the trough. She doubted he would go near his corral for a while—though the pen would even not hold him until she repaired it, since he'd kicked off the top pole of one side and jumped over the lower bars. Then she snatched up the bucket and sat down with the loudest nanny, while the other continued to complain.

Ruth finished the milking, strained and set the milk inside, then walked to the bank of the wash, ready to start back to the North Fork and the task of rebuilding the road. She stopped at the bank long enough to take a breath and look across to Jim's grave, sighed again, remembering the vow she took there years ago. She had kept her promise to become more intimate with this place her lover was a part of. She had become nearly as conversant as he was with its plants and creatures, knew now how to roast young yucca stalks and prepare the shoots of cattail that grew near pools at the willows in spring. Knew which plants to use to ease pain or soothe stomachaches. But something was lacking in that intimacy, leaving her unsatisfied. Yet when the image came to her of David Stone rising from the dust under his car, she pushed it from her mind.

Caught in a dust devil of thought, Ruth left to rejoin the miners, walking down toward the North Fork. Blue loped alongside and around her for the first two bends. She ignored him until he came up and gave her a playful nudge with his nose. She stopped and looked at him, saw that his annoyance had dissipated. She had been forgiven.

She took hold of his mane and propelled herself upward, managing to swing one leg over his back. "Too bad you didn't get over your tantrum sooner," she told him. "Then I could have used a bridle." As it was she gripped his mane, leaned forward and wrapped her arms around his neck, letting her legs tighten around his belly. He took off at a run down the washed-out road. She clung to stay astride, relishing the rhythm of raw animal muscle and power between her legs as the horse carried her, tightening her thighs around him as he thrust her upward, then brought her down solid again and again, all the way to the North Fork. All the while, she was helpless to stop the shocks of pleasure that spread through her with each jolt. When he came to a halt on the far bank of the North Fork, she slid down from his back to solid ground, as shaky on her feet—and in her soul—as if she had just been delivered from a journey through some forbidden place. Was this what being alone had reduced her to?

She could hardly meet the miners' eyes when they looked up to greet her. As for Juniper Blue, he trotted off to graze as if nothing had occurred. And as far as she was concerned, nothing had, or ever would again.

While the miners attacked the steep banks on each side of the deep wash with pickaxes and shovels, Ruth stationed herself in the bed of the wash, tossing off rocks mounded on top of what had been the road, and dragging away debris of brush and branches half buried in the sand among and under the piles of rounded rocks. The labor comforted her, brought her back to herself. While she worked, tugging and lifting until her back muscles quivered from the strain, she wondered what she would have done without help from these neighbors who pitched in without her asking. J.B. and Maddie could have walked home with her, she supposed, then she could have made many trips back to the car for the supplies.

It took so many supplies nowadays, with the two children and all the animals she had. Her life was far more complicated than in those days when she could carry most of what she needed in a back satchel. But she had to quit thinking that way, she told herself. Things were different now; that's all there was to it. Somehow, the freedom she had sought had been transformed into responsibilities, and somehow, she didn't quite understand how, those responsibilities built a barrier between herself and the land that she loved. Yet it did her no good to whine about it—even to herself.

At noon, the work crew quit and drove back to the Olsens', where they knew Kate would have a hearty lunch waiting. Like a jealous lover, Blue stayed behind the Model A all the way to the Swedes', then disappeared to wait in the willows when she went into the house. After devouring a huge bowl of beans and stuffing herself with Kate's fresh-baked bread, Ruth wanted nothing more than to curl up for a nap. But there was no time for such luxury if she was to get the children home before dark. So after a short sit, the crew got back on the road.

After the miners left, Ruth had one more cup of coffee with Kate, since this was the last time she would see her until spring. Ruth gave her two cans of peaches she had picked up at the store, in lieu of the new Indian foods she had promised Kate they would bring back from the feast for her. Then she rounded up the two children and said her good-byes. The thought of Kate and John being gone, of her Indian friends having disappeared so abruptly, left Ruth feeling even more empty and alone, and she hugged the big woman fiercely. Maddie refused to let go of Kate, so she lifted the girl and set her inside the car.

After several more hours of back-wrenching work, much of the time J.B. and Maddie doing their small part to clear away the smaller rocks and debris, the crew had finished what they hoped was a passable road. The angle up the far bank was still quite steep, even though the miners had hacked away at the top and greatly rounded off the final few yards. Ruth took the Model A up it by herself, while the children waited in the wash.

She got a good run on the steep ascent, racing down the first bank and across the wash bottom, the Model A bucking and bouncing over the rough road as she held the steering wheel tight to stay seated. She gunned the engine hard when she reached the high steep side, but the car slowed considerably about halfway up, even though she pressed the gas pedal to the floor. Her momentum continued to drop until she thought her children could have walked faster than the car was moving. John Olsen and Olaf ran up behind her, followed by Ingmar and Karl, ready to give a push if necessary, but the car continued up the incline at a crawl. Near the top, when the Model A reached the spot the miners had rounded, a bit more gas kicked in. The men moved back, and Ruth took the car over the top at nearly the speed an adult could walk.

She stopped and set the handbrake, then got out to thank the miners, who had taken so much time out of their preparations to leave in order to get her home safely. They looked tired, though all were smiling over their success.

"We take little more off the top now, ya," John Olsen told her as J.B. and Maddie came running up the road, their strong little legs bringing them up the incline faster than Ruth had driven it.

Ruth gave John Olsen a huge hug good-bye, then went on to hug each of the others, who reddened and shuffled. The miners were more comfortable demonstrating their affection with J.B. and Maddie, giving each a kiss and a hug, before the children got into the car. Ruth went around to the back and pulled out one of her jugs of whiskey.

"Here," she said, holding it out. "You men deserve this." John Olsen hesitated, though from the expression on his face, Ruth could see he wanted it. "It's the least I can do. I'll feel better if you accept it." With that, he swept the jug from her and handed it to Ingmar.

"See you in the spring," she told him, then switched on the ignition and headed home, Juniper Blue trotting ahead of them, innocent but proprietary. He was innocent, she reminded herself, remembering her vow, and so was she. Even so, Ruth couldn't turn her mind completely from the fact that she was heading toward winter's deeper isolation, and her concern that isolation was shaping her in ways she had little control over.

CHAPTER EIGHTEEN

A lot of good burying the pipes two feet deep did, Ruth mused the first morning that no water came when she turned on the spigot at her sink. And after all the trouble of putting in the new windmill system. Well, she wasn't quite back to melting snow for water. Not yet, anyway. She had kept full the old fifty-gallon tank she'd used before the windmill was in, left it sitting in the corner, though it took up so much space she had almost chucked it. Only the possibility of this being that "doozy" of a winter changed her mind. Now she was glad she could count on that supply before resorting to melted snow and icicles. But it looked like there'd be no real baths for a while for any of them. Sponge baths would have to do. Not that it mattered much, with snow up to the fenders of the Model A, and more coming down every day; who would see them?

Each morning, snowing or not, Ruth reshoveled her way out to

Juniper Blue and the goats on paths she had carved from the snows that started a few weeks ago. While she milked, J.B.'s and Maddie's job was to spread chicken mash and gather eggs—Maddie, of course, talking chicken squawks and brawks the whole time. On the level, the snow came to Ruth's waist, though the sides of the pathway reached nearly to her shoulders with all she'd removed from underfoot. She had shoveled out a pathway to the Model A also and made the children play there, instead of on the main path, since J.B. kept carving out caves in the sides to play in, which made more work for her. J.B. and Maddie loved to play in those pathways whose walls reached far above their heads, enjoyed going out to the Model A and peering in the windows to see the dark cavern inside. On some days, if she was feeling generous, Ruth would tug open the driver's door and let them play inside—although they seemed happy enough just crawling beneath the running board and playing in the natural shelter beneath the car.

She was grateful that the two of them occupied themselves so easily. Even so, being cooped up with them daily—without anywhere to go or anything to do beyond the tasks required for survival—left her restless and oppressed. Especially once she'd gone through all of the new novels she had stashed for her winter reading. She began rereading the old European books that had belonged to her father, some of which were better the second time around. Things picked up for a while when she remembered the huge Russian tome and began rereading it. She even tried writing in her journal again, talking to each page as if it were another person, but found herself distracted and annoyed by the constant sounds of her children's play, only a few feet away. Maddie's animal sounds especially grated on her, and Ruth sometimes snapped, "Stop those goddamned mouth noises" before she could stop herself.

There were good times, too. In the beginning the three of them had made snowmen and snow houses, but soon the accumulation became too deep for that. Some days they would bake together, then eat hot mesquite breads and rolls while she read to them from books Kate and John brought back from San Bernardino, fairy tales and fables that kept the two children at rapt attention, stories where characters were drawn toward dangerous fates. Each time Ruth finished a story, Maddie and J.B. would want to know how words worked on the paper.

It wasn't long before they could both pick out most of the common words in each story by themselves, then guess what the rest might be, amazing Ruth with their bright curiosity.

Yet her amazement at their antics had worn thin by the day the pipes froze, as if that fact signified an even deeper isolation to come. She stood looking out the window above the sink and could barely make out the barn and corral behind the slanting white curtain that was falling heavier than any she'd seen this winter, so heavy that she decided to forgo the cup of coffee she usually had before the milking, and get the chores done first. While gusts of wind pinged icy crystals against the panes, Ruth made sure the fire was securely ablaze, then wrestled the children into their jackets and mittens, put on her own, and ventured out into the storm.

Through ferocious cold, the three of them made their way toward the barn and goat shed. Wind-driven flakes targeted their faces and eyes, made even the path in front hard to see. Ruth shoveled the worst of the new accumulation as they went, though she found her-self mistakenly shoveling into the snowbank more than once before they reached the animals' shelter. Maddie and J.B. gathered eggs, while Ruth fed Blue and the nannies, but she didn't let them take the eggs back to the house or go play by the car as she usually did when she milked. Instead she had them stay close by her in the shed, J.B. creat-ing a tiny town out of snow that had drifted in through the cracks and Maddie driving Ruth to distraction by conversing with the animals. The fact that the creatures responded to the girl only encouraged her.

When she finished the milking and settled the children back in the cabin and had the fire in the stove replenished, Ruth went back out for more wood. Instinct told her she should bring in an extra supply for this storm, a supply she decided to take from the stack inside the barn, rather than the closer pile beside the house, which would be easier to get to if the snow got worse. All the while she was loading armful after armful and carrying the wood into the cabin, Blue kept running and kicking up his hind legs, whinnying and carrying on, in the small cor-ral space she kept cleared and he packed down with his hooves. Ruth knew he wanted more attention than the pats and hugs she had given him before she began hauling in the wood, but she had no intention of trying to ride him in such deep snow.

His capering finally got to her as she was carrying in the last armful of wood, a few pieces of the pitchiest chunks of pine for starting fires, and rather than heading out the barn door for the house, Ruth trudged into the corral, struggling her way toward the gate on the roughed-out trail Blue's hooves had sculpted in his many trips to see if the gate was open. In a burst of empathy, she decided to unlatch the gate and let him try bucking through the snow on his own. But she couldn't push the unlatched gate open enough for him, with three feet of snow banking it shut—not even when she leaned against it with the added weight of the pine chunks. It moved only a few inches before snow caught and held it fast.

Still determined, she climbed the willow pole gate and jumped down onto the snow that held it shut. Her jump did pack the snow down some, though not enough to escape reach of the gate's bottom rung. Another jump might just do the trick. Ruth stood a moment considering, her face numb from the falling flakes, her feet already far beyond feeling. Maybe she should simply get the shovel and clear the space that way—but the thought of remaining longer in the storm deterred her. Instead, she remounted the gate, opting for the easier way.

This time she balanced herself on the gate's top rung, weaving a bit in the wind as she prepared to make one last leap into the snow. Then, just as she bent and tensed to jump, she heard something crash inside the cabin. Caught in the momentum of her leap and unable to abort it, she twisted around at the sound, tossing up the wood and toppling off the gate still half turned. After the initial jolt of shock at losing her balance, Ruth started to laugh as she fell, at the idea of landing in a bed of soft snow. As she hit, she felt her knee pull, heard a small snap. A chunk of wood thumped against her head.

Head pounding and the side of her face pressed into unsympathetic snow, she turned to right a leg that seemed askew. Excruciating pain shot into her knee, leg and hip, and she gasped out loud into the icy quiet surrounding her. Laughter floated out from the house and was swallowed up into the silence. Flakes brushed against her face, and she felt a chill on her neck, where ice was gathering along the collar of her coat. The only heat came from the pain in her leg. Ruth glanced over and found Blue looking down on her from behind the gate, his eyes alert and watchful.

This was ridiculous. She had to get up, straighten her leg. Once she did that, everything would right itself.

The snow offered no support for rising, so Ruth set her jaw against the hot knife of pain that brought tears to her eyes each time she moved. She rolled onto her back, reaching around to grasp the bottom rung of the gate and pulled herself an inch or two toward it. Each time she felt herself growing dizzy and the white world around her about to turn black, she stopped, lay still a moment, then dragged herself a few inches closer. Stopped again. Dragged again.

When at last she could reach the support pole for the rungs, she turned and began to pull herself upward, careful not to place any weight on her leg. She couldn't keep tears from forming with each lurch she made upright, nor stop the spells of faintness that came over her. Blue whinnied and stomped back and forth nervously, finally coming over to nudge her affectionately, reaching through the rungs of the gate with his muzzle. So unstable was she by this time that he almost knocked her back into the snow. Only by clinging tight to the gate against the pain roaring into her leg was she able to remain upright.

Woozy and weak, she could barely beg him to stop. Then she had a thought and wrapped one arm around his neck, then the other, grasping his mane in one hand and letting her weight fall forward onto his strong body.

The horse took a few steps backward, which pulled her through rungs into the corral again. He stopped when she cried out with the torment of it, clinging to his neck in a half-swoon, and crying softly. "Oh, Blue," she whispered. "What am I going to do? I can't even stand up."

When the anguish eased some, Ruth braced herself and said as commandingly as she could, "Take me in, Blue. To the barn, Blue," and hoped the animal would understand her.

It seemed a miracle when the horse began to move backward again. "Slow, go slow, Blue," she yelled out, though he was barely moving. But the agony of her leg being dragged over the hoof-pocked snow was almost too much for her, and she was afraid she might lose consciousness and drop down into the snow that kept trying to claim her. A great part of her was ready to let go of the horse's warm neck and sink into the sleep that pulled at her. The only thing that seemed real was her own suffering, keeping her awake, and at the same time pulling her toward oblivion.

Ruth was shivering violently by the time the horse had brought her closer to the door that led out of the barn to the pathway she'd dug to her cabin door. She noticed her own shaking calmly, as if it belonged to someone else. The same way she noticed that Blue could not get through the narrow doorway to get her out of the barn, as if she'd just discovered that fact, instead of having planned the building that way.

So how would she get the rest of the way to her cabin, she wondered, with the same detachment. By now, she wasn't even sure it mattered. She wondered vaguely what her children were doing, what might have crashed in that warm place, which at the moment seemed to belong to some other world, maybe the world of dreams, or one from the pages of a novel.

Even as she wondered, Blue was edging her toward the barn door, which she'd left open, thinking she'd be going back through it in a moment. Already, a patch of snow had drifted onto the barn's dirt floor. She looked down the path toward her cabin doorway, the scene thickly blurred by falling snow. The cabin appeared a thin and distant memory of itself, something that might dissolve if she touched it, nothing like the warm place she had been inside of only a short while ago. The distance to that doorway seemed insurmountable.

Ruth reached out and grasped the wooden jamb of the barn door. When she held it securely, she planted the foot of her uninjured leg and released Blue's neck, letting some of her weight shift toward the wood. But when her shoulder bumped against the jamb, her foot slipped backward in the patch of snow, and Ruth felt herself pitch forward, pain wrenching her beyond standing. She heard herself yell out just before the path floor came up to smack her.

It was hurting that brought her back out of the blackness. She heard voices and the horse whinnying, felt herself being pulled, then let go, pulled, then let go again. Each time she moved excruciated her further. "Stop. Leave me alone," she heard herself mumble, when the dragging started again. She opened her eyes to find out who had hold of her arms at the shoulders, had hold of her coat really, to inch her forward. It was her children, one on each side.

"You have to come inside now," Maddie told her, letting go of her coat sleeve.

"We thought you got dead," J.B. said, still holding on to the other side. "We heard you yelling."

"Being dead wouldn't hurt this much." Ruth looked up toward her cabin door, which her children had left wide open. She was not much closer to it than she had been when she fell—a foot or two maybe.

"Get back," she said, raising up onto her elbows. "I can make it now." When she stayed still, her leg remained numb and painless on the icy floor of the path. "Shut that cabin door. You've let out all the heat." Ruth found it a comfort to order her children around, something that woke and strengthened her.

"Look at you. You don't even have any mittens on. And your jackets aren't zipped. Get back inside. Put some wood in the fire," Ruth told them as firmly as her shaky voice would allow.

She clenched her teeth and used her elbows to move herself forward, finding that her legs slid nicely on ice buried beneath the new inches of fluff on the path, and that her injured leg hurt less when she was able to negotiate her own movement. She managed to use the foot of her good leg to help propel her, but when she tried bending that knee to boost herself, it caused such torment in the injured leg that she almost passed out again.

"Get inside, I said, Maddie," Ruth snapped at the girl when she got her breath back. Maddie had only walked a few steps closer to the cabin when her brother went in, but had remained outside. Her daughter didn't respond, and Ruth looked up to see the girl standing, arms folded and jaw set tight, her usual defiant position whenever she ignored Ruth's requests.

"Not until you do," she said, her teeth chattering so hard the words came out staccato.

Infuriated, Ruth pulled herself forward toward her even faster, using arms and elbows like a swimmer moving through water. And for a few more strokes, as fury fueled her, pain became irrelevant.

The girl stepped back as Ruth inched forward, stopping just in front of the closed cabin door to wait for her. Ruth's crazed drive gave out just before she reached the door, and she lay panting and gasping, groaning as the pain caught up with her. She put her head down on her arms in defeat. Enveloped in this white world, tinted with blue shadow, she could not pull herself one inch closer.

Ruth heard Maddie open the cabin door, felt her house's heat pour out on her. She looked up to see both children standing just inside, watching her. "I fixed the fire," J.B. told her. "Come and see." He turned toward the stove, where Ruth caught a glimpse of flame from a burner he hadn't quite replaced right.

"Come on, I said," her daughter told her, in perfect imitation of Ruth's daily tone and phrasing. "You have to come inside now." All around her, the world was a blur of wind and white, except for that space just inside her cabin door, that place where confusion cleared, the way it had for that one moment in the dust storm so she could turn toward shelter. The bright place in front of her beaconed like fate in a fairy tale, felt equally magical and unreal. And Ruth swam toward it, just ahead of the wave of pain about to crest over her, gliding her body over the strip of wood at the doorway and onto her own concrete floor. The last thing she heard before the world faded and darkened was Maddie latching the door behind her.

CHAPTER NINETEEN

What she wouldn't give now for that same world she had been so discontented with a mere three weeks before, Ruth realized. She held tight the shovelcrutch and tried to ease her rear onto the milking stool without causing too much pain in the leg that was still far from healed. It hurt less, certainly, once she splinted the knee area with rungs from the chairback she'd cut up and bound to her with strips of sheet. She'd used the top bar of the same chairback to attach to the shovel handle once she'd sawed off the shovel to shorten it some. It wasn't much of a crutch, but the best she could do for outside, and the blade kept her steady on the icy path. Usually. Once she hadn't dug it deeply enough into the path's bottom and fell into the side that now rose well above her head. It had been a painful ordeal to extract herself from snow that kept caving in as she tried to push herself up against it. After that, she took more care where she placed the blade and how deep.

She even found that with the children's help—they held her steady as she shoveled—she was able to use the makeshift crutch to clear snow from the path.

Inside the cabin, Ruth used another improvised affair put together from the rest of that poor chair, a cross slat from the bottom nailed to a pole made of its legs. She pulled bits of rubber from jar rims to stabilize the bottom surface, otherwise it kept slipping out from under her on the concrete.

All the chores she had done so easily before—so easily that she had considered them boring and monotonous—were now incredibly difficult. She never knew for certain if she would actually make it through the arduous journey out to milk the goats and back again. And the children had to carry in the pail. There was less milking now, though. One of the nannies, the one she'd named Natasha, had gone dry after Ruth could not get out to milk for nearly a day and a half, and she was just barely able to bring back the other nanny's milk. The children did their share, carrying in wood and feeding the animals while she directed. They helped in the house too, handing Ruth what she needed while she stood cooking or washing dishes and, only occasionally, a few clothes. Determined to make the water last as long as she could, she had the two of them heap up the dishpans with snow each day, and used the inch or so of water that resulted for cleaning.

Yet the burden of extra effort to do the chores did not distress her as much as the continuing ache of the injury, which still kept her awake a great part of each night. She did her best not to put weight on that leg, but inevitably some situation would call for it—usually to keep herself from falling facefirst onto the floor or the frozen pathway. Maybe if she didn't have all the chores to do, the leg would heal faster. But what if the problem was that the leg needed more attention than she was able to give it? Getting to a doctor certainly was out of the question.

Initially, she had been relieved to find that, except for a swollen area around the knee, the leg appeared fairly normal. There were no kinks or places askew at the joint. That seemed a good sign. Yet she was no expert. She got out her medical book and read all there was about bones, but that didn't tell her much more than she'd learned in nurse training. She couldn't be sure if she was dealing with a broken or cracked bone, or some tearing of ligaments around her knee. Or both.

Either way, the most she could do was splint it and keep weight off the leg as much as possible.

She had come to on her cabin floor that morning of the injury, both children standing over her, tugging on her clothes to rouse her. Maddie had already covered Ruth with her comforter, and J.B. had just made her the worst cup of coffee she ever tasted, though she hadn't been focused enough to try it before it got cold. She'd spent the rest of the day in bed—which cost considerable agony just to get into. And getting out to use the slop jar almost made her pass out again. But Maddie and J.B. fed her and themselves from the bread and rolls she had made the day before. In the evening, Ruth opened up a can of Hereford Corned Beef they brought over to her, so they could make sandwiches. The animals went without, and even with the strong wind whipping flakes against the house, Ruth could hear their complaints. It wasn't until the snow stopped the next morning that she let J.B. and Maddie go out to feed, while she directed from the doorway. But the milking had to wait that day, which was why now her morning's milking was cut in half. A mixed blessing, she thought, as she squeezed streams of white liquid into the bucket, watching foam grow around the edges. The milk's mild goaty odor wafted upward, overriding the more pungent smells from the manure of cooped-up animals.

When she had wrung the last drops from the nanny's teats, Ruth called Maddie away from her chicken squawking and J.B. from the tiny houses he was making with hay and had them take the pail into the house, carrying it one on each side as they high-stepped down the snowy path. Only once had they slipped and tipped the bucket.

Her fingers whitenumb and without feeling, Ruth rubbed blood into them before she slipped them back into mittens and snatched up her shovelcrutch. She pulled herself upward, tears forming when she had to use her injured leg to catch her balance, gritted her teeth and hobbled to the barn door to feed Blue.

The sun had finally made its appearance over the high ridge, where it hid for all but a few hours on winter days, and was now scattering glitter over the surface of the snow. The row of icicles on the eave above the cabin door ignited with light, and a spear of that icy light dropped down from the eave. Ruth watched it disappear into the deep snow. Not so long ago, such a sight would have moved her, she realized, would have lit her up as brightly as sun lit the ice; now she just wished she could get through the drifts enough to collect those icicles—they would melt down to so much more water than did the pans of snow. Would that joyful part of her return with the healing of her leg, she wondered, as she thrust her shovelcrutch into the snowpack, the blade beating metallic chinks against the ice?

Still, the bright ice did its job, despite her denial of its effect, and she went through her cabin door wondering if the worst of the winter might well be over now—it hadn't snowed in days. At the same time she noticed that the #8 tin tub was almost half filled with water from the several loads of snow she'd had the children carry in the day before. Maybe it was time they all had a bath. All she needed to do was heat enough of it in pots on the woodstove.

By afternoon, they were settled in more comfortably than they had been in weeks, the children quietly picking words out of the book Ruth had read to them earlier, and Ruth immersed again in Moscow's snowy winter. Bathing had not been easy for her, standing with her good foot in the water, the other resting on a chair beside the tub, while she poured warm water over her body from a bowl the children filled and handed to her. But nothing had felt so good for a long time. Afterward, she fixed chicken and noodles, using half of the old hen they had helped her slaughter the day before. The other half was still frozen in the outside cupboard.

The food and comfort had made her sleepy, and she was just forcing herself to read on a bit further, when she heard Juniper Blue whinnying. He'd been fed; she didn't know what that horse could possibly want now, she told herself, breathing in the aroma of the hot bread that was still cooling, mingling with the smell of chicken and noodles left on the stove to finish off for dinner. Outside the wind had picked up again, whistling into cracks in windows and doors. She had no desire to rouse herself from comfort's cocoon to see what the horse's problem was out there, and instead set aside the book and snuggled into her pillow. Although the whinnying became more insistent, so did her desire to ignore it, and she was just slipping away into some warmer world, when the sound of someone pounding on her door interrupted.

She lifted her head, not yet sure from which world the knock came.

She looked over and found Maddie and J.B. staring intently at the door. Then came more pounding. Someone from outside called out her name, though mixed with all the whinnying going on, it was impossible to know if she recognized the voice or not.

"Who's out there?" she yelled, but with the wind and whinnying—and it sounded like two different horses—she couldn't make out the reply. She was just wondering if she should reach for her rifle or her crutch when Maddie spoke.

"It's that man," she said.

"With the broke truck," J.B. explained.

"Ruth. Are you in there?" This time she recognized his voice as well.

"Of course I'm in here," she said, reaching for her inside crutch. She pulled herself to her feet, still shaking disbelief from her head, and crutched to the door. "But what are you doing out there?" she asked, jerking the door open.

By this time both children were beside her, and the three of them could only gape at the sight Stone presented as he stood before them, nearly as snow-covered as any snowman they had made. Every surface of his clothing was frosted over, including his cap; his eyebrows and lashes were caked solid. And it wasn't even snowing.

"What did you do, Mr. Stone, fall off your horse?" Ruth and the children moved back, so he could enter.

"David," he said, stomping off snow and blinking it from his eyes. "And you try riding eight miles through several feet of this stuff. Just look at the poor horse." He gave a couple final kicks to the doorjamb to uncake his boots.

She peeked around him, at the two horses that were calling to each other and pacing in small circles on either side of the corral fence, though their pacing came in lunges and leaps as they packed the snow down around them. The horse Stone had ridden looked to be a bay, though attached patches of snow made it appear somewhat like a pinto. Some kind of bulging saddlebag contraption, also partially snow-blanketed, was slung over the horse's rump.

"Stand still, then, and let me uncover you," Ruth said. "J.B., bring me the broom. Maddie, get me that towel off the chair there."

She shut the door behind him and took the broom to the top layer of snow on his clothes, then told him to remove his coat and boots and put them near the fire. When Maddie handed the man a towel for his face, he gave the girl a wink and ruffled J.B.'s hair. Ruth watched the way the children's faces brightened at his attention as they walked with him toward the stove. He did have a way with them, she remembered, as she reopened the door and quickly swept out the chunks of snow.

Stone looked over as she made her way to where he stood warming his hands over the burners. His face jolted with shock when he finally noticed her splinted leg and crutch. "Oh my god. I knew I was right to come. I just knew it."

Ruth scooted around and sat in one of the two wooden chairs that remained. "And just why did you come all the way up here in several feet of snow?"

"Juniper Valley has just over two feet. I measured three at the Rimrock crossroads, where the grader stops. But it just kept getting deeper here in the canyon." He pulled over a crate and sat down on it. "But tell me what happened to you. I don't suppose you've seen a doctor?"

"You still haven't said why you came."

"I kept worrying about you—the three of you—all the way up here alone in this snow. Then I was talking with some folks at Matt's store, Larry Hudson, from the Rimrock area. He told me how he and some neighbors had brought provisions up for you once in a bad year like this."

"Did he say he arrived to find that I had plenty of venison and could have managed just fine?" She ignored her memory of how welcome the coffee and beans and other goods had been that terrible year.

"Anyway, when I heard there was another storm coming in, I started thinking you might need a few things to get you through it, stew and coffee and butter and such. After all, you were willing to help me when I needed it. Hudson even offered me his horse. And it certainly appears I did the right thing by coming. You can use some help."

"Actually, we've been managing just fine since I fell. It was hard at first—still is, I guess. Pain is the worst thing. But the children help with chores. You'd be surprised what they can do." She stood and poured water into her enamel coffeepot, set it on the burner. "But what's this about a storm coming in? It was calm and sunny when I went out to milk this morning."

"The radio said a big one is on the way. I know it doesn't look like it, but the wind came up about the time I passed the Olsens' place. You can see a few clouds moving in over the ridges." He glanced down at the splinted leg she had stuck out to one side. "But what about your leg—did you set it yourself? You need to see a doctor."

"Just how would I do that? Ride out on Juniper Blue in the snow with the two children, splinted leg and all? I'm sure that would have helped matters." Ruth hobbled back to the chair and sat again. "And I don't even know that it's a break anyway. I can't see anything out of place. It could be I pulled loose some ligaments. Nothing I read in the medical books was much help in telling me which it is."

"You couldn't have gotten a very good look at it, Ruth. I can't see how. Maybe I'll be able to tell more."

"You're not a doctor any more than I am. Less, in fact."

"But I can get a better view of that leg. And, actually, I am a doctor, though not of the medical variety."

"Doctor of old pottery," Ruth said. "Anyway, I'll think about it." She stood and picked up the can of coffee. Stone rose with her, put his hand around the can.

"No need for you to do that," he said. "I can pour in the grounds."

She snatched back the can and pulled the lid off. "I'm not crippled, Mr. Stone."

After she stirred in grounds and pulled the pot to the side of the burner, she softened. "I know you're trying to help," she told him. "But I like to do for myself. I always have."

"I understand that. But that leg might need a rest so you can keep doing for yourself." He looked over at J.B. and Maddie, who were absorbing his every word. "And don't forget that you've had to do for them too," he said.

"They've been doing for me as well," she reminded him, reaching for the cups. "Besides, you've come a long way to get here. You must be exhausted."

"At least let me pour, Ruth. Let me do that much."

Ruth sighed and sat back down. She crossed her arms, gave him a look, and rolled her eyes. "Be my guest, then, Doctor," she said, trying not to smile.

"With pleasure, Madam." For the first time he broke out in that smile she remembered so well. She couldn't help but laugh at the sight of something so out of tune with the mood of her winter confinement.

Over coffee—his largely untouched—Stone caught her up on local news. He'd been driven from his dig by the snows some weeks ago, but said the same snows had stopped work on the new movie town after only a few of the buildings had been framed. Before that, he said, movie people had been coming into Juniper Valley and Two Bunch Palms spending money and promising to bring work for the folks in the area. Ruth filled him in on her encounter with the creator of Frontiertown in the sandstorm, and what she'd learned at the Cricket Club.

Thoroughly enjoying real conversation, Ruth hadn't kept track of the day's passing until she noticed twilight darkening the snowy brightness out the window. It took another moment before it occurred to her that Stone couldn't possibly ride back out of the canyon in the dark. Her concern caused her to lose track of what he was saying, until his prolonged silence brought her back.

She looked away from the window to find him watching her. "I'd wondered about getting up here and back in one day, too," he said. "In all this snow. I threw on my bedroll and an extra blanket just in case."

Ruth said nothing, looked out the window at the horses, who had now made friends across the corral fence. "Your bedding must be covered with ice. You better bring it in and hang it by the fire," she told him then. "If you dig out the corral gate, you'll be able to get your horse into the barn for the night." She stood and began making her way toward the door. "I have to get the goat milked. Maddie. J.B. Get your boots and coats on and follow me out with the bucket." She pulled their coats from the hook and tossed them toward the children, then pulled down her own and hopped to the bed with it.

"No sense in both of us going out there," Stone said. "I can do the milking once I shovel the gate open."

Ruth stopped in the middle of pulling on her boot. "You ever milked a goat before?"

"No."

"A cow?"

"No. But it can't be that hard."

"If a woman can do it, you mean." She yanked up on her boot, then slid the foot of her injured leg into what was left of the matching boot she'd had to cut off and split in half to get on.

"That wasn't what I meant," Stone said. He rose and got into his jacket, then reached down and began to help Maddie zip hers.

"She can do that herself," Ruth told him, but he zipped it nonetheless.

"What in the world is that?" Stone said, when Ruth opened the door and grabbed up the shovelcrutch beside it. She looked back and gave him a wry smile, shrugged her shoulders, then without answering, chinked her way down the path to the goat shed and barn. Maddie and J.B. trailed behind with the milk pail. She noticed that the twilight sky was completely overcast, and a few flakes whipped by on the wind to slap against the skin of her face. The feel of storm was now strong in the air.

Ruth and the children had the routine down; while she milked, they doled out the feed and gathered up any new eggs and put them in their mackinaw pockets. By that time, she had the bucket ready for them to carry back to the cabin. David Stone was just leading his bay into the barn when Ruth and the children started down the path toward the door.

"Here. Let me help you," he said, hurrying after them.

"You can see we're managing just fine," she said, stabbing her shovelcrutch blade into the icy pack ahead of her and leaning on it to pull herself forward. She rested her weight on the good leg, then stabbed again into the ice pack. He caught up with her and took hold of her shoulders, throwing her off balance.

"David," she yelled. "Stop. Let go of me." When he did, she toppled sideways into the bank of snow beside the path.

"Goddamn it," she yelled, struggling to extract herself. Stone reached in and pulled her to her feet.

"Being out here is dangerous for you, Ruth. In your condition. I told you I should be the one doing the work in this storm," he announced, brushing clumps from her jacket.

"It is dangerous—with you around," she sputtered, spitting snow and blinking it from her eyes. "I was doing just fine, I told you."

"Doesn't look like it to me." He shook his head and took firm hold of her shoulders. "Come on, I'll get you into the house."

"I can get there on my own, really I can," Ruth protested as he guided her forward. "I do it twice every day. Sometimes more." But she was helpless to stop his good intentions and let herself be half carried along to the cabin door, where the children stood watching. As soon as they were all inside, he went back out to bring in the saddlebag and supplies, then to load up on wood for the stove. Ruth flopped onto the bed and sat there shaking her head. She didn't know whether to laugh or cry. How could she ever convince this well-meaning blockhead that his help was a hindrance that threw off the delicate balance she had worked hard to achieve? She supposed she would just have to ride this thing out, let him give her the help he insisted on until he left tomorrow.

Snatching up her inside crutch, Ruth made her way over to the stove and began preparing dinner. In one of the saddlebags he'd brought in she found a can of stew to heat up along with the rest of the chicken and noodles she had planned, since there were now four people to feed, and one of those quite large. Maddie and J.B. came over to help without being asked, the two of them seeming excited about having company. Ruth had to admit that even she found the prospect of a night of sociability a welcome relief that overrode the disruption Stone's visit had caused. Certainly, there were worse people to have for company. And the evening passed pleasantly enough, with Stone telling the children stories after dinner, then he and Ruth sitting up to share their own stories far later than she had stayed up for several years, while wind magnified its whine through cracks in the cabin's walls and windowpanes.

She learned Stone was originally from Chicago and the son of a minor industrialist, that he had become fascinated with archaeology on visits he made to the West to stay summers with an uncle in Arizona. He had spent those summers searching around old Indian ruins, trying to put together their history. When he was sent to the East to finish his education—presumably to enter into the business world—Stone said his reading and coursework drifted away from the prescribed direction, much to the chagrin of his prosperous father, though his growing passion for archaeology was secretly encouraged by his mother. There had been a break with his father when he had been offered and accepted a position at the University of California, though Stone said fences were pieced back together somewhat a few years later, and they were on civil terms again. It had been a treaty greatly facilitated by the mother.

Ruth was content to listen as Stone embellished his tale, feeling increasingly familiar with the characters he drew of his parents and of the renegade uncle in the West. The family dynamics he described were completely alien to her experience, and she found herself unable to imagine what it would be like to have such a commanding father to reckon with, but especially what it would be like to have a mother who supported dreams and desires, rather than trying to thwart them at every opportunity. Ruth tried to explain this to Stone, but sketched out only the briefest of outlines of Cally's life, and the rivalry with her sister over Ruth's late father. She left out the sordid details of Cally's infamous reputation in El Paso, told instead of her mother's persistent requests for Ruth to return to El Paso, mentioned that Cally had recently gone to live in Boulder City. She didn't mention the loan she had given her to do so.

Ruth evaded as long as she could any mention of Jim's murder and her rape here at Glory Springs. Stone did not pry after facts—indeed seemed to know them without her telling—but was more interested in the effect the terrible events had on her. She was not accustomed to such probing, gentle as it might have been, and skirted around the more profound areas, places she had not explored herself. Eventually she found herself telling him how her commitment to Glory Springs had been deepened by all that had happened. She had given herself over to it completely, she told him, after Jim's death. The place was the core of her life, she explained; she was married to it now, though the marriage certainly had its faults.

The freedom she had sought here had thinned out, she told him, the way she heard romance did when confronted with the ordinariness of daily married life. And sometimes she found herself discontent, having forgotten her own reasons for living in the wild in the first place. She couldn't seem to help herself: content beyond imagining one day, restless and dissatisfied the next. Even as she explained these things, Ruth found herself comforted by the act of putting them into words, as if that arrested her turbulence, made it easier to tame and control.

"It's no wonder you get restless, Ruth, way up here by yourself. Responsible for two small children," he said, when she paused. "That doesn't seem strange at all."

"Well, you spend time alone yourself, out at those digs," she said, defending her assessment. "I don't hear you complaining."

"Men are different," he told her. "Besides, I do get restless once in a while. Then I go on into town for company. That usually takes care of it."

Ruth hadn't heard much beyond his first statement. "So you're saying women are different—that they get restless more easily?" She tried to quiet the heightened volume of her voice so she wouldn't wake the children. "Men are more easily content?"

"I meant different in the complaining of it, Ruth. You said that you didn't hear me complaining, so . . ."

"Then you're saying women complain and men don't? Men are the tough ones?"

"I'm not saying that, exactly. You always think the worst of anything I say, it seems. But, yes, I think maybe women get to complain more. We're taught not to, that's all. It's certainly not because we're tougher."

"So your own mother complained a lot?"

"No. She didn't complain at all. My father did all of the complaining in the family, and he complained about everything." He gave a sudden show of white teeth and stopped speaking, scratched his head. "I guess you win, Ruth. I just disproved my own theory."

"I've never much liked the idea of roles laid out for people, for men or for women. I don't see why people can't just be themselves, be the way they are. That's what I set out to do when I came here." Ruth looked over at the bed where Maddie lay sleeping beside her brother. "Then things happened I hadn't counted on," she said.

"That seems like sophomoric reasoning to me," Stone said, gently. "Did you ever consider that maybe there is no real freedom, Ruth? Maybe no one is free to be only who they are. Maybe who we become only happens in part because of others around us, beginning with our families. Because of the things that happen to us. Like injuring your leg, for instance." His smile was gone now and his face wore a somber look. "Things like what happened to you before," he said. "Surely you must have changed because of it."

Ruth felt a welling up at his words. She swallowed it back and took in a breath. "A person can't let such things win," she said. "Even something like injuring a leg." She caressed her thigh with one hand. "It hurts, but I have to go on the same as before. Like I did after . . ." She looked away from him then. "Only some things can't ever be the same."

Stone leaned forward and lifted her hand from her thigh, held it between both of his own. She glanced back to find liquid glazing his eyes. Ruth felt the force of his probing gaze, felt it break through to touch something she held inviolate inside her. She wrenched her eyes away and closed them tight.

For a moment she wondered if this was real, this man here holding her hand while snow scattered icy crystals against the windowpane. The ache inside her was real enough, but the man in her cabin seemed entirely out of place and time. Maybe she was really asleep and would wake to find that the last five painful years had never been. But the firmness of Stone's grip anchored her, and she opened her eyes and found the present real again.

Tears spilled over as she looked back at him. "Did you come here to dig for artifacts in the ruins, Mr. Stone?"

"I don't see any ruins, Ruth. I see someone beautiful and strong, but stubborn beyond reason. Someone who could use some help but won't admit it."

"What is any of this to you? What makes you come way up here through this kind of weather? I can't understand it at all."

"I can't either, to tell the truth. Who's to say why we care about what we care about." He looked away, his face coloring slightly, a half smile threatening his lips. "I just had to see if you were okay. Maybe I just had to see you. All I know is I couldn't get you off my mind."

"You weren't on mine at all. Well, not much anyway. I've just been trying to hobble through this winter." She pulled her hand away and grabbed for her inside crutch. "We better get some sleep," she said, steadying herself on her good leg. "You have a long way to go in the morning."

Not that she could sleep for a very long time. She lay awake, acutely aware of the stranger on a bedroll next to her stove, which he had banked well for the night. She was aware also that he was as awake as she was. She heard no sounds of snoring, nor even the deep breathing of sleep emanating from his direction.

Ruth assessed and reassessed her impression of this man. He could be a well-meaning boob, who frustrated her with his own set of stubborn but insensitive actions. Yet she had appreciated him going out in the storm to do his business, so she could use the slop jar before climbing into bed. Tonight he seemed more substantial than ever, and that unsettled her. He was harder to dismiss, and she lay thinking over what had been said between them and what hadn't. Gradually, drowsiness found her, and her last thoughts were that in the clear light of day, everything—her little cabin, and this man who had intruded—would return to the ordinariness of before.

CHAPTER TWENTY

In her dream she was kneeling in warm sun, grinding something on a *na'dai*. A group of Indians surrounded her, and she was one of them. Like the other women, she was wearing nothing more than the grass skirt John Olsen had described to her. Jim was there too, over by the *kit'catact,* standing with Thomas and some other men. The scene was saturated with such warmth and happiness that Ruth fought hard against the other reality threatening to break through. For some time, she had been vaguely aware of voices and laughter, of small children and an occasional adult, though the sounds blended nicely into the scene of her dream. It was only when they were joined by other sounds, sounds familiar to life in her cabin—the scraping of iron burners on her stove and the metallic clank of pots being moved—that she roused herself from the world her mind had made.

She opened her eyes and looked around. Outside the window, fat white flakes fell steadily between the row of long icicles hanging from the eave. J.B. and Maddie stood on a chair by the stove beside David Stone, who flipped a pancake in the air, then another, eliciting bursts of delighted laughter. The smell of coffee mixed with the sweet fragrance of browning pancakes.

It shocked her to find that so much had gone on in her cabin without her awareness. Usually, she was up making coffee and heating the cabin before the children woke. This morning, the room was already comfortable, even with what looked to be a blizzard out the window.

"Good morning," Stone said, when he saw her struggling to sit up, using the heels of her hands to pull herself upright without paining her leg. "Coffee's ready."

"So I smell. And more." She watched him shuffle pancakes onto a small plate in front of each child. They were plates she had fashioned by hand last summer and fired in the campfire along with the ollas. Their surfaces had turned out to be a bit rough and bumpy, but she liked using them anyway.

She scooted her legs around to the edge of the bed and rubbed sleep from her eyes. With Stone in the room, how would she ever manage to use the slop jar—which she had to do in the worst way? Before she could decide what to do, he walked over with a cup of coffee. "I'm going out to feed the horses," he said, getting into his coat. "I'll get the chickens and goats while I'm out there."

"Not the wet nanny," Ruth said. "She has to be fed while I milk her. Otherwise she won't stay still."

"I'll milk her, then." He returned for the pail under the table. "Just have your coffee. I can do it, Ruth. I'll fix you some pancakes when I come back in." He was out the door before she could protest.

Fix her pancakes, indeed. Though she was annoyed at his presumption, Ruth was grateful he gave her privacy. What more harm could he do out there than lose the morning's milk—should he happen to get any out of the goat? Even Ruth sometimes had to tie a loop around the nanny's back legs so she couldn't kick the bucket. Most likely Stone would come in with an empty bucket, and Ruth would have to do the job. Meanwhile, she had her cabin back for a while.

After she'd taken care of her bladder and dressed herself for the day, Ruth crutched her way over to the children at the table next to the stove. J.B. was licking the maple syrup from his empty plate as if it were the greatest treat in the world, though Maddie had scraped all remnants of the sweet goo from her pancakes before eating them. The girl had never been one for sweets, other than roast agave and cactus apples and occasionally tomato jam.

"I like him," Maddie announced.

"Me too," J.B. put his plate aside long enough to say.

Ruth ignored them and poured out two small glasses of last night's goat's milk, set one in front of each child. "Shall I fix you more pancakes?" she asked, leaning over to get a better view of the snow out the window. The final few inches of the Model A's roof had been buried. It appeared that almost a foot more had fallen during the night, and it was coming down fast now. What if Stone couldn't leave after all?

"I want him to cook them," Maddie said.

"David is feeding the animals." Ruth pushed the hot coffeepot back onto a burner and dumped in more grounds, stirring them in thoroughly. She hoped his pancakes were better than his cowboy coffee, which was as weak as ladies' tea—and about the color of fresh morning urine. After testing the griddle with spit, she spooned on several small pools of batter and stood watching them sizzle around the edges, her stomach rumbling at the smell of browning batter.

She slid another pancake onto each child's plate and started a stack at the back of the burner for herself and Stone. Meanwhile, J.B. was slathering on enough butter for three pancakes from one of the lumps David had brought up. She reached over and wiped off half of it with a knife, before the boy poured on the maple syrup—also furnished from Stone's saddlebags. They had been out of butter for some time, and Ruth wanted the two lumps to last a while.

Maddie hadn't touched the new pancake Ruth made, and sat looking at it with her arms folded. "*He* made faces on them," she said, jutting out her chin. "These are ugly ones."

Ruth shrugged and turned her face away, feeling heat rise to her cheeks. She took in a deep breath to bring herself under control. "Suit yourself. Too bad, though," she said, pulling from the shelf the last jar of beavertail cactus jam she and Kate had put up last summer, a not-too-sweet treat that even Maddie loved. "I thought you might like to put this on it." She spooned more batter onto the griddle, wondering why she needed to win this one enough to sacrifice that treat. It was almost a relief to hear Stone kicking snow from his boots against the wooden doorjamb outside.

"Smells like this would draw anyone in out of the storm," he said, swinging the door open. A gust brushed a sheet of flakes in behind him before he closed the door again. He set the pail down by the door, leaned over to untie his boots and step out of them.

When he carried the pail to the table, Ruth was surprised to see it half filled with foaming milk, about the amount she would have brought in herself. "Took a while to get the hang of it," he said, with more than a tad of triumph in his tone. His smile revealed teeth that nearly matched the flakes he brushed from his shoulders.

"You can grab us down some plates. I'll have these ready in a minute." She checked to see it if the grounds had settled, then poured each of them a cup of coffee, taking a quick sip of her own to make sure her doctoring had improved the brew. This time it was at least drinkable.

When she spatulaed the pancakes onto their plates and sat at the table, she found Stone with his face scrunched up, coffee cup still in one hand.

"Whew! Guess I made this a mite too strong." He actually shuddered after swallowing.

Ruth shook her head, laughing to herself as she reached for the butter. She didn't feel like explaining, though for a moment she was afraid Maddie might tell him about the added grounds. She silenced the girl with a look, noticing that Maddie had resolved their pancake standoff for herself by creating a face of her own on the pancake out of the cactus jam. "Don't concern yourself. I like it strong," Ruth said, carrying the first bite of pancake to her mouth. "Try adding some milk to weaken it if you like." She nodded toward the jar of strained milk.

"Good idea, but not that goat's milk." He made a face. "I prefer the dry milk I brought up for the pancakes."

"Suit yourself. It worked well enough in the pancakes. They're very good."

He rewarded her with another flash of teeth. "That's the first nice thing you've said about me. You can be a hard woman to please."

"Maybe I don't want to be pleased," she said, her voice edging toward bitterness. "Maybe I just want to be left alone."

For a few minutes they ate without speaking, though J.B. and Maddie kept up enough conversation with Stone that their silence didn't become awkward. When they'd finished, Ruth refilled the coffee cups—enjoying the near horror on Stone's face at the thought of having to drink another cup of it, though he let her pour. The children went off to occupy themselves with building blocks.

"You know I can't very well go off to leave you alone until this storm abates," Stone said glumly. "And even when it stops, the going will be rough with all the additional snow." He heaped powdered milk into his cup. "I'll stop trying to please you till then."

The hurt in his voice made Ruth both ashamed and angry. She wanted to take his hand and tell him she was sorry—and at the same time to sock him so hard he'd fall off his chair, the thought of which made her laugh out loud. He looked over at the sound, his expression becoming more hopeful.

"It looks like we're stuck with each other for now, then," Ruth said, in a sudden burst of humor. "The hard woman and the nice man who rode through miles of deep snow to please her."

It amazed her to see Stone's face completely conquered by her smile. How easily she made this man happy, almost as easily as he irritated her.

"I know you've had a hard time of it, Ruth." He put his hand over hers. "I just want to make things a little easier for you. But for some reason you don't want to let me."

She felt the contact, extracted her hand. "Why should you want to?"

"You asked me that before. You're so damned stubborn. If I had any sense I wouldn't even bother trying." He started to take her hand again, but stopped. "But you chase all sense from a man, Ruth. Look how I came all the way up here in this snow. And I never even rode a horse before."

"Never? Not even a little? It's a wonder you made it," she laughed.

"Hudson had me practice around his place the night before. Showed me how to take command of the animal." He swiped a hand though the dark curl of his hair. "I hadn't milked a goat before this morning, either, remember. I'm a quick study, it seems.

"As a matter of fact, I never chased a woman before—they always chased me. Mostly I concentrate on my work. But I never met anyone like you, Ruth. No one anywhere near it." He stopped and glanced at her. "I don't suppose you want to hear any of this."

"What about your friend Clara Gooden? She's the one who sent you up here in the first place." The words rushed out before she could stop them. She bit down on her lip in shock.

Stone blushed deeply. "You *are* full of surprises, aren't you, Ruth? How in the world could you know about Clara? You said you hadn't heard of her." He took in a breath and shook his head.

"Clara was a classmate at UCLA. We share many of the same interests and I—we—I—" He stopped struggling for words and focused on her. "It's you that interests me now. All I can think about, it seems."

"Seems to me you'd be better off with Clara Gooden, or someone like her." Ruth swallowed the last of her coffee and reached for her crutch. "The two of us don't have much in common." She stood and began her clumsy journey across the room.

"Please let me look at your leg, Ruth."

She stopped, looked back at him askance. "Now you are getting forward."

"You know I don't mean it like that." He got up to follow her.

She positioned herself at the edge of her bed. "You do know I've had nurses' training in El Paso?"

"No. I didn't know. But you still can't possibly see that knee the way I'll be able to close up. You can't even bend it." He kneeled beside the bed.

"It is getting better every day, you know. That has to be a good sign."

"Things can heal wrong as well as right. I had a grandfather whose arm healed at an angle. He could hardly use it the rest of his life. All because he was too stubborn to see a doctor."

"So what if you *do* find my leg is healing crooked? How would I get to a doctor? It's better to just let it be. What good would the knowing be to me?"

"Knowing is always better than not knowing. At least that's what I believe. Please, Ruth, be sensible." He stopped speaking and simply looked at her, one hand on her bed as he remained on his knees in front of her.

For a moment, looking at the man on his knees beside her bed, something in her did want to know. She sighed and eased back onto her pillow, pulling up her skirt on that side to mid-thigh.

"I'll have to take your splint off to see," he said, starting to untie the strips of sheet holding on the wooden slats.

It was more than she could do to remain prone and let someone do for her. She had to get onto her elbows to watch. But watching was a mistake—and in a way she had not expected. She felt her body respond to the sight of this man now sliding his fingers gently along the skin of her knee, his touch sending shivers through her. Ruth looked quickly away, but that didn't stop the heat she felt when his fingers traveled to the skin just above her knee where her thigh began.

"I don't see anything too much amiss here," he said, touching her tenderly, his voice innocent of her arousal. "Except for this hot knot all around your knee. I don't like the way that looks at all, but there's no way to tell what's happened in there. I'm afraid to have you try and bend it."

She looked over to tell him "I told you so," but when he saw her flushed face, his expression changed. All she could do was draw in a breath and hold it until they could pull their eyes away. He reached over and wrestled her dress back down.

"I'm sorry, Ruth," he said after a few moments.

"It's not your fault," she said. She thought she saw him suppress a smile at her admission—which irritated her, and she clung desperately to that patch of irritation, as if it might save her.

He looked at her, then, his clear eyes breaking through the cloud of desire enveloping them. "I think I can construct a more comfortable splint than what you've got here," he said, his voice ringing with a determined sincerity that overrode what had happened. Ruth appreciated his effort.

"I think I'll just wrap it back the way it was," she said. "At least for the time being." She reached for a chair slat, but he put a hand over hers to stop her.

"Fine. Put them back yourself, but I want to cover each slat with cloth wrap before you do. That way you'll be a little more comfortable," he told her.

She allowed it and later found that movement was indeed less painful for her without hard wood pressing into her already sore knee. Stone had been right a little too often for her to dismiss him as easily as before. The world where Stone's role was that of a well-meaning fool had not returned as she had hoped it might last night. Instead, she had shocked herself with her own behavior. How starved for touch she must be to betray this place she loved with lust for an outsider.

His helpfulness continued to irritate her throughout the day, starting with the way he went straight to doing dishes—with both children helping him—while Ruth remained helpless, rewrapping her leg. He was even smart enough to be as sparing with dishwater as she was, and he and the children heaped the #8 tub with fresh snow afterward. It annoyed her also when she made a trip to the outhouse, to find he had already shoveled out the path. Certainly, it made her trip out there easier, especially carrying the slop pail, but she didn't trust the easiness. It was something that would have to be paid for, she was sure. And the idea of being dependent on this man was more than she could rest easy with.

Ruth gritted her teeth and resolved to get through the day—or days—until he could leave. So what if he helped out until then? And her response to his touch meant nothing, except that she was deprived. And so the day went by pleasantly enough, Stone building block structures with J.B. after lunch, and letting Maddie show him her collection of dried plants. Then he read to them and put them down for their nap. Ruth tried to read as much as she could during all this, but the situation seemed so unnatural that she couldn't concentrate.

When the children were asleep, he and Ruth shared coffee and conversation. He talked more of his work and how he recorded it in his journals so he could eventually make it into a book when he finished the dig. He wanted to create a "big picture" of the way early human cultures had lived on this sparse land, he said. Ruth was struck again by the way he seemed to regard the abstract version—his drawings, descriptions and speculations—as more real than the materials he dug from the ground, and she was comforted enough by this perversion to find distance for herself again. She began to relax into his company.

The nights were harder, though, and the longer she lay awake each night, the angrier she became at the way her body was betraying her. It had betrayed her in the past, so this should not have come as a surprise. She almost wished for the pain in her leg to return and distract her body from its need for pleasure. Stone lay awake, too, as she could tell from his tossing about. She could not sleep until his tossing stopped, and then she was as likely to encounter him in a dream as not. Sometimes she would be running her hands over the muscles of a male upper torso, shirtless and tanned the way she had seen him by the road last summer, enticing him to touch her. In one dream she was lying with Jim, but when he entered her, she looked up to find it was Stone, which woke her at once. She lay in the dark for a long while, warring with her desires.

It was with much relief four days later that she heard him tell the children he would be leaving the next morning. "The last few days have been wonderful. They've meant a lot to me," he said later when Maddie and J.B. were asleep, and Ruth sat with him over coffee by the fire. "Being up here with you. I hope I've been a help to you as well."

"Of course you have," she said. "I only hope you haven't spoiled me for what needs to be done. It was hard to be done for so much."

Stone smiled. "I'm surprised you didn't ask me to leave days ago. As soon as the snow stopped, and the sun came back out. Just kicked me out the door into six-foot drifts."

Ruth looked away. "I was surprised you didn't leave earlier on your own. After all, you have a life to get back to, your work and all."

"You should get out to see a doctor as soon as the snow melts some, Ruth. Maybe I could get the WPA grader. Hudson's been . . ."

"You've done enough. More than enough."

"More than you wanted, you mean."

Ruth looked back to see that smile again. "I didn't say that. But I couldn't accept a smidgeon more from you, David Stone. Stop now and we'll be all right."

"You said 'we.'" He picked up her hand.

She laughed, took back her hand but continued to look at him. "We can be friends, David. Beyond that I don't know."

"Certainly you know. How can you say that after . . . after what . . ."

"A burst of lust means nothing at all."

"Is that all it was for you, lust, then? I don't believe you. And I sure didn't ride ten hours in a snowstorm out of lust, Ruth." His face reddened and he clenched a fist, started to bring it down on the tabletop, then stopped.

"Damn it to hell, Ruth." He leaned toward her and took hold of her shoulders. "Look at me, will you? You make me feel like such a fool sometimes. But you're the real fool, hoarding yourself away up here like some kind of hermit, even with someone falling all over himself to show his—"

"Don't say any more, David. And take your hands off me, before I knock your block off. No one's talking about love here—not even you, Mr. Noble. Not that I—" She closed her eyes so he wouldn't see the tears starting to form.

"Maybe you should see a doctor for your ears as well as your leg, then," he said, gripping her shoulders even tighter.

"I said let go of me," she hissed, her tears already sucked away into her own firestorm.

"No, damn it. Not until you hear me."

Staring daggers into his eyes, Ruth brought up a fist and sunk it into his belly before he realized what she was up to. For a moment she thought he would double over and release her, but he caught himself and stood up, pulling her up with him to her feet.

It all happened so fast, him looking at her with such undisguised longing that it shucked off the anger she had carefully cultivated. Then he was kissing her and she could no more resist her own passion than she could will herself to stop breathing in large gasps of air. Somehow, they were on the bed—he must have carried her—then he was gone again and the lantern was out and he was back unbuttoning her, then they were *both* tearing away the reluctant buttons. She worked her hands under his shirt and ran her fingers over the skin she had dreamed of, then unbuckled him and took hold of the prize she wanted so badly.

He was kissing her breasts and moving his lips down slowly over her belly. His fingers had already found the inside of her. She tried to move him over and into her, but he held back. "No. I'll hurt your leg," he whispered.

"I don't care," she said, sliding her palm over her damp prize and using her other arm to move his buttocks toward her. "I don't care. I want you inside me." And she didn't care, at the moment, if it split her in two with pain. She had gone this far, nothing would stop her now. She would force it, if she had to. They would get this over with for good, she reasoned wildly, this inappropriate attraction between them.

"I care," he said, thrusting himself into her palm, but not her body. "I care," his fingers reaching deep enough inside to arch her back. She opened wider to his fingers and cupped her hand as he thrust against her again and again, all the while kissing her neck and breasts. "I love you, Ruth. I love you," he kept murmuring into her flesh.

Reason deserted her. If this were to be her last act, she would not regret it, she thought, releasing an explosion of pleasure within her. Then Stone's moans joined her own, and they both had to drown their chorus in pillows so as to not wake the children.

But of course it was not her last act, and she spent another sleepless night lying awake with the aftermath, the alien sleeping unaware at her side, while she strained to find some comfortable position. What had she gotten herself into, she wondered? She hadn't meant to incite a profession of love, nor to give over control of her body to him. Thank god he had not pushed himself inside her as she had demanded. Where had her good sense gone? Could she ever trust herself again? She worried herself wide awake until nearly dawn. What if he didn't leave now, after all? Worse yet, what if he did go and she began to miss him?

When morning came, she was pleased to see him making preparation to leave as planned, and even more pleased that she wanted him to. She went about the milking and breakfast making as if her routine had never changed, though she noticed him watching her, as if to reassure himself she could still do these things. It wasn't until he had saddled up and come back in to hug the children that he finally put his arms around her and looked into her face.

"Take care of yourself, Ruth," he said. "You don't know how hard it is for me to leave. I'll miss you." Light reflected from tiny tears at the corners of his eyes.

"Same to you. You're the one riding out through several feet of snow, David." She could hardly bear the tenderness of his smile.

"Don't worry about me. I'll be back," he said, pulling away. Then he was out the door, crunching through snow.

Ruth stood with Maddie and J.B. just outside the door as he

climbed aboard the bay and rode off, the children calling after him as the horse went lunging through the snow, Juniper Blue whinnying after the bay.

The drifts were more than belly deep on the horse, despite the sun and warmth of the last three days, and her concern for him mingled with gladness at having her place back again. Ruth looked forward to the challenge of handling the chores alone once more. She did not think she would miss him much.

CHAPTER TWENTY-ONE

Ruth drew in deep breaths of fragrant air. Each one seemed to lift her higher from the ground she stood on. The luscious scent left by the brief morning thundershower made her want to nibble at the land around her, to take whole bites out of nearby rocks and shrubs. How glad she was to be back in Black Canyon again. She loved the place almost as much as her own canyon now. What a relief it had been to find the road rebuilt and the camp intact after last fall's flood, to find her friends back again, the *ki'takiis* and the *kit'catact* made anew for the summer.

She'd had to fight David to come here. He was still trying to control her with his protection, so much so that at times she regretted letting him into her life. She had tried to resist his efforts when he showed up with Hudson and the big WPA road grader, two weeks after riding off in the snowstorm. But she hadn't prevailed. He'd been determined to rescue her—when she no more wanted to be rescued than to set fire to her cabin. Yet somehow he persuaded her to leave so she could see a doctor for her leg, and she packed up a few things and got into the Model A—J.B. and Maddie in the front and four hens stuffed into a crate in the rumble seat, and let the grader inch them down the snowpacked road by rope. The goats had to be tied to the back bumper, but Juniper Blue followed after of his own accord. Then she and the children spent a miserable two weeks in the Hudsons' tiny spare room. She lost both goats and two of the chickens there to coyotes and had to replace them—the Hudsons not being set up for animals the way the Swedes were. If only Kate and John had not been gone.

And after all that, the doctor in San Bernardino said there was nothing he could do for her leg short of surgery to rebreak the bone and sew back some ligaments—and even that might not improve things after so much time had passed.

As soon as the snows had melted in the spring, she had wanted to drive over and see if her Indian friends had returned, but she'd had to wait until her injured leg healed enough for her to get around, albeit with a considerable limp. At least she no longer had to support herself with a makeshift crutch or the walking stick she had used after that. Walking still pained her knee, but she was determined not to let mere pain get in her way. She had faith that in time that too would be gone, and she would be as before.

As soon as Grandmother Siki spotted Ruth hobbling over from the Model A, doing the best she could to diminish her limp, the old woman had called to Brenda to gather a few yerba mansa leaves. Siki and Martha had wrapped and bound the large, soft leaves around Ruth's knee. Almost immediately, Ruth felt improved. By afternoon, she found she could bear enough weight on her knee to kneel in front of a *na'dai* herself and pound mesquite pods to flour like the other women who worked in the shade of the ramada.

A few of the girls worked along with the women. Usually Maddie would have been there, but today she was helping the old woman. Maddie followed Grandmother Siki in much the way she had once followed Kate, imitating her ways. With Kate, Maddie had watched and learned better than Ruth how to make pastry crusts thin and crisp. From Grandmother Siki, Maddie had first learned how to grind and prepare the different flours to sunbake into breads. Now she seemed more interested in the medicines the old woman concocted from different plants, and she stuck close by her side, like today, watching Siki crush the dry red root of deer brush. They also had something simmering in an olla hanging above the fire. Every so often the old woman would nod in that direction, and Maddie would get up and stir whatever they had there. Although the two of them spoke occasionally, much of their communication went on without words.

At first Ruth couldn't help but resent the way the old woman had adopted this strange child, teaching her things that even some Yuiatei didn't know. She had wanted to get up and snatch Maddie back to her. What right had she to know these Indian ways? Twice Ruth came close to clarifying the girl's lineage to her for once and for all. But gradually she had gotten used to Maddie's role with the Yuiatei, as unfair as it was to J.B. And he certainly didn't seem much interested in learning about plants of any sort.

Both he and Maddie had more command of the language than Ruth did, though she had to admit that Maddie had more than J.B. Still, both of them seemed to understand what was said before Martha translated, while Ruth could only get the gist of things and needed help with the details.

Ruth's knee was already aching by the time Martha came over and squatted beside her with a bowl of acorns. With a section of broom plant, she brushed the flour into her bowl and relinquished the grinding stone Martha had let her use.

"Tomorrow we do the *jaa'ii*," Martha explained. Ruth was trying to remember what the *jaa'ii* might be when Martha said, "The cactus fruit, Dlah'da," as if she read Ruth's thoughts.

"Prickly pear," Ruth said, remembering the fat red cactus fruit growing around the camp. She'd eaten the dried strips and many foods flavored with the juice or pulp at ceremonies, but had never been in on the preparations. She and Kate had made jam from the beavertail cactus fruit, but Ruth was especially interested in learning the ways the Indians prepared their cactus for preservation, ways they used before glass jars with airtight lids were available. It seemed like valuable knowledge to have on hand.

Martha tossed handfuls of the dried halves of shelled acorns into the depression and came down on them with her *a'dai*. Ruth sat admiring the rhythm of her crush-and-grind motion as Martha swept her arms down and out, the acorns crumbling under the smooth rock she wielded. Ruth's own motions felt awkward in comparison, but got the job done eventually. Martha had been quiet today, and Ruth saw that her eyes were puffy and red-rimmed. She thought it had something to do with whatever Grandmother Siki had said to her earlier by the *ki'takii*, but was afraid to ask about it.

Ruth gathered up more acorns and set them next to the *na'dai* for Martha to grind. The acorns were much larger than those of the scrub oak and came from the tall oaks high up on the mountains. Even these needed to be soaked and dried before grinding, and the coarse flour made from them had to be rinsed several times as well, which could be tricky. Still, there was always a residue of bitterness that Ruth found unpleasant. She greatly preferred the sweet mesquite flour.

Ruth was glad that wild food preparation was being taken so seriously this year. It was an opportunity to learn more, though the scarcity that caused it made her sad. In recent years only enough was prepared for the ceremonies. Usually only a few people, like Grandmother Siki, would use it when they went to the lower desert for the winter. Martha said most of the others bought food from stores while they lived down in the desert valley to work at their jobs. But so many jobs had disappeared with the Depression, at least the better ones. She said even the picking jobs were being taken by truckloads of people coming in from other states, and others coming up from Mexico. Ruth knew that many of the Yuiatei had taken to selling their beadwork and baskets beside the highway into Palm Springs.

"It's getting so hard," Martha had told her, shaking her head. "But maybe it's a good thing in a way. People will remember how the old foods can get them through."

Ruth saw other signs of the hard times that Martha didn't mention, smelled it in the odor of alcohol that often wafted through camp, especially when groups of men gathered behind the dwellings. Earlier, Ruth had heard men yelling out there. She thought she recognized one of the voices as belonging to Martha's husband, Jackson. Later Ruth saw him stagger out and fall asleep under a creosote bush. Maybe that was what Martha and Grandmother Siki had been talking about.

While people were settling around the evening campfire in early twilight, Ruth was startled to see Thomas and three other men walk into camp carrying rattles and bull-roarers, the skin of their chests and backs covered with painted designs. Martha was in her house tending to her daughter's sick baby, so Ruth remained puzzled until Thomas and the others came back out of the *kit'catact* dressed in everyday clothes. Even then she felt shy about asking directly—pure curiosity was not seen as a reason to probe into Yuiatei practices—so Ruth had learned ways to discover whether probing was appropriate. And Thomas was both friend and *cafika,* but she never knew for sure which one she was talking to.

"When I didn't see you," she told him, "I wondered if you and the others were still down in the desert picking." He had taken the rock next to her that Martha had vacated, and Ruth had waited until he was halfway through his plate of food before she spoke.

"We finished last week. There'll be nothing more until the dates in the fall." He did not turn his head to look at her when he spoke. This seemed a clear sign she was not to ask more, so she was surprised when a few minutes later he told her, "We were putting out marks so the bear will know we are her friends. We keep finding her tracks around the camp."

"Even with all of you here? That seems strange." Ruth knew the black bears had come into her camp only when she was gone.

"Grandmother says she is an angry bear. In trouble. The men up there"—Thomas nodded toward the mountains behind San Bernardino—"keep hunting her. Grandmother thinks the bear comes to us for help. She says this is the last bear."

"But there are lots of bears. I've seen them in Rattlesnake Canyon many times and . . ."

"Not this kind of bear, Dlah'da. This isn't a black bear."

"But it must be. The last grizzly was killed near Big Bear the year I homesteaded, 1929. At the logging camp. I saw pictures. He was a giant."

"Maybe this was his mate. Maybe they didn't know about her. But somebody up there saw her tracks, I guess. It's hard to hide when you're as big as she is. That's why Grandmother wants to make her an unseen one." He took a cautious drink from his tin coffee cup, and Ruth wondered if she could make her friends cups from clay, cups that wouldn't burn a lip when the coffee was hot. "At least invisible when it comes to Teske," he said.

Ruth winced. "We Peeled Ones. But you haven't actually seen the bear yourselves. How do you know it's not just a huge black bear?"

Thomas laughed. "How about I show you the tracks in the morning. Then you'll understand."

After everyone had bedded, Ruth stared up at the maze of stars for a very long time. With no moon, they were exceptionally bright. She remembered that there were bears up there somewhere, Ursa Major and Minor. She had heard of them, but could never untangle them from the rest. With so many pinpoints of light, how was she to separate one figure from the others? She knew bears were somehow part of the dippers—which for some reason she could pick out easily. The bears, however, remained a part of the bigger mystery above her.

In the morning, Thomas took her to see the tracks just behind the camp. After that, Ruth had little doubt that they belonged to a grizzly. The prints were nearly twice the size of the largest bear track she'd ever seen, the steps farther apart and set much deeper into the ground from the weight of the animal. When she wandered out to join the others picking prickly pear fruit, the amazement was still strong in her. The idea of coming upon a creature of that size as she went about her life in Glory Springs sent a chill down her back.

Since others were using clumps of broom plant to clear spines from the cactus fruit before picking them, Ruth broke off a cluster of the plant for herself. She knew she was supposed to thank the plant, but she still felt silly doing it. She managed to utter thanks in Yuiatei, which she thought more appropriate for the occasion anyway—and it didn't make her feel quite as foolish.

Although she'd brushed most of the spines away, by the time they brought the fruit back to camp to prepare, Ruth's fingers were dotted with the nearly invisible hairlike bristles that cushioned the bigger, easily seen spines. But the tiny ones buried themselves under her skin in small reddened patches that stung whenever she touched anything at all. They were nearly impossible to remove, even with her teeth.

Grandmother Siki looked up and laughed when she saw Ruth doing it, said something in Yuiatei, then went back to using the sharp edge of a stone to peel the rind off the fruit. The others used knives.

"Wait, Dlah'da. We'll put mud on them after we get them peeled," Martha said. "Grandmother said it only makes them worse to try it now."

Fuchsia-colored juice ran between her fingers and down her arms as she worked through the afternoon under the ramada, peeling, then splitting open each fruit to remove the seeds, plopping the seeds into one of Martha's buckets, the pulp into another. Maddie, like the other children, sampled the pulp, red juice streaking down from the corners of even redder lips. Ruth found the pulp edible but a bit bland for her taste. It made sense later when she saw the way strips of the fruit were dipped in honey water before they were dried like jerky. Other pulp she saw was mashed for fermenting, and the rest mixed with gobs of sweet baked agave, various seeds and coarse meal to be preserved in flat cakes. Throughout the afternoon, Ruth kept trying to store all she was learning in the larder of her mind.

They were just finishing the last bucket of fruit when the sound of a commotion came from behind the settlement, where the older boys had gone to make rabbit sticks. A minute later, the boys came running and shouting into the area where the women were working.

Grandmother Siki maneuvered faster than Ruth had ever seen her move. Thomas caught up to the old woman as she bustled out toward the edge of camp. Then Ruth saw the creature they were approaching, and her insides squirmed. The huge bear raised up and bellowed, and she thought her heart might melt into hot liquid. Yet Grandmother Siki and Thomas continued their resolute march toward the animal. Without hesitation or reflection, Ruth rose with the others and started out in the same direction. They moved together, the whole of them, as if they were one and the same person, stopping only when they came up behind Grandmother Siki and Thomas. The old woman began speaking in low tones to the bear, who had come down on all fours again and stood watching her.

The rank scent of absolute wild wafted past, as Ruth gaped at the sublimity before her. Its small, dark eyes held something ancient and unutterable, something that made her want to drop to her knees in worship—and at the same time, turn and run from it as fast as she could. This was a far different bear than the black one she'd found in her camp, with its soft and glossy coat. Breeze refused to riffle this creature's coarse fur, the stippled bristles standing staunch against the elements, retaining an integrity that rightly belonged to a scouring brush. Confronted with something entirely beyond her experience, Ruth felt herself turn to quaking jelly inside.

What she saw before her was something she'd sensed the day she first set foot on Glory Springs, on small rocks rising—as if this enormous bear epitomized the wildness that civilization had been built to conceal. Her civilization, that is. The people of Black Canyon were conferring with the bear, Grandmother Siki talking to it as if she were an ambassador negotiating with another nation. Ruth felt her chest swell as she watched the way this fragile human community came to terms with this emissary of a wildness they still belonged to.

Thomas began to chant beside the old woman, gently rolling his gourd rattle in rhythm to his words. Occasionally he stopped to sprinkle pollen from his medicine bundle. Ruth's ears rang with the collective tension in the air. She wished she better understood the words Thomas and Grandmother were saying, so she could be as much a part of the ceremony as the rest. Ruth looked over at Martha for help, but her friend's eyes were intently focused on Grandmother and the bear. When she looked back, the bear was disappearing into the high chaparral. Soon all that remained of that magnificence was the thud of heavy feet lumbering through the brush.

PART III

CHAPTER TWENTY-TWO

Dust devils had been spiraling about all morning in Frontiertown, their whirling columns carrying loose weeds and debris high into the pale desert sky. That's what happened when people scraped away all the chaparral to make some silly town. Ruth had been watching the wind's mischief as she ground acorns in the cove of boulders at David's dig. It was hard not to look over, with all the bursts of fake gunfire blasting from the place every few minutes. After more than two years, she assumed they must finally be doing a movie shoot.

The so-called town had been completed by the end of last summer, but only now had she noticed much happening there. In early spring she and David had driven over to take a peek at what had been wrought, but left as soon as they saw that people actually occupied some of the wooden buildings that lined the wide dirt street slicing the pretend town in half. A large sign identified the road as Mane Street.

How corny could they get? Before they left, she caught a glimpse of signs proclaiming Livery Stable, General Store, Dirty Dog Saloon, and Land Claims Office. All were overly prominent, unlike signs that graced the streets of a real western town—if Juniper Valley were any example. There were more shops, but she couldn't register them all in the short time they were there. And each time she'd driven out to visit David at the digs since then, she'd seen trucks hauling in god-only-knew-what.

Ruth wet a finger and tapped it on the pile of acorn flour, brought it to her tongue to test the taste, which was still bitter with tannic acid. She would have to leach the flour thoroughly before it could be used in bread—or even to thicken stews and soups. She glanced over at where Maddie and J.B. were helping David dig for artifacts. Maddie had deserted the small pile of meal she'd made from catclaw pods last week. Ruth had never used catclaw pods before, although her friends in Black Canyon occasionally ground them into a coarse meal. She wet her finger again and leaned over to dip a finger in the small heap the girl had left in the depression. The taste was spicy and a bit bitter, nothing she wanted to include in bread making, the way she added some of the other wild flours—desert willow pods, chia, and mesquite being her favorites—but it might be used to flavor stews. For special-occasion breads she liked to throw in a bit of pinyon nut and sumach berry meal. Just the thought of such bread, chewy and wild-tasting, made her stomach rumble.

Ruth had planned to leave for her cabin first thing this morning, but the children had begged to stay at David's camp for another day, so she had compromised and agreed to stay until afternoon. Now that the sun beat down from directly overhead, it was time to gather up and get back home. Their visit was supposed to be a brief overnight after spending three days with their friends in Black Canyon, but J.B. became fascinated with the rock dwelling David was uncovering when they arrived. She didn't have the heart to squelch his excitement. After all, she'd left the goats and chickens free to peck and graze. She just hoped they had sense enough to get out of the way of predators. Juniper Blue usually did a good job of protecting them for her, and David told her all was well when he went up to feed early yesterday. She was still leaving the two new kids to nurse with the nannies, but would have to wean them soon if she wanted to have milk.

It had been easier for her to make her trips to Black Canyon before Kate and John left for Montana to work in the mines there. It wasn't their care of her animals she missed most, though; she missed stopping by for coffee and conversation, missed knowing they were there. It saddened her every time she drove past their place and found it deserted. And who knew when they would return?

She was determined not to let David seduce her into spending another night here. Besides wanting to get home, she was finding it hard lately to fully enjoy their times together when she wore the new device. It frustrated her to no end that she had to either plan ahead and put the diaphragm in before time, or stop and do it in the middle of things. David had been infinitely patient with her over it, and it didn't seem to dampen his appetite. She knew they'd been lucky that her herbal methods had worked for the last two years. Still, she found it odd that the same device that allowed safety in her pleasure also changed and detracted from the very experience itself.

As she expected, David and the children fought her efforts to return home, lining up solid against her will. She might have been persuaded to at least stay for lunch if they hadn't been so unified. Their determination served to increase her own tenfold, and a half hour later she had them in the car heading out, Maddie's and J.B.'s silent expressions screaming that they'd like to shoot her. David stood looking after them, his face making it clear that she'd wounded him.

She had to hold her ground, though. From the beginning, the three of them had pitted themselves against her—starting two winters ago. When David had shown up with Hudson and the WPA road grader, the two children began gathering up their things even as she'd argued with him. Now he'd enlisted them in his campaign to marry her—which he had been carrying on for the last two years as well. She held firm against it but sometimes wondered if it weren't their alliance that so determined her. Sometimes when she saw them working together, she had a urge to creep up and listen to what he might be telling them.

Ruth pulled up to the Rimrock road, but before she could turn onto it toward home, she had to wait for a fancy gold roadster traveling so fast over the dirt that it left a long, curling trail of dust. As she might have expected, the car was heading directly for Frontiertown. A woman leaned over and waved casually as the roadster passed. Then the woman's hand froze in motion, and her face took on the same shock of recognition Ruth herself felt.

For a moment, as the roadster was skidding to a halt and backing up toward her, Ruth couldn't recall the woman's name, though she remembered their meeting vividly. Not until Esther had unfolded her lanky frame from the car and came striding toward them did the name return to match the face. Ruth opened her door and stepped out before Esther reached the Model A.

"Oh my god, it *is* Ruth, George. I told you it was Ruth. And that adorable cricket child and her brother," she called back to him as she came.

The woman threw an arm around Ruth's back and hugged her. "Imagine running into you way out here. I was planning to make inquiries tomorrow as to just where your little cabin is situated. You never returned to us as you promised, you naughty thing." Bracelets jingling, she held Ruth out to examine her. "Just as lovely as I remember her, isn't she, George?" Esther announced to her brother as he walked up beside her.

"Indeed," the movie producer said. He reached for Ruth's hand and brought it to his lips in what seemed to be an act of ironic formality.

"George thought I might like to watch some of the first day's shoot. There's to be a small celebration afterward." Her face brightened, and she put a hand to her chest, where it came to rest on a mammoth silver necklace, cousin to the gold one she'd worn at the Cricket Club. "Oh, this is wonderful, just wonderful. You could come too, Ruth. Couldn't she, George?"

Ruth was just forming her refusal, searching for words more tactful than the truth of the matter—that she never wanted to set foot in that foolish movie town—when from inside the Model A came the definite sound of a cricket chirping.

Esther let out a burst of laughter. "Oh, my dear child," she said, reaching into the Model A, where Maddie had invaded the driver's seat. Esther lifted the girl off the seat and squeezed her to her chest, then set her back again. "How enormous you've gotten in just two years. Or is it three?"

"That's what children do, Esther. How are you, young man?"

George reached into the car and shook J.B.'s hand. "How would you like to see movies being made?"

"They've never seen a movie. I doubt they even have any idea what a movie is," Ruth said before the boy could respond. "Seeing one made wouldn't mean a thing to them. I've only seen three myself, and that was years ago in El Paso."

"Never seen a movie! We can't have that, can we?" He tweaked the boy's ear and turned to Ruth. "We have to fix that. Movies are the voice of the future calling out to us. It's especially important for young folks to be listening."

"I don't know that it's the future children should be listening to. Maybe they should hear what the past has to say first."

"Hear! Hear!" Esther laughed. "Brava, Ruth. Not that I agree, but it takes a valiant spirit to argue with my brother, especially when he's using his voice of authority."

"You never let up, do you, Esther? You've been after me since I uttered my first sentence."

"Actually, George, I was too young for such a thing at two years old."

"Hah. I don't believe that for a minute." He looked at Ruth. "So you would object to my treating the three of you to a movie in the Springs?"

"It's not their seeing a movie I would object to. Palm Springs is long way to go for mere entertainment, though I take them even farther for things more instructive."

"My dear girl, if you think movies are mere entertainment, then you *are* living in the past," Esther said, pausing to light a cigarette that sat at the end of a long holder. "After all, film is the latest form of art."

"I like living in the past, if that's what you want to call it."

"You need to spend more time out of this wilderness," George announced in an avuncular tone. "Though wilderness does have its place in art. But there's a modern world out there, sweetheart, and it's getting more modern by the moment. The past ceases to be relevant. Now that automobiles have arrived, how important is it to know how to ride a horse? Things like riding horses become mere entertainment, much the way film renders the written word obsolete—or at least inferior."

"It's exactly that kind of modern world that makes me want to live in Rattlesnake Canyon. It's the only place that feels real to me. Except maybe for Black Canyon."

"I really have to see this special canyon of yours, Ruth, dear. I'd like to understand why it has such a strong influence on a spirited woman like you." Esther put a hand on Ruth's arm. "I feel somewhat the same way about the Springs, but certainly not without the right people—and all the other accouterments, of course."

"It's time I got home to milk the goats. And I have chickens and a horse to feed—and perhaps even to ride," Ruth added. "For my own entertainment, of course. You see, Mr. Golden, I don't have time for watching some movie being made—art or not. I'll never see it." She opened the door of the Model A, then, in a burst of guilt, turned back to Esther. "Thanks for inviting me, though, Esther. I'm still grateful for the time you gave us such warm refuge from the sandstorm."

"It was a delight. I'm so glad the wind blew you up on our doorstep that day." She leaned over and gave Ruth a quick hug before she let her get back in the car. "Now I just hope a small breeze blows you into our little movie town."

"Maybe some other time," Ruth said, shutting the door.

"How disappointing." Esther gave an exaggerated crestfallen look and snuffed out her cigarette on the road. "Here I run into you after all this time—and you'd rather go milk a goat." Then she smiled and set a hand on Ruth's shoulder. "You will come to the completion party, though, won't you? When will that be, George?"

Her brother began explaining the reasons why he didn't know just when production would be over, and in such detail that Ruth felt her eyes glazing. She switched on the ignition. "Just write me when you do know—care of Matt's General Store in Juniper Valley," she said. "I'll see if I can make it."

"But tell me where *is* this wonderful canyon that you have to get back to?" Esther insisted.

Ruth pointed toward the mountains, then gave a wave good-bye and pushed down on the gas pedal. "Bye. Bye," came Maddie's voice beside her.

"Good-bye, old man," J.B. shouted after them, though his words were muffled in the wind—which was a shame, Ruth thought.

"Why did you call him old man?" she asked, when she stopped laughing.

"He called me *young* man."

"That's different."

"But he is old," J.B. said. "Like David. And you."

Ruth looked over and studied her son's face. She saw no rudeness nor disrespect there, though his sincerity cut even deeper. She didn't want to think about how fast the years were passing. Was she really almost thirty years old? It wasn't that far off. Ruth sighed, and concentrated on her driving. Yet Golden's words kept coming back to her. Even Esther said she was living in the past. Of course it was true. She celebrated it. Why should craving to learn more about the way the Indians lived and ate on the land be living in the past when it was new to her? And there was so much more to learn.

Since the day she first set foot on Glory Springs, she had loved speculating about how people had once lived there—without even the conveniences that gave her comfort, the buildings, this car, and water piped in from the windmill—things she wasn't about to give up, despite the qualms she had about creating her own little city in Rattlesnake Canyon. She wanted to learn all she could about how people lived when such things weren't available. And who knew if she might need to know some of these things soon, the way her money was dwindling. Things weren't getting any better with the economy either. wpa road building was not an option for her. And she couldn't stomach the thought of going away somewhere to find work as a nurse.

The drive to Glory Springs soon scoured all pondering from her head. Ruth relished the sight of Juniper Blue galloping toward them at the bend, the clucks of excited hens and the bleating of goats—she almost ran over the new two kids when they darted out in front of the Model A. It was not until the next day that any thought of Esther and her producer brother visited her, and then only because she nearly collided with the gold roadster as it came around the bend just as she—on Blue at a dead run—reached it on the other side.

Ruth yanked the reins to one side just as Blue, without any direction from her, swung around so fast it almost flung her from his back. She tightened her legs around his sides and leaned forward into his neck as he made a sudden leap over sage and rocks in his emergency detour. The horse sprinted down the wash until Ruth brought him back under control, turned and galloped him back to the bend, where Esther and Golden sat watching her in the roadster.

Still shaking from the close call, Ruth brought the horse to a stop beside the car. A good portion of her wanted to yank Golden out of the roadster and shake him. "How ever did you find me?" she managed to ask, with forced civility.

"There *is* only one road that goes up into these mountains. So-called road. I must say, just traveling on it was an adventure in itself." Esther took off her hat and fanned her face with its brim, a cluster of jingling bracelets glinting sun with her movement.

"We could be back at the Springs by now, enjoying the pool," her brother reminded her. He pulled out a flask and tipped it back. "I don't know why I let you talk me into this," he said, screwing the cap back on.

"It's not my fault your little starlet had an attack of appendicitis, although I'll admit it was convenient for my agenda." She turned to Ruth. "I didn't know if you'd ever get around to inviting me, so I came on my own."

"I'll meet you at my cabin. It's up the road there by those pinyons." She pressed her heels to the horse's flank, held on as he took off up the road ahead of the vehicle. Partly to calm herself and partly for the hell of it, she rode Juniper Blue past the cabin, then swung him around and bolted back to the yard before the roadster got there.

J.B. and Maddie were standing on the table rock watching the roadster drive closer, Maddie engaged in that annoying chirping until the car pulled up. Esther flung open the door and held out her arms, welcoming the girl onto her lap. Maddie let out one last chirp that even brought a laugh from Esther's reluctant brother. J.B. walked over and held out his hand for Golden to shake.

Ruth slid down from Blue and gave him a pat on the rump to head him toward the corral. As she stopped to coddle her injured knee, she observed the way her children behaved around these two people. How quickly they took on whatever was required for attention—as easily as they did with the Swedish miners or the Indians in Black Canyon. The two of them were entirely different here at home, kept to themselves more. But they seemed to open up around other people. Even odd little Maddie became someone Ruth hardly knew.

"It may be mere entertainment, but you certainly can ride. I'll say that for you." The producer swung open his door and stepped out of the car. "And your little place here would make a great location. It looks like something out of a tale of the Old West—minus the vehicles, of course." He blocked the cars from his sight with one hand. "There," he said. "Maybe an old wagon out by that barn."

"Funny how everyone looks at this place and sees how it could benefit them, not what it is in itself. The last person who arrived here unannounced wanted to dig for artifacts."

"That's the way the world works, sweetheart. Always has. You can't blame that on modern life either." He walked farther into the yard and continued looking around. "But, damn. This is a sweet spot you have here."

"Lovely," Esther said, walking up beside him with Maddie gripping her fingers. "Though extremely isolated. How ever did you find such a place?"

Ruth invited them in for cowboy coffee as she outlined the history of her homestead quest and construction of the cabin, while she lived in the little tent. Golden's appreciation of Glory Springs helped her to forgive the egotism that saturated his every remark, cushioned the anger his attitudes stirred up in her, so she was able to give her story the embellishment and omissions it needed to impress her guests even more. Ruth fully relished the mastery of taking linguistic control of the events that had dramatically altered her life. It pleased her to see the man go quiet and appear to actually listen. As for Esther, she broke in occasionally with questions that elicited even more shaping of the story.

With the coffee, she campfire-toasted special-occasion bread made from mesquite and sumach berry meal, with a few pinyon nuts thrown in.

"What is this delicious bread?" Esther asked. "I don't think I've ever tasted anything quite like it."

"Someone knows how to bake." Golden reached for a second slice.

When she described the ingredients, he stopped chewing and

stared warily at the bread he was holding—as if it might turn around and bite his hand.

"How marvelous, Ruth. You are a wonder," Esther said. "Could you teach Mary how to make this? Serving it at the Cricket would be such a conversation stopper."

"Maybe a guest stopper, too, Esther. You might as well put roasted lizard on the menu as tell people they're eating weeds and bushes." George put down the slice of bread he'd been buttering.

"If they tasted as good as Ruth's bread, I'd do it," Esther told him.

"It wouldn't be easy," Ruth explained. "These kinds of flours don't come packaged at the store. We have to grind them ourselves."

"Really! But it's so savory."

"I'll show you," Maddie said. "Come see my *na'dai*—that's a grinding rock. It's over there." With a nod, she indicated across the wash, the way a Yuiatei would.

Maddie beamed when Esther called her a "little Indian." Ruth felt like rolling her eyes.

As they made their way across the wash, Ruth explained how they'd learned to make the foods from the Yuiatei. "They were able to feed themselves with wild foods, plants and animals, for hundreds of years before there were stores here," she said.

"Well, they had no choice," Golden laughed. "They were savages."

"They were more civilized than you think." Ruth stopped, turned back to look at him. "Civilized to this place. I'd like to see you live without grocery stores or cars. You wouldn't last two days."

"That's not what being civilized is all about, young woman. Surviving in a place. That makes no sense."

"What *does* being civilized mean, then?"

"Come on." Maddie tugged at Esther's hand. "I want to show you."

"Just hold on, Maddie." Ruth reached out to push the girl's hand away from Esther, then pulled back. "We'll get there soon enough."

When they reached the spring, Maddie scrambled up the rocks to the *na'dai*. Ruth and Esther skirted the trail around the boulders, while Golden and J.B. waited for them in the wash. Maddie was already at work on mesquite pods by the time Ruth boosted Esther over the fallen Joshua tree beside the girl and her *na'dai*. She planted herself on a flat rock, and the two of them stood watching as the girl ground powdery meal from the long pods, tossing away fibrous strands and pounding down on the hard little beans inside.

"My goodness. That *is* a lot of trouble."

"It's worth it, though. And not just because of the flavor," Ruth told her. "I've come to think it's best for people to eat the foods that grow in the place where they live—instead of arriving in trucks from god-knows-where. Maybe people need what's in the soil around them to stay healthy. They become a part of the land that way—literally."

"That rock makes quite a soapbox," Golden chided from down in the wash. But how could she expect these city people to understand the joy that intimacy with the land provided? Even David only smiled tolerantly when she tried to explain it. Oh, he knew all the fancy botanical names for things, but he remained foreign to the place, refused to eat many of the dishes she made from the wild.

"Oh, let her alone, George. I like her odd ideas. At least they're original."

"You want to see what I made?" J.B. said suddenly.

"Don't tell me you grind up weed beans too?" Golden laughed. J.B. shook his head.

"Come see," he said.

Golden looked pleadingly at his sister but to no avail. "Of course we will," she said.

"First taste this." Maddie appeared beside them with a pinch of mesquite flour. Esther sampled it, nodding in approval before they headed down the trail.

They followed J.B. across the wash to the hidden place where he had constructed a group of small *ki'takii* made of brush and willow boughs. Ruth had not realized he had gone from making minuscule huts to those of a size that he and Maddie could sit up in, his own little settlement.

Suddenly, she was proud of her children, of both of them, with their wild-loving ways. They had planted their feet firm against this rough granite sand, would stand with her against encroachments of that modern world that these and other people brought to their very doorstep. Soapbox or not, they were, like her, emissaries of this wild place.

CHAPTER TWENTY-THREE

Ruth threw the letter into the drawer with the others. Cally's agreement not to contact her again included letters, at least as far as Ruth was concerned. And there had been three in almost as many weeks. She slammed the drawer shut and walked outside to round up J.B. and Maddie for the milking. Both children loved the act of pulling and squeezing milk from the teats, though they had a way to go before she would be able to turn the chore over to them. Meanwhile, teaching them was making the process take twice as long for her—and often resulted in spills and less milk.

She had no obligation to open Cally's letters. She just wished she could get them off her mind. Yet they sat in the drawer hissing at her like a nest of rattlers. Cold coiled in her belly every time she thought about opening one. At the same time, she was half afraid not to. What if Cally were to show up in her life unannounced? Get a ride to Juniper

Valley and have someone bring her the rest of the way? That other option her mother mentioned. The idea was terrifying, but she knew Cally was not so far away as El Paso anymore. Some of her neighbors' husbands in Juniper Valley had gone to work on that dam and still managed to make visits home occasionally. God knew if any of them had visited her mother's "business."

Neither the nannies nor the children were in sight, though Ruth assumed J.B. and Maddie must be in the little settlement J.B. had built. They spent much of their time there lately. Ruth crossed the wash and went through the scrub oak into the draw behind the boulder pile that hid it from the canyon. Sure enough, the children were there. What she didn't expect was that they had the goats in a little pen fashioned from yucca poles and sagebrush and were trying to milk them. They hadn't noticed her, so she stopped where she was to watch them.

In place of hay, Maddie had placed a bowl of acorns in front of each animal and hobbled their back legs so they couldn't kick the milk buckets borrowed from the shed. The children had the situation in hand all right, the only problem being hands—theirs were not large enough to extract the milk efficiently. Still, they managed to get small streams out of the teats, J.B.'s a bit more substantial, maybe because he had been outgrowing Maddie lately, growing to look more like Jim as well, Ruth realized, as she watched him bend down to reach beneath the goat. His dark hair was long enough to slide over his shoulders and fall along the bare skin of his arms and back, and something about the way he moved was enough to make Ruth's heart contract. Oh, Jim, she thought, I wish you could see him.

David wanted to cut that hair, to chop it off and send J.B. and Maddie down to the one-room schoolhouse built across from the general store. Ruth had fought against cutting her son's hair. She didn't think J.B. wanted it cut, but he did want to please David—who would have won, except that J.B. also didn't want to look different from the boys he played with at Black Canyon. But Ruth knew the battle wasn't over yet. And as for school, she didn't know how much longer she could hold out.

"You want to have supper with us?" Maddie called, peeking out from under the nanny. Her auburn hair dropped down dangerously near the bucket of milk.

So they had noticed her. She should have known. Ruth began walking toward them, seeing now the spread they had laid out on their makeshift table, a crudely woven tule mat on the ground, like ones women made in Black Canyon. She wondered whether Maddie had woven it. Both children worked to create their own little Black Canyon here, minus the people, of course.

"What are you having?" Ruth asked, bending to inspect what was on the mat table. Nothing cooked, she hoped, since she didn't want them starting fires over here.

"It's a surprise," Maddie said, squirting milk into the bucket in weak spurts. The nanny struggled to free her hind legs, but Maddie bleated her still again.

"Do you want me to finish the milking?"

"We can do it." J.B. said, his back still turned to her. His small streams of white seemed more steady. "It just takes us longer. You have big hands."

Ruth looked down at her hands, smiled as an image of Cally's perfect painted nails came to her. Ruth's own fingers ended in jagged nails, with slices of dirt embedded beneath. She prided herself on their difference. "Bigger than yours, anyway," she said. Ruth lowered herself onto the ground in front of the mat, feeling much like a guest in her own canyon. But this was their piece of that canyon. They had made it so.

Who were these little people, really, she wondered, apart from her own conception of them? This odd little girl Ruth couldn't quite forgive, and this boy who resulted from the love that had changed her—but who, in reality, was a being completely separate from that love. From the love she bore him. Separate also from Jim, as Maddie was from her father's evil. Why was it so hard to remember that, and why did the mere thought of it squeeze tight her chest?

When the children finished the milking—at least to their own satisfaction, they unhobbled the nannies and brought the buckets over to her. Not too bad, Ruth thought. Though she could have gotten more out herself, she let it pass.

The supper Maddie had prepared consisted of some kind of sun-baked meatless pemmican she had concocted from prickly pear apples, wild grape and acorn meal. Their beverage was one common in Black

Canyon, mesquite pods soaked in water, which resulted in a sweet and tangy drink the Yuiatei called *lik'ii*. Ruth sometimes wondered if the drink fermented a bit as it sat day after day in Black Canyon, with only new mesquite pods and water added each morning.

"Mmmm. Good. Where did you learn to make this, Maddie?" Ruth took another bite of the pemmican.

"I figured it out." A gust caught hold of her hair, lifted the red mass away from her face.

"She watched Grandmother," J.B. said. "That's how she always does it."

"Grandmother Siki, you mean?" Ruth asked.

Maddie nodded. "Not Grandmother Kate."

"Kate's not your grandmother. Neither is—"

Maddie's face became defiant. "She is. They both are." She put down her cup and folded her arms.

"A grandmother is your mother's mother," Ruth began to explain. Already she regretted intruding on the subject.

"That's a different kind of grandmother," J.B. said. "But don't you have a mother? What about your mother?"

Both children sat watching, waiting for her answer, while Ruth struggled, now hobbled by her own challenge. "Okay, Kate and Grandmother Siki can both be your grandmothers," she said, forcing a smile as she got to her feet.

"But why won't you tell us?" Maddie asked. "Why can't we meet her?"

"Because she's far away," Ruth said, "That's why." And running a brothel in Nevada. Ruth started down the draw, but J.B. came after her.

"Well, we have a car. Let's go see her." He tugged on Ruth's arm from behind, as Maddie came up beside him.

"Yes, let's. Why can't we?" Maddie said.

"No." Ruth stopped and turned toward them. "We are not going to see her. Ever! She is not your grandmother."

"But you said—"

"Never mind what I said. I was wrong. I wouldn't let you near that woman. Don't ask me anymore," she said, helpless before the bewilderment on their faces. She turned and rushed back across the wash, imagining their accusing looks as she fled.

Relieved that they didn't pursue her, Ruth built a small blaze in the fire ring and put on the coffee water to heat. Then she went in and got the letters, took them out with her to the camp chair. She tossed the first one into the fire, picked up the second, hesitated, then threw it, too, into the flame that seemed to open up and swallow it whole. Already, she could breathe easier, as if a weight had been lifted from her chest. She smiled and reached for the third, which was the first she had received.

As her arm opened to throw it, a gust loosened a cone from the pinyon and dropped it onto the envelope, knocking it from her hands. A chill ran up Ruth's back as she bent down and picked up the letter. When she did, she noticed the wavery handwriting of the address. Inspecting the envelope more closely, she made sure the writing was actually her mother's, which it seemed to be, she finally decided. Still, its condition aroused her curiosity. Setting the letter on the rock table, she picked up the coffee can and dumped grounds into the boiling water, pulled the pot to the side, and sat watching the envelope.

She should simply throw it in the fire with the others and forget about it. But could she get it off her mind? Especially that wavery handwriting. Had something happened that caused Cally to break their agreement? Maybe she should read the letter, then burn it. Yet she had no inclination to open the envelope, so she sat sipping her coffee and trying not to think about it. At deep twilight, when the children came in from across the wash, the envelope remained unopened on the rock.

Sliding the letter out of sight beneath the coffee can, Ruth heated some stew and leftover biscuits to supplement the "supper" the children had prepared. After she had them bedded down on the cots moved under the pinyons for the summer, she went over and refreshed the campfire, reheating the coffee. Enhancing her cup with a healthy shot from her whiskey jug, she picked up the letter and brought it with her to her chair. She was on her second doctored cup when Blue came over and nudged her shoulder with his muzzle.

Ruth leaned into him and rubbed her cheek against the soft velvet fur between his nostrils, turned to plant a kiss on it. "Oh, what should I do, Blue? Should I read this letter, or throw it in the fire with the others?" He nuzzled her neck but gave no answer, so Ruth did neither. After more whiskeyed coffee, she went inside, put the letter back in the drawer, then came out and crawled onto her cot beside the children.

For the next two weeks, Ruth thought little about the letter, except on evenings when she was alone at the campfire. Then, instead of enjoying her time by herself as she usually did when David wasn't up for dinner and spending the night, she sat fretting over the damned letter. She had told herself that if something was really amiss, surely Cally would write again, but when another week passed without a letter, Ruth had still not been able to put it out of her mind. Finally, she could stand it no more, and after fortifying herself by the campfire, she tore open the envelope.

Ruth, the letter began curtly, *I am in trouble and need your help. You must send me money immediately. You owe me at least that much. And if you'd given me the two thousand I asked for in the first place, I wouldn't be in this mess. The stake you did give me was barely enough to set up the kind of establishment near the dam needed to be successful. Customers in the ratty makeshift place were slow in coming. Eventually business boomed, though, and by the time the dam was finished, I was making even more than I had in El Paso. If it hadn't been for that infernal fire, I would have had enough funds to set myself up somewhere else when the dam finished, and you wouldn't be hearing from me. But the fire took everything I'd built. All the money I'd put aside as well—since there was no bank anywhere near that ramshackle settlement. As if that wasn't enough, I came down soon after with lung fever. I am recovering now, but slowly. That isn't surprising, given the conditions I lived in before I found my way back to Las Vegas. It was ungodly hot in that shack I took refuge in—one of the many abandoned by the workers after the dam finished. Las Vegas itself is not so civilized as El Paso, but here there is at least an attempt at it. Electricity and phones for those who can afford them. It will do. I need enough funds to set myself up again when I recover. The prospects are good here—and the town is a growing one. But I cannot survive without some means to make a life for myself. So ask yourself if you want a sick and defeated old woman to show up on your doorstep—that is if you even have a doorstep in that godforsaken place.* The letter went on to give an address to send the money and a phone number to call if necessary.

Holding the letter as she would a hot handle, between the thumb and index finger of one shaking hand, Ruth carried it over to the rock table, picked up the coffee can and hid the danger beneath. Grabbing up her jug, she poured the rest of its contents into her cup, not bothering this time with the coffee, and began pacing in front of the fire, her thoughts and feelings too intense and entangled to sort out.

She couldn't get the image of Cally out of her head, saw her sitting under these pine trees spewing out her poison on J.B. and Maddie, their faces at rapt attention as she trapped them with stories from her sordid life. Their grandmother come to them at last.

She wanted to choke the woman, and for a moment she relished the idea of wringing the life out of Cally's neck with her own hands, like she would some chicken. Cally's promise to leave Ruth alone had meant nothing to her—and, true to form, she even managed to blame Ruth for that. But would Cally really make good her threat to show up on this doorstep? In the end, that was what mattered. Just how sick with lung fever was her mother? Too bad not sick enough to die from it. Ruth slammed the rest of the whiskey and went back over to see if she could drain another drop from the jug. A drop was all she got. She picked up the jug and hurled it into the wash, listened as it shattered on a rock. Staring after it into the dark, she felt tears creep up to overrule her anger—but she wouldn't let those harbingers of helplessness have their way.

She could never send Cally that kind of money. Even though she wasn't sure just how much was left, she knew the pile had been dwindling, getting smaller each time she reached into the bottom drawer for more. It had been some time since she'd actually counted it, but she knew the improvements on her place had taken more than she'd expected. Then there were the car parts she had to purchase so John Olsen could get her Model A in good shape before they left for Montana. Parts for the Olsens' truck in payment. And years of buying supplies and gasoline had slowly worn down her stash. Gasoline, too, for the many trips to Black Canyon.

She would have to make do with fewer supplies, eat even more of the wild foods she loved—and that cost her nothing. Economy had not been the point to begin with, but now she was grateful for that aspect. She had thought that with what she had left, she could last out another few years before having to consider anything drastic, such as returning to nursing care. She wanted to stay in her canyon and live the life it offered as long as she possibly could.

She supposed she really ought to count that money again. Simply feeling the size of the pile was not an accurate measure, and not knowing no longer served her. But merely the thought of knowing what was actually left sent her stomach into upheaval. Then she would have to face what had to be done.

It could be, she told herself, as she got onto her cot beside the children's, that there was more left than she expected. But she didn't believe it.

And even if there was enough to send Cally some of it, what guarantee did she have that it would be the end of that woman in her life? Cally just might write again in another four years asking for more.

Ruth closed her eyes and set her mind toward sleep, but her lids popped open again. She stared up between the pine branches at pinpoints of light peeking through the needled openings. The air was warm and calm, and the crickets seemed to be celebrating the situation. How she loved this place, this life. Much of the oppression she'd felt for so long after the children's birth had lifted once J.B. and Maddie became more self-sufficient. Then it was only David, loving, helpful David, that she had to guard her independence against. At least, that's what she'd thought before she read Cally's letter. Now the idea of her mother showing up without warning seemed a much bigger threat.

There always seemed to be something that threatened her living the life she desired. Lack of funds was certainly one thing that had been lurking at the back of her mind lately. She hadn't seen it as imminent until Cally's demand. She couldn't imagine her mother as the sick and helpless woman Cally had presented in the letter. If she was so sick and helpless, how did she get to Las Vegas? Was it her phone number she'd given—or a friend's? Cally always seemed to have a man around somewhere, smitten enough to take care of her. But there had been two letters after the one Ruth read, and then no more. What else might those letters have told her—if only she hadn't burned them. And why hadn't there been more? What if her mother was on her way here right now? The thought chilled her thoroughly.

For much of the night, Ruth lay awake with her turmoil, watching the Big Dipper move across the sky, dozing occasionally, only to confront Cally's mocking face in her dreams. She was relieved when she spotted a sliver of dawn over the ridge down canyon. She got up in the dim light and made her way to her cabin door, lit a candle and took it with her to her chest of drawers. Once she knew how much money she had left, and the children were awake, she would drive down to the general store and call the number Cally had given her.

CHAPTER TWENTY-FOUR

Far beyond simply sick at heart as she waited for the operator to
connect her call, Ruth felt her stomach was about ready to heave up
its contents—if there'd been any. She hadn't even dared coffee before
they set out for town. Then, when she got to the general store, she
found it hadn't yet opened for business. She'd had to wait almost an
hour to make the call. Maddie and J.B. amused themselves chasing
the whiptail lizards that were plentiful in the chaparral behind the
store, while Ruth sat and stewed for a few minutes, then got out
and paced circles around her Model A, playing out scene after scene
where she told Cally to go hang herself. By the time Matt drove up
to open the store, she was contemplating the idea of prying up one
of his windows to get in. She could barely force herself to engage in
the expected pleasantries, asking after his wife and new baby. Their
history together didn't help matters.

As if things couldn't get worse, the ringing on the line continued without any answer on the other end. Finally the operator came on to tell her that she should try her call again later.

"No luck, huh, Ruth," Matt said as she handed him back the phone.

"A long trip in for nothing," she said, without meeting his eyes. She didn't want to confront the question she knew would be there. It was none of his business.

"Must be important. Maybe you should stay around and try again later," she heard him say as she walked toward the door. She clamped down on her urge to turn back and spew expletives at this former flame who dared pretend to give a damn—and made sure the door slammed behind her.

But as much as she hated to admit it, he was right, and once she got J.B. and Maddie back in the car, she headed for David's dig. She could spend some hours there, then drive back and try the call again this afternoon.

As she expected, David was delighted with her unexpected visit, and the children were, as usual, happy to play in the miniature rock city they'd constructed. Everyone, it seemed, was pleased with the situation, except Ruth. But going all the way home was ridiculous, and she had to do something to keep her sanity while she waited to make that call. Pummeling mesquite beans into submission seemed particularly suitable. Besides, she didn't even know what she was going to say when she did call. Certainly, she wasn't going to tell Cally she'd send the thousand dollars, since she'd found that she had just under a thousand herself. She could only hope that if she told her mother she no longer had much money, the woman wouldn't bother showing up in the area in the first place. Hoped, but didn't count on it.

David's welcoming hug comforted her, so she agreed to a cup of his warmed-over breakfast coffee—which at least had gained some strength from sitting a few hours in the pot. Yet even as they sat in the shade with their cups, Ruth's hands were itching to attack the bean pods in one of the *na'dai* David had uncovered.

"I keep waiting for you to tell me." David's words brought her out of her thoughts.

"Tell you what?" She blinked, took a sip of coffee to focus.

"Well, you don't usually show up unannounced midmorning without *some* reason. And you seem distracted." He took a drink, puckered his face. "Whew! This will put hair on your chest. Better not drink it, Ruth."

She rolled her eyes at his feeble humor. Of course, any humor would seem feeble at the moment, she imagined.

"Come on," he said, laying his free hand on her arm. "Why so glum? You can tell me."

So she did, despite her better judgment, letting it all spill out of her, at first a trickle through the crack in the dam that held it, until it pushed open the crack, the dam falling away to let the torrent rush through. Until now, she had revealed only a few details of her upbringing and her mother's character. Now she told him everything that flooded into her mind, that in fact bypassed her mind and poured out on its own. Told him of her meeting with her mother in Los Angeles, the money she'd borrowed for her business and the promise Cally had made—and now her demand for even more out of the meager remnants of Ruth's inheritance. Each word she spoke was carried out on a rush of conflicting emotion that had her in tears before she finished.

David got up and kneeled by her chair, put his arms around her, and for a few moments Ruth felt wonderfully empty, washed clean of all her turmoil. Then he spoke, and she remembered why she hadn't told him in the first place.

"Would it be so bad if she did come here?" he asked. "I would really like to meet this woman you came from." He reached up to wipe the tears from Ruth's eyes. "But if you want to give her the money to stay away, then do it. And marry me, Ruth. You won't need that money. We can get by just fine on my salary."

Ruth smacked his hand away and jerked up from her chair. "Didn't you hear anything I said?" She began pacing. "I should have known better than to come here," she muttered, then turned to him. "Didn't you hear what that woman is like?"

"Calm down, Ruth." He got to his feet and started toward her. She began backing away. "You know I love you. I'd do anything for you," he said. "All I want to do is take care of you so you won't have to struggle so much up there in that canyon. Make things easier for you." He stopped moving toward her, and his arms dropped to his sides. "Please let me."

"I like my life up in that canyon, goddammit," she all but shouted. "Why do you think I homesteaded that place? Why do you think I'm afraid she'll ruin the life I've built?" Ruth looked over to find J.B. and Maddie had stopped what they were doing to watch. Taking in a deep breath, she said, "Go back to what you were doing, David. I'm going to work on the *na'dai* for a while," and left him standing there.

Kneeling over the grinding rock, Ruth couldn't punish the mesquite pods enough. She'd snatched a batch from the cache she and Maddie had gathered around the digs last season and thrown a handful into the depression, then borne down with the *dai,* rock against rock, the tough bean pods between soon ground to powdery meal. Feeling a bit better, she ground another batch and another, and was just brushing the pile of flour into a bowl, admiring her efficiency and its resulting quantity, when she noticed the gold roadster turning off the main road and heading toward the dig. She left the bowl on the rock and stood up, watching Maddie and J.B. get up from their play and run for the approaching roadster. Already the girl had begun those damned cricket chirps. Would she never grow up?

Ruth was disappointed not to see Esther beside her brother when he pulled up near David's worktable. David put aside his drawings of the pottery on the table and walked up to the car as Golden got out. She picked up the bowl of flour and started in their direction.

"I saw your little yellow car over here," Golden said when Ruth came up, "and thought I'd stop. It always reminds me of one of those sunflowers that grow by the road." He chucked Maddie's chin and shook hands with J.B. "Anyway, finding you here saves me from making the trip up that damnable road again."

"But where is she?" Maddie asked, her face fallen. "How come she isn't with you?'"

"Esther's in the Springs, little one." He bent down and rechucked her chin. "I know she'd love to see you. You too," he said to J.B. "Why don't you have your mother take you down there? You can see a movie too, my treat. I bet he'd love *King Kong,* Ruth."

"Why did you stop here, Mr. Golden?" Ruth asked.

"Glad you asked," Golden said, turning back toward her. "I won't beat around the bush, then. As a matter of fact, I have a proposition for you. Esther and I think we've worked out something that will benefit the both of us—you and me, that is.

"Truth is, I couldn't get out of my mind the way you rode that horse the other day. I could almost see that scene on film, kept bringing it up to Esther. Then one day she asked why I didn't just write you into my new picture. At first I laughed. Esther never had a good idea in her life—as far as movies are concerned. But her idea stayed with me. Finally, I talked with my scriptwriter, and damned if he didn't come up with something terrific."

Golden walked over to the roadster, fished around behind the seat until he came up with a sheaf of papers, which he brought over and handed to Ruth. "See what you think," he said. "It's a bigger part than I originally had in mind—but that means it will be more lucrative for you. Say seven hundred dollars' worth. That's not peanuts these days, you know."

"Indeed," Ruth said, staring down at the script in her hand, too stunned to say anything more. She looked up and found David frowning. "But I'm not an actress," she told Golden. "I told you I haven't seen but three movies and . . . and . . . ," she stopped herself from saying "and I hate your phony little town and its movies." She didn't think there was reason to insult him. In fact, she felt flattered by his offer. It was out of the question, though, went against everything she'd built her life around—even if the seven hundred dollars might save her.

"The role involves riding in and out of scenes, for the most part. And with your looks . . . well, you won't have to do much acting. But you don't have to say yes now," he said. "Read the script and think about it. I believe you'll like the role. Consider seriously what it might mean to you. This kind of thing could change your life." He shook his head and smiled. "Anyone else would be fainting with joy to have this offer, you know, kissing my feet." He got back in the roadster and switched on the engine. "By the way, the remuneration is negotiable. Well, you know where to find me."

"What a ridiculous idea," David said, as soon as the roadster was out of sight. "I hope you know that, Ruth. The nerve of that man, trying to involve you in—"

"Oh, shut up, David. Of course I know that. I don't need you to tell me what I should do." She looked down at the bowl forgotten in her arms, reached in and ran her fingers through the floury meal. It had an odd feel to it, she thought, as she walked over to put it with the bulk of flour she had ground here over the last few weeks. She remembered the way she had pounded her rage and hate into every particle, and it dawned on her that she had poisoned this bowl of flour with her own pain. Anything made from it would be toxic.

Rather than adding it to the rest, she climbed to the top of the boulder pile and tossed the flour into the afternoon wind, hoping that might dilute the contents and keep it from harming anyone else. Then she gathered up her children and drove back into town to make her phone call.

At the general store, Matt stood discreetly shelving cans on the opposite wall while Ruth tried her call. Not that he wouldn't be able to hear every word, nonetheless. She almost wished there would be no answer again as she stood, stomach churning as the ringing continued. Then she heard the dreaded voice, and all else became irrelevant.

"Who's there?" the voice asked, without any pretense of greeting.

"It's Ruth. You asked me to call."

"And it is about time, I'd say. I could be dead by now, no thanks to you."

"I called to tell you that I don't have the money to give you. It's been four years. I've had expenses and—"

"Just how much *do* you have? Send me what you have. I can pay you back with interest once I get on my feet here again."

"I can't. I won't send you what I need to live on. It's my money. Remember I have children to think of."

"I have to have money, Ruth. How else can I get a business started again? I should have stayed in Vegas in the first place. It's more my kind of town."

"But I told you I don't have it. I can't send you what I don't have to send."

"I'm sure you have something put away. I know you, Ruth. You've always been devious. Now, do I have to come there and wring it out of you myself? Don't think I won't. And if you really don't have it, then at least I have somewhere to live."

"Well, come ahead, then. You'll find nothing left to wring out. I simply don't have—"

"Maybe I'll just do that, then. You leave me no other choice." The phone clicked off on the other end.

Near tears, Ruth set the receiver on the hook. She swallowed hard and took in a deep breath, then turned and walked out of the store. Stopping on the front step, she stood watching J.B. and Maddie crawl on their knees after lizards. She didn't yet trust her voice not to break when she called them to her.

What had she done? Why had she dared Cally to come when it was the thing she most dreaded? She pictured her mother getting out of a new Ford where a man waited behind the wheel, barging through the cabin door, a cigarette clamped firmly between those white fingers with their blood-red tips. Cally would home in on the money in the bottom dresser drawer the way a fly finds shit in the wilderness. Ruth shuddered. She would hide the money in a better place. Another picture came to her: Cally with suitcases in front of the cabin while the Ford that brought her drove away without her.

Suddenly her gut filled with writhing snakes. Her knees barely held her. She couldn't let that woman anywhere near Glory Springs. She didn't care what it took.

CHAPTER TWENTY-FIVE

Ruth wriggled away the itch from sweat gathered between the bare skin of her legs and the horse's coat, shook off the liquid tickle in the crevice between her breasts. She struggled to keep Juniper Blue still as she sat clad in the silly faux deerskin dress they made her wear. With fringe, forgodsake. She thought about how Martha and Grandmother Siki would laugh if they saw her now. How different she looked from the Indians she knew in Black Canyon. Was she really about to streak bareback through the crowd that lined Mane Street? She felt an urge to turn the horse around and ride off. Yet she remained under the makeshift arbor without heeding her own instinct. She had to be practical, she told herself, had come this far, how could she not to go through with it? But with Blue stamping his hooves in restlessness, she only hoped the director would signal soon.

From her position between the phony land office and bank, she could see David with J.B. and Maddie on the wooden porch of the Dirty Dog Saloon, watching two supposed cowboys pretend to fist-fight in front of the cameras. It was a odd sight, these men coated with makeup, their shirts and slacks stiffer and cleaner than any cowboy's. Even their felt hats stayed perfectly shaped, looked nothing like the scrunched and sweaty hats that working cowboys wore. Again and again the two actors faked pummeling each other, until the director was satisfied. In the next scene—also repeated into excruciating bore-dom—one pulled his pistol and shot the other with a loud *pop* that sounded more like fireworks than a gun. Though the blank shots came from fifty yards away, Ruth felt Blue quiver with each pop. Realizing what might happen if the horse were closer to the guns, she'd had Golden and the director promise that no shots would actually be fired while she and Blue were in a scene. He said it would not be a problem to add the sound later.

Golden had done everything possible to persuade her to make the movie. The extra money he'd agreed to had allowed her to send Cally almost what she had asked for—leaving Ruth nearly a thousand left of her own. If she was careful, that should last some years. Yet it wasn't only the money that convinced her, she told herself, but the role it-self. Her part was that of an Indian woman who rescues the white hero, Roger Rider—a laughably ridiculous hero in her eyes, but in a harmless sort of way—when he lies near death in the wilderness. She appeared several times in the movie, her last appearance just when townsfolk are about to hang Rider before he can clear his name.

Even though the role didn't involve speaking a word, the idea of playing an Indian woman who saves a white hero appealed to her. It wouldn't change the way most people thought about Jim and the Yuiatei People, but such a thing might help them see Indians in a new way. At least she hoped that would be the case. It irked her, though, that she was too busy playing Indian to go see her real Indian friends, especially since something inside was nagging at her to go to them—it felt suspiciously like a heart-calling.

She wondered if lies were a part of any work of art. If the same kinds of lies were a part of the books she had come to love? If she could go back to those places in the novels, could walk the streets of Moscow or London fifty years ago, would she find the places as described on the pages? Or would those places be as far from the truth as the film's depiction of cowboys and Indians? She hoped not.

A group of actors dressed as townsmen began milling about the land office, waiting for their cue. Among them was Ben, the bootlegger from Los Angeles—well, she supposed he couldn't be a bootlegger now that prohibition had ended. She had nearly been shocked off her horse when she saw him that first day on the set, playing one of the gang of thugs out to get the film's hero. The role seemed appropriate enough. He hadn't recognized her at first. When he did, his face flushed, and he mumbled an apology for the night in L.A. She'd only nodded, then ignored him, although she was pleased to have such an effect on him. He couldn't possibly know the way seeing him had sped up her heartbeat. In fact, he seemed intimidated by her status in the film.

Finally, it was time, and the director gave her the nod to ready herself. A group of men strode out of the land office, and she felt her muscles tense. Reaching down to pat Juniper Blue, Ruth reassured him it would be over soon. Her first appearance was to be brief, Golden said, merely to introduce her presence and create curiosity for her role later in the action. After watching so many takes of the scenes before hers, she hoped there wouldn't be too many repeats of her action. If only she could somehow get it right the first time.

The director's arm came down, she pressed her heels to the horse's sides, and Blue took off so fast she almost slid off. She gripped her legs tighter as they ran down the middle of Mane Street to approach the group of men—where she was to turn her horse and ride off between the buildings. But when she reached the group, she was startled by the loud *pop* of a blank, followed by two more in quick succession.

Juniper Blue came to a sudden stop, his hooves skidding up dust. Ruth tightened her legs around his sides and clutched his mane with one hand for all she was worth. She felt him rear back, so she leaned forward and clung tight as he raised both front legs and pawed the air. Everyone on the street seemed frozen into a snapshot, while Blue whirled slightly and whinnied, then dropped down and ran off between the buildings. She looked back over her shoulder at the dumbfounded crowd just before he carried her out of sight through the chaparral.

When she finally brought the horse under control again, he had almost reached the road that turned up into Rattlesnake Canyon. Then it took all her persuasion to get him to head back in the direction they had come from, back toward that awful little town. Only her fury at the moviemakers gave her the motivation to return, otherwise she would have gone on home. Sure, David and her children were still at the shoot, but they would find her easy enough should she continue on toward Glory Springs. Yet she had a few things she wanted to say to those idiots before she left—and the money for the film could just be damned.

And she'd be damned if she was going to subject Juniper Blue to scene after scene of retakes in order to satisfy some director's whim in someone's fantasy of the West. Not when he was stupid enough to allow his fake gunshot sounds to spook the devil out of poor Blue. Ruth patted her horse's neck, leaned down and kissed his mane at the thought, as they galloped through the brush back toward Frontiertown.

She trotted Blue between the Dirty Dog Saloon and the general store, toward the group of actors already being positioned for the next scene. David and her children were nowhere around, but the director caught sight of her approach and all action stopped. She was surprised when the entire group, Ben among them, broke into applause as she rode up and brought her horse to a halt.

"Young woman, that was the most perfect first take I've ever done. A brilliant addition to the script," the director called out to her. "Brava."

"Very good, Ruth," Golden told her. He started toward her, but Blue backed a few steps away. "Usually I discourage such spontaneous inventions, but this—"

"You said there wouldn't be gunshot," Ruth half snapped, the edge of her anger dulled by the reception she had received. And it looked like the director wanted no retakes. "Or whatever those phony sounds really are."

Golden looked sheepish. "That was merely an accident on the part of a technician," the director said, coming up alongside them. "The guns were supposed to be emptied of blanks."

"It scared the devil out of my horse. I told you I wouldn't take part in this film if gunshots were part of any scene Blue was in." The horse was still high-stepping nervously. It was difficult to make him stay.

"I'll see that it doesn't happen again," Golden said. "If that's what it takes to keep you. After a scene like that, how could we afford to lose you?"

"If it was an accident, young woman, it was certainly a magnificent mistake. We should have more accidents like that." The director shook his head in admiration.

"There *can't* be any more accidents like that," Ruth said, a bit unsettled at the way her words were keeping the door open. When she'd ridden up, she had not intended to continue in the project at all. "I won't have it," she managed to say with more conviction.

The two men seemed eager to meet her demands, and before she left, Ruth allowed Golden and the director to mollify her. They swore there would be no more "accidents." No one would fire a loaded gun in any scene her roan was in. Was it the money that so determined her to do this thing, to go against her better judgment? she wondered, as they discussed the issue.

Ruth had also wondered vaguely as she talked to the director where David and her children had gotten themselves to, was puzzled that they never appeared. Afterward, she rode behind the saloon where his truck had been parked and found it gone. A technician near the saloon said he'd seen David speed off after Blue bolted. Of course. She should have known. Why did the man always think she needed to be rescued?

She had ridden about halfway to the Swedes' when she heard the truck engine just in time to pull Blue off the road as David's truck came racing down around the bend from up canyon. No doubt he had gone clear to the cabin to find her and was now returning—more frantic than ever since she hadn't been there. The man wasn't hard to predict.

Ruth steadied Juniper Blue as David skidded the truck to a halt just past them. The resulting backfire caused Blue to rear again, but she was ready, held tight to bring him in check. David all but leapt from the driver's door and sprinted toward her before the dust had settled. Behind him, J.B. slid down from the seat to the ground.

"Are you all right? Where have you been?" he shouted as he came. "When I didn't find you back at the cabin, I—"

"I'm just fine, David," she told him when he reached her. "Despite your damned van. You really need to get that thing fixed. It's louder than a shotgun blast."

"I saw Juniper Blue heading toward the canyon. You couldn't seem to stop him." He lifted his arms upward to pull her to him from the horse, but she stiffened to avoid him.

"I did stop him, David, eventually. Then I rode him back to Frontiertown."

"But—but—" He stopped and simply looked at her helplessly. "We were worried, Ruth. You scared the bejesus out of the three of us." Beside him J.B. watched her with bewildered eyes. Maddie observed the drama calmly from the running board.

Ruth lifted a leg over and slid down from the horse. "You're the one who scared these kids," she said. "They know I can take care of myself. If you weren't around, they wouldn't think a thing of it." She smoothed J.B.'s hair and gave him a smile, then started toward the truck.

"I told you from the start making that picture was a bad idea. That Hollywood crowd means nothing but trouble. I thought you agreed."

"Trouble and money, David. Don't forget the money. And I need it too, after what I sent Cally."

"You're limping again, Ruth, do you know that? Dammit, Ruth. Why are you doing this?"

"I always limp when my leg is tired, you know that. Don't try to make more of it." She reached the passenger door, where Maddie had pushed down the handle and swung out on it, hanging half out the rolled-down window of the open door. "You'll wreck that door, Maddie. You're too big to do that anymore," she said, pulling the girl off and setting her roughly on the car seat. The smile on Maddie's face shriveled into a pout, shooting Ruth through with a familiar burst of annoyed guilt.

They started up canyon, leaving Blue to follow on his own.

"You know you don't have to have that money, Ruth. Why put yourself through hell for it? It pains me to see it. I've told you I make plenty enough to keep the both of us. And neither of us has many expenses."

She didn't bother to respond, or even to look over at him. They had been through this many times before. She would not be a kept woman; she had already made that clear to him. Another Cally. Not that he wanted to make her a kept woman, exactly. But a wife was far worse—and he'd turned up the pressure since the university was pressing him to return to Los Angeles and teach the coming fall term.

"I don't know why you have to be so stubborn about everything," he said, after a long silence. "To your own detriment."

"It's not for you to say what's detrimental to me," she said. But she shouldn't have responded. The last thing she wanted was to be pulled into a rehash of the subject.

"It's not? I'm the man who loves you, Ruth. Sometimes I wonder if you do." Out of the corner of her eye she could see him shaking his head. "Love yourself, I mean. All this nonsense I hear about not ending up like your mother. Not being dependent on men. Even on a man who adores you."

"I don't want to talk about it, David. At least not now."

"You never want to talk about it." He slammed the truck into a lower gear and gunned the motor up the far bank of the North Fork. "Sometimes I wonder if you even want me around. Maybe you think you'd be happier on your own." He looked over and she met his eyes. "But I think you kid yourself, Ruth."

"Quit putting thoughts in my head, David," she said calmly. But she *had* wondered about it. Yet she didn't think she wanted him gone altogether. She just didn't want him smothering her with his attention and care. If it was this bad when they lived apart—at least officially apart—what would it be like if she became his wife? If she became anybody's wife? Not that she'd had any other offers—or wanted them—since the two of them had become . . . she wanted to find another word for it, didn't want to use the word "lovers" since that was the word for what she was with Jim. Yet "lovers" was certainly the term she found in novels. And the physical act was still decent between them—or would be without the damned diaphragm.

Yet she resisted the word. She had loved Jim with all of her being. Nothing before or since had come close to what she felt for him. David, she loved too, but with reservations. Sometimes, in the middle of their lovemaking, she would think about some particular moment with Jim, and remember how she would have given up anything to stay with him, would have faced down the entire world if need be, and the difference in her feelings would leave her face wet and her insides hollow. At times, David had noticed her tears and kissed them tenderly from her cheeks. She supposed he thought they were part of the passion she felt for him. She almost wished they were. He was a good man, except for wanting to control her. At least he wasn't a rogue, like that bootlegger, and he certainly was attractive.

When the tension lessened between them in the late afternoon, they sat under the pinyon, while stew simmered on the campfire. It was far too hot to cook inside. While J.B. and Maddie were occupied across the wash, Ruth explained to David that at first she really *had* resolved to pull out of the part, but had gone back to all that applause—and the absolute promise of no more gunshots in her scenes, which had convinced her to continue.

"The shooting will be finished before winter," she reminded him. "I don't even have to go in for a shoot again until next week."

"Don't trust those people, Ruth," he said. "I can't be over there with you anymore." He glanced sheepishly away, then brought his eyes back. How somber he looked, she thought, remembering the flash of smile that never left his face the first few times they met. How it used to annoy her. She rarely saw it anymore. "Leave Maddie and J.B. with me at the dig," he said.

"If you like."

"There's nothing I like about it either way. Nothing I can do about it either, it seems." He reached down and picked up a twig from the ground, began sketching a rectangle in the dirt. "My thoughts on the matter seem to carry little weight with you."

Ruth suppressed a bitter smile, thinking of the day she'd first arrived on her site and Matt Baxter drew a rectangle in the sand to correct her own. "Just turn your house around," he had said. Some things never changed. And this was still *her* life, despite David's intrusion into it. She would make her own decisions. The more he pressured her, the stronger grew her desire to go the other way. Even in the beginning, when she had strong misgivings about taking part in the film, his being set against her doing it had helped convince her to go through with it.

"You're a hard woman to be with, Ruth," David said, bringing her back.

"You knew that from the start. No one forced you." She got up from her chair to check the stew, took a step, then turned back. "In fact, I clearly remember warning you off."

She was relieved to see a sudden flash of white teeth and brightening of his eyes. He leapt from his chair and snatched her to him. "That you did," he said, his eyes glazing as they dropped their gaze to her breasts. "Didn't slow me down a bit." He began covering her neck and shoulders with kisses. "It never will," he murmured into her skin. She felt his hand snake through the opening in her blouse to cup her breast, his thumb fondling her nipple.

Sparks chased each other down her back and up her thighs, working their way inside to ignite a full-fledged wildfire. She glanced across the wash to be sure her children were still occupied. "I'm not the only one who's stubborn, then," she reminded him, just before his lips covered over and quieted hers.

CHAPTER TWENTY-SIX

"You were magnificent in that part, Ruth. You looked just like a real squaw." Esther's bracelets jangled as she reached over to pat Ruth's cheek. "I'm so glad George came and got me. I just had to see your scene." She turned to her brother. "Don't you think she looks as real as any Indian squaw, George? And the way she jumped on that horse and rode off—as if it were something she did every day."

"It *is* something I do every day. And several times a day here on this shoot. We did five takes on that horse-mounting scene," Ruth told her. "It's a wonder Blue allowed it."

"You should have seen her first scene, Sister, where the horse reared back. Now that was magnificent." Golden shook his head and forked fried rice into his mouth. "I don't see how she can top that."

"Why should I want to?" Ruth took a taste of her fried rice. She preferred it to the vegetable dish, but she was not used to such foreign food. Frontiertown's Chinese restaurant seemed the crown jewel of unreal in this fanciful movie town. Even its name, the Golden Palomino, was a fiction that belied the cuisine. The place would be more appropriately called the Golden Dragon. And it perplexed her that the movie crew should be in here eating plentiful and rich foods—had in fact brought the restaurant here with them in the first place—while much of the country went hungry. How could she ever forget those breadlines and suffering faces, especially with newspapers being brought up daily for the crew to remind her? In the past, her access to newspapers had been an occasional glimpse of an old one at the general store in Juniper Valley. It used to be much easier to ignore the awful things outside her canyon.

She sat at the table with Golden, his sister, and the director, while other crew members occupied tables around them. She had noticed Ben come in with two men a few minutes before and found him watching her each time she glanced over. Such a small world, the movie community was. She never would have believed when she met him several years ago that they would someday be in a movie together way out here in the Rimrock—or anywhere else, for that matter. Even now, there were times when she thought she might wake up and find this whole movie thing a dream. A familiar feeling. The makeup that the men were wearing enhanced that unnatural feeling, but it worried her that she was getting used to men with makeup masks. Everything here, even her own self, was unreal. How quickly fake had come to seem natural to her. Only when she went home to Glory Springs could she remember what real was. Then she would look at her costumed self in the mirror and laugh.

"You will, won't you, Ruth?" Esther had hold of her arm. "Come stay at the Cricket once the shooting is done?"

Ruth looked up to find the three of them staring at her. "I'm sorry," she said. "I guess I drifted off."

"Indeed," Esther said. "I hope it was to a pleasant place." She let go of Ruth's arm and picked up her cigarette holder, waited while the director lit it. "We were talking about the cast party we'll have down at the Springs when all this is over. It will be a splendid shindig! You simply have to come stay for the weekend. And bring that wonderful little girl, both wonderful children. And that man friend of yours, if you like."

"I'll have to see," Ruth told her. "There's so much to do up at my place to get ready for winter. Maybe."

"Nonsense." Esther looked at her firmly. "One weekend away won't make any difference. I'll hear no more maybes out of you."

Ruth smiled in spite of herself. Her plan was to take J.B. and Maddie with her to Black Canyon as soon as the shooting was over. Maybe she could make the Cricket Club a stop along the way. She knew she'd better get back with her Indian friends before she started picturing them wearing fake fringed clothing. She'd been away far too long, ignored too many dreams where Thomas and Grandmother Siki were holding out their hands toward her. She was sure she had been called and felt shame for not yet answering. But the trip was too far to make on weekends, since it took the better part of a day to drive each way. Soon, she'd kept telling herself, soon. Now, soon was almost here.

David, she supposed, would pout about it when she told him, but she had decided not to take him with her to Black Canyon. In the beginning, she had all but pleaded with him to come with her to meet her friends, to meet the actual people whose ancestors' artifacts he dug up. She wanted to cure him of the cultural abstractions he was inventing. But he had no interest in Black Canyon then. Now that he had, he couldn't understand her reluctance to take him there. She wasn't sure she understood it either.

The scene she appeared in after lunch had only a small part for her. She was to be sighted again between buildings on Blue, observing unseen the crowd of men—led by Ben and another bad guy—as they hustled the white-hatted hero into the jailhouse. The plot called for planted evidence to be found linking him to the earlier bank robbery and murder actually done by Ben and his cohorts. Even though all she had to do was sit there in the heat on Juniper Blue, then swing him around and ride off as the men were herding the hero into jail, that task became more of a challenge than she expected. After many takes, the repetition might have bored her to sleep, except that Blue became increasingly restless, and she had to work to make him stay put until the actors got the scene right. Ben's acting, she noted, left a lot to be desired, but so did the others'.

Juniper Blue was still high-stepping and trying to twist around, letting out a snort each time she gave the light kick to his sides that told him to take off. She had let him run a short while each time before bringing him back, knowing the director would need a few minutes to set up for the next take. Ruth patted his neck as she rode him back, hoping this would be the final take. She remembered the dreams she'd once had of riding Blue over the mountains, his hooves barely grazing the surface of the earth. How different these boring scenes were from the freedom she had felt riding him in those dreams—rather like the realities of her life when compared to the idea of freedom that had inspired her to homestead Glory Springs.

She returned to find the director setting up for another scene entirely. He'd finally been pleased. All she had to do now was say goodbye to Esther before she and Golden left for the Springs, then she could ride over to the dig, where David was keeping J.B. and Maddie. She had ridden Blue as far as the Dirty Dog when she heard someone call her name. She turned to find Ben at the porch railing of the saloon, looking ridiculous dressed as a cowboy. She suppressed a smile. The hardscrabble city boy was as out of place here as she'd been in L.A.

"Wait up, Ruth," he said. "Could we talk a minute?"

"What about? Blue wants to get out of here. And so do I."

"How long are you going to stay away from me? I've told you I was sorry about what happened in Los Angeles."

"No need. You can see that these calluses come in handy for spurs," she said, lifting a foot out from the horse. She ran a hand along Juniper Blue's side to calm him, her palm filling with sweat and bits of short hairs she swept from his hide.

Ben gave her a cocky smile. "How about a beer, cowgirl? Or should I say Indian maiden?" He swung a leg over the railing and dropped down beside her. "I keep picturing what you'd look like up on that horse in the gown you wore that night."

Ruth hadn't thought about that silly gown in years. No one would ever dare wear a thing like that around Juniper Valley.

"How about it, then, doll?"

"How about what?"

"The beer." He nodded over his shoulder. "There. In the Dirty Dog."

Juniper Blue took a few fast steps sideways, causing Ben to leap for the high porch rail, as Golden's roadster approached. Laughing at the sight of the cardboard cowboy hanging on to the rail, attempting to fling his leg and shiny black boots back over, Ruth managed to calm the horse before Golden shut the engine off. She had thought Blue would get used to the new things here, but he had become increasingly edgy around this place lately. Thank god she had only the big rescue scene to go before the film ended. She didn't think she could control the animal any longer than that.

Once Ben had scrambled back over, Ruth slid down and tied Juniper Blue to the porch rail. She walked over to the roadster to tell Esther good-bye. Ruth liked this tall bony woman for some strange reason—maybe because she was liked in return. Maybe also because Esther was like no other woman Ruth had met; she had her own ways, as genteel and different as they were from Ruth's. Yet, like Ruth, she did not let others dissuade her from following her inclinations.

The idea of a cold beer had sounded good the first time, though she had been about to refuse. But when Ben came up beside her again as she waved Esther a final good-bye, Ruth consented. "Not in a brown paper bag this time," she goaded.

"Only the legit this time, I'm afraid. Those lucrative days are over for me, unfortunately. But I am getting more parts now." He gave her a crooked smile and took her arm as they walked toward the saloon. She noticed he gave Blue wide berth. "Nice horsey," he said as they skirted around him.

One beer led to another, and Ruth felt herself relaxing in a way she couldn't remember doing in some time. Even Ben's talk about other roles he'd played in the last few years and about losing his income from bootlegging began to fascinate her, enhanced as his stories were with that frequent asymmetric smile and the hank of dark hair that kept falling across his forehead, like the forelock of a horse. That, of course, reminded her of the dream she'd had in Los Angeles, where he had other horse features as well, and she hugged the humor of that memory to her like a happy secret.

She told him about her trips to Black Canyon and all she had been learning about wild foods from her friends, and was surprised to find that he listened intently, with interest, to what she was saying. At least she thought so, until she felt his hand on her thigh. She lifted it off and went on talking as if nothing unusual had happened—but not before she felt a hot shiver of lust between the thighs she had just declared off limits. She felt her neck and face heat, but stayed with the story she was telling. Then he took hold of her hand and interrupted her midsentence.

"I'd still like to show you a good time, dollface," he said. "I mean it. Just say the word." She became aware then of a flush in his face to match her own, and the image of what might lay under the table in his lap suddenly lost its humor, whetted instead a libidinous curiosity.

He looked out the window, then back at her face. "The camera tech said there was a man with you on the first shoot. Children too."

"I'm not married to him, if that's what you're asking," she said.

His hand slid up from hers to her upper arm, massaging it as the back of his hand pressed against her breast, intensifying her heat. "What's stopping us, then?"

Ruth drew her arm away. "I have to get back," she said, moving her chair away from the table. She lurched to her feet, suddenly feeling dizzy. The room around her blurred slightly.

"No you don't." He stood beside her and wrapped an arm around her waist. "Let's go somewhere, doll."

"I am going somewhere—but not with you." She sucked in air and marched toward the swinging doors of the saloon, knocking them open with her elbow. Outside, the world had blurred a bit, too, she realized, as she floated down the porch steps. Blue whinnied and stomped his forelegs as she came toward him.

Ben caught up, and she felt his arm lock around her waist again. She opened her mouth to protest, just as he swung her into his arms and clamped his mouth over hers. Her legs went rubbery as his tongue tickled its way inside. The large hardness pressed against her pelvis compelled her attention. When he released her mouth, his lips worked their way toward her ear. "You want it too, don't you, baby? Come on. I know a place we can go," he huffed into her ear, his breath tingling the skin left sloppy by his tongue. "God, I'd love to screw you."

His crude words showered cold snow on her hot body, cooling her heat in mid-melt. She pulled back her arm and whacked the side of his face so hard he had to take steps to keep his balance. By then she had Blue untied and was astride his back, the alcohol lubricating her every motion. As she galloped off, she heard the man call out her name.

She kicked the horse into a run. With air pushing her hair back and Blue's motion jerking her up and down, the world felt even more dreamlike. She heard her own laughter swallowed up in the wind. She had rescued herself in the nick of time, she thought, whatever a "nick" was. Thanks to Ben's vulgarity. Yet that was what she had wanted all right—to "screw" him. She tried on the word, something she hadn't heard since she left El Paso. "Screw," she thought, letting the images arise, "screw," and found it had power to arouse her. That and the horse's pounding motion.

Not Blue again: she thought David at least kept her safe from that. But they hadn't had a good—she tried on the word again—screw since that day he'd panicked and gone after her. Maybe that's what she needed, a "screw," she told herself, a "screw," "screw," "screw," the word creating a frenzy of drunken desire that she didn't even try to bring under control. Better Blue than Ben, she told herself, as she lost all will to fight the deliciousness enveloping her. And there was no one to rescue her from the rivers of pleasure that flooded through her.

Shame had reasserted itself before she reached the dig. Sobered now, she had no more lust left in her to counter it. What in the world was happening to her that a rake like Ben could bring out such appetite? Sometimes she couldn't make sense of herself. Bringing Blue to a halt, Ruth dismounted and led him on foot the last half mile. The horse didn't seem at all affected by her predicament.

David came rushing over the minute she appeared between the boulders. "Are you all right, Ruth? Did something happen again?"

"I just thought I'd give Blue a rest from riding him. After all, I've been sitting on the poor horse all day." She laid the reins back over his neck. "I hope that's all right with you," she added, when he came up and put an arm around her shoulders.

Her words brought him up, and she could see the wounding on his face. "You smell like beer," he said.

"I had one with some of the crew," she told him, "though it shouldn't concern you. If you don't want to keep Maddie and J.B., I'll take them out to the set with me. They're practically big enough to stay by themselves at Glory Springs."

"Why are you acting like this? I don't know what's got into you lately."

"Maybe it's what's not getting into me that matters." She cupped her hands and called out her children's names as she walked toward the boulders.

"What's that supposed to mean?" he called out, though he didn't follow her.

"Not a thing, David, not a thing," she shouted back. "Come on now, Maddie, we have to get home," she yelled. The girl, as usual, was taking her own sweet time coming down from the rocks. J.B. was already at the bottom of the boulder pile.

David walked up to the Model A as she herded the children into the car. He patted their heads, then followed her around to the driver's door. "I don't suppose you want me to follow you home," he said.

"Do whatever you want to," she told him, pulling her door closed. "It's not up to me."

"That's ridiculous."

"I want David to come," Maddie chimed in. Ruth stifled a desire to backhand the girl and turned the ignition.

"I wish you'd never gotten mixed up with that movie crowd." His hand gripped the open frame of the window.

"It's almost over, David. One more scene next week, and I'm through with *my* part." She pushed in the clutch and put the car in gear, careful not to look at him.

"That remains to be seen." He let go of the window frame.

Maddie and J.B. laughed, though Ruth didn't think he intended the wordplay. She felt her anger easing. "Of course you can come up, if you want to," she conceded.

"But do you want me to? I don't want to come otherwise." He shrugged, dropped his arms to his sides, where they hung abjectly.

"I don't know, David. I do and I don't. Take your pick." Ruth met his eyes. "I'm sorry if I'm being mean, David. It was a hard day over there. I can't wait for this thing to be over."

He nodded, and some of the melancholy lifted from his face. "I'll think about it, then. Maybe I'll come up later."

Ruth let out the clutch and the Model A jerked forward more abruptly than she intended, nearly flinging J.B. out the window. "Don't lean out like that, I told you, J.B. You can wave from inside the car."

The boy continued to wave good-bye to David as he hung halfway out the window. Maddie leaned out to join him, ignoring both Ruth's words and her mood. Maybe that was a good thing. She had been moody since this movie job started. Something about it seemed to be stirring things up in her, and Ben's being there didn't help matters. She didn't mean to be so nasty to David. The alcohol was no excuse. But his niceness grated on her for reasons she couldn't quite fathom. It wasn't the niceness itself. Jim had been just as wonderful to her as David had, and she enjoyed him without question. But there it was again. David was not Jim. She wished she could quit blaming him for that.

She was wrong to blame David for the sex, too, she knew. Her response to the diaphragm was not his fault. It had been good between them before that, despite her reservations about his not belonging to this land she loved. But their sex had never been the way it was with Jim, and suddenly she was filled with images of the ways she and Jim had made love, on rocks beside the lake, in the water, against trees. . . . The road in front of her blurred, not from alcohol this time.

As she drove on, Ruth vowed to not blame David for things he couldn't help not being—no matter how strongly she felt about them. She didn't like this meanness she felt growing in her. First with Maddie and now with David. Too much like Cally for comfort. Ruth had worked hard not to blame Maddie for her father's evil. Sometimes she even managed to like the girl. But she was always catching herself with ugly impulses.

And David was completely blameless, really. Was his only crime that he loved her? Was that what made her disdain him? Maybe, but his lack of love for the land saddened her also, as well as his disinterest in the Indian friends who were so important to her. Then there was the control issue. Was she imagining it? Other than that, she could not fault him for the way he treated her.

For the first time, she wondered what might have twisted her mother into meanness. She had always assumed it was just the way Cally was. But now she thought about the way her mother must have been treated by Ruth's grandfather's legitimate white family, who brought her up after Lolinda's death. Thought, too, about what Cally had said about Lolinda's treatment by her own people and by whites. Maybe these things made Cally the way she was, warped her out of shape. Ruth would never know. She kept finding more and more that life was not as simple as she'd thought. Like the petroglyphs on Rocky Mountain, stories carved into stone, life remained hard and unfathomable.

CHAPTER TWENTY-SEVEN

She had been feeling smug for days, couldn't help but gloat a bit whenever the opportunity arose. The shooting was over for her—and it had ended without any of David's dire predictions coming to pass. They weren't really predictions, she supposed, simply an overall pessimism about her making the movie. He had been convinced that more trouble was on the way, which made her positively triumphant the day her final scene ended without further incident. She nearly floated over to the dig to tell David. He had seemed glad enough, but Ruth had the feeling he was disappointed to be wrong.

She was even looking forward to tonight's cast party, had dug out and washed her old red dancing dress. It wasn't too out of date, she hoped, picturing herself whirling around the dance floor in it. Afterward she could get back to her real life—and as far as she was concerned, a trip to see her friends in Black Canyon would be the perfect way to start. To make it even more perfect, when David found she intended to make the cast party a first stop on her way to Black Canyon, he withdrew his earlier request to finally go meet her friends. So she didn't have to fight him about it. He had no desire to attend the party, and she could tell by the way his face tightened that he was holding back protests over her own going.

J.B. and Maddie had been disappointed that he wasn't coming with them, but they seemed to have forgotten all about it now, as they stood at the passenger window counting barrel cactus on the way through Devil's Garden. Even though it was late fall, Ruth could feel a light coat of sweat seep from her pores long before she reached Palm Springs. How much warmer it stayed down in the lower desert—it was a good thing Esther had sent word to come early in the day because she had some kind of surprise planned.

When they arrived at the Cricket Club, Esther greeted the children with gifts, a wooden cricket for each of them—which solicited more chirping than Ruth cared to hear, a doll for Maddie and a toy truck for J.B., though neither had much interest in ready-made toys. The books Esther presented did make them happy, though. Both had come to read well on their own. David continued to press her to send the two of them to the new schoolhouse in Juniper Valley. Education, he insisted, was crucial for their development. But there was more than one way to be educated, she thought. Besides, they read everything they could get their hands on. And who knew what the town's children would subject them to.

Ruth assumed that the scrumptious lunch prepared for them must be the surprise. A dubious surprise, given her predilection for foods natural to the area; everything in front of them had been imported from hundreds of miles away. Yet Ruth enjoyed Esther's delight in directing its presentation. The salad with its avocado, shrimp and crab, the cups of chowder, and the tender mignons of beef served with new potatoes were more than any of them could eat, even without the breads that were served alongside. Then raspberry sherbet for dessert. "But this is nothing," Esther told her, when Ruth protested that such plentiful and fancy dishes were much more than was necessary. "Wait until you see the fare for tonight."

While the table was still being cleared, her friend turned to her with a mysterious smile. "Now for your surprise," she said. Ruth followed her to a small shop that occupied the far corner of the lobby. "You're to borrow any gown and shoes you want to wear for tonight. Jewelry too, of course. Then Stella will do your hair. She's quite superb."

Ruth explained that she had brought her own dress, but Esther insisted on seeing it. When Ruth pulled it from her satchel, Esther blanched and clutched a hand to the ample gold necklace on her chest.

"Oh, Ruth. Surely you're joking. And where are your heels? Surely you aren't intending to wear those boots. Or were you planning to walk into the ballroom in rags and barefoot like the Indian squaw you play? For heaven's sake, Ruth." Even the dress shoes Ruth brought out would not do, Esther said. In the end, Ruth had to agree to dress, shoes, and jewelry—and to having her hair "done" later that afternoon, though the very idea of being "done" to—sitting still while someone fussed over her—made her question her decision to attend the party in the first place. The potluck dances in Juniper Valley suddenly seemed a lot more fun, even with their repetitive two-stepping. All the fuss and rigmarole here over trivia bored her, and she couldn't help but have qualms over the money she saw being spent on such things. The evening event suddenly appeared to be simply something she had to get through before she could leave for Black Canyon.

J.B. and Maddie seemed to have no such hesitations, though, es-pecially once they found the swimming pool, a place quite different from the small, muddy ponds at the Willows or Barker's Tank where Ruth sometimes took them. Esther and Ruth joined them for a time, Ruth wearing a borrowed suit. How amazing to see clear to the pool's bottom as she swam, to find no strips of green scum or fungus float-ing around the top to avoid sucking in. Though she enjoyed the feel of cool water on her body, the water smelled strange and didn't seem natural to her. After a few laps across the pool she got out.

The children continued to swim off and on through the afternoon. Ruth sat for a while under an umbrella with Esther, until it was time to put her good slacks and blouse back on and have her hair done. She had never done so much sitting around waiting in her life as she had during the making of the movie and here at the Cricket Club, she thought, then sat waiting an hour or so more inside while Stella fussed over her hair. Esther seemed to assume it was natural to be served and done for. Ruth thought about the lines of hungry people who waited on city streets for bowls of soup. The ways of the modern world seemed extremely odd. She pictured Martha and Grandmother Siki grinding flour and patting it into bread in Black Canyon—and Kate making pastries. Herself making biscuits and bread at Glory Springs. What happened to the satisfaction of that in a world where everything was made for you somewhere else?

All this sitting around made her think too much. She'd rather be doing something. Maybe when her hair was done, she should just gather up her things, get J.B. and Maddie in the Model A, and drive off. She knew she wouldn't do that to Esther, but the idea that she *could* do so gave her relief.

The result, when the rollers were finally out of her hair and Stella had finished and turned Ruth to the big mirror to view it, was enough to make Ruth catch her breath. The swirling shiny mass swept up atop her head with strands left to dangle at the neck looked more like a wig than her own hair. She had been turned into some other person, and now appeared as unreal to herself as did the rest of the place around her. She sat amazed in front of the mirror while Stella went to call Esther in. Who was this strange woman? What role was she to play tonight?

"I knew it. I just knew it," Esther raved when she rushed into the room. She clapped her hands together. "Oh, my dear girl, you are a regular glamour queen now—or will be when we get you dressed right. Just wait until George sees you."

Still stupefied, Ruth let herself be guided out into the lobby, where she gratefully accepted a glass of red wine. "This is the best of the reserve," Esther told her. "To celebrate your transformation."

Ruth had never tasted anything quite like it. It was as good as any belt of whiskey. Her earlier resolution to stay away from such drinks until she was safely in her own canyon did not deter her from enjoying this one thoroughly. After all, she *was* celebrating a transformation of sorts—not the one Esther thought, but a return to the life she had set aside to do the movie.

When her glass was refilled, she enjoyed that one as well, and it wasn't long before she was not nearly as bored as before, nor as concerned with the artificiality of her surroundings. They soon became, as a matter of fact, quite comfortably ordinary, as if this were her natural setting. By the time her glass was refilled again, she was more than willing to go along with things the way they were.

By late afternoon, other members of the cast had begun arriving and were settling in to their rooms. After a snack of plentiful lunch leftovers, meant to serve as the children's supper, Ruth took J.B. and Maddie to the suite Esther had provided and began laying out her clothing. While they sat on the bed reading to one another, she allowed herself a luxurious soak in the porcelain tub, not once thinking it out of the ordinary. This was a time to simply enjoy herself, to ride out the evening in style. Tomorrow would be time enough to go back to the life that was real to her. Wine had rounded off the rough edges that had troubled her earlier, and she soaked for a very long time, immersed to her neck, drowsy and comfortable, her head with its fancy hairdo safely above the water, having no thoughts at all. Despite the excitement of being at the Cricket Club, the afternoon's swimming had worn the children out, and they fell asleep soon after Ruth finished her bath. Pulling a light blanket over each of them, she quietly closed the door to their room. Now she was truly free for the evening.

Ruth slid on her satin gown and pulled up the hose Esther had insisted she wear. She felt herself back in the spirit of playing a character in a novel—or movie, much in the same frame of mind she had succumbed to that night in Los Angeles. The woman she saw in the mirror was certainly not anyone she knew. No fringed dress for her, either. Then where was her maid, she asked herself laughingly, as she strung the sparkling necklace across her chest. Dangling earrings gave this woman in the mirror an air of glamour, and she turned her head from side to side to make the earrings swing.

There was a light knock, then Esther's voice at the door. "Ruth, it's me. Can I come in?"

"I thought so," Esther said accusingly when Ruth opened the door. "Not a stitch of makeup on. Not even lipstick."

"I don't have any makeup. I don't like wearing it."

"Well, you don't usually need it. But with that dress it's absolutely essential." She waved a little cloth bag in the air.

Ruth went along with her. The makeup job, light as it turned out to be, was simply another aspect of the part she would be playing tonight, Ruth told herself. Maybe she should give herself another name for the evening, Rachel or Rosalinda. Palm Springs was too warm a place for a name like Natasha.

When she walked into the ballroom, Ruth had no trouble sensing the impression she made. As the role of her character required, heads turned, and a momentary hush occurred before the voices picked up again, much like the descriptions she'd read of such entrances in many novels, modern and otherwise. She liked this setting infinitely better than the nightclub in L.A., she thought, surveying the grand chandeliers. Walking in beside Esther on shoes that felt like miniature stilts, Ruth smiled at no one in particular and at everyone in general as they made their way over to the buffet table, where Golden was standing. He turned away from the men and women he had been conversing with to greet Ruth with enthusiasm.

Ruth's head had not fully cleared from the afternoon wine—in truth she did not want it to—and when someone handed her a glass now, she happily accepted it. She wanted to drown out the memories that nagged, reminding her of other times she'd thrown caution to the wind and the disasters that followed. For now she would enjoy herself. She held out her wineglass for more whenever a waiter passed.

The table beside them was replete with everything from lobster—something Ruth had only seen pictures of—and gigantic hunks of beef, served by men with stiffened collars, to so many other dishes it confused her to sort them out with her eyes. Aside from her usual disdain for such foreign foods, eating did not seem a part of the role at the moment. Then who was this woman she was playing? She would figure it out as she went, she told herself, letting the evening open out in front of her like a novel being written as she lived it.

Golden introduced to her to many in the crowd that seemed to follow them across the room. Ruth could not seem to remember a single name or title held by any of them. *His little rustic star in the making,* he kept calling her. She went through the motions of being there, smiled and carried on light conversation. Yet, after a while, even the idea of playing a glamorous role bored her, and her attention drifted to the orchestra and the small number of people who were dancing in front of the band platform. The music was almost as boring and unreal as the rest, but at least it was something.

Eventually, someone asked her to dance, and once out on the dance floor, she was able to put her role aside and actually enjoy herself, especially when the slow beat of the music picked up. She began to let go, to dance without having to carry on conversations with any of the men who cut in. In their tuxedos, they reminded her of those strange arctic birds she'd seen once in a magazine. Someone was always waiting to ask for the next dance and keep her out on the floor. How glad she was that her injured leg held up; it seemed completely healed tonight, except for an occasional twinge in the knee.

Ruth had noticed Ben watching her from the sidelines. He looked especially seductive in the formal tux that could barely contain the scruffy slum boy inside it. She turned her head away and refused to meet his eyes, the way she had done whenever she saw him after the fiasco of their last encounter. Now, though, she had to repress a smile at the thought of it. Let that Chicago bootlegger eat his heart out at the way she looked tonight.

Not until the orchestra took a break was she escorted again to the sidelines by her final dance partner, a tall man about her age, with dark hair. He kept up a steady stream of talk about the plans he had for himself as a film star as they walked toward the table of food. This guy had no idea of releasing her, she realized, as she took a plate and began loading it up—dancing had given her quite an appetite. At the moment it didn't matter where the food came from; it was there, and she would eat it. She was just wondering how to escape her captor when Esther showed up to rescue her.

"There you are. Come away to our table," Esther said, hooking her by the arm and whisking her away from the dance partner, who stood like a statue, his mouth locked open in midsentence. "George has been telling everyone just how good you are with that horse of yours."

Ruth snatched one last bun from the basket beside her as they moved away. "Thanks for rescuing me," she said.

"We were about ready to come out and pull you off the dance floor."

"Oh, I'm glad you didn't do that. Dancing is what I love best." She plucked a strawberry from her plate and popped it in her mouth. She hadn't eaten a strawberry since the ones she sneaked out of her Aunt Myrtle's garden in El Paso, she realized, savoring the tart-sweet flavor exploding against her tongue.

After Golden introduced her, people in the group began asking questions about her life in the canyon; apparently she had been much discussed in her absence. The last thing Ruth had wanted was to talk about her life in the canyon tonight—especially with a plate of exotic food in front of her, and at first she only answered politely between bites. But everyone seemed eager to hear her stories, and soon she relaxed into her tale and began shaping ordinary incidents into dramatic form that fascinated her listeners completely. Another glass of wine encouraged her to further enhance the details.

"But how can you live in such a place like that all by yourself?" a woman wanted to know. "With two children, for heaven's sake."

"And no man around," the woman's director husband said. "Surely a man would make things easier."

"Oh, I bring up a man occasionally, when necessary," Ruth said, in a burst of wickedness. "They do have their purposes." Esther and Golden beamed with the success of their evening's entertainment.

Ruth's glass had just been refilled when the music began again, and her feet began to keep the beat under the table as she talked. "Hello, Ruth." A melodic voice sang out the words near her ear. Electric fingers sent tingles across the bare skin of her shoulder. "What do you say we go cut up another rug?" The mirror in front of her broadcast an intriguing mischief in his eyes.

"Don't take her away, Ben. Things were just starting to get interesting," Golden told him. "She's been riveting us with her stories."

"I'll be back." Ruth took one last sip of the wine and got to her feet. "The dance floor is calling me." Along with something else.

Ben whispered something as they walked, his hand caressing her waist, but she couldn't hear the words through the voices and music, didn't need to anyway. He pulled her close on the dance floor, and she felt her body snuggle against his hardness, but they had hardly begun when someone cut in. He resisted surrendering her until Ruth wondered if there might be a fight. Then Ben moved off but cut back in again and again between her other partners, all of whom kept trying to start up conversations. After a few tunes, the beat picked up considerably, and she kicked off her shoes at the sidelines.

How she loved to give her body over to the music, let melody and beat get inside to drive away all worry and thought, until there was nothing left but music and movement, not even herself.

When the orchestra took another break, it was Ben who took her arm as she reclaimed her footwear. He began leading her from the floor, but in a direction other than the table they had come from. Ruth glanced over to see Golden and Esther immersed in conversation with a man who had taken over her chair. The idea of returning to the table to resume stories of her life in the wild did not appeal to her in the slightest, though she knew letting Ben guide her away from the crowd might not be entirely wise.

"Let's get out of this joint," Ben was saying, as they went out the door onto an unlit patio. "I want you all to myself, Cinderella."

"But I'm having a good time. Only until the break is over. Then—"

He put his finger to her lips to quiet her, looked down at her with dark eyes she couldn't quite see into. They looked more like shadowed alleys that she could get lost in. "We can have a better time out here," he said, then took her arm and led her to the edge of the deserted patio, sat her on its wall.

"Wait there. I'll be right back." He rushed in again through the open door.

Ruth set her shoes on the patio wall, peeling off what was left of the stockings she'd worn and stuffing them into the shoes. She looked up at the stars and the pale sliver of moon. These stars were dimmer and fewer overhead than in her canyon, where there was no surrounding light. But the sky was so huge here; the Milky Way extended out to a desert horizon unhindered by canyon mountains. The view of the sky behind her, though, was blocked by a mountain even larger than Rocky Mountain, the Milky Way seeming to pour out of its black peak and stream across the sky. Night had cooled the desert's heat, and she took in large breaths of flower scent on the balmy evening air. Gradually, she began to remember what was real again.

Ben appeared in the lit doorway carrying a bottle and two glasses. "Let's walk, before someone finds us. I saw Golden looking around the room for you." Walking sounded like a fine idea, she thought, as they climbed over the low patio wall.

Traipsing out onto the lush grass, Ruth savored the feel of soft blades under her soles and between her toes. The last time she'd walked on lawn was in Los Angeles. "This is more fun than walking on glass, I'll bet," Ben laughed.

She laughed with him. "But the effect is not nearly as dramatic." It had taken several days for her feet to heal after her act of drunken bravado.

They sat on the grass near a large leafy tree of some kind, nice but certainly not one she'd seen in the area, Ruth mused, as she looked up at the fanlike leaves. She heard a sucking *pop* and looked over to see Ben catching liquid from the bottle in one of the glasses. "I scored some champagne," he said.

"I think I've had enough to drink," Ruth told him. "My head's finally beginning to clear."

"Oh, you don't want that. Not yet anyway. Besides, this is the good stuff. Half a glass won't hurt you." He stopped pouring and handed her just over half a glassful. She remembered the champagne from the novels. She never got to try it in Los Angeles. Ruth turned the glass slowly, letting light from the door and big bay windows reflect color onto the bubbles. Against the light, she could see constant streams of tiny globes coming out of nowhere to rise to the top of the glass.

"It's like some kind of magic potion. Small bubbles rising," she laughed, knowing he wouldn't understand the allusion.

"A toast." Ben held up the glass he'd just poured himself. "Here's to us," he said, "and good times together." He touched his glass to hers.

Soft light from the windows brought shadow and form to his face, giving the illusion of depth. "Depends on what you mean by good times," she said. "I want to be sure what I'm toasting."

"I think you know," he said.

"Maybe." She pulled her eyes away and pressed her glass against his, took a sip to quell the knowing below her belly. Champagne was indeed fine, even if it did tickle the inside of her nose. And so light as to be inconsequential, like this attraction between them. She took a more substantial swallow.

"What's maybe about it?" Ben asked. He moved closer and let his finger trail down her arm, leaving a row of sparks behind. "Unfinished business. Isn't that why you came out here with me?"

"I don't know why. Not for sure." She polished off the rest of the champagne, held out her glass. "I just don't want to do anything more that interferes with living in my canyon. It's my whole life," she said when he picked up the bottle to refill their glasses. "Working in that film was enough interference."

He pulled his hand away. "So my competition is a canyon? Then why do you keep leaving the place? Like coming here? And the time you came to L.A.? For a woman who claims to love some wild place, you certainly travel a long way to escape it."

"I didn't go willingly to L.A." Ruth sipped at her champagne, relishing the bubbly liquid before swallowing it. "But maybe I'd been reading too many books about the glamour of the modern world. Lies," she said. "I found L.A. a scary place. I have everything I need in my own canyon."

"And what is that? What could you possibly find in some desolate spot that isn't in a place like L.A.?" He ran a hand down her back, let his fingers rest just inside the material of her dress. "L.A. has everything Chicago didn't. At night, it's the bright lights, in the day, perpetual sunshine."

She shrugged it away. "L.A. has champagne, and dancing and movies and big buildings and department stores, and trolleys, and people everywhere. But it doesn't have everything. It doesn't have acorns or bobcats or bear or pinyon pines or mesquite or chia. It doesn't have the music of wind in the pines. And it surely doesn't have quiet."

"Well, I'm glad of that. Who wants quiet? It's all about excitement, baby." His hand ran down her arm and trapped the back of her hand against the grass. "That's what I want—and an exciting woman . . . I need that too," he said. She could feel his eyes scrutinize her body. "You should be wearing that dress in the movie instead of the idiotic fringe." He set down his glass and turned her toward him, let one finger make its way down alongside the neckline of her dress.

"We'd better go in. Esther must be wondering where I've gotten myself to." Fighting the fire growing below her belly, Ruth edged away and got to her knees, then stopped to allow a sudden dizziness to pass.

"Let's just finish up the last of the champagne first. It'd be a shame to waste it." He tugged suggestively at her hem and held out the bottle. "There's only a little left. Where I come from, we don't waste something this fine."

"My head feels full of bubbles already," she said, but he filled the glass in her hand anyway.

She took a sip when the dizziness passed, then began struggling the rest of the way to her feet. The dress was in her way, and another short spurt of vertigo came over her, so she lifted the skirt above her knees to maneuver. Still slightly off balance, one leg brushed against the man on the ground below, her weight pushing against him.

"For someone who's trying to leave, you're sure tempting me to keep you here." Ruth looked down to find his face centered between the thighs she had half bared. Before she could drop the skirt of her dress, she felt his lips graze the inside of her thigh just above the knee. She meant to step away but felt her knees loosen, loosen further as his lips traveled higher. His hand gripped her buttocks, and she felt him easing her back down on the grass. Brought fully into her body, rational thought deserted her, and she knew only her own raw heat and warm night air on her bare skin as he pushed her dress up and pulled it over her head.

Soft grass prickled under her back while he kneaded her breasts, kissed and sucked them until her fire raged higher. And those words he kept whispering in an endless stream, some she had only heard spoken in her mother's brothel, intensified his every touch.

The shock she registered when she felt lips then a tongue where no tongue had been before was overridden by the explosion of lust it generated. When he pushed himself inside her, it was not the horse length of her dream, but it fit her exactly.

She wrapped her legs around him to push him deeper yet, but he resisted and began to tease her, holding her back while he made abbreviated thrusts, even as she used her hands to force his pelvis closer. As frustrated as she was overheated, Ruth twisted around and rolled him over.

She began jamming herself down on him. "That's right, baby. Do it, you wild thing you. Screw me good, now." So she did. Yet just as pleasure was about to overtake her, she felt herself lifted away slightly and returned to have the grass under her back. The abbreviated thrusts started up again, mechanically, as if by a machine. She was being "screwed," she knew. That's what this contest was for both of them. "Fight me for it, that's right," he said, bringing his tongue up between her breasts.

All right, city boy, she thought, you asked for it, and twisted around again, trying to roll him over. But he had positioned himself firmly this time and wouldn't budge. "What are you going to do now, baby?" He laughed. "Let's see what the wild woman's got in her."

Ruth began using her legs to kick each thrust deeper, until he let go of her breasts and held her legs away. Yet that gave her room to maneuver her arms and upper torso and soon she had the two of them at least on their side. Yet the controlled half-pumping continued uninterrupted, as her craving intensified.

"Okay then, baby," he whispered, gripping her cheeks and yanking her into him again. "Like that? Huh. Isn't that what you want?"

They began pulling and pushing and ramming at each other in a way Ruth had never before experienced or imagined, as if she had left herself behind and returned to some prehuman state. She grabbed and bit and pulled, raking fingernails across his flesh, as Ben jerked her body around like the limp carcass of some rabbit she had shot. She wanted to destroy him, to erase this denizen of dirty back alleys. Teach him what wild was really about.

When the explosion between them came, it was more powerful and unsettling than anything she had known before, so intense it seemed to blow apart something sacred inside her, leaving her in a wasted heap beside him on the grass.

A hot welling filled her eyes. This was not the part she had intended to play tonight—nor ever. For a moment more, she lay quiet on her side, her silvery dress only inches away from her face. A hiccuping sob escaped her. What had she done? Who had she become? Where was the Ruth who had loved Indian Jim? What else might she be capable of, disconnected from the man and the place she loved?

Ruth snatched up her dress and ran toward the building. Ben didn't make a move to stop her as she left. Almost sober now, she headed away from the windows, toward the side with the swimming pool, and opened the gate to the darkened pool. Could even this much water ever wash the shame from her? She stood for a moment watching stars afloat on the black fluid, then dropped her dress on the cement and jumped feet first into the liquid sky.

CHAPTER TWENTY-EIGHT

It was full daylight when the children's voices pried sleep from her mind. Ruth fought consciousness for a while, shying away from the ache waking brought to her head and heart. She tried to slip back into the one remnant of dream left to her—a glimpse of Jim descending the bluff across the wash at Glory Springs, as he had the first time she saw him. In the dream, she was filled with joy at his return, had fully believed he was with her, that the voice and touch she loved would be hers to enjoy again. Waking reminded her better. His being at the bluff was real, all right—he was buried beneath it. That was what was real.

The remainder of the heart pain she felt came from blurred memories of the night before. How could she have come so low? Betrayed herself and all she and Jim had shared. It occurred to her that it should be David she felt she betrayed, but it was not David who owned her heart, and so her body. She could receive him without desecration, yet he did not belong there any more than he belonged to Glory Springs. But what had made her consort with the likes of Ben? Was her wanton appetite so enormous she couldn't contain it?

For such a long time after the rape and births, she had been deadened to her core. No man tempted her in the slightest. It had been Ben who first aroused her in L.A., but she had managed to escape entanglement. She had blamed the incident on her reaction to her mother. But last night's tryst had no such excuse. None at all. And Ben's questioning her loyalty to Glory Springs still troubled her. For all her talk, and the effort she spent making the canyon her soul's lover, she had belied her promise with every association with the Hollywood crowd, with the phony town that was a mockery of the place she loved. Perhaps once she had compromised by taking David as a lover, she had set something corrupt in motion.

How grateful she was to be finished making that film. Sitting by the pool late into the night before, letting the balmy air dry her, she was kept from despair only by the knowledge that in the morning she would leave this place and the Frontiertown movie crowd behind. At last she could answer the heart-calling she had ignored the last few weeks in order to finish the movie and go see her Indian friends. Never again would she let a moneymaking pursuit get in the way of what was important.

By the time Ruth finally decided to open her eyes, J.B. and Maddie had dressed themselves for Black Canyon and stuffed yesterday's good clothes into their satchels. "Let's go see Grandmother Siki now," Maddie said, when she saw Ruth was awake.

"And Billy and Frank. And Thomas," J.B. added.

"Yes, let's," Ruth told them, smiling suddenly. "Let's get out of this crazy place before we all forget what's real." She sat up and swung her legs over the edge of the bed.

The three of them were in the hallway, walking toward the lobby, a few minutes later. But as they passed the dining room doorway, Esther's voice called out her name. Ruth took another two steps forward, curtailing an urge to break into a run out the hotel door when Esther called out again.

"Ruth. Ruth, you aren't leaving yet, are you? Not without saying good-bye?" A certain bewilderment filled her voice.

Ruth stopped, looked down at Maddie and J.B., who had stopped as well. "I guess we have to do it," she sighed. Without a word, they all turned and trudged into the dining room, where Esther sat at the table with her brother and another man.

"We were just going out to put things in the car," Ruth lied as she approached. "The shoes and jewelry are still in the room." That at least was true.

"Come here, dears," Esther said to Maddie and J.B., setting down her cigarette and holder. She caught them up in a hug when they reached her. "Put that stuff down and climb up into one of these chairs. Tell Mary what you want for breakfast."

"We're not staying for breakfast," Ruth told her. "I brought along some jerky and flatcake to eat on the way to Black Canyon."

"Nonsense. What kind of breakfast would that be? I won't hear of it. Now take a seat." She patted the chair next to her.

Ruth and her children glanced helplessly at each other, then did as they were told. Ignoring Esther's request would be impossible without insulting her—and they liked her too much for that.

"Where did you run off to last night?" Esther asked, once Mary had gone to fetch their breakfasts, leaving Ruth a cup of weak and tasteless coffee. Esther pushed the cream and sugar toward them, the copper balls on her necklace clattering as she leaned forward. "We were afraid we'd offended you somehow. Maybe something said to you at the table?"

"Oh, no, of course you didn't offend me. You've been wonderful to me. I just . . ." Ruth swallowed back her first thought and said, "I'm not used to being around so many people for so long." That, too, was partial truth.

"Someone said they saw you go outside with Ben Philips, although I didn't think his type would appeal to you." She gave Ruth an odd look.

"That didn't last long," Ruth told her quickly. "I wanted to be by myself." Yet another half-truth.

"Maybe that's why he looked so gloomy when he came in later," Golden said. "It must have been the rebuff you gave him."

Ruth felt herself coloring and was relieved to see Mary heading their way with juice and toast. "I certainly don't care to see any more of that man. Thank god the shooting's finished."

Golden exchanged glances with the man next to him, then turned toward Ruth. "Well, that may not be quite the case, Ruth. Jack's been telling me there's been a problem with your last scene."

Ruth wanted to stop up her ears as he continued, explaining how a camera mistake had ruined what had otherwise been a perfectly good take of her scene, one that now needed to be reshot.

"But I thought I was through. You said it was a great take. Surely there was more than one camera there," she fairly sputtered. The blood rush in her ears nearly blocked the rest of his explanation, most of which was so technical that she couldn't understand it anyway. The upshot she understood clearly enough, but she could not accept it.

"I can't do it," she told him. "I won't. You said the film was finished. At least my part in it."

"I thought it was. The whole damned film." Golden took a drink from his coffee cup so Mary could refill it. "Look," he said, "this is just as inconvenient for me as it is for you. More so. All it takes for you is a few more hours in an area near where you live. I have to bring back the camera crew and actors et cetera, to a place nearly a hundred and fifty miles from home base. Over those goddamned dirt roads. But the film can't exist now without your scene. And no one gets paid until it does."

The development cast a pall over her whole day, over all of her life as well, she felt, as she drove toward Black Canyon a short while later. J.B. and Maddie felt it, too, Ruth could tell by their continued silence. The breakfast conversation had lightened a bit after Golden's initial announcement, but Ruth's equilibrium, fragile as it had been in the first place, hadn't returned. And though she hadn't actually agreed to the reshoot, she had stopped saying no after he brought up the issue of pay. How could she afford to say no? Although she'd vowed not let her need for funds seduce her into making *another* film, she damn well needed to get paid for this one.

The children's faces brightened some when she turned off the main highway onto the dirt road to Black Canyon, and that lifted her spirits as well. "We're almost there," she said as lightly as she could manage.

"It won't be long now." So much depended on the salvation that lay up in this canyon.

Their life had been thrown off balance by her making the film, and reconnecting with their friends in Black Canyon seemed the only way to bring it back into balance. Not that their life had been harmonious before the film: There was always tension—her conflictedness about David, the residue of resentment with Maddie, the pain of Kate and John's move to Montana for work, and her own bouts of restlessness. But somehow all of that held together—until the film came along.

And now she faced having to redo that scene.

Ruth knew well that her desperate need to see her friends did not bode well, remembered driving up this road in a similar state of mind several years ago and finding everyone gone. Sometimes she wondered if desperation drove the things she needed away from her.

In the rumble seat were the two ollas she was bringing for Martha to sell. Her friends had been amazed when she brought down some ollas to show them a few months ago. Except for Grandmother Siki, whose hands were too arthritic to work now, knowledge of olla making had been lost. Maybe, Ruth thought, it was the desire to work with clay earth—and the time to do it—that had been lost. The next time she came, she brought an assortment of plates and bowls that she had fashioned for them. She had already made plenty for herself and the children. Martha had sold two of the larger ollas—her friends called them *niaha*—and asked Ruth to bring others if she had them. The old style, it seemed, was still valuable, and Ruth felt privileged that they let her contribute. It made her feel one of them.

When she rounded the bend that brought the little settlement into view, the three of them let out their breaths in a collective whoosh of relief. "Look, Maddie," J.B. cried out. "They *are* home." At least it appeared so, with all the cars and people moving about. Ruth tromped harder on the gas.

"Where is she?" Maddie asked in a quiet voice. "Grandmother Siki? I don't see her."

"She's probably inside. Look, there's Martha coming out of the *ki'takii* now," Ruth told her. She thought it odd that Martha would be in traditional dress, knew of no ceremonies at this time of the season. The old woman did not come out behind her either, Ruth noticed.

She parked the car alongside the rusted pickup and walked with the children toward the center of the settlement.

The fact registered that no other children ran out to greet hers, and that she heard no one call out her name as she approached, but it wasn't until she had entered the small community that the full extent of the somber mood registered. She saw the sadness on their faces, then, heard it in air absent of laughter and voices.

"Grandmother Siki," Maddie yelled, running off toward the woman's other house and *ki'takii,* while J.B. ran to the group of boys who were quietly playing a game with acorn cups.

Martha glanced down at Maddie running past her, then lifted her eyes to Ruth's, who nearly winced at the sadness in them. "What happened, Martha? Is Grandmother Siki ill?" she asked softly, hoping for an answer that would put an end to the cold knot growing in her.

Martha shook her head slowly. Her eyes welled above lips that trembled slightly. "Today is her *nonach'ili.*" She took in a breath, and tears rolled down her cheeks as she looked at Ruth, yet beyond her, as if to some place of great grief. Ruth closed her eyes, unable to look at her friend's pain. The *nonach'ili,* where relatives did the first burning of the person's precious possessions, took place a month after death.

"You need to get dressed," Martha said. "In the *ki'takii* this time."

Stunned, as if she'd just smashed facefirst into solid rock, Ruth followed Martha toward Grandmother Siki's *ki'takii.* Maddie was running back toward her from the other house. "Where is she? Where is she?" The girl's voice was frantic. "She's not in there."

Ruth cleared her throat and held up a hand to stop her. "This is the day of her *nonach'ili,* Maddie," she said. Ruth reached out her arm, but stopped in mid-motion. The girl seemed to go empty before Ruth's eyes. For a moment, Maddie seemed on the brink of tears, then she swallowed it all back, as if her feelings had been sucked into the dry sand of a wash. Maddie turned away and shuffled to the edge of the clearing. By the time Ruth reached the *ki'takii,* Maddie had sunk to the ground and sat there, limp as a plucked yucca blossom. Ruth almost went to her, though she suspected she'd be rebuffed, so she turned and went into the brush dwelling to get herself properly dressed to honor and respect the beloved old woman.

Grandmother Siki's presence still filled the *ki'takii.* Ruth's throat choked and a hot lump swelled her chest. Now she understood where all this heart-calling had come from, the strong pull that she had ignored in order to make the film. While she was playing fantasy Indian for a celluloid illusion, the real Indian woman was here dying. Or somewhere dying. She sensed that with Grandmother Siki's death the core of everything here died as well. The utter finality of the event bore down on her—along with the irrevocable effect of her decision to delay coming here. To have been summoned one last time—and not come. And if she *had* known what was happening, would she have left the film to see the woman? She would like to think so, but she was no longer sure of herself.

When she came out of the *ki'takii* wearing the green dress, she noticed that an older girl had joined Maddie at the edge of the clearing. They didn't seem to be conversing, as Maddie ran dirt through her fingers, but her daughter's back, Ruth thought, was straighter now. J.B. had joined the boys in what had to be the most silent game of weighted acorn cups she had seen played here. On her way back to question Martha, Ruth saw Thomas and Lemuel walking into the large *kit'catact* in the community's center. Above the traditional ceremonial loincloth—now worn over white trousers—a slash of long dark stripes ran diagonally down and across Thomas's bare back. She didn't remember that paint design from the other *nonach'ili* she'd been to. Maybe Grandmother Siki's would be different.

Martha kept her eyes from Ruth's face when she joined her and three others, her sister and two cousins, spreading foods out on a table under the arbor. Ruth took it as a sign that the woman did not want to converse, though Ruth was anxious to know what had happened. Grandmother Siki had seemed so healthy, so full of life only two months ago. How had she sickened so quickly? Or had something else happened? But no one seemed to want to tell her, so Ruth held her questions and worked along with the rest. From the Model A, she fetched the pemmican and goat jerky to go along with the other traditional foods already on the table. The knowledge that she had ignored the heart-calling weighed on her chest like a stone. She had the feeling the others knew.

The afternoon plodded on like the dirge she supposed it was, and Ruth plodded with it. Even the air hung heavy as it moved sluggishly

286

through the canyon, as if saturated with a thick glumness. The notion of balance and lightheartedness that she had been so desperate for had fallen away, and Ruth was left with a more intense sense of the world out of kilter than before. More than just *her* world now, a larger world that she counted on seemed to be in danger—as if she were witnessing the fading away of something profoundly precious. She tried not to put thoughts to the feelings churning through her, hoping they would soon settle to the bottom like coffee grounds when a pot stopped boiling.

Her intuition seemed confirmed when she heard Martha telling her sister about her husband, Jackson. From what Ruth could piece together, Jackson was now in jail in Banning. It wasn't just for drunkenness this time, although Martha said he had been drunk when he got the notion of going to the liquor store to reclaim what had formerly been Yuiatei land. If only he hadn't taken that rifle with him, even if it wasn't loaded. Later the sheriff had found him passed out by the whiskey section. No wonder Martha seemed so distracted, Ruth realized. She didn't want to probe her for details about Grandmother Siki.

It wasn't until early evening, when the burning ceremony was about to begin, that Ruth found out some of what had happened to her, and only then when she was startled to see a huge brown bearskin—the largest Ruth had laid eyes on—brought out of the *kit'catact*. Lemuel and three other men walked out in front of Thomas to place it with other objects beside the newly lit campfire, Lemuel's limp, as always, distinguishing him from the rest. When Thomas passed her, she was aghast to realize that the long dark lines on his back were not paint but half-healed scabs and scars, some with thick stitching visible, and that another set had been scraped across his cheek. The shock knocked her back a step, against Martha, who had come up beside her.

"It was that bear," Martha whispered. "The one they made unseen. It came back here wounded." She stopped, and Ruth heard her pull in a breath. "Grandmother tried to speak to it again, to tell it to go back and hide from the Teske who shot it." Ruth heard the sob buried beneath the words. "But she was too angry, that bear, and she hit Grandmother across the belly. Like this," she said, and Ruth felt the impact of Martha's blow, the rake of nails that didn't penetrate the cloth of her dress the way the bear's claws would have penetrated the old woman's belly. Even so it nearly knocked the breath out of her. She barely heard Martha's next words, they dwindled away so softly into air. "The bear was mad at us because the peeled man with the gun saw her. Sometimes making unseen doesn't work, you know. That's what Grandmother said."

The woman's face was scrunched up now, her eyes squinched shut against the words she whispered. "Thomas jumped in there and covered Grandmother with his body, but it was too late. Then Lemuel put our big gun to the bear's eye and shot her brain."

The men were following Thomas back into the *kit'catact,* as images of the bloody scene tumbled through Ruth's head, the ripped belly and Thomas's tender back trying to shelter Grandmother Siki from the bear's attack. "She stayed with us for two more weeks, Grandmother did. Wouldn't let us take her to the hospital in San Bernardino. It hurt her so bad, but this is where she wanted to be at the end, she told us. So we stitched her here, with yucca. Thomas too. You must have felt her calling," she said matter-of-factly. Ruth could only turn her face away and let it burn.

All through the burning of Grandmother Siki's possessions, as the loved ones shuffled more than danced around the campfire, Ruth remained rigid with shame. Ruth had nothing she could contribute to the ceremony, since she had not answered the heart-call, and she could only stand and watch the mourning dancers with regret, not even allowing herself the tears she saw glistening on Maddie's cheeks from the other side of the campfire. Not all of the old woman's possessions were burned, only selected items that she had asked loved ones to put into the fire. But when Martha lovingly offered her grandmother's traditional dress and shell bead jewelry to the flames, Ruth suddenly felt a sensation of movement in her arms. It was as if she were alongside Martha offering the dress. The sensation was so strong, Ruth had to look down to make sure she hadn't unconsciously moved her arms, yet they remained motionless at her sides. When Martha faced her again as she circled the fire, Ruth thought she saw her glance over. Perhaps it was only the reflection from Martha's glasses.

Thomas did not circle the fire with the mourners, but stood chanting and shaking his large gourd rattle at them as they passed by him. Now he put the rattle aside and sprinkled each of them with pollen from his feathered bundle as they passed, until they had all been blessed. Then the mourners went around again, and he stopped each in front of him, holding up the bowl of liquid to take a sip from. Ruth's heart caught when she saw that it was one of the large bowls she had made and given to the people the last time she was here. However small, its use meant she was part of the ceremony, and she allowed herself tears then. On the final round, Thomas turned each mourner in front of him and brushed face and shoulders with an eagle feather.

Ruth admired him in his role of *cafika*, a part he played reluctantly— because it was needed, and because there was no one else capable. Yet he wasn't playing a part in the way the actors in that film played their parts, the way she had played the Indian woman. Thomas actually took on the power of a *cafika*. His ability to affect his people was unmistakable. He was Thomas, yet more than Thomas. She wondered if it happened because that power was naturally in him—or because his people granted it to him. Or both. But however it happened, it was as real as breathing.

When the mourners had gone around again, Lemuel led them away to join the others gathered around the fire. At this point in the other *nonach'ili* Ruth had seen, Thomas returned to the *kit'catact*. But this time he remained standing where he was.

He began speaking in Yuiatei, then stopped and repeated in English, "There is something I must say now," for Ruth, and no doubt for some of the young people who didn't know their own language well. Then for a long time he went back to speaking in Yuiatei again. Ruth could understand enough to know he spoke of Grandmother Siki and of the bear, but much of the meaning was lost to her. She was greatly relieved when he began again to speak in English. Yet even in English, he formed the phrases as in his own language.

"We are sad that Grandmother Siki has been taken from us," he began. "That the bear took her. Sad too that we had to take the bear. Grandmother was like that bear. She was the last of the old ones, the ones who knew the ways well. She tried to save that bear, but it didn't work." He paused for a moment, then continued. "Sometimes it doesn't work.

"Sometimes it feels like things are coming apart, that our life is like the spiderweb that has been ripped in the center, and now all the strands are flapping in the wind and will be blown away soon. And something like that is true. The strands are coming apart. But if we hold on to the ways the best we can, hold things together, maybe the spider can repair the web again. That's all we can do, and we must do it."

He stopped for a moment and looked at the people gathered in front of him. When he spoke again, his voice took on a more intimate tone. "Things are changing fast all around us," he said. "Faster than ever before. People around us don't know how to live with the ways of the land; they have learned to hate and live against that land. When we are out there living among them, we take on some of those hateful ways too. You have to ask yourself, are you living with the land—or against it? Are you helping to hold the web together?"

In the silence that followed his words, Ruth thought about that question. She knew participating in the film was not holding the web together. But just what was this web he spoke of, she wondered? She was convinced his words were true, yet she didn't understand them entirely.

"You think Grandmother Siki is not here with us anymore. But our Grandmother is not gone," he went on. "Not dead. She has gone into the land around us, and the land is our true Grandmother. Ancient Mother—this is what our word *ona'dahada,* grandmother, means. As long as this land is alive, Ona'dahada Siki will be alive in the plants and animals, in the air." His gaze followed the sweep of his open arm that encompassed the landscape, then for a moment focused on Ruth. In that fraction before he looked away, she felt she was seeing into depths she sensed, yet had not experienced, depths that reached in and touched her own.

"Ancient Mother will take care of us. But we have to take care of her too," Thomas said. With a slow turn of his head, his eyes took in each person in front of him. "The ways of the old ones, the ways of Grandmother Siki and the bear, were the ways Ancient Mother gave us to live here. We must not forget those ways. Must not put them aside because they are too hard. If we lose those ways we will be lost too. We will die. Then even our real Grandmother will die, for her ways are our web. Ask yourself with each thing you do, are you keeping our Ancient Mother and her ways alive?" Thomas stood without speaking while his words continued inside the people. Then he turned and walked back into the *kit'catact.*

His words, like his glance, brought thoughts and feelings rumbling through her. Ruth had always understood what drew her to Jim and to his people, why she felt connected to them. They loved the land as fiercely as she did. But she understood now that they thought of the land in a way very different than she did. While she saw it as her lover, for them it was not a lover but a grandmother. Ancient Mother, Thomas had said. In some way they were like a family, and this was their way of thinking about the world. But these were not her people. She had never had her own people, none that she felt were her own, and she had disowned her own mother. Even the photograph she now had of her grandmother was only a flimsy piece of paper. Her imagination could not change it to flesh. These people were the closest she'd come to family—and they were coming apart fast in the world she saw shifting around her. Shifting into something Golden called *modern,* a word that made her shiver.

It occurred to her that in her whole life she had never cared about anything beyond her own desires—except in her love for Jim and her canyon—and even those things were bound up with her desires. Now she could not imagine herself anywhere else other than Glory Springs. Somehow, despite her selfish view, she had stumbled onto the place that could save her from her own selfishness. The place that was in her—even if she hadn't understood it. Somehow she had been changed inside by this wordless knowing.

Gratitude spread through her. She was thankful that she had Glory Springs to go back to, even if she had strayed from her life there. She had based her life on that place, though she had never understood why until now. How much better her life there would be now that she understood the reasons for it. All she wanted at the moment was to go back to her land and lead the life she was meant to lead there. Without having others to show her the proper ways to live on that land, she would have to discover them herself as time went on.

A slow-rising joy overruled her earlier sense of shame and despair. Ruth closed her eyes and let tears wash her clean. It no longer mattered what she had done last night—or any night before that. She basked in the community around her. These people were not any more perfect than those in Juniper Valley, but they understood something the others didn't. And in some way she was a part of that understanding. Ruth opened her eyes and looked at the people with her around the campfire, feeling a love so strong it was hard for her to bear it. Her eyes fell on Maddie and J.B. Her son had taken his sister's hand, and they stood quietly looking at the bearskin in front of them. The love she felt covered them with the rest. She knew she had been much lacking as their mother.

But she would change all that. She would go back to Glory Springs and start her life fresh again, this time with clearer purpose. She would do her part to hold the web together, to keep alive this Ancient Mother—and yes, it was hers too. Now she had a past to connect with—an actual grandmother, though much remained obscured by mystery. But she *could* connect with the past of her land, a history that was secreted in its soil, in its plants and animals, bring all that knowledge into her present life.

When Thomas came out of the *kit'catact* sometime later, the canyon had darkened. He walked over and took the sitting rock beside Ruth at the campfire. She was grateful for his presence; it seemed a kind of forgiveness. Yet for a long time neither spoke, and she continued to think over what he had said, as she watched J.B. and Maddie playing with the other children. Though somberness still hung in the air, she could feel normalcy returning.

"I'm glad you came, Dlah'da," Thomas said finally. "She wanted you to be here."

Ruth turned her head and made herself look at him, at the bear slashes across his cheek that seemed to intensify the knowing in his eyes. "I'm so sorry I didn't come sooner, but so much was happening that . . ."

"All that doesn't matter. You're here now." When he looked at her, fragments of light reflected from his dark eyes, reminding her of firelight dancing on the ceremonial bowl. She held his eyes for a moment, but could not bear the weight and depth she saw there for long.

"You were hurt bad, too," she said, moving her gaze to the campfire.

"That bear marked me pretty good, all right. She woke me up."

Ruth didn't ask what he meant, didn't know how to.

"Maybe I'll come over in the spring," he said, and she felt a warmth spread through her.

"You mean when you gather the 'bee hee,' or whatever that is?"

"Maybe. Or maybe I'll drive over in the truck. I don't always travel like a wild Indian," he said.

Ruth laughed, studied his face more closely. It was the first time she'd seen him smile. "There's nothing wrong with being wild," she said, finally, watching his smile broaden, bridging the distance between them. "Nothing at all."

CHAPTER TWENTY-NINE

Ruth's renewed sense of purpose remained as she drove home the next morning. She woke early, the old injury to her knee complaining about sleeping on the hard ground. After waking her children, she said good-bye to their friends and gave Martha a farewell hug, telling her she hoped for the best with Jackson. Martha nodded, swallowed back any response other than the liquid that gathered in her eyes and was magnified by the lenses of her glasses.

Ruth couldn't find Thomas anywhere, but even that didn't dampen her eagerness to get home and start anew. Exactly what changes she would make, and why, she had no idea, but she had faith they would come when the time was right. And she would see Thomas again in the spring.

She had ample time to think over the long miles, and the one issue that troubled her as she drove was David Stone. Just where did he fit into her new life? That had always been a question, but she had kept it tamped down, where it only smoldered. He was a good man; she sometimes liked being with him, though not as often as he did her, nor as intensely. J.B. and Maddie certainly loved him. Yet she was always having to fend off his constant need to take care of her, and to suffer through his unhappiness whenever she fought loose.

But if he actually did go back to the university next month, there might no longer be an issue. She supposed she would have to fight one last battle over returning with him as his wife. He would not give up without that, she was sure—even though she had made it clear she would not go. He had accepted it somewhat already, she thought, or he seemed to. After all, he'd been hauling up hay and chicken feed for her in his van each time he came. Winter was not far off, and who knew when another bad snow might come, he kept telling her. While he lived in the city, she would see him only occasionally, which would give her time to understand what he meant to her. Then she could better decide what to do.

"Can we go out to the dig to see David first?" J.B. asked, as the Model A chugged up the long hill into Juniper Valley. The car seemed to take the hill more slowly each time—showing its age, she supposed.

Ruth shook her head. "He said he'd go up to feed the animals and wait for us there." She reached over and gave her son's shoulder a squeeze, already sorry that he would soon be missing this man who had as much as adopted him.

J.B. ducked away. "Can we get in the rumble seat yet?"

"Not till we turn off into the canyon," Ruth told him.

"Aren't we going to stop for supplies? You need gas."

"No I don't. We have enough to get up the canyon. We can always coast most of the way out again. I don't want to waste any time. I really want to get home." The thought of parking the Model A under the pinyons around her cabin brought a swell of joy. Her image of the sweet scene did not include David's tan van, though she knew it would be there.

"But Maddie wants a pickle, don't you, Maddie?" He gave his sister a look to enlist her, but the girl turned her head away.

Ruth laughed. "You wouldn't be wanting licorice or anything

would you, J.B.? That wouldn't be your real concern now, would it? What do you think, Maddie?"

Maddie looked straight ahead, with a face that appeared expressionless, yet sad at the same time. Ruth couldn't remember her saying a word since they left Black Canyon, even though her brother had tried to involve her in the usual driving games. Ruth knew it would take her some time to recover. Maddie had taken Kate's leaving hard, but that loss was supposed to be temporary. This loss was far more final. For herself as well. Yet at the moment what she had gained seemed far more important.

Ruth pulled up to the general store. She supposed she could use a bit more coffee and wheat flour to go with her mesquite and acorn meal. Maddie didn't come in with them, but Ruth bought one of the big dill pickles Maddie loved from the jar on the meat counter anyway, left it to J.B. to coax her into eating it. Yet the girl wouldn't even acknowledge its existence when they got into the car. He laid it on her lap, where it sat until Ruth stopped at the mouth of the canyon to let them climb into the rumble seat. She was relieved to see that Maddie at least wanted to do that.

It was all Ruth could do not to tromp the accelerator, but with the children bouncing around in the rumble seat, she didn't dare. Yet she kept catching herself pressing the pedal down harder than she should. She pulled her foot off—after hearing J.B. shout out a cowboyish "Yy-eeehaaa" as they sped down a gulley and bumped back over the top. The rest of the way she drove slower; Glory Springs wasn't going anywhere, she told herself.

She was nearly to the North Fork when she noticed a little curl of what looked like smoke above the ridge ahead. It disappeared when she went around a bend, but came in sight again on the other side. Her initial thought was that David must be there cooking for them, though she was surprised that smoke from her little stove could be seen from this distance. But then she'd never before come up the canyon while she was cooking at her stove to see it.

The small plume was blocked by the mountain as she went on, but when she drove around the next bend, it appeared again. It seemed like a lot of smoke for a woodstove. A chill crept up her neck. After glancing back to make sure J.B. and Maddie were sitting down, Ruth gassed the car enough to get decent speed for the last stretch between her and home. Rounding the final bend, she caught a whiff of acrid air just as the sight of its smoldering source came into view.

She blinked her eyes dry, jerking the wheel back when her tires sank into the sandy edge of the road, stomped on the gas. Steeling herself, she kept her eyes trained on what she could see of the smoking remnants of her home.

Ruth skidded up and jerked to a stop behind David's van, leaping out of the car at a dead run, without as much as switching off the motor or setting the brake, almost tripping on some kind of steel cylinder that lay outside the rock wall, directly across from where her kitchen was situated inside. At the sound of a cough from inside the cabin, she jumped over the cylinder, calling out David's name as she ran. Smoke still billowed upward, but she could see no flames—also no roof above the kitchen area, though the sooted rock walls around it did appear to be mostly intact.

"I'm in here, Ruth," he coughed out just before she reached the door.

With a hand on each side of the doorjamb, she braced herself, taking in the ruin inside as David stumbled toward her, kicking aside the wet and charred debris that had been the roof over her kitchen. The wall behind the stove had been burned as well. "Need more water," he said, rushing past her with a bucket in each hand. "Quick, before the embers catch again. The tank in here is out. The pipes to the windmill are gone now."

Ruth registered his blackened face beneath singed hair and reddened hands along with the rest, stood blank and stunned a moment more, then turned and ran out to get the other bucket and milk pails from the barn. "Come on," she shouted to Maddie and J.B., who stood wide-eyed in the front yard. "Help us put out the fire." David was already running back to the house with water he'd drawn from Blue's tin watering trough. Blue was pacing and whinnying in his pen.

She sank her bucket and pail under the water, drew them up, and rushed after David. The children were already submerging their pails when she left. She met David coming out the door again, left him her water pail and ran back to fill the empty ones he'd held. As the buckets filled, Ruth looked up at the small tank that fed the trough, hoping it would be enough to finish dousing the fire.

When the inside of her house around the kitchen was saturated to such an extent that only a few places barely smoldered—and those they could extinguish directly by careful pouring—the full force of the calamity rained down on her. Much of what had once been her home was now blackened rubble. The center of the damage had been in the kitchen and extended outward from there. Her chairs and table were gone. Soaked and charred, the kitchen walls and most of the furniture that remained intact appeared unfunctional, the place uninhabitable. Everything reeked of wet charcoal.

For some time, none of them spoke as they numbly searched beneath pieces of burned roof timbers to see what was left to them. The children's blankets had gone up, but the clothes in their scorched dresser were undamaged, except for the smell of smoke that permeated them. Ruth's dresser and everything near the far wall by the door had fared somewhat better, and her comforter looked together beneath the mess that had fallen on it. The books under her bed beside the door had survived, without damage, as had the ollas. Yet nothing in the disorder seemed truly useable. Was this some terrible dream, Ruth wondered, and she would wake up to find everything whole again? But the black streaks on her arms and her soaked clothing felt too real for any dream. She longed to drive down to Kate's and be consoled like a small child—but Kate too was gone. Ruth felt a helpless rage moving through her, a feeling that almost comforted her with its familiarity.

They began carting anything salvageable out to the front yard. So much of the cabin she loved had been destroyed. When she left here such a short time ago, her home was all in one piece. She had expected it to remain that way, had counted on it without knowing it. David would be looking after things for her.

At the thought, an icy anger solidified inside her. In her panic, she had thought of nothing more than saving what she could of her home, then of seeing what was left to salvage. Now, for the first time, she wondered exactly what had happened. The image of the metal cylinder came back to her. And why was her own woodstove sitting out beside her front door? She looked over at the twisted metal where her woodstove had once sat and began to suspect—then to understand. She should have known, should have listened to herself about him long ago.

David was dragging her bed out the front door. His reddened hands appeared badly burned. When the fire was out, she had suggested he stop and cover them with yerba mansa leaves, but he only shook his head and began sorting through her belongings. His forehead seemed to have been burned some also, around his singed hair, though his face was so black with soot it was hard to tell. His struggle to save her house from the fire had been quite literally etched into his skin. When he put the bed down and came back through the doorway, Ruth saw what else was etched there. The moment he saw the look of understanding on her face, his own crumpled with guilt. She did not have to say a word. She might have killed him on the spot if her guns had not burned in the fire.

"What have you done, David?" she whispered when he came over and stood before her.

"I'm so sorry, Ruth." His eyes were swollen with tears, which spilled over the red rims to make light tracks down his cheeks. "So very sorry." He reached out a hand, then drew it back when she stiffened. "I'll do everything I can to make it up to you." He looked up around, scanning the open roof and walls. "We'll make this place as good as new, you'll see," he said without conviction.

"I told you I didn't want that bottled gas. I told you that." Her voice, the only weapon she had left, had become a steel knife to slice him as deep as she could. "But you did it anyway." As if sensing something, J.B. and Maddie came over to stand beside them.

"I wanted to make things easier for you. So you wouldn't have to be chopping and hauling in wood for cooking all the time—having to go out and get it in the snow. After what happened to you out in the corral three years ago when I wasn't around to help . . ."

"So you decided to bring up gas canisters that I have to buy and haul up clear from Juniper Valley?"

"I was going to take care of all that, Ruth, I—"

"I heat this house with wood, too—or I did. Did you think of that, David?" She managed a cool calmness that belied the turmoil inside her.

"I did, Ruth," he said, sounding glad for the chance to explain.

"I thought we could bring a little oil burner into the middle of the room—hook it up to barrels outside the window there—make the heat more central to keep you warm at night. I was going to cut a new hole for the pipe right there." He looked up into the singed pinyons above what used to be the kitchen ceiling. It was a wonder the trees hadn't ignited too.

"I guess you won't have to worry about that now," Ruth said. She shook her head. "Bottled gas and an oil burner—when I was perfectly happy the way things were. I don't understand it. Why on earth . . . ?"

"I got the letter yesterday, Ruth, from the university. They want me back down there week after next, told me to finish things up here." He swallowed and looked at her with such pained intensity that she had to steel herself against bending. "Since you keep refusing to come with me, I wanted to make sure you were comfortable before I left. I thought I'd surprise you."

"You did *that*, David. But did you actually believe that coming home to find a bottled gas stove and an oil burner would make me happy? And you think you know me, David. You claim to love me—and you don't know how much I would have hated those things—even if you hadn't burned my house down putting them in?"

"He didn't mean to," J.B. said. He stepped closer to David and took hold of his pant leg. That was the last straw. Ruth snatched him back.

"I want you to leave, David. Right now."

"But . . . but . . . there's all this to clean up, Ruth. Calm down and think about it. I can't leave you in this mess—"

"Yes you can. And you will. Your being here is not a help. You've done quite enough."

"You're being crazy, Ruth, you—"

"That's my right, isn't it? This is my place, remember—or what's left of it, thanks to you."

"Why can't he help us?" Maddie asked. She and J.B. stood together holding hands and looking up at Ruth with determination.

Ruth clenched her teeth. "You little fools," she said.

"As you just said, I'm the one responsible for this," David told her. "I'm the one who should clean all this up and make it right again. Not you."

"Make it right? In two weeks, David? This will never be right again.

Never." Ruth closed her eyes tight against the flood that threatened to wash away her resolve. She couldn't even run him off with her shotgun, she thought, with a dark laugh to herself. She would run all three of them off in a minute if she had that gun, these uninvited intruders into her life.

Ruth set her jaw and looked at them. Was it only this morning that she had started out invigorated with purpose? Everything had seemed so clear to her then—though at the moment she couldn't recall just what it was that she'd felt at the time, only that she'd felt it. Whatever that understanding was, it was gone now, was as ruined as her home. How ever could she hold any strands of web together or help keep any stupid Ancient Mother of the land alive—with her house burning down around her, and her children standing solid against her with the intruder who burned it? She shook her head and marched out the door toward the barn.

Swinging the corral gate wide as she opened it, Ruth took two steps toward Juniper Blue, who was trotting over to meet her. She hooked an arm over his neck and swung up on his back, the way she'd practiced so many times while making the movie. Then they were out the gate and racing up trail to the *ciénaga seca* and there was only the wind's roar in her ears and the horse's powerful muscles contracting under her as the animal carried her away.

CHAPTER THIRTY

She *would* rebuild, would get that roof and wall repaired, Ruth told Esther and Golden over lunch in the Golden Palomino. And she would accept David's money to have it done. He certainly owed it to her, though it had taken several days to come to terms with the idea. Meanwhile, the four of them had cleaned most of the debris from inside her cabin. When the shoot was over this afternoon, she announced, she would drive into Juniper Valley to see if she could hire someone to help her with the rebuilding. That might not be easy to find now, despite all the unemployment. Many of the men were off working in L.A. or had moved their families back there entirely. Others, like Larry Hudson, were busy building roads for the WPA. If not, she would do it herself—except she knew little about putting on a roof, she explained, beyond what she'd learned at her house raising years ago. What she did know was that winter was almost upon them.

Any time now, the weather could turn for the worse. How much cooler it was today, Ruth reminded them, than for the last shoot, such a short while ago.

Golden had brought his sister up as a surprise for Ruth, knowing how unhappy she was over having to redo the scene. And Esther's arrival had been a ray of light on this day Ruth had been dreading. Of course, she pretty much dreaded every day now, dreaded waking up to see again the destruction inside her cabin that made her heart ache anew. Ruth's story of the fire had left Esther appropriately shocked and sympathetic. Golden had a more practical approach.

"Nothing would please me more than if you changed your mind and continued on in another film," he told her. "What you'd earn would certainly help with any rebuilding costs. You could even add more rooms and a few conveniences as well." He picked up the bottle of wine beside him and poured some into his sister's glass, before refilling his own.

Ruth gulped down the rest of hers and held out her glass for more. After all she had been through the past week, she needed it. This was the first time she'd felt herself breathe since the fire disaster.

"Thanks for the offer, but no. David should pay for the damage." How could she tell this man she'd rather go live in a tent on her property than take part in another film? She had woken up that morning finally ready to face the challenge of repairing her home. At first the fire had seemed like nothing but another senseless disaster to cope with. But she had remembered her desire to come back from Black Canyon and start afresh. She would certainly be doing that now—in a more literal way than she had conceived of. And maybe it was right, she told herself, that a piece of the roof Jim had helped build over her was gone—even if that absence mirrored the hole in her chest each time she looked at it.

"You don't have to make up your mind today," Golden told her. "The offer stands."

"Here's to you, Ruth." Esther raised her glass. "And to success in whatever you choose; you know what's best for you."

Ruth smiled and tapped her glass against Esther's, then Golden's. Yet something in his face told Ruth he had some plan in mind as his glass touched hers. The man always seemed to have agendas that took time to decipher. Not that it mattered; after today, that needn't concern her.

Ruth dressed in her silly outfit for the last time, blocking out all thought of the way she would look to her friends in Black Canyon. The way she looked to herself—web or no web. She simply had to get through this scene one more time and it would all be over. Yet Thomas's words chased her as she rode Juniper Blue into position to wait for the director's cue. She knew she wasn't holding any strands together here.

Roger Rider was already standing under the noose while Ben and the others were getting into position in the middle of Mane Street. What a rogue that Ben was, but the business between them was finished. She felt nothing more than relief that she would not see him again after today. The fire had put things into perspective. She could get through this, she told herself, as she watched David's van approaching from the digs. He must have come to make sure this was her final scene.

She could get through the next few days until he left too. Her anger toward him had settled into a cool politeness that he seemed almost grateful for. But she would never forgive him, never, and anything at all made her anger flare up again. She had ridden Blue back that night to find the three of them by the campfire eating beans from a can they'd salvaged. She watched them from across the wash for a while, resentment for their bond churning in her again, but in the end it was overruled by pity at their forlorn faces. When she rode up, their eyes lit with relief. Even Maddie seemed glad to see her.

Ruth smiled and rolled her eyes when the men in the street swung into action at the sound of the director's cue, transforming themselves from frozen manikins to moving manikins, she mused. It was always such a odd sight, but the wine made it bearable today. Of course, her part was the oddest of all. She was to ride into the crowd when they had the hero on the scaffold. In the surprise of her appearance, the hero would leap from the platform onto her horse, while the sheriff was distracted. Then she would carry him off, while the sheriff and his deputies fired silent shots from behind them.

It was the awkwardness of Roger Rider's leap that had caused so many retakes the time before. He was such a terrible rider that she could barely ride away between the two buildings with him before he fell off the back of the horse. Twice he had slipped partially off before they were out of sight. And the man's extra weight was something Juniper Blue had never cottoned to either, even if they had to go only a few yards. The horse stayed jumpy and nervous on the set.

When the director gave the signal, Ruth touched her heels to Blue's flank and galloped down the street into the crowd, which always over-did the shock of her appearance, she thought, and fell away as if they were rabbits at a spring when a mountain lion appeared rather than gun-toting men when a mere Indian woman rode up. She brought Blue alongside the scaffold and Roger Rider plopped down behind her with the most perfect timing yet. Her nose prickled at the strong scent of makeup and cologne as his arms clasped her waist with a despera-tion Ruth knew was not forced. She tapped Blue with her heels, and they took off toward the alley between the buildings, the silent shots going off behind them.

"Hang on, Roger," she whispered. "We're almost there."

Just as they rode out of sight, a blast of sound came from behind the building. That damned van, Ruth thought, as Blue reared back so fast she barely had time to hunker forward, grasp tight his mane and neck to stay on as he rose and pawed the air. Rider had one arm clamped around her as Blue's whinny screamed in her ear, and she felt herself slide back with the weight of the rider who was pulling her down with him. Then Blue whirled back around. Letting go one hand from the horse's neck, Ruth strained to peel from her waist the grip-ping fingers of the man who was already sliding off Blue's rump. But he had her in a death grip.

She felt the horse rise higher, looked up to see his smoky blue back above her, where the sky should be. All she could do was shift her weight to one side as the horse came down on top of her. She felt the hard ground and tried to twist out of the way, but the crush of the horse was already upon her.

Once, she opened her eyes and found nothing but white around her. She worried that winter had come before her house was finished. An-other time, she thought she caught a glimpse of bars and wondered whether they'd put her in the movie jail instead of Roger Rider. Sometimes she heard voices, but there was always so much dust in the room she couldn't find anyone there. The rest of the time she was in an empty place that kept pulling her back into itself.

She kept hearing voices calling her name, though she couldn't understand what they wanted and didn't feel like rousing herself to answer. But one voice kept coming back again and again, wouldn't leave her alone. It was a voice that hurt her head to hear, and she tried hard to ignore it. Yet sometimes she felt a touch on her face and forehead that the voice brought with it. The touch made the voice harder to ignore. Finally, she had to tell it to stop bothering her.

She felt her arm being lifted away from herself. "What did you just say, Ruth? I heard her say something, nurse." Lips were kissing her hand, and she had to pull it back again.

"What was that, Ruth? She just said something again."

Why didn't he hear her? She was practically shouting. She shouted it again. *Stop.*

"I think she said 'stop,' nurse. Stop what, Ruth?"

She could barely see David's face swimming through the dust around it. Didn't he understand anything? Her head ached so bad. Everything about her hurt. She closed her eyes again, welcoming the quiet darkness. His next words barely reached her before she retreated into oblivion.

"Oh, thank God, Ruth. Thank God."

The next time she opened her eyes there was less dust in the air. She was in a strange room somewhere. Someone was there with her. She was sure it was a dream, so she closed her eyes and waited for it to end. Gradually she became more aware of how much her head hurt. And one of her arms. Her leg. She tried to move her arm, but it wouldn't budge. Opening her eyes again, she saw her arm was held up in the air and attached to some wires. Something white wrapped around it. Puzzled as she was, it hurt her head to figure it out. She closed her eyes again.

"Ruth, we know you can wake up now." She felt a big hand tapping her lightly on the cheeks. "Ruth, you have to wake up now. Come on, we know you can do it," the loud voice said.

She looked up into the face of a strange man. The room behind him had cleared of mist. "Stop hitting me," she said. "Your voice is hurting my head."

"Good girl," the voice boomed back at her. "Stay with us now."

"Why should I?" This man was making her angry.

"Because we want you with us, that's why, Ruth," that other voice said. She felt a squeeze of her hand and turned her head to see David on her other side.

"Do you know where you are?" the booming voice asked.

It hurt so bad to think, but she realized she didn't really know. She looked more closely around her at the white room. "Is this a jail?"

"Do you remember what happened?" David asked.

Ruth tried to remember, but the pain in her head stopped her. "Get back, David. You're breathing my air," she said.

"Can you remember, Ruth?" This time the booming voice.

"If you'll stop shouting maybe I can."

"Frontiertown," David said. "Do you remember that?"

The word brought light to what had been dark. She closed her eyes and saw Blue's back coming down on her, felt the man's hand clutching her waist. She remembered pain, such pain. Remembered people running and shouting. Esther shouting her name. Remembered lying on a car seat where every bump stabbed into her as someone drove. After that, nothing at all.

"Blue," she said. "What happened to Blue?" She tried to sit up, but the arm in the air wouldn't let her, and her leg shot through with pain. "Why is my arm tied up? Where are J.B. and Maddie, David?" Tears were coming too easily, and they hurt her head even more than the voices did. "Why am I here, David? Take me home right now."

"Maddie and J.B. are with me, Ruth. Don't worry about them, they're—"

"What do you mean, with you?" Despite the pain, she got to one elbow and looked around. "I don't see them anywhere." She collapsed onto the pillow with the effort.

"I mean they're here with me in L.A., like you are. Except you're still in the hospital. Golden is paying all the expenses. He brought Esther to see you several times, but you wouldn't wake up. But, finally . . . oh, thank God, Ruth. I hope I can take you home soon."

He leaned in and took her face between his hands. She could see tear tracks down his cheeks. "I was so afraid I'd lost you, Ruth." He kissed her forehead and she felt a splash of wet on her skin. "We'd almost given up hope."

"L.A.? Why are we in L.A.? I hate that city. Take me home, David. I want to go back to Glory Springs, where I belong."

David exchanged a glance with the booming voice, which had now gone silent. "It's winter now, Ruth. You've been here for weeks."

Weeks? She'd been in this hospital for weeks. How could that be? "Well, I want to leave now," she told him, but puzzlement weakened her conviction.

"Your cabin is burned, Ruth, remember? It's no place for you to live right now—no roof over the kitchen. Some of one wall is gone too. Remember that?" He looked over at the doctor. "I haven't had time to repair it yet—and the animals are sold. I've been over here with you when I wasn't teaching or with Maddie and J.B."

"You sold my Blue, David. You sold Juniper Blue?" It was all Ruth could do to contain her outrage.

David shook his head. "Not Blue. After the accident . . . he . . ." He stopped, his face a mask she couldn't see behind. "Someone had to . . . well, you know, Ruth. His leg was no good at all."

Ruth caught her sob and held it inside, though she felt her chest might burst apart with the pain of it. Her wonderful blue roan, her dreams of magical travel above those flying hooves, gone. "Home, David. I want to go home." She kept trying to blink her tears away. "I don't need a roof or water tank. Or even animals. I lived there before without them." She yanked on her arm to free it from the wires, but it pulled back from her. On one elbow now, she tried to swing her legs over the bed's edge, but one wouldn't come, wouldn't come at all.

"Not with children you didn't . . . and not with . . . not without . . ."

"What he's trying to say, Ruth," the booming voice said, gone quiet and gentle, "is that you can't live in a place like that in the shape you're in now. Not without help. Not ever again." He put his huge hand on her chest, the other behind her, and eased her down against her pillow. Reaching down, he laid a hand on each leg. "Your left leg is non-responsive, Ruth. See? You can't even feel my hand massaging it, can you? We think it might be something in the spine—I'm very sorry. Likely you'll never use it again."

Ruth reached down with her free arm and squeezed her left leg again and again, slid her hand under the blankets so her fingers felt the cool skin. It was like touching a limb that belonged to someone else.

CHAPTER THIRTY-ONE

David and J.B. kept up conversation as the four of them drove past endless small towns and groves on their way to the desert, J.B. asking about buildings and automobiles as they went, and David manufacturing answers and explanations. Ruth blocked out their voices, drew in a large breath of orange blossom from the groves alongside them. Beside her, Maddie sat as silent as herself. The miles between the city's edge and Glory Springs stretched interminably before them. Yet Ruth's impatience to see Glory Springs was tempered by her fear of what seeing it again might stir up in her.

She went through most days in silence now, with David at the university and the children at school. But she stayed nearly as silent when they were around. On the best of days she was numb, on the worst, submerged in murk. She trudged through the motions of being alive, but something in her had gone bone dry, and she could find nothing to revive her. In L.A., there were no calls of quail and jays, no fuss of chipmunks among the rocks on the mountain. All she heard around her was noise, the cars and trolleys on the streets outside, the voices of people on the sidewalks. And everywhere she looked under the dull, gray sky, she saw people or the things that people made and owned. No place existed for its own sake. Except for a renegade weed in the yard, nothing was wild.

Glory Springs had thrown her out of its heart, would not let her live there. But no wonder—she had betrayed the place with her dalliances—first with David, then with Frontiertown . . . and Ben. But was it irrevocable? Was this exile forever? She ached for her home with the whole of her—or what was left of her. Sometimes she closed her eyes and pictured a squirrel she had watched run up a pinyon, or a lizard skittering across a rock. When she imagined deeply enough, she could make herself smell the pine air, breathe in the scent of a moonlily blossom, or hear the song of an oriole, the yipping howls of coyotes. It made her ache to think that the orioles might return to sing in the spring without her there to hear them. And through all the painful days, David went on acting as if nothing had happened, as if her whole world hadn't dissolved. He flashed that hated smile regularly, now that he had her entirely under his control.

She had fought him off at first at the hospital, still believing she could get back to her place on her own. But of course she was too injured, too weak from her long unconsciousness for that. When Golden came to pay the hospital bill and to give Ruth the money she had earned for the film, Esther had offered her a permanent room at the Cricket Club. Ruth considered it, but even though Palm Springs was closer to her homestead, she felt that place was at the heart of all that had led her astray. She went with David instead. The ten big bills Golden gave her, though, she secured behind the lining of her purse, where she kept Lolinda's photograph.

The physical pain she came home with had dwindled over the months. Now, except for an occasional phantom stab in her useless leg, it wasn't the physical pain that tamed her; she had already been accustomed to phantom attacks from her past. These were merely more corporeal. But she hated the idea of that worthless limb with a passion, sometimes wished that doctor had just cut the thing off. She'd rather have what was left of her fully functional than to have a part of her numb and unable to move. Yet the rest of her wasn't much better. Without her life in Glory Springs, they might as well obliterate the entirety of her. Why couldn't David understand that?

At first, he pretended to go along with her idea of returning to Glory Springs; like the house he had rented for them, the situation was temporary, that was all. But as the weeks passed and she gained some strength, she began to realize what he intended. Still, she was too trapped in blackness to argue most of the time. It was David, though, who finally goaded her out of it long enough to fight.

"I think it's time we set a date for our wedding, Ruth," he said to her one night after the children had gone to sleep. She had sought shelter in a book all evening and hadn't wanted to let his voice in. But his request assaulted her sanctuary, and she looked up.

"What are you talking about, David? Marriage was never a part of our arrangement."

"That's not fair, Ruth. I've always told you I wanted marriage—from the very beginning. I can't count the times I've asked you."

"That was before—you haven't since . . . since my accident." She looked down at her lap, where the withering limb lay covered over with a flowered print dress. Beyond her knees, the angle of the cloth dropped off into nothingness, the way her life had. "Why would you want to marry me now, a woman with a useless leg? And inside, I'm more useless than this leg, David."

"I'd want to marry you if you had no legs, Ruth. I love you. What more do I have to do to prove that to you?" He rose from the stuffed chair he'd been sitting in.

She sucked in her breath at the image of her he'd just presented. "Funny thing is, David, I still wouldn't want to marry you." She winced inwardly at the flash of pain she saw on his face, relished it at the same time. "What I want is for you to take me back to the canyon and have that cabin rebuilt the way you promised. With a few adjustments, I can live there, even without . . . even with this leg."

"That's ludicrous. Just to think of you—the way you are now—in that canyon trying to care for your children. You can barely manage the crutch yet with your injured arm."

"That's for me to decide. You've always wanted me out of Glory

Springs. I could have lived there once—even like this—if you hadn't burned the place down."

"You know that's not true, Ruth. You've needed a lot of care. You almost didn't make it." He kneeled beside her chair and took her book away, placed it on the table beside her. He picked up her hand. "But it *is* true that I've always wanted to marry you, to keep you with me. That didn't mean out of the canyon. At least until the accident happened."

"If the accident hadn't happened, I wouldn't be here with you right now. You don't really want to marry me, David. You just think you do for some reason. Maybe you truly did want to before, but what man would want to be tied to a bitter one-legged woman with two . . . two bastard children."

"I love those children, I told you before—almost as much as I love you. Look, I know what kind of a woman you are, Ruth. And that doesn't make a bit of difference to me."

"What kind of a woman am I, then, David?" she spat. "Since you seem to have a label for it. What am I?"

"Well, you . . . you . . ." He shook his head. "You scared me most of the time, Ruth. It never mattered what you might have done in the past. But I never knew what you might do on any given day. Never knew if you'd come back to me. All I knew was that I didn't want to be without you again. That won't ever change."

He kept on until he wore her down; she agreed to consider his suit, and, in return, she extracted his promise that in the spring he would take her back to Glory Springs for the day, so she could make her peace with the place—or at least enough peace to get her by for a while. Besides, he said, he wanted to make sure her Model A was still intact at the cabin, and to see if he could advertise it for sale at Matt's store. Yet spring had almost become summer before she could get him on the road.

After what seemed like forever, they finally reached the desert and drove into Devil's Garden. Almost immediately, Ruth felt something in her revive, and she could feel the same spark in Maddie, who began watching out the window, even responding occasionally to her brother's and David's remarks. Most of the time in Los Angeles, Maddie stayed nearly as glum as Ruth. How odd Ruth had found it, that it would be this rapist's child who sat silently beside her the whole while, sharing with her the pain of being away from Glory Springs. The girl had even stopped making those annoying animal sounds. Ruth found she missed them.

J.B. had become distant from her. At first he had even asked if she was the same mother as before the accident. The question had shocked her, but it shocked her even more to realize she could not reassure him. She had been wondering the same thing herself. It was only when she smelled the pine pitch caught in her old shirt pocket that she felt anything at all come back to life in her. She discovered that the heat of an iron brought out the aroma and had pressed the cloth so fiercely and often that the scent was all but gone now.

When the Swedes' rock house came into view, Ruth realized how much she'd secretly hoped to find that Kate and John might have returned—especially since she had been noticing fresh tire tracks in the road. But the tracks continued on past the old homestead, which remained deserted, unbearably forlorn without cooking smoke wafting from the chimney and goats running across the road in front of them. All tracks and signs of life had long ago been washed from the ground. She and Maddie turned their heads to keep the place in view until the next bend snatched it away.

The rest of the way to Glory Springs, Ruth could hardly sit still. David's truck couldn't go fast enough around each bend. She wanted to jam the foot of her good leg down over David's on the gas. He was driving so slowly and steadily up the canyon that Ruth had the feeling he was deliberately holding her back from getting there. But then slow and methodical was the way he did everything—from digging up artifacts and making notes, to wooing her.

At last they came around the bend, and she caught sight of Glory Springs. The pinyons around her little cabin came into view, and, for a moment, Ruth expected to see its intact roof resting beneath them, rather than the layer of brush that the wind seemed to have swept there. Then she remembered that neither of them was whole anymore. Even the custom yellow Model A parked under the pinyon seemed tired and worn, layered over with pine needles and splotches of pitch.

The yard around the house, though, was covered with spring flowers, lupine and mallow and countless others, just as it had been the first time she saw the place, and the minute the truck stopped beside the house, her hand was at the door lever. "Get me my crutch, someone," she yelled, wishing David had not put it in the back of the van. She turned and swung her leg out. Maddie scrambled past her, Ruth's purse tumbling out onto the ground. Ruth kicked it away, undid her sandals, and placed her sole against the dirt, both soles, but only one knew the feel of sand beneath it.

Not able to wait a moment more, she stood on her good leg and hopped over to the pinyon, grabbing hold of its rough trunk to keep herself from falling. Hugging the tree tight to her, Ruth rubbed her cheek against the bark, savoring each scratch it gave to her skin. She felt a sharp sting on her arm and looked down to see a pine ant biting her, then another, pests she'd wanted to rid herself of years before. She could have kissed them now.

Such a flood of emotion washed over her that her leg buckled at the knee, and she sank down from the pinyon. Laying her face against the granite pebbles, she let her tears soak the dry ground. She turned her head and pressed her lips to the earth, with her tongue tasted the place her heart lay.

"Oh, for heaven's sake, Ruth. Get up from there." David leaned her crutch against the tree. He reached for her arm, but she slapped his hand away.

"Leave me be, David. I'll get up when I please," she choked. She heard his footsteps crunch away on the sand toward the cabin. A moment later she felt a faint pat on her arm, gentle as a blessing feather. She looked up to see Maddie standing beside her. The compassion on the girl's face penetrated the armor that encased her the way stones had once shielded Jim's grave, touched Ruth to her very core. It took everything she had to gird herself again, so she could rise from the ground and do what had to be done.

As she crutched her way toward the cabin, the view through the open doorway appeared to house the same ruins she'd left the day she rode down to finish the movie. She could see how winter rain and snows had cleaned some of the soot from the rock walls, and washed it to the floor, where it had dried in odd-shaped patterns on the cement. But by the time she came through the doorway, she could see the amazing change that David was staring up at, and the wonder of it rooted her where she stood. The huge hole in her roof had been repaired, lain over with bare planks and covered inside with the skin of the grizzly. Planks also had been secured over the hole behind her stove. And her woodstove itself had been put back into its place, along with the other furniture and a familiar table, the one from the *ki'takii*.

For a moment, Ruth stood dumb with astonishment, her head not able to grasp the significance. This had to be some kind of dream, like the ones where her injured leg miraculously recovered. The Swedes were still gone, and ghosts of lovers did not rise up to repair burned houses. She hobbled over and put her palm against the rough planks that had been nailed into place above the rock bottom of her cabin, let splinters enter her skin as she swept her hand across. Still, she did not wake. Then she spotted the little leather bag with its feathers lodged against the rafter, left to strengthen the new section of roof. A blessing bag.

Still in wonderment, she turned around to find Maddie had come in and was smiling up at the ceiling. It was the first real smile Ruth had seen on her since they left. Then Maddie turned and ran out calling to her brother.

"They came, J.B. They were here, Thomas and the others to fix it," she shouted. "Come look, their tracks are all over the yard."

Ruth dared not say a word, fearing she might break whatever spell she was in. Instead, she sank down on her bed, which had been outside with the rest of the furniture the last time she'd seen it. Before she'd left to shoot the scene, she and David had already torn down and hauled out the burned timbers, and David told her that after the accident, he had gone back and piled what was left of the furniture and belongings in the corner by the door—where the roof was most intact—and covered the pile with tarps. But all that had been unpiled, cleaned, and put back into place now.

David had yet to comment when J.B. came running in, his face reflecting the same hope she and Maddie felt. Her own intensified when her son came up and took her hand. "Thomas came to find us," J.B. said, and Ruth remembered Thomas's promise to drive over in the spring.

"Well, that was very nice of him—or of whomever did this," David said, finally. "But we better finish up here so we can get on the road before dark. It's a long way back."

"We just got here, David," Ruth said. "I'm not going anywhere yet."

"I didn't say leave immediately. In an hour or two will be fine."

"But I don't see why we have to leave at all, now," she said. "At least not today."

"Why can't we leave in the morning?" J.B. asked. "Everything is fixed now."

"Not everything. The roof is fixed, but not well, it appears. There's still no water tank. Who knows if the windmill still works? I shut it down at the house months ago. And remember that the pipes to the sink are broken off. Besides, we didn't even bring any food with us for dinner."

"I don't care." Maddie stood framed in the doorway, her long red hair lifted out around her by the afternoon breeze. "I'd rather stay here than eat."

"Well, I wouldn't," David said. He sniffed the air. "The place still smells like smoke."

"Thanks to you." The words slipped out, but they quieted him. Ruth made her way into the yard, David and J.B. following behind. She turned to look at him. "I'm going to stay right here tonight, with or without you. If the smell bothers you, we can cook and sleep outside. Why don't you drive into Juniper Valley and pick up some supplies for dinner and breakfast? You better hurry, though, the store closes early. Might as well fill up these old water jugs while you're there, too."

David's face darkened as he stepped out into the yard, his mouth contorted. "I was afraid this would happen if I brought you back to this place. You always get so stubborn when you're here." He gave one of his helpless sighs and shrugged his shoulders, then stood scowling and shaking his head. "Okay. I guess that will give you time to get things ready to take back with us," he said. He picked up two of the water jugs and began walking toward the car. "But we leave first thing in the morning," he insisted. Opening the van door, he turned back. "Don't anyone get any ideas." He was still shaking his head when he drove off. It was the first time since the accident that she had prevailed.

Ruth watched him disappear around the bend, the afternoon blossoming around her. The three of them stood looking at the space the van had vacated, feeling the canyon expand in his absence. For the first time since David had come into their lives, Ruth felt the man's hold on her son lessen, saw it in his smiling face as David left. Maddie was smiling too, but her loyalty to David had ended when he took them from this place to L.A. Ruth breathed in air overflowing with spring flowers and listened to the voices of windblown pines telling her she was home.

But not for long, she reminded herself, and felt some of her joy began to fade. Then she brought herself back into the moment and hugged her children to her. Now. They were here now.

The next thing she knew, J.B. and Maddie had pulled away and were running across the wash and up the draw to see what was left of their settlement, Maddie chittering with a chipmunk as she ran, and Ruth was left alone in front of her homestead. Oh, if she could only take all this back with her to L.A. Leaning on her crutch, she stood looking at a wispy white cloud forming overhead, and ignoring the nagging in her head that said she had much to do here and little time to do it. Instead, she hobbled over to the old campfire and sat on one of the rocks beside it, continuing to observe the cloud gathering itself together, as she dipped her hand into the sand and let the grains sift back through her fingers, like the memories filtering through her. She watched the cloud's shape continually change, gaining substance and form, then losing it, gaining and losing, as it drifted across the canyon, sometimes stretched apart by the forces surrounding it, sometimes holding its integrity. When it disappeared behind the ridge, she pulled herself up, drew in a deep breath and thrust her crutch out in front of her.

She attacked the practical tasks, slid her box of books out from under the bed and gathered some of the items of clothing that David had missed when he retrieved her things before bringing her from the hospital. She piled the clothing on the bed, then pulled down one of the small ollas from the ledge between the walls and roof, leaving the rest beside the large one Jim had made. Although she longed to have Jim's with her, she would never take it from this place.

Remembering the jars of mesquite and acorn flour stored in the barn, along with pinyon nuts, and other favorites, Ruth made her way toward these outbuildings that were being built the day David first arrived at Glory Springs, this man who might soon be her husband. Might. She crutched her way along, keenly aware that this complex had been meant to house the horse that had come like a gift into her life, reviving her dreams of freedom, then left her life, constraining her permanently. She wished Blue had fared better with his injuries. Somehow she couldn't believe that her beautiful Blue was dead. Gritting her teeth, she went through the corral and out the gate, letting her thoughts savor and chew the bitter residue, the way a goat ruminates its cud. Then her eye caught a patch of abundant green just beyond the gate around the water trough, and she hobbled over to examine its cause.

A shock of laughter burst loose at the explosion of green leaves growing wherever the old willow wood met ground around the leaking trough. Something in her lifted at the sight, and more laughter burbled out, like spring water onto dry earth. Ruth eased down and touched the tender new leaves that had insisted on coming back to life. Displaced from the wash near the Swedes', these willow poles she had thought dead had learned to draw up nutrients from this hard place, had somehow sent down roots to stake their claim. Suddenly this ordinary event seemed miraculous—anything at all might be possible. And, on a more practical level, she knew this meant there was nothing wrong with the windmill itself. It was still filling the old trough.

The tasks she had been set on deserted her. They were not what brought her here, she realized. Ruth looked across the wash to Jim's grave. It would be a long way across that wash, she knew, dragging the inert leg that constantly threw her off balance over several piles of rocks and flood debris strewn along deep sand that was itself difficult to cross by crutch.

She had barely made it past the trail down the bank of the wash before she fell the first time, having jabbed her crutch into the sand too hard and too fast to catch herself with her stable leg. Once she'd righted herself and mastered crutching through sand, she found a greater challenge just getting past the first pile of rounded rocks and flood debris, the bottom of her crutch sliding off the loose rock and pulling her off balance. Her fall was harder against the rocks, and a sharp snag of broken branch managed to push itself into the skin of her hip as she landed. She turned and yanked it out, then had no choice but to drag herself and that leg until she reached the next patch of sand, wincing each time her weight rested on the good knee that pressed against rock and debris. Ruth smiled darkly when she looked back to see that the stick had gouged a path along the calf of her dormant leg, leaving a trail of red. At least she couldn't feel its pain.

When she got to another patch of sand, she struggled to her feet and made her way over to the next rock pile. This time, she didn't wait to fall before beginning her crawl-and-drag routine to reach the next patch of sand. Only two more rock piles, she told herself, but each one tired her more, and plunging her crutch in and out of sand was not much easier. Would she ever fully recover the strength she had lost with her accident? She was exhausted by the time she clawed her way up the far bank, didn't bother to get to her feet when she reached the top, but pulled herself by knee the short distance to Jim's grave.

Eyes blurring the way before her, Ruth continued by feel until she could put a hand on the ground covering the grave, finding the hard dirt softened by a cushion of plants. Wiping her tears away, she saw that they were tiny purple and gold flowers. She gave a little laugh, leaned down and kissed them, then flattened herself over the length of the grave. Laying her cheek against the silky little petals, she breathed in their quiet fragrance.

With a finger she touched the minute velvety lobes. It amazed her that each of these tiny flowers embodied something of the ground that created and sustained it, as did the little hopping bugs disguised as pebbles that this place had once been named for—small rocks rising. These flowers, too, had risen from rock turned soil, as had everything else around her, every other plant and animal. Jim had now dissolved into that soil, was now part of this canyon. She was breathing him in with the fragrance of these flowers.

David's words came back to her: *I know what kind of woman you are,* he had said. But did he really? Ruth thought not. He did not understand this core of her that was not so different from these flowers, from the willow leaves growing along the bottoms of the corral posts. And like these things, she needed her roots buried in the soil of this place to stay alive. Roots could not reach beneath the concrete of Los Angeles. That place would kill her if she went back there.

She remembered clearly her first instinct about David when he drove up in his steaming van—viewing him as a foreigner, an intruder who was not a part of the place she loved. How different that feeling was from the one she had the first time she saw Jim descending the bluff above his grave, as if he had come from the very rock itself.

She should have taken her intuition more seriously. But she had done other things besides affiliate with David to move herself away from here. She had chosen that path away from here herself, the way Thomas had described at the ceremony. Somehow she had to forge a way back. And something in her had not given up. Something inside was growing new leaves.

Ruth stayed quiet a long time, letting thought and words slip away from her. The grave's calm beneath her body seeped into her. Some time later, she heard small footsteps scaling the bank of the wash and looked up. She was grateful to see J.B. and Maddie walking toward her. She sat up, but none of them spoke for some time.

"Is this where our father is buried?" J.B. asked solemnly. That wasn't really his question, Ruth realized; she had pointed the place out to him a long time ago. She looked at Maddie by his side and the question in *her* eyes, before nodding—to them both. She did not think Jim would mind.

"He was a good man, just like I told you. The very best in the world."

The children stood looking down at the grave. "I wish you could have known him," she whispered.

"We know his people," Maddie said. "Was he like Thomas?"

Ruth shook her head and swallowed hard. "He was beautiful in his *own* way. But Thomas is a good man too."

"But what about David? Isn't he our father now?" J.B.'s face was a mixture of pain and confusion. "He takes care of us. He . . . he . . ."

"Loves you? I think he does." Ruth felt a chill come over her at the admission. "Do you want him to be your father?" She cringed against the answer she expected.

"How can he be," Maddie said, "when he's not?" Her jaw was set against it. "We can only have one father and he's right here."

Ruth winced, bit her lip until she tasted blood, said nothing.

"I don't know," J.B. said. "Maybe."

"He'll never let us come back here," Maddie said. "You said you wanted to live here again, J.B."

"I know." J.B. squatted down beside Ruth, looked over at the grave blanketed with flowers. "I want to. But how we can live here now with her hurt leg?"

"You sound like him." Maddie put her hands on her hips and looked down at them. "Why can't we? We can help her. We did before, and we were little then." She looked at Ruth for support. "You want us to stay here, don't you?"

Ruth had a bizarre image of Maddie with her foot on the gas pedal as Ruth drove the Model A. Countless protests rose up: broken pipes, no wood chopped for cooking, her animals gone, no gun anymore, on and on, as if David were in her head directing her thoughts, and she wondered just when was it she had lost herself so completely. How deeply the man had insinuated himself into their lives.

"You can start by helping me back across the wash," she said. "Then you can gather some wood for the campfire, and we can talk more about it."

Lodged between the two of them, it was difficult to use her crutch, but they kept her from falling several times, and she made it across the wash in about a third of the time it took to get across by herself. Not an easy journey, but certainly easier than the first. It pained her to lean so much weight on their young shoulders. But if that's what it took to make it across upright, lean on them was what she must do.

Once they had gathered wood and hauled out what pots they could find intact to cook in, Ruth brought her purse inside the cabin and called J.B. and Maddie to her. She reached behind the lining and extracted the money, set it beside her on the bed. "This is all we have left," she told them, "but if we're careful we can get by for two or three years—maybe more. Especially if David pays to repair the damage he caused."

J.B. picked up one of the hundred-dollar bills and felt it between his fingers. "Gosh," he said.

Seeing their wide eyes, she explained, "I know it looks like a lot to you, but money goes quickly." Then she noticed the photo exposed under the bill J.B. had taken. She had almost forgotten it was there.

Maddie snatched the picture. "Who's this?" she demanded. She held the photo up to Ruth's face.

"She looks like you," J.B. said. He put down the bill. "But different too. She looks kind of . . ."

Ruth was tempted to alter her family tree, lock Cally out of their lives forever, to give them a grandmother worth having. "She's my grandmother. Your great-grandmother," she told them.

"She looks like Daddy's people, doesn't she, J.B.?" Maddie's face was lit with excitement. "Can we go see her?"

"She died a long time ago. I never got to meet her."

"But where's our real grandmother? Your mother," Maddie persisted. "Is she dead too? You said . . ."

Ruth hadn't intended this conversation, felt pressed by the weight of it. "She's not dead. But she's nothing like . . . like Lolinda here."

"Well, can we see her, then?" Maddie was adamant. J.B. stood studying Ruth's face.

"Why don't you like her?" he asked.

Ruth took the photo from her daughter and gathered up the money, slid it back behind the lining. She thought carefully before she spoke. "Maybe someday you can see her," she said, reluctantly. "But not quite yet. Until then, Lolinda can be your grandmother."

The whine of an engine became audible in the distance. Ruth sighed. Too bad David hadn't had a flat tire, or gone off the road and got stuck in the sand for a while. "Come here," she said. She reached out and took each of them by the hand.

"Listen, both of you. Think carefully about where you want to live. It won't be easy if we stay here now, for any of us. But we can figure it out."

"I know I want to live here," Maddie insisted. "I can help you all by myself. Without J.B." Her eyes teared, but she blinked them dry. "Please can't we stay home?"

"Do you think Thomas and those guys will come back?" J.B.'s tone was almost wistful. Ruth weighed her answer.

"If they came once, I imagine they'll come again. After all, they did fix the roof for us, left us the bearskin and blessing bag." She looked up at the rough ceiling, understanding now that the brush she had thought windblown onto the roof when they drove up had been a layer of woven fronds and tule, laid for protection on top of the crude planks and skin visible from the inside. "If they don't, we'll have to find a way to go see them," she promised.

J.B. looked down at her leg, his expression dubious. A honk sounded down at the bend, and they walked out to watch the van wind around it.

"Here's what we'll do," Ruth said quickly. "Let's just enjoy being home for now. You can think about it. I'll make up my mind in the morning." She needed more time to prepare for the battle she knew was ahead. Why start it prematurely?

"I don't need to think about it," Maddie said.

David returned with a cheerfulness that seemed designed to keep them on his side, handing out candy bars and Cracker Jacks to have after dinner. He noted that not much preparation had been done for leaving, and Ruth glossed over it, reminding him that he had driven off with most of the boxes. Not that she'd once thought of them.

They brought the cots out under the pines, the children insisting on dragging out their own, which Ruth allowed despite David's objections. She heated the can of stew he had purchased, and the four of them ate by the fire in the twilight, watching the full moon rise. As they had so many times before, she and the children kept track of the moonlily plant beside them, watching its blooms open in the twilight. David insisted it should be called datura, albeit sacred datura. Whatever it was, Ruth loved watching the almost visible movement of those large pinwheel-like buds as they transformed into huge white trumpets to herald in the night.

Impatient for an early start in the morning, David tried to get them into bed before the blooming was complete, but Ruth fought for their right to watch until every one of the evening's thirteen blossoms had opened fully to the moon. And she remained up afterward, despite his protests, not about to give up a moment of her time here. When she heard him start to snore, the evening was finally her own.

The moon rose high from the horizon, its glow luminescing each iridescent blossom. Ruth leaned over and touched a soft bloom. Such intoxicating fragrance! The flowering plant returned each year to regale the night with a seductive scent that drew huge hawk moths into its reproductive process, and tonight, like so many nights before, Ruth watched the shivering quiver of blossom and wing under the moon, this union of plant and insect in the ecstasy they had been designed for. It was a ruthless design, really. The pollinating moth would soon come back to lay its own young, green horned demons who would devour the leaves of this plant, chew the stems to nubs. But they also nibbled open the prickly seed pods, so that the plant's progeny were released. Life wasn't easy. It seemed brutal sometimes, especially in its parts. Maybe she hadn't fully understood that before. But the plant came up again each spring, and the moths always returned.

She stayed up remembering and pondering, until her mind exhausted itself and her thoughts lost coherence. She sat at last without language, in the pure knowledge that she was at her Glory Springs, the place of small rocks rising. In her wordless intimacy with this place, she remembered the taste of its plants and animals, remembered the energies these things brought into her body. She felt the place knowing her back and finally understood that only in this place was she fully herself.

When at last her eyes would not remain open, she moved her vigil to her cot, fitting into the small space left to her beside David, and tried to tune out the man's snores.

The next thing she knew, Thomas was there, wrapping her injured leg in soft yerba mansa leaves and giving her a dark potion to drink. Pollen was in the air. All around them were the birdmen, flapping their wings and making bird calls. Maddie and J.B. were dressed as winged things too, and Maddie's bird calls were the best of all by far. She saw Grandmother Siki over by the fire, then realized it was Lolinda instead. Ruth longed to get up and join her and the rest of the creatures, but her leg was holding her back. Suddenly she remembered this was a ceremony for letting go of the dead, and she looked up at Thomas in shock. "Then come back to life, Dlah'da. Come back." His blessing feather became eagle wings that he waved over her, and their wind tingled the skin of the leg she had thought dead.

When sun opened her eyes, the first thing Ruth did was reach down and caress her leg, for the first time with compassion. Though the limb remained numb as ever as she ran a finger down the path of yesterday's dark gouge, her will did not—and she took up her crutch and made her way over to her children, who had already started gathering wood for the breakfast campfire. "We're not leaving," she told them. "I've decided." Maddie was ecstatic.

J.B. looked down, shuffled his feet. "Okay," he said.

"Don't be ridiculous, Ruth," David said, when she told him, then continued carrying her box of books to the van.

She hobbled after him. "Bring the books back, David. I said I'm not leaving." He set the box in the back of the van, then turned and started to walk past her.

Ruth reached into the van and pulled the box toward her, then out the back of the van. Box and books tumbled onto the ground at her feet. "These books aren't going anywhere. And neither are we."

"For Christ's sake, Ruth. Have you gone completely out of your mind?" He crouched and began shoving books back into the box. Ruth reached down and shoveled them out again. He pushed them in.

With the crutch, she flipped the box over and batted it away. He grabbed hold of her crutch, then, held it still, and the two of them glared at each other. "Are you going to take this away from me, too, David?" she asked with sugar-coated acid.

He took his hand from her crutch and stood up. His shoulders drooped. "I've never taken anything from you, Ruth. All I've done is try to take care of you and the children." The pain on his face squeezed her heart. He put out a hand to touch her arm, but she pulled it away.

"While I was driving into town I was even thinking that maybe I'd find someone to make this place livable—for a vacation spot at least." He sweetened his look. "You couldn't manage here alone, but I don't see why we can't drive out once in a while so you could spend time here in the summer—since you love it so much," he said. "Would that make you happy, Ruth? Would you forgive me then?"

"You promised to repair this place months ago."

"But that was before everything . . ."

"And I don't want a vacation spot, David. I want my home back. This is where I live—and by God, I'm going to stay right here. I lived here before there *was* any cabin"—she swept an arm out—"or windmill, or pipes, or . . ."

"Things were different, then, Ruth. You know that. Sure, you could do it with two good legs—and without children. And if it hadn't been for that damned movie—"

"It wasn't the movie that backfired, David. It was the truck you never bothered getting fixed until after it was too late."

"That's not fair, Ruth. And it doesn't change the fact that you only have one good leg now."

"I can live here with *one* good leg, David, and *with* children. You just watch me." She stuck the crutch under her arm. "Besides," she nodded toward the children laying the firewood, "I have six—well, five good legs now." She started toward the campfire.

"That's the thing, Ruth," he said, following after her. "You can't do this to those children, bring them back out to this wilderness. Can't take them out of school, for one thing. J.B. especially. He's doing so well. I won't let you do this."

"They're my children, David. Mine, not yours. Their welfare needn't concern you. And school is almost out for the summer anyway." Maddie took her hand as she came up to the campfire.

"What about it, J.B., Maddie? Surely you don't want to stay here." He stared down at her son, who looked at the ground. "Go on, tell her."

"I want to," Maddie said, her face and voice defiant, her hand tightening around Ruth's fingers.

"J.B.?" David's voice poised in the air above its target.

Ruth wanted to reach out and hold her son to her, do something to lessen the conflict and confusion playing on his face, but she knew he had to come to it himself. Finally, he looked over at her. Seeing his resolve, she smiled and nodded her support.

"I guess I want to stay, too," he said, then amended at the sight of David's pained expression, "Well, for the summer anyway. Maybe after that . . ." His voice dropped off.

David began pacing in front of the unlit campfire, shaking his head in furious disbelief. Ruth turned and struck a match to the wood, set on the pot of water Maddie had brought out. She was letting herself down onto one of the old sitting rocks when David marched over and took hold of her shoulders. He pulled her up and held her there, her crutch clattering from the rock to the ground. "I'm not going to leave you here, Ruth. I just won't do it."

"What are you going to do, then? Drag me kicking and screaming?" she asked, as Maddie brought the crutch over and held it at Ruth's side.

"If I have to." He gave her a small shake for emphasis. "There must be laws against what you propose to do with these children, yank them out of school and cart them off to some godforsaken place where you can't even take care of them. If there aren't laws, there should be."

Ruth gripped tight the crutch Maddie held out. "If you do try to drag me, David, be prepared to lose that battle. You'd have to kill me before you could take me out of here. You would kill me if you took me away from this place."

"Kill you? Oh, Ruth." His face saddened. "It's only because I love you that any of this matters." He looked down at the children. "Otherwise I wouldn't care what happened. But you're my family now. I have to take care of you."

J.B. walked over from where he stood by the campfire. "Then let go of our mother," he said quietly.

Ruth thought she saw tears in the man's eyes as he loosened his grip on her and sank back against the table rock. He buried his face in his hands, made no sound, but they could see his shoulders heaving. She felt herself weakening, and the misery on J.B.'s and Maddie's faces told her they were too. The litany of difficulties in living here echoed through her head. Yet none of them went to him.

Then, in the pinyon overhead, an oriole sang out, filling the air with its song, and the three of them looked up at the bright spot of yellow and black balanced on the high branch. Sunlight filtered through the branches around the bird, illuminating clear drips of pitch on the pine needles surrounding him, and creating countless drops of bright light that shimmered in the slight breeze. They stood looking at one another, breathing in the fragrant air, and letting the canyon strengthen them.